THE CRITICS RAVE ABOUT SIMON CLARK!

"This guy Simon Clark is something special. It's time to find out what you've been missing."

—*Hellnotes*

"Not since I discovered Clive Barker have I enjoyed horror so much."

—*Nightfall*

"One of the best contemporary British horror writers. Watch this man climb to Horror Heaven!"

—*Deathrealm*

"Clark may be the single most important writer to emerge on the British horror scene in the '90s."

—*The Dark Side*

"Clark is worth seeking out."

—*Fear*

AMONG THE GRAVES

A section of fence had collapsed inward, giving easy access to the graveyard. He paused. Here, bushes and trees clustered across the face of the cemetery so densely it was as if they tried to hide some deadly secret. A breath of air stirred them. The sound made him think of something massive moving through the trees; an unseen prowling *something* that watched him from the shadows.

With a shiver he entered the cemetery; the lush grass reached his elbows. This was akin to walking through a green ocean with the tops of gravestones breaking the surface like shark fins. They were dark, predatory shapes. Soon they surrounded him as he moved deeper into the cemetery. It was silent now, except for the lone cry of a bird. Soon he'd passed from sunlight to shadow beneath the trees. Hell. It was dark as sin in there.

It took a moment for his eyes to accustom themselves after the transition from brilliance to near darkness, but at last they did. And by the headstone of a family burnt to death in a house fire stood a figure.

"I didn't think you would dare come," said the figure. "Follow me."

He did as he was told. And followed the figure along a path that weaved between graves, deeper and deeper into the heart of the graveyard.

Darkness Demands

SIMON CLARK

LEISURE BOOKS   NEW YORK CITY

A LEISURE BOOK®

July 2001

Published by

Dorchester Publishing Co., Inc.
276 Fifth Avenue
New York, NY 10001

ISBN 0-8439-4898-1

The name "Leisure Books" and the stylized "L" with design are trademarks of Dorchester Publishing Co., Inc.

Printed in the United States of America.

Visit us on the web at www.dorchesterpub.com.

For Helen Clark,
A wonderful daughter and an amazing source of
inspiration. This one's for you, hon!

Darkness
Demands

Chapter One

One

One day you might disappear.

It might be just another everyday kind of morning. You get out of bed, you dress, you eat toast and drink some coffee. Then you leave the house.

And you never return. As simple as that. You vanish. You're history. No body is found. No clues. No nothing. Gone.

OK. So it might not happen this week, or this year, or even this decade. But it does happen, sometimes men and women vanish, never to be seen or heard of again.

And, yes, you know only too well, it could happen to you. It could happen today.

"Dad, can I play out in the field?"

John Newton turned away from the words on the computer screen to see his nine-year-old daughter leaning in through the doorway.

"OK. But no going out of the field and no talking to strangers."

"All right, Dad. See you later."

John Newton gazed at the computer screen for a moment before hitting the keys again.

"Dad?"

"Yes, Elizabeth?"

His daughter swung on the doorknob again, the breeze wafting papers on his desk. He held them in place by slapping both palms down on them.

"Dad?"

"What is it, hon?"

"Can I go out on my bike?"

"Hmm?" His attention had drifted back to the screen again. Maybe that first sentence could be punchier: *One day you might disappear.*

"Can I take my bike to the field?"

"No."

"Why?"

"The grass is too long."

"I can manage."

"No. The grass gets all wound up round the cog. It'll make a mess."

She considered this as she swung back and forth on the door handle. Her long hair brushed the wall with a whispery sound.

Dreamily, still gazing at the words on the computer screen, John murmured, "Don't do that, hon, please. Dad's working."

"A new book?"

"Yes."

"What's it about?"

"It's about people who've disappeared." He smiled at her, wiggled his fingers, and imitated a Vincent Price voice—badly. "People who have mysteriously vanished from the face of the earth."

"Oh. So it won't be about Sam, then?"

"No. I don't think I could write a whole book about our dog."

"How many pages?"

"Lots and lots."

"Have you nearly finished it?"

"No."

"Halfway?"

"No. I've just started the first page."

"Can I read it?"

"Not yet, hon." He shot her a smile. "Would you like to finish off what's left of the cake?"

She stopped swinging on the door handle. "All of it?"

"Go on, be a devil, there's only a couple of slices left."

"I'll take it into the field and have a picnic," she said before running away down the hallway.

John tore his gaze away long enough from the screen to call after her, "No leaving the field . . . no talking to strangers, remember? Elizabeth, do you hear?"

But she was already gone.

John straightened the papers that had wafted across the table before returning to the keyboard. A bang from the direction of the kitchen made him look up. It didn't sound like a splintering crash, so there was every chance nothing had broken (and he remembered the cake was on a plastic plate, so that was unbreakable anyway), and there was no scream from Elizabeth advertising disaster. He listened for a moment longer, waiting for the call of "Dad . . . Dad . . . *Dad!*" It never came. So he guessed that Elizabeth had merely tossed her empty cup into the sink. Well, distracting, even mildly annoying; but no catastrophe. Not this time anyway. Back to the book.

Page 1. Chapter 1.

The new book.

An important book. If his publisher didn't give him a contract for this, he was effectively out of a job. Until, that is, he found another publisher. Which wouldn't be easy, despite his track record of half a dozen successful books. Especially the latest, which had funded the move from their old home to this pretty water mill in a village that looked as if it had just jumped from an Agatha Christie movie.

There was plenty of hot competition out there in the world of books. Whole battalions of ambition-fueled writers would happily write a book for no advance in the hope of simply becoming a published author.

This then, this screen full of words in front of him, was important. And it was important he got it right.

But it wasn't easy. Thursday looked as if it might be a total bust. Val had had to leave early for work; his son, Paul, had decided to go swimming (which would have meant John being taxi driver for the morning); Paul had eventually been part-persuaded, part-bribed to take the bus into town to meet friends. But what the hell a bunch of seventeen-year-olds would do was anyone's guess. Then there was the home front. Elizabeth, even by midmorning, was at loose ends.

So this was the start of a new book. An important book. A book of towering, Empire State Building proportions in John Newton's life. He had to have the first chapter and outline at his agent's office by next week. His agent never liked going empty-handed to a lunch with the publisher. With that all-important first chapter Tommy might clinch a new deal by the time the ice cream arrived.

Yet, today the world had started to conspire against him. Already unseen forces, it seemed, had launched their attack to prevent him from writing that first page.

Like any writer, he'd gone through the pre-first-line rituals. Made a jug full of strong coffee. Looked out through the window at the glorious summer's day before closing the blinds of his study (a room that everyone else insisted on calling "the box room"), then switched on the computer.

First, the computer refused to come to life as it should. An on-screen message told him there was a fault, that there would not be enough memory to continue safely. Which was crap because the computer wasn't yet three months old.

He'd restarted the damn thing two or three times until the opening screen at last satisfyingly appeared as it should.

Second. His daughter wouldn't be able to entertain herself for more than ten minutes in a row.

Third. The dog had taken an insane dislike to a flowerpot on top of the wall. Now Sam was determinedly barking himself stupid. OK, so he could remove the flowerpot or shout at the dog—or both. Only, he'd reached that magic moment when every nerve in his body urged him to sit at the computer and type and type and type until that first chapter was done. Then he'd be happy to play with Elizabeth and throw a ball for the dog.

But right at this moment he itched to wrench back the curtains, throw open the window, and yell out at the world, "*I'm mad as hell and I'm not going to take it anymore!*"

He paused, smiling to himself. Even his own thoughts were distracting him from writing now.

"Come on, Newton," he told himself. "Work." He even raised his eyes to a strip of paper pasted to the top of the computer monitor.

WRITE, DAMN IT. WRITE. IT'S THE ONLY
THING YOU'RE GOOD AT.

Maybe it wasn't kind, but there were times when he needed every kind of encouragement, whether a carrot or stick, to keep him sitting in front of the computer when sane people were taking trips to the coast or firing up a barbecue.

He rubbed his face with both hands. "Come on, Newton. You can do it." Then he typed: *Where some people wind up, when they might disappear without trace, can be guessed. Bandsman Glen Miller probably vanished into the sea shortly after his plane took off in 1944 from—*

But which airfield did the doomed Miller fly from? John returned to his research notes spread out like so many fallen leaves across the table. Elizabeth swinging the door had sent them fluttering out toward the wall. A couple of pages had even escaped to the floor.

Swiveling round in his chair, he scooped them from the carpet. One of the pieces of paper didn't belong to his research notes. How it had got there, he didn't know.

He looked at it. Straightaway he was distracted from his golden mission of the day: to write that first all-important page of that all-important book. A book that, if bought by the publisher, would meet mortgage repayments, keep the car in gasoline, and put meals on the table. But there was something about that piece of paper. . . .

It was a page that looked as if it had been torn from an exercise book. The paper was heavy, silky to the touch. For some reason, and he didn't know why, he'd concluded the paper was very old—antique, if you can have such a thing as antique paper.

It had been stained from the dew on the patio where he'd found it two mornings ago. Weirdly, it had been left beneath a fragment of gravestone. He'd laughed out loud when he first read what was written on the paper. Why someone should go to the trouble of writing such a letter to him seemed inexplicable.

Absently he sniffed the letter, as if it might contain a whiff of perfume, but there was no discernible smell.

"But it does reek of one thing . . . *mystery*." He shook his head. "My God, you can never resist a melodramatic turn of phrase, can you, John Newton?"

The letter must have arrived beneath its stone weight in the dead of night, which added nicely to the mystery. While he'd had every intention of simply dropping it into the trash, there was something about it. Something compelling that drew him back to read it again and again.

He turned it over to look at the words written in pencil.

Dear Messr. John Newt'n . . .

"Oh, no, you don't," he told himself. "No more distractions. Write, damn you, write."

At that moment the telephone rang. And that was probably the moment that it all began. Not with the call. But what he saw through the window.

Two

The caller was his agent. He wanted to know how the first chapter of the book was going.

"No problems, Tom." John grimaced at the sound of the lie slipping so easily from his own lips. "You'll have the first chapter by Tuesday."

"I can't say I'm happy about this one, John."

"I know, but trust me, it'll turn out fine."

"It's just a bunch of stories where people disappear without trace. Where's the center to it? What's going to be so special about it that makes a publisher reach for the checkbook?"

"Don't worry, Tom. I've got something up my sleeve." *Yeah, my arm.* John nearly added the dry riposte aloud. He realized there was nothing earthshaking about his latest book. Unless inspiration came on swift wings, it would be the kind of book that's sold off dirt-cheap in hardware stores.

Changing the subject, he asked, "How did the book fair go? Any business?"

"Do you want the good news or the bad news first?"

"Bad."

"The Dutch people are only offering a five-hundred-dollar advance for the translation rights of *Blast His Eyes*."

"Jesus Christ. After Goldhall has taken his cut, that leaves . . ." John tried to calculate the percentage.

"Yeah, I know—enough for a couple of ice creams."

"Don't keep me in suspense then. The good news?"

"Dellargo in New York are taking *Blast His Eyes* after all."

"That's a certainty, Tom?"

Simon Clark

"Consider it signed, sealed, and delivered."

"Thank God for that."

"Just don't hold your breath for the advance check. These things take months to come through. Don't you love being a writer?"

John smiled. "Absolutely. Wouldn't change it for the world." He said it in a flippant way. But it was true. He did love being a writer. Seeing his book in print for the first time was still a hell of a thrill. Even the smell of new paper as he flicked through the pages of a virgin book sent him into a kind of gooey-eyed ecstasy. Val would smile as she watched him. "Why don't you wear that expression when you look at me, John?"

Tom continued. "Oh, John, I've got the sales figures through for *Blast His Eyes*. I was going to put them in the post, but I thought you'd be like a cat on the proverbial hot tin roof waiting for them."

"Sure. Fire away, Tom."

"As you know Goldhall has reprinted five times now—so write me another *Blast His Eyes*, you idiot," Tom spoke with his voice liberally laced with good humor, but the challenge was there. John's latest book was a humdinger of a success. He couldn't follow it up with just a so-so potboiler.

As Tom ran through the sales figures—these included overseas sales, library sales, book club sales, high- and low-discount sales—the full schermozzle, Elizabeth came into the room and pressed a sticker onto the front of his T-shirt. John mimed he was busy talking on the phone. It was obvious that he was anyway, but he hoped Elizabeth would take the hint and do something else until he'd finished.

He glanced down at the sticker. It showed two monkeys copulating. A caption ran: *Monkey See, Monkey Screw.*

He covered the mouthpiece and hissed, "Lizzie, where did you get the sticker?"

"Paul's room."

"You know you're not allowed in there."

"Can I get my bike out?"

"Lizzie. Can't you see? I'm on the—"

"Hello, John," came Tom's voice in his ear. "Are you still there?"

"Yeah, sorry, Tom. Just a little interference at this end."

Elizabeth persisted. "Dad. Can I take my bike out onto the lane?"

He held up a finger. *Just give me a moment . . . PLEASE.*

"I'll take that as a yes, then." She darted from the room before he had chance to contradict her.

Meanwhile, Tom had wound up reading the list of sales figures to John. "Oh, before I go," Tom said. "Pat was telling me that you've been receiving some strange fan mail."

"Fan mail? Hardly that. It was more a demand-with-menace kind of note."

"You've reported it to the police?"

"No."

"You should, you know. There's some strange people out there."

"As I told Pat, it was just a bizarre message left in the garden."

"It was addressed to you personally?"

"Yes."

"So take it to the police. You can't be too careful with this kind of thing. I remember when a lunatic stalked one of my authors for months. It ended up with this nut trying to set fire to her house."

"Tom." John stood up to open the blind. He saw Elizabeth peddling like fury down the drive, her hair flying out. "Tom . . . it's just a prank by some kids."

"How do you know that? It could be a letter today; tomorrow it could be—"

"Waking up with a horse's head beside me?"

"You've got a beautiful family, John."

"Tom. Listen." John smiled, amused that Tom could take the thing so seriously. "Listen. I'll read it to you."

19

He picked up the sheet of paper. "Dear Messr. John Newton."

"What was that? Messer?"

"Yeah, it's an old-fashioned version of Mister. In fact a lot of the words are spelt in an archaic way; the sort of thing you'd see in an eighteenth-century manuscript."

"Weird."

"I suppose it added to the fun for whoever wrote it."

He read the letter in full to Tom, pointing out the idiosyncratic spellings as he did so.

"Dear Messr. John Newt'n,
I should wish yew put me a pound of chock latt on the grief stowne of Jess Bowen by the Sabbath night. Yew will be sorry if yew do not."

He rounded off by telling Tom that it was unsigned and undated.

"Very mysterious," Tom mused. "What do you make of the phrase 'grief stowne'?"

"A quaint way of saying gravestone, I guess."

"And there really is a gravestone of this Jeff Bowen somewhere nearby?"

"Jess Bowen. I don't know. Perhaps. There's a massive cemetery not far away from here."

"What does Val make of it?"

"I haven't told her."

"Why?"

"There's a big audit going on where she works. I didn't want to bother her with this when it's just some dumb practical joke."

"John. Take this seriously. Someone's sent an anonymous note that clearly contains a threat."

"For what? A bar of chocolate? The whole thing's absurd."

"That might be, but they're saying you'll be sorry if you don't comply. Take it to the police, John."

"OK. I'll phone them." The lie slipped out as easily

20

as the one earlier about having a great, dazzling, winning idea for the next book. Nevertheless, John was genuinely touched by Tom's concern. But come on . . . could he really complain to the police about a quirkily written note demanding chocolate? He could just imagine it. The desk sergeant listening gravely before disappearing into a back room from which an embarrassed John Newton would hear a huge burst of laughter as the sergeant shared the story with his colleagues. No, thank you.

The telephone conversation was winding down. Tom aired his thoughts about overseas rights. Meanwhile John looked out of the window. He didn't want Elizabeth out on in the lane with her bike. Not alone anyway. True, there was nothing in the way of traffic, yet it still made him uneasy.

At that moment the village of Skelbrooke looked dreamily peaceful. As summers in England go, this was turning out to be a good one. The church blazed white in the sun. Trees billowed a luscious green, half hiding the red roofs of the cottages dotted here and there. Jet vapor trails looked like white chalk lines scrawled across the sky. There was a hush and stillness about everything.

But at that instant, beneath that blanket of tranquility, John realized something was wrong somewhere.

As Tom outlined his killer strategy for a new book deal, John leaned forward, his head thrust forward to look through the grass. His muscles tensed. And he didn't know why. The voice of his agent still sounded in his ear, but he was listening hard for sounds beyond the window glass.

His eyes searched along the lane for a glimpse of Elizabeth. He willed himself to see her comically pedaling legs and flying hair as she zoomed along.

But there was no sign of her. He tilted his head the other way.

Stuff's happening, John, came the voice in his head. Stuff is definitely happening.

But what?

He couldn't see anything.

21

But why have all the birds stopped singing?

Why does it feel—in your heart of hearts—that an evil dark cloud has murdered the sun and drowned the world in shadow. . . .

Come on, he told himself, cut the melodrama. I can't see anything wrong.

You mean not a little kid lying crumpled on the road under the wheels of a van?

His imagination fired volleys of images into his head.

It's just that old parental thing, he told himself. As soon as you clap eyes on Elizabeth peddling happily along, it will explode that sense of doom into a billion pieces.

But that's exactly what he did feel. Doom.

DOOM. In capital letters. DOOM written large and black in the sky. DOOM engraved in dark coffin wood. A word that would sound with all the ominous power of thunder at midnight.

Christ, why do I feel like this? Is this the openers for a coronary?

And still Tom spoke into his ear; this time about a city-by-city book promotion tour.

John leaned forward until his forehead pressed against the glass. Looking down to the right, he could see his neighbors on the driveway of the house. On the one hand, they were doing something perfectly normal. On the other hand, it made no sense at all.

Turning his eyes back to the lane, he saw an elderly man, dressed in pajamas and wearing a straw hat, walking as fast as he could manage up the hill. His legs were shaky as if walking was a fearsome struggle. His dragging feet raised a dust cloud around his ankles. And all the time he frantically waved one arm, clearly telling someone (still unseen) to leave him alone.

And where in God's name was Elizabeth?

John couldn't hold back any longer. "I'm sorry, Tom. I'm going to have to go. I think the neighborhood has just gone insane."

Chapter Two

One

After the hurried good-bye to Tom, John Newton replaced the handset of the phone, then shot another glance at his neighbors' antics from his study window.

It could have been a scene from a silent comedy. The Haslems appeared to be preparing for a vacation. They carried suitcases out of the house. They were packing the car.

That, on the face of it, would have been perfectly normal. But it was the way they were going about the process that was so damned weird. Everything was conducted in a mad rush. Keith Haslem, a tiny plump man with a roundly bald head, was running around throwing suitcases into the trunk. His face flared red. His mouth was opening and shutting in a frantic goldfish movement. It took John a moment to realize the little man was yelling at his kids, but the double-glazed window of the study sealed out the sound, hence the silent-movie effect.

John watched in bewilderment as the whole Haslem family—Keith, Audrey, three daughters, and the dog—ran from the house to the car and back, packing in a wild frenzy of activity. When the suitcases were in the trunk, so higgledy-piggeldy there was no way in hell they'd ever shut the lid, Audrey Haslem appeared carrying piles of clothes, which she tossed into the rear seat, as if she was determined to empty the whole house into the car.

And all the while the now-purple-faced Keith Haslem yelled at his family, urging them to move faster.

But what the hell for?

When John had spoken to Keith at the weekend, Keith had told them they weren't going on vacation until August. Now it looked like . . . well, it didn't look as if they were going on vacation at all; it looked as if World War III had been declared and Keith and family were hurling their possessions into the car before heading hell-for-leather for the hills.

Shaking his head, John headed downstairs and into the garden. Looking for Elizabeth was his priority now. Even so, the maelstrom of activity next door tweaked his curiosity.

Now he could hear Keith's high-pitched rant. My God, thought John, the man is in a panic. He sounds terrified. Maybe John wasn't so far wide of the mark about the World War III scenario. These people were running in fear.

"Katy! Katy!" came Keith Haslem's high-pitched screech. "Get into the back of the car . . . no, move the damn box so Stella can get in. No! She has to sit in the middle, for chrissakes!"

"Keith? Keith? What about the bird?"

"Forget the fucking bird!"

There was a wail of cries from the girls in protest. "He'll die if we leave him!"

"There's nothing for him to eat!"

Keith yelled louder. "I'm getting out of here in five minutes flat."

"But Dad—"

"We'll get another fucking bird, OK?"

"Keith..." Audrey's voice, calmer, but still trembling. "Keith, stop swearing at the girls... please."

Keith's voice cut through the air sharp as a knife. "Audrey! Get in that fucking car!"

"I still haven't locked the back door of the house. I thought—"

"For pity's sake, woman..."

John took the path to the lane, keen to see if Elizabeth was still there, but he walked with his head to the right, trying to look through the hedge at the fabulous sequence of events unfolding next door. The hedge was too thick. All he could rely on were the sounds of the fear-shot voices. This time it was like listening to an old-time radio play.

Keith screeched, "Stella, where on earth are you going? Stella! Get back in that damn car. Now!"

"I'm getting Archie."

"I told you! Forget the bird..." Then under his breath, but loud enough to carry through hawthorn, "Oh, fucking Jesus H. Christ."

If the Haslems operated a swear box (as once the Newtons had tried to do, when Paul went through a "shit this" and "bastard that" stage when he was eight), then Keith Haslem was well on the way to personal bankruptcy.

"Get back in the damn car!"

"Keith, stop swearing," Audrey begged piteously. "The neighbors will—"

"I don't care about the fucking neighbors. If the neighbors had any fucking sense they'd be clearing out, too... Stella... Stella! Oh, all right, then, but the cage will have to go on your knee. Credit cards! Credit cards! Audrey did you pick up the credit cards?"

If the neighbors had any fucking sense they'd be clearing out, too.

John's curiosity was wriggling like a toad on a hook

25

now. Why the hell should we be leaving the village? What on earth was happening?

John quickened his pace. That tickle of disquiet had become a full-blown itch. He'd rest easier once he'd seen Elizabeth.

Meanwhile, in a break in the hedge he glimpsed Keith's bald head, now a dangerous shade of blueberry and slick with perspiration. If the man didn't slow down, he'd drop dead in his tracks, with a ruptured aorta spurting like a garden hose.

The man shouted, "Audrey, get a move on! If we don't get away from here now, we'll be too late!"

The world, John decided without a shadow of a doubt, was turning very weird, very fast.

Two

John opened the garden gate. Up the lane to the left, the old man in pajamas and straw hat still hobbled up the lane in tiny mincing steps as if his life depended on it. Now John saw Martin Marcello, who ran the village post office. He was following the old man, that much was clear, but he was walking slowly enough not to gain on him.

"Curious." John murmured to himself.

There was no sign of Elizabeth up the lane. He decided to turn right downhill. Possibly Elizabeth had cycled toward the village on the off chance she could find one of her playmates. Even so, she'd been told dozens of times not go into the village without John, Val, or in a pinch, Paul.

Seconds after heading downhill along the track, John nearly lost his life to the hood of the Haslems' car as it sped out of the driveway. John leapt back. Like a photograph, the image stayed glued to his mind of the terrified-looking family in the car: Keith clutching the steering wheel, his eyes wide, his mouth still hammering away in overdrive as he shouted at his family and maybe the world in general. Only, the sound of his voice was now drowned beneath the howl of the car's motor.

At least with a nod toward neighborliness, John lifted a hand at the Haslems in greeting, but they ignored him. They were locked inside some private drama; nothing else mattered now. Seemingly, they were on a mission from God (and running well behind schedule), or they were fleeing for their very lives. John noticed the canary in its cage on the lap of one of the little girls. In the end it hadn't been left to starve.

John continued down the hill, the loose stones rolling and grating beneath his feet. The lane itself, according to a plaque at the junction, was two thousand years old. Roman road engineers had run this track as straight as a pool cue ninety miles across what would be England's waistline linking Leeds with Whitby on the coast. Along it had marched conquering legions. Most of the road was lost beneath fields and cities now, of course. But here, for half a mile or so, it still ran straight and white as bone. Faint grooves could be seen that marked the wear of ancient chariot wheels. Over the centuries it had been downgraded to little more than a track, and the once-mighty Via Constantine had even been demoted by name to merely the Back Lane. Where travelers once might have seen a discarded legionnaire's javelin, or come across a coin bearing the head of Caesar, now there was the usual scattering of gum wrappers, cigarette butts, and shards of broken beer bottles that caught the morning sun in bursts of dazzling light. Across an edging block that an Etruscan worker would have levered into place with hands as hard as boot leather, there was a condom. It had been stretched out of shape to near-shocking dimensions. ("Oh, look, Dad," Elizabeth had exclaimed on seeing it yesterday. "Someone's lost a pink balloon!" "No, sweetheart, don't pick it up." "Why not, Dad?" "You . . ." He'd paused. "You don't know where it's been, hon.")

Flanking the lane were the houses of bank managers,

lawyers, businessmen—and one writer of true-life crime stories, namely one John Douglas Newton, age thirty-five. A man with a little more than three days— that's seventy-two little hours—to find a follow-up to *Blast His Eyes*. His agent had telephoned John after reading the *Blast His Eyes* manuscript and announced, "The book's going to be big box office . . . damn big box office. . . ." And he'd been right. Damn right. Was his agent right now? Already Tom was predicting *Without Trace* would be dismissed as a warmed-over collection of missing persons stories. Hell. Tom had sowed the seeds of doubt. John was beginning to catch a scent surrounding his new book. And that scent was definitely hinting Crock O' Shit.

This wasn't a nice experience.

As if seeing himself from outside his body, say from that sparrow's view as it sat high on the telephone line, he saw himself walking down the road in a T-shirt, jeans (with a fist-size hole in one knee), and wearing untied shoes that flopped on his feet.

Witness one John Douglas Newton. In three days Mr. Newton must deliver a hotshot idea to his literary agent. Meanwhile, he's in search of one absent daughter, age nine, with a passion for killer whales and strawberry ice cream. John Douglas Newton, a man innocently walking along a peaceful country lane in the old country. A lane that will take him into a territory populated with fear and misery . . . a place that lies between darkness and light . . .

Yeah, he thought, all that's needed right now is the pitter-patter notes of the *Twilight Zone* theme to come tiptoeing out of those trees across there.

Ignoring the mind chatter, John pressed on. Now the main road that cut across the Back Lane was in sight. Beyond that, the village proper with its stone cottages, pub, and green bounded on one side by a pond. It would be the English Tourist Board's vision of an idyllic rural village if it wasn't for the vast Necropolis— aka City of the Dead—on the hill. A hundred-acre cemetery once served by its own miniature railway system that passed beneath an archway on which was inscribed: *BOUND FOR GLORY*.

Now there was a sense that the old lane was getting ready to run underground. The level of the lane dropped; the banks rose so he was fully enclosed on three sides with only a strip of open blue sky above him. In the distance came the tolling of the cemetery bell.

It was then that he found Elizabeth.

As simply as that.

Her bicycle had been dropped on its side. Elizabeth lay on her back on a sunlit swath of dandelions and clover.

John Newton took one look at her, and in a curiously dislocated way, and more in surprise than shock, said to himself: "My God. Her throat's been cut."

Chapter Three

One

Her throat's been cut. . . .

At that moment the world vanished. Or at least to John Newton it did. The lane, the trees, the stone cottages, the swan on the village pond, even the blue sky. Everything blurred and was sucked to some other place.

Everything, that is, but Elizabeth.

He stared down at his daughter. She lay with her eyes wide open. Blood covered her throat in a broad wet slick. From there it drenched her yellow T-shirt.

There was so much soil mixed with the blood. It looked as if a handful of brown dirt had been poured onto it, so it still stood proud and dry of the blood flooding down his daughter's body.

Her throat's been cut. . . .

The words churned through his mind. Now they made no sense to him.

All he could do was stand, stare . . . while those

dumb, meaningless stupid words rolled around the inside of his uncomprehending skull.

Her throat's been cut. . . .

At that moment Elizabeth sighed. She pulled herself onto one elbow as if she were in bed waiting for her good-night kiss.

All of a sudden words gushed from his lips. It was the question parents always ask: "Elizabeth! What happened to you?"

The world rushed back into focus around him; he was down on his knees beside her, helping her sit up on the grass.

Elizabeth struggled to draw breath; then she said, "I fell off . . . stupid thing!" She tried to kick the bike.

Elizabeth's answer seemed as obvious as John's question. But at least it explained everything.

"Jesus, Lizzie," John said, feeling concern burst like a bomb inside his chest. "I thought you were—" *Dead?* Seamlessly he moderated what he was saying. "I thought you were really badly hurt."

"I am badly hurt," she retorted. "It's that stupid bike. It's no good."

"Here . . . let me have a look. No, hon, lift your chin up for me . . . uh . . . that's a bad cut, sweetheart."

"Are my shoes spoilt?"

"No, they're okay, hon."

"I'm not going to hospital."

"I'm afraid you are." Now he could see what looked like a second open mouth just under her chin. The skin had well and truly split wide open. Still, he found himself shocked by the amount of soil in and around the wound.

"You've really taken a tumble, haven't you?"

"Am I going to die?"

"No." He quickly hugged her and made sure she saw his reassuring smile. "But we've got to get it sorted out . . . or you'll end up bleeding all over the furniture."

"Stupid bike."

"How did you fall off?" Again he realized it was an-

31

other one of those all-too-obvious parent questions (it belonged in the same file as "If you break your legs, don't come running to me").

"A stone," she said, now more angry than shocked. "There was a stone that did it."

He looked. There was no stone. More likely she'd just been going too fast, then simply lost control of the bike. His priority now was to get her to hospital. He didn't like the way her blood trickled so freely from her chin. If anything, those ruby red drips were coming faster than ever.

"Come on, Elizabeth," he told her gently. "Let's go and get you sorted out."

Instead of waiting to be helped to her feet, she grabbed the bike, stood up, and began pushing it back up the lane in the direction of home.

"Wait . . . it's all right, hon. I'll do that," he told her quickly, surprised at her resilience. If anything, she seemed angry rather than hurt. But then she'd always had a high pain threshold. Visiting the dentist never fazed her; she hadn't even cried as a baby when she received her infant inoculations. Mingling with the shock of seeing her as bloody as this, he also felt a good shot of pride. Elizabeth was made of tough stuff. If she could take life's knocks with such aplomb, she'd go far.

He'd taken the bike from her by now, and he wheeled it along the lane. Elizabeth walked with her head held high, seemingly defying the injury to ruin her self-composure. She walked with her hand cupped a few inches below her face, catching the dripping blood, until a pool of glistening red formed in her palm.

God, she was a tough cookie. He shook his head in wonder and followed his daughter along the grooves worn by the long-gone Roman chariots.

Two

In the front of the car, Elizabeth sat calmly on the bath towel he'd spread out for her. Another towel covered her lap, while she held a fistful of kitchen tissue to her still-bleeding chin. She looked like a midget Santa Claus figure complete with bushy beard.

Patiently she gazed in front of her as he rushed round the garden, urging the dog into the kitchen, where he'd have to stay penned until their return. John tried telephoning Val to let her know what was happening. Her mobile was switched off. No doubt she'd be embroiled in a meeting. He thought about leaving a note for Paul, but took the gamble he wouldn't be back for a long time yet.

By this time John allowed himself the luxury of trembling a little, which must have been partly relief at finding Elizabeth more or less in one piece. Even so, he was just about holding everything together, and made a point of locking shut windows and setting the burglar alarm. But then canceling it because he'd forgotten his wallet and some coins. Even though you might have broken your leg or gashed open your head, the hospital still demanded that you pay to park your car there.

At last he switched on the radio in the kitchen (the dog would bark and worry the rugs if left alone in silence), then reset the alarm before going out to the car. Now Elizabeth's kitchen-tissue beard had turned red against her chin as the blood soaked through.

When he jogged to the end of the drive to open the double gates, he heard agitated voices—one male, one female—coming from the lane itself.

Despite his urgency about getting Elizabeth to the hospital, he found himself tuning into what was being said. Perhaps it was the emotion in the voices that caught his attention. If anything, the woman's voice sounded fearful, while the man's veered more to anger.

"I tell you," the still unseen woman was saying, "it was the letter. That's why he was so upset this morning. He's never gone off before like this. The letter must—"

"Why on earth did you show it to him, then?"

33

"I didn't intend to. I left it on the table. But he came in asking for breakfast while—"

"Breakfast! He's always asking for breakfast."

"He saw the letter and—"

"You should've thrown it away."

"I didn't have time, Robert. When he saw it he just cried out. He was like a little boy screaming as if he'd hurt himself."

"Dear God." The *Dear God* was laced with irritation.

"Robert, he was terrified."

"He read it, then?"

"Yes."

"Why on earth did you let him run off like that? In his pajamas! We must be bloody laughing stocks. Why can't . . ."

John now saw the couple as he swung open the driveway gates. The man had seen John, too, and clammed up.

John showed that he wasn't paying any attention to the couple. But the truth of the matter was the writer side of him never switched off. Even in the present circumstances, with his daughter dripping blood into a towel.

It wasn't deliberate on his part; it was fully automatic now. Even at funerals some part of his mind would absorb details for future work, whether images, the things people said, or peculiar incidents.

Now it was the middle-aged couple hurrying red-faced up the hill. John didn't know their names, but he'd seen them before in the village. The woman was mousy, dressed plainly, and struck him as being shy; certainly way down the list when it came to saying boo to a goose. Her husband was sturdily built, smiled a lot, and spoke loudly when he came to into the pub. He was one who'd call out, "Usual, love!" to the barmaid no matter how many were at the bar before him.

Today they looked like yet another Skelbrooke family in crisis. On seeing John, the man shifted his expression from fuming irritation to broad smiles. The pair continued by as if enjoying nothing more than a walk up the lane.

But once they'd gone by, John heard the woman whisper, "Robert. Ask him?"

"No . . . do you want everyone to know?" This was also whispered, but Robert's whisper was the kind that people in the next street hear.

"Robert, please . . ."

"Uh . . . all right."

By this time John had the gates open and was heading back to the car.

"Eh . . . excuse me . . . ah?"

John turned to look back at the man.

"Sorry to trouble you," the man began, the voice gruff, no-nonsense, not apologetic in any shape or form. "But we're looking for . . . uhm . . ."

"We're looking for my father." This time the wife had plucked up courage to speak. It was probably fear that did it. Her voice was quick-sounding, breathless. "I wonder if you've seen him. He was wearing pajamas and he's a bit, well—"

"Forgetful," the man said, tactful at last.

John nodded. "I did as a matter of fact."

"Oh, when?" The woman sounded brighter now.

"Just a few minutes ago."

"Oh, you couldn't show us where, could you? We're ever so worried about him."

She looked worried. *His* eyes still carried a flash of anger.

"I'm sorry. I can't. My daughter's had a fall from her bike. I need to get her to hospital." As soon as he said the words, he felt like an unfeeling shit; an uncharitable shit at that.

"Oh, no, don't worry." The woman sounded embarrassed for having asked. Her dark mouselike eyes darted nervously as she spoke. "Don't let us keep you. I'm sure we'll find him."

Guiltily, John Newton walked back to the car. Elizabeth's injuries weren't life-threatening by any stretch of the imagination. Perhaps if he spared a few moments to help look for the old man? John felt a sudden sympathy for the woman. Certainly her husband wasn't showing much in the way of compassion. The man was standing on the grass banking, a hand shielding his eyes as he scanned the meadow. He looked more like a hunter searching for something to kill rather than a man looking for his elderly father-in-law.

But the moment John saw Elizabeth, he knew where his priorities lie. She looked pale now. Shock had started to kick in. The tissue had turned a soggy mass of red.

"Come here, hon," he said, climbing into the car. "Let me take that tissue away. There . . . use the towel instead."

"But it'll get messed up with blood."

"Don't worry," he said gently. "It might help stop the bleeding."

"Will it wash?" She sounded anxious.

"I'm sure it will."

"Are you sure my shoes aren't ruined?"

He didn't give them a second glance; instead he gave her a warm, reassuring smile. "They're fine. The important thing is that we get that chin of yours fixed."

Holding the towel to her chin, she nodded. "I'll be glad when we get to hospital."

He figured from that that the wound was starting to hurt. Starting the car, he reversed out onto the lane. The couple were standing on the grass bank looking over the hedge into the meadow.

As he turned the car he saw a pair of figures moving slowly—very slowly—down from the top of the lane. There was the elderly man in striped pajamas. His head hung down with exhaustion. Helping him carefully by the arm was Mr. Marcello from the post office.

The daughter and son-in-law hadn't noticed the pair yet. Both still stood looking over the hedge.

John, relieved to be of some help, touched the horn long enough to catch the couple's attention. When they looked at him, he pointed in the direction of the old man and Martin Marcello. The couple saw the old man immediately. The woman shot John a grateful smile.

As John drove forward down the lane toward the main road, he said to Elizabeth, "There's my good deed for the day."

"What good deed, Dad?"

He smiled. "It doesn't matter. How're you feeling, hon?"

"Fine. It doesn't hurt."

Which he interpreted as her chin was hurting, only she was trying hard to be brave.

What a day! And it wasn't even halfway through yet. His neighbors had fled from their house, apparently half crazy with fear. He'd witnessed a geriatric runaway. His daughter had opened up what looked like a second mouth under her chin—blood everywhere. He even felt its sticky grip on the steering wheel. But he'd no need to worry now. The hospital would fix the wound. Soon she'd be back watching cartoons. John decided to buy some comfort food for her on the way home. Perhaps one of those bright green fondant frog cakes from the baker's in the village.

Turning onto the main road, he told himself it had been one of those crazy days . . . or crazy mornings, he corrected . . . when everything had either gone wrong, or had been downright weird. Already he half-glimpsed a pattern to the weirdness, as if the runaway old man and the fleeing family, and maybe even his daughter's accident, yearned to be connected together into a coherent pattern. But he was still too shaken by all that blood to think about it right now.

As he accelerated away from the village, Elizabeth asked if she could listen to her favorite CD. He said she could. Then he tried to concentrate on the road ahead. Not the redness that bloomed like a flower through the towel she pressed to her chin.

Chapter Four

One

The old man called from the bedroom window. "Harry, the letters have started. Go up to the Water Mill and warn Mr. Kelly . . . he'll know what to do. There'll be trouble if we don't do anything. Harry? Where are you, Harry? Why won't you answer me?"

In the garden below, Robert Gregory shook his head behind his paper.

The old man called again louder, "Harry? It's me, Stan Price, why won't you answer me, Harry?"

"Because he's been dead for the last five years. You went to the funeral, you stupid old goat."

"Robert? Did you call me?" The mousy woman came out through the back door. She was carrying a bowl full of potato peelings.

Robert Gregory jerked his head at the bedroom window where the old man leaned out. "He's been calling from that window for the last twenty minutes. Can't you do anything to quiet him down?"

"I'm sorry, Robert, he's never like this usually. It's probably that nasty letter. Whoever sent it wants locking up."

"I've told you, Cynthia. It'll just be kids. But can't you do anything with *him?*"

"Robert, he's confused."

"He's upsetting the neighbors, Cynthia."

"He's never usually like this. It's the—"

"The letter, I know." Robert returned to his paper, staring gloomily at the sports pages. "But we can't have him yelling out of the window all day. I won't be able to show my face in the pub at this rate."

"Once he's had his dinner he'll quiet down."

"Lord, let's hope so."

The old man's voice sprang up again. A notch higher, as if in desperation. "Harry! Harry! The letters have started again. Go up to the Water Mill; warn Mr. Kelly. Harry?"

"Jesus wept," Robert Gregory muttered.

Cynthia Gregory looked up at the window. "Don't go upsetting yourself, Dad, please."

"Harry!"

"Go back to bed, Dad."

"Harry! It's the letters!"

"Oh, Dad, please. I'm making your dinner."

"Harry. It's Baby Bones . . . Baby Bones is back."

Robert muttered to himself. "Christ. It's a damn madhouse . . . we'll all be as bad as him before we're through."

"Robert." Cynthia sounded wounded. "It's not his fault. He's suffering from dementia."

"It's not him that's suffering from dementia," Robert grunted. "We're the ones suffering from it."

"Harry! Come to the window, Harry! It's the letters again. Tell Mr. Kelly."

In a tight voice, Robert Gregory spoke to the old man in the window. "Dad, don't you remember? Harry's dead. He died five years ago. You went to the funeral."

"Harry . . . *Harry!* I got a letter! Harry, I'm frightened!"

"Poor Dad." Cynthia's eyes watered.

"Poor us."

"He's calling his old friend," Cynthia said. "They were friends before they even went to school together. Harry lived in the house there, just over the back fence. Dad used to tell me he'd call Harry from his bedroom window just as he's doing now, then they'd go fishing together."

"Harry! Har . . . reee." The old man's voice cracked. He sounded close to weeping.

Cynthia sighed. "Oh, I better go up to him, I suppose."

"Harry! Listen to me. It's Baby Bones . . . He's back. He's back!"

"Dear God," Robert Gregory murmured into his newspaper. "If I ever get like that, put a bullet in my head."

Two

John Newton had returned home from the hospital by early afternoon. He had managed to get a message through to Val about Elizabeth's accident. She'd called in some favors to finish work early. As they made sandwiches in the kitchen at the Water Mill, he ran through the day's events. He told her about the departure of the Haslems, and seeing the old man attempting to flee the village up the back lane. How Martin Marcello had followed him from the post office, after noticing old Mr. Price, shuffling away from home in his pajamas. And how the old man had finally been reunited with his daughter and son-in-law.

Val washed cherry tomatoes in the sink. Her mind was still firmly with Elizabeth. "Did they say anything else at the hospital?"

"No, apart from not getting the wound wet for a week."

"And they're certain she doesn't need stitches?"

"No, they used tape to hold the wound together."

"There's bound to be a scar."

"There will. But it will be right under here." John pointed with the tip of the knife under his chin. "No one will see it."

"God, I'm away a couple of hours and all hell breaks loose."

"Hey, you're not blaming me, are you?"

"No, John." She smiled, relaxing a little. "I know these things happen. She's going to be all right, that's the main thing."

"And perhaps a bit wiser, too," he said. "She might not go so fast on her bike again."

"And pigs might fly. Just make sure she wears the helmet, John."

Val slipped effortlessly back into the mother role again after a few hours of being the highly efficient export manager at the kitchen utensil manufacturer where she'd worked these last ten years. A company flippantly referred to within the family as Pots 'n' Pans R Us.

As they talked, John buttered the bread and watched his wife move around the kitchen with that seductive walk of hers. She'd loosened her shoulder-length hair from the clip, teased her blouse from her skirt, so he caught glimpses of her bare waist when she reached up to the top shelves for the glasses. It may have been the aftereffects of a chaotic morning, but he found himself craving to stroke her bare back before slipping off to bed to grab a few steamy moments alone with her.

"John? John, you've not been listening, have you? Did she need a booster?"

The image of Val lying naked on the bed, smiling sexily up at him, reluctantly sloped away from his mind's eye. "Booster?" he echoed, scrambling to pick up the thread of the conversation.

She shot him a smile. "Booster, yes. Did Elizabeth need a tetanus booster?"

41

"Oh . . ." He was back on track. "No. The one she had as a baby is still good for a few years yet. Do you fancy orange juice to go with the sandwich?"

"No, let's go mad and have a beer."

"God, I could do with it."

"The accident really shook you up this morning, didn't it?"

"You can say that again. I thought she'd cut her throat. I really thought she—"

"Put it behind you." Kissing him, she slipped her hand around the back of his neck. "Mmm . . . muscles are tight. If we get a chance after lunch, I'll see what I can do to relax you."

He found a grin working across his face. "Is that a promise?"

Her voice dropped, sounding so husky and warm that it sent a shiver up his back. "We'll have to wait and see, won't we, my little glamour boy?"

He slipped a hand under her blouse and stroked the skin on her back. It was deliciously silky and deliciously cool despite the summer heat.

"Mm, John . . . you know I demand gratification . . . and I will begin with that cold beer. You get that. I'll bring the sandwiches."

His heart purred inside his chest. Somehow she always made him feel like a teenager again; one just about to experience a naked clinch for the first time. Perhaps it was that erotic flash in her eye; or the way her lips would grow larger, redder, and so compelling he could hardly take his eyes off them. Hell, yes, it was all happening at an animal level. But hallelujah to that. After seventeen years of marriage, they still enjoyed moments in bed that were nothing less than electric. And now, with a promise of generating a little more electricity upstairs that afternoon, he went through into the lounge of the Water Mill with a spring in his step and memories of the blood-sopped morning thankfully blunted.

Three

"*Sexy Paul . . .* Sexy Paul Newton!" There were four girls of around fifteen sitting on the wall that flanked the cemetery gates. He knew them well enough. They called themselves the "Paul Newton Fan Club." He knew full well that they were just taking the piss.

"Sexy Paul. Sexy Paul Newton," they sang again as he walked by. He gave them a deliberately nonchalant wave. Immediately they whispered amongst themselves and then broke off into giggles.

He hoped to God that they didn't follow him today. He didn't really mind them, but what they'd see would go round the school like a dose of measles.

Thankfully, they didn't follow. So he quickened his pace, following the line of the cemetery railings. ("Is that to keep us out or *them* in," his father was overfond of saying. But it still got a laugh out of Elizabeth.) Anyway, today Paul Newton had a secret meeting with someone he would prefer wouldn't become known to the Paul Newton Fan Club. Or to his family (who thought he was mooching around town with friends). Because today was going to be different.

A sun-drenched path took him further uphill. Open fields lay to his left, while on his right the cemetery clung to the hill. Through the iron fence he could see darkly shadowed places beneath masses of trees that erupted from what had been once neatly tended pathways. Tree trunks even burst from the graves themselves. With the imagination he'd inherited from his father, he pictured the tree roots worming their way through rotted coffins and right into the bones of long-dead men and women. Maybe a big taproot forced its way through the jaws of a man rotted by syphilis. And his skull was encrusted with pouting florets of milk mold . . . while the bodies of a million maggots lay there like dried rice, filling the casket from top to bottom. . . .

Cool, he thought, smiling. Maybe he would follow in

Dad's footsteps after all. But he'd write horror movie scripts. And in a movie that would take the world by storm the syphilitic corpse would burst from the grave like a missile, showering the neighborhood with maggots. They'd come down rattling on roofs and cars and burrow into dogs' coats.

Exceedingly cool. He grinned in an easy, handsome way, enjoying the flow of thoughts through his head. Picturing his fantasy movie, he moved on to another scene. A guy and a gal are making out in the backseat of a car; the guy kisses her nipples; they're hard and they're dark . . . the guy and the girl are getting close to that moment . . . *that moment* . . . she's naked now. . . .

But isn't this supposed to be a horror flick? Paul Newton was miles away. He'd even forgotten about his secret rendezvous; well, for the moment anyway. But the Great God Sex that rules all heads (from twelve to eighty) had taken control now.

A scene did suggest itself where the guy, hearing that rain of maggots on the roof, exclaims, "Hey, what's that noise?"

"Don't stop now, Jim" (or Joe or Bert or whatever the frig the hero of the movie is called). Then he leaves the car, pulling up his pants as he does so. Sees the maggots writhing on the ground, then hears a noise in the bushes. "I can hear something," Jim, Joe, Bert (or whatever the hell he's called) says to the naked and still hotly panting girl. "I'm just going to see what it is. I'll be back in a minute."

The girl groans with sexual disappointment. Boyfriend disappears into the bushes where he's glimpsed something shuffling along in a postmortem kind of way. There's a scream. . . .

But Paul Newton realized the sex scene playing in his head was far more interesting than the horror angle now. The girl would be standing naked by the car, nipples hard as cherrystones in the cool night air, her feet placed apart, pulse throbbing as . . .

Hell. He was here. So soon, too.

A section of fence had collapsed inward, giving easy access to the graveyard. He paused. Here, bushes and trees clustered across the face of the cemetery so densely, it was as if they tried to hide some deadly secret. A breath of air stirred them. The sound made him think of something massive moving through the trees; an unseen prowling *something* that watched him from the shadows.

With a shiver, he realized that today was that single point in time when his fantasies and reality would collide. Licking his lips, he entered the cemetery; the lush grass reached his elbows. This was akin to walking through a green ocean with the tops of gravestones breaking the surface like shark fins. They were dark, predatory shapes. Soon they surrounded him as he moved deeper into the cemetery. It was silent now, except for the lone cry of a bird. Soon he'd passed from sunlight to shadow beneath the trees. Hell. It was dark as sin in there.

It took a moment for his eyes to accustom themselves after the transition from brilliance to near-darkness, but at last they did. And by the headstone of a family burnt to death in a house fire stood a figure.

"I didn't think you would dare come," said the figure. "Follow me."

He did as he was told. And followed the figure along a path that weaved between graves, deeper and deeper into the heart of the graveyard.

Four

"Is that Harry?"

"No, Dad, it's me." Cynthia Gregory walked into the bedroom. She sounded tired. It had been a horrible day.

"I need to see Harry. It's important."

"You can't, Dad."

"Why not?"

"Don't you remember, Dad?" Her voice, despite her woes, was considerate. "Harry died five years ago. You were at the funeral. Now, Dad, sit down to the table. Robert's bringing your meal. Do you want to go to the toilet first?"

"Is it supper time?" The afternoon sun streamed in as the old man sat on the bed. "Is it supper time? I'm hungry."

"Yes, Dad." The old man's daughter sighed. "It's supper time. Now, do you need the bathroom?"

"I want to speak to Harry. It's important."

"Oh, Dad . . ." She placed a tablecloth on a table that faced the window. Then she set out a knife and fork. "There. You come and have something to eat."

He rose to his feet, then went to the window, where he stared out with filmy eyes.

"I'm hungry," he said. "It must be supper time by now."

"Robert's coming up now. Meat pie all right? And there's a crumble to follow."

"And bread and butter?"

"Yes. Just as you like it."

"I don't like brown bread. Never have."

"No, it's white bread."

He spoke about food as he always did. It was one of his few interests in life. Yet he looked out of the window as if he expected visitors. She shook her head. Despite everything, she loved her father. He'd been good to the family. Their mother had died young, but he'd never neglected his children once. Often, he'd work from home so he could be with them. Summers he'd take them swimming to the lake at the water mill. It was a place that drew him back time and time again. He'd known the Kelly family that owned the place then, and he'd spend hours talking to Dianne Kelly; so much so that Cynthia wondered if there was romance blossoming between the widower and the spinster.

Now the old man looked out of the window. His lips moved as he whispered nonsense to himself. Cynthia tried not to ask the question, but she found it tumbling from her lips anyway. "Oh, Dad. Why did you run away from the house this morning? You scared me half to death disappearing like that."

He didn't reply. His eyes were on the cemetery in the distance as if he looked for someone there.

"What was it about the letter that frightened you?"

"Letter?" His milky blue eyes were innocent.

"Yes, the letter you saw this morning. It was a wicked thing to do, but it was just some silly prank by children. They should have known you're in no state to go leaving bars of chocolate in the cemetery. If you ask me, it was just plain cruel and I've a good mind to—"

"Letter? Letter!" The old man remembered; a light flared in his eyes. One that shone with fear. "It's the letter. The letters have started again." With a shocking suddenness, he struck the window with his fist. "Harry! Harry! *It's come back. The letters have started again. Go warn Mr. Kelly. Harry . . . Harry, why won't you answer me?*"

"Oh, God," Cynthia murmured in utter defeat. "Dad, I wish you wouldn't say these things."

"Now, now, Dad, what's all this, then?" Robert Gregory breezed into the room with the tray. "Don't go upsetting Cynthia, there's a good lad. Eat your dinner while it's hot."

"Harry . . ." The force had gone from the old man's voice now. Deflated, he allowed himself to be led by the elbow to the table. "Why won't Harry come round to the house anymore? He hasn't visited me in months."

"Now, Dad," Robert Gregory boomed louder, as if sheer volume would have a calming effect. "Tuck in. There's crumble and custard for afters."

"I've told him," Cynthia said in that tired, distracted way of hers. "But he's still worrying about that letter."

"Now don't go fussing about silly letters, Dad." He helped the old man sit at the table. "Eat up, there's a good chap."

Cynthia went to sit on the bed. She crossed her arms,

rubbing her elbows with her hands, troubled.

Robert Gregory dropped his voice to a stage whisper. "Cynthia. Go down and have your lunch."

"But I don't think Dad will—"

"Don't you worry. I'll sit with him. You go down and unwind for a while. You've really been through the mill this morning, you know."

With a grateful smile, Cynthia went downstairs. Soon Robert Gregory could hear the clink of cutlery as she ate. He waited for a moment, shuddering at the sloppy sounds as Stan ate the mashed potato. Then he went across to the table, where he glared down at the man attacking the full plate of food. "I think you've had enough of that, don't you?"

Robert picked up the bread, dropped it onto the mound of steaming potato, and then took it through to the toilet, where he silently scraped it into the bowl. It took three flushes, but at last the food was gone. After that, he put the empty plate in front of the old man, who stared at it in confusion.

A little while later Cynthia returned to room. "All done?" She sounded brighter.

Her father looked down at the plate. His eyes were puzzled and sad-looking.

"Is it supper time yet?" he asked. "I'm hungry."

Five

Paul Newton felt electricity in the air. It crackled down his nerves from his scalp to his fingertips. The figure beneath the trees turned to look at him.

The eyes enchanted him—they were huge, luminous things that locked onto him and wouldn't let him look away.

"I thought you'd have preferred to be with your friends," she said.

He couldn't take his eyes off the slender figure, or her eyes, or her curling hair that cascaded down over her shoulder onto one breast.

"Is there something wrong with my T-shirt?" she asked, looking down.

"No . . . *no.*" Good God. Like some lovesick kid he'd been staring at her breasts. "No. I thought you looked . . ." He swallowed, then added lamely, "Nice."

"Thank you, Paul Newton. You look nice, too. New shirt?"

"Yes." His mouth stayed dry. There was a real danger now his tongue would stick to the roof of his mouth, leaving him making groaning sounds like some zombie wanna-be.

"It's lovely," she said, reaching forward to touch it. "Cotton and summer go together like strawberries and cream, the perfect combination."

"Your hair looks different." Oh Christ, why did he sound so lame? He clenched one fist behind his back. This was his first real date, for Chrissakes . . . and with Miranda Bloom, the most gorgeous girl of his year. And here he was babbling nonsense. He tried to look calm, cool, and collected. He leaned back against a stone angel, which rocked with a grating sound. Alarmed, he grabbed it around the waist to steady it.

Miranda giggled.

"This place isn't safe." He grinned. "The whole lot's falling down."

"It's full of dead people, too. More than eighty thousand if I remember rightly."

"Hell, that's a lot of bones."

She smiled. Paul Newton found it was a breathtakingly cute smile. His heart hammered.

"You've never been here before have you?" she said, stroking back a swath of curls.

He shook his head. "It's always been locked. I mean . . . I mean the main gates have always been locked." Hell, he was even stammering now.

"They've been locked years. The place isn't used anymore."

"At least this lot will rest in peace, then." He nodded at the acres of headstones lying beneath the trees.

Simon Clark

"Maybe not. Lots of people come here after to dark to be alone." She gave that beautiful smile again, her dark eyes catching the glints of light falling through the branches. "There are always couples sipping wine in the graveyard at midnight, if you know what I mean?" She wrinkled her nose.

He nodded and said that he did, while frantically sifting his memory for the meaning of the expression. But the look in her eye was interpretation enough. She meant people made out here. He thought of naked bodies lying entwined on the grave slab of *Nathaniel Benjamin 1863–1938, Mayor of Dewsbury and husband to Mary. Peace after great suffering.* Dear God, how could you keep your finger on the button when you could picture Benjamin's skull leering up at you through six feet of grave soil?

"Come on," she said. "I'll show you round."

Then she did something surprising, yet wonderfully exciting—she took his hand in hers. Then they walked hand in hand amongst the headstones—alone but for the bones of eighty thousand dead.

Six

While his teenage son was moving deeper into the graveyard, and at the same time beginning to cross that boundary between boyhood and manhood, John Newton sat in an armchair at the Water Mill eating a sandwich. Val, from beneath a smoky fringe of hair, shot him glances with come-to-bed eyes.

Meanwhile, Elizabeth, with her bandaged jaw, lay on her side like a Roman aristocrat, her top half propped up on one elbow as she drank from a carton of juice. She'd chosen to lie on a glass section of floor that was the window to the millrace. Through it you could see water running beneath the house. It was certainly this square of glass, some four feet by eight, that had sold the house to them all those months ago. One look at it

50

as he and Val walked in for the first time, and *Wow!*
They were well and truly snared.

Both had gazed in wonder. The glass panels set in
the floor were incredibly strong. "You could march elephants across those," the agent had told them. "It
won't so much as crack." But still, John Newton found
it an effort of will to actually stand on the glass floor
and peer down into what amounted to a pit of darkness. It didn't make it any easier when lights beneath
the glass were switched on to reveal torrents of water
cascading through the stone tunnel. In years gone by
the flow would turn the waterwheel, which drove the
millstones that ground wheat into flour.

So, Val and John had toured the house, then climbed
back into the car, telling the agent that they'd other
properties to see. They'd driven all of thirty yards when
Val turned to him and said, "John, we've got to have
it, haven't we?"

John had nodded. The Water Mill was irresistible.
They'd gone straight back and made the offer.

Of course, as in the rest of life, nothing ever goes that
smoothly. They'd offered less than the asking price. The
agent had haggled. Then they'd sat and drunk coffee
over the millrace again, gazing in wonder at the hundreds of gallons of water tumbling just feet beneath
their feet, then—collapse of stout party—they'd caved
in and offered the agent's asking price. After a pro-
tracted song and dance between banks, lawyers, struc-
tural engineers, surveyors, and for some reason the
lady who lived down the street, it was all settled. Five
months after clapping eyes on the place, the Newtons
moved in. For weeks afterward they'd switch off the
TV to gaze down through the glass floor at those speeding waters. In the light of the spot lamps, the torrents
never looked the same twice. If it were sunny for more
than a day or two, the water would take on a hint of
green from algae in the water. If it rained heavily, clays
in the streambed dramatically stained the water blood
red.

The effect was nothing less than magical. It hadn't even been dampened when Paul gleefully told Elizabeth there was a local legend that children had drowned there in the tunnel beneath the house. Threats of grounding plus removal of the computer from Paul's bedroom encouraged him to retract the story.

Still, Elizabeth would gaze down through the glass at the waters swirling just four feet below and ask thoughtfully, "Dad, do you think anyone has ever drowned down there before?"

John always made a point of laughing as if the idea was just plain silly; then he'd distract her by changing the subject.

Elizabeth lay on her favorite spot on the glass, directly above the rushing stream. Even though the thick glass shielded her completely from what must have been a considerable roar, Elizabeth told them she liked to feel the vibration of it tickling her behind as she sat there.

Once, after a particularly heavy downfall of rain (and when both Paul and Elizabeth were at school), John made love to Val on the observation window. The vibrating glass certainly did have a stimulating effect. Even if the image did linger in John's mind of the glass giving way beneath their combined weight, and plunging them into the torrent below.

"How's the chin, hon?" John asked.

"OK," Elizabeth replied, more interested now in what was happening to *Tom & Jerry* on the TV than the state of her chin.

"Does it still hurt?"

"No."

John smiled and shook his head. The girl was made of iron and steel, all right. He only wished she'd develop a greater sense of self-preservation. She sucked on the carton straw; some juice dripped down to stain the dressing bandaged there beneath her chin, so a blotch of raspberry contrasted with the rusty brown of the bloodstain. The dressing was maybe a bit too big for her chin, forming a projecting shelf onto which crumbs from her lunch had dropped. These John had to carefully remove with the pastry brush so they wouldn't become stuck in the drying gunk that was forming a scab.

"How's the book going?" Val asked.

"Not bad," he said, telling a little white lie. "I've written the first couple of pages." The last thing he wanted to admit right now was that he doubted if it would be even half as good *Blast His Eyes* and that already he'd begun to harbor fears that they might end up losing the Water Mill before they'd even grown used to calling it home.

So, that was where the little white lie came in. It was there to protect Val, not deceive her. He didn't want her worrying needlessly at this stage. Hell, didn't he go through this crisis of confidence with every book he wrote? That came with being a writer. Once you became cocksure about your talent, that was when you fell slap-bang on your face. Like taking an exam, or going for a job interview, a little fear was good for you. It spurred you on to make a greater effort. At least that was what he was telling himself now.

"John . . . John?"

He looked up, snapping out of his gloomy trail of thought.

"John." Val gave him a direct look. "Seeing as Elizabeth is engrossed in watching television and Paul's out." She smiled. "I thought I'd have a shower. Come up and have one after me." Her voice was silkily casual. "Finish your coffee first; it will give me a couple of minutes to get ready."

Elizabeth was *completely* engrossed in the TV—the wonder that was Cartoon Network would keep her entertained for another hour at least.

Shooting him a provocative glance, Val left the room. Smiling to himself, he cleared away the plates to the kitchen, finished his coffee, returned the salad to the refrigerator, then locking the house doors, told Elizabeth he was going up to shower.

"Mum, too?" Elizabeth asked in a disinterested kind of way. She'd seen this before.

"Yes, hon. Shout if you need anything."

His daughter nodded her bandaged head. "Enjoy yourself," she added obliquely.

He found himself coloring a little as he climbed the stairs.

Val lay beneath a white sheet. She lay on her back, hands behind her head, gazing up at the ceiling.

"Right on time." She smiled and pulled back the sheet so he could climb in.

Her body looked taut, almost catlike, as she lay there naked. As he shed his own clothes, she stretched luxuriously. "I think we both need this." Her voice grew husky. "It will be therapeutic."

"I need some special therapy, I can tell you." Smiling, he slid in beside her. Once more he marveled at how cool her skin felt against his. Her touch was deliciously gentle. Instantly the heat of sheer desire prickled through him. Lightly he kissed her breasts, paying particular attention to her nipples, which he feathered with his tongue. God, this felt good after all the shit today. The dull wearing ache of that two-hour hospital wait evaporated. He didn't think about the book. Or about anything in the world outside.

He was going to escape into passion. And passion as hot and as sizzling as he could make it. Already Val breathed deeply into his ear as she squirmed beneath the workings of his tongue. His hands joined in, either firmly massaging or caressing lightly.

"Oh, John," she sighed, pulling his head down to her nipple. Gently he took the bud of hardening skin between his teeth and applied pressure.

"Harder." She moaned. "Bite harder."

The cry that came from her lips was powered by sheer pleasure.

Excited now, feeling a flame crackle through him, he

rolled her fully onto her back. Her thighs closed around him, gripping his waist. He looked down at her face; her eyes were closed, her mouth partly open. Now her lips had grown big and red and moist. Her hair was a crazed veil half hiding her face.

"Now," she said urgently. *"Now!"*

He gripped her waist and drove himself into her. With every push of his hips, with every surge of her breathing, with every moan of her pleasure, the outside world—along with his baggage car of cares—receded into the distance, and finally died away to nothing.

Chapter Five

One

Sunlight struck her face. It seemed nothing less than a physical blow as she ran from shadow to open ground. The place was an infestation of weeds, bushes, creepers, vines, and acre upon acre of gravestones bulging from the ground like scabs.

Jesus Christ, where is it?

She paused, sweaty, hot, breathless, a pain digging so deep into her side, she cried with every breath she took.

Where the hell was it? It had to be somewhere near here. She'd seen it plenty of times as a kid; she'd even freewheeled her bike across it once. It was a dare all local kids had scared themselves with at one time or other. Now the graveyard looked different to her. But then again, it was fifteen years since she'd actually been in the place. The last time had been to offer up her virginity on some godforsaken tombstone shaped like a four-poster bed. The Virgin Buster, they had called it . . . that was where many a Skelbrooke teenager had finally cut loose from Planet Childhood . . . hell, she was rambling like a lunatic. This thing was hitting her hard. Oh, Jesus, she was so scared; she'd never been so scared. But where in Christ's name was the stone? She needed it now. She needed it so badly.

She took a path that forked to her right downhill. Trees reared over her once more like beasts from a nightmare. Stone angels were overgrown and over-whelmed with bindweed. Nettles all but exploded from this tract of earth that held more than eighty thousand dead. As she ran, the carrier bag swinging from a balled fist, she read the headstones.

Corporal Stanley Harold Strong. Died of his wounds, Somme, 1916. A glorious death . . . Alice Wincanton Good-all, wife of Montgomery Nesbit Goodall, yielded the spirit, December 25th, 1879 . . . Huxley Peter Wrathler, released by the Lord God of his suffering 1867, aged 93 . . . Victoria Sef-ton, aged 6, drowned in the Water Mill Mere, July 2nd, 1911—short was her race, the longer is her rest, God called her hence because he thought it best, weep not for me, my parents dear . . .

"Damn." The path ended, blocked by a pyramid-shaped tomb that was a full ten feet tall. Turning, Mary Thorp retraced her steps. She was thirty years old. Too young to die.

Again she toiled up the path, plunging into shadow before bursting into sunlight, sunlight so bright it felt as if laser beams were burning right through her eyes to sear her brain.

Dear God, where is it? It must be near here. She re-membered the pyramid tomb; she remembered the stat-ues of children on the Necropolis wall.

. . . sweet little children taken into the arms of the Lord . . . not dead, but sleeping . . . don't weep for us, parents dear. . . .

She was a slim blond woman, she looked fit, but this was taking a toll of her. A dozen different pains speared through her thigh and buttock muscles. As she ran, a branch speared the carrier bag, dragging her to a dead stop.

"Shit! You bastard shit!"

Startled birds flew up from the bushes.

After dislodging the impaled carrier bag and checking that her precious gift was safe, she ran on, stopping every so often to read a headstone inscription before howling with frustration. Mary Thorp prayed she found what she was looking before he found her. *Him*. Joe Budgen. That bastard was hell-bent on tearing her apart. So she didn't wait for him while he was in jail. What was she supposed to do? He'd gone down for eight years. How did she know he would be out in four? Damn prisons. Why don't they keep killers behind bars forever? Everyone knew that Joe Budgen had gone up to Harrison's place with the intention of killing him. Cops were so fucking blind.

Now Joe Budgen was out. He'd learned she was living with Stevo; that she'd had a kid by him. And Christ, Joe hated Stevo; he blamed him for grassing him up to the cops over that Ecstasy scam. And Joe would be even more pissed if he found out that Mary fell pregnant with Liam within about three weeks of Joe being sent down.

She cut from the main path to wade through long grass. Sunlight forced her to squint so tightly, she barely saw at all.

Where was that damned thing?

She had to find it soon. Had to.

Because now that was the key to everything.

She paused long enough to look around. Hell, the cemetery looked different from when she was last here fifteen years ago. Trees that were mature then had toppled in winter storms; those that were saplings would now be full-grown trees, altering the look of the place entirely. And there was that damned ivy; it was everywhere, snaking up over the faces of angels and cherubs like some spidery green cancer.

She climbed onto the back of a fallen Virgin Mary,

trying to find some high point where she might see that distinctive tombstone. The one with the statue of the little weeping kid. Of course, it might be gone now. Some kid showing off to his girlfriend (no doubt bound for the Virgin Buster) might have simply shoved the thing over into the nettles.

"Oh, Christ, no . . . not yet."

The words came out in a groan. She hadn't seen the gravestone with the weeping kid. Instead she'd seen a denim-jacketed figure striding up the hill. Although he didn't wave or shout, she knew that he'd seen her.

"Oh, Christ," she groaned again. "He can't have found me that quickly . . . shit, shit."

She looked around. There was no one in sight. No one to run to. Not that it mattered. He was a fucking head case. Once in the early days when they were together, she'd badmouthed him in a pizza restaurant and he'd simply leaned forward, stuck his fingers through her lips, and tried to tear out her tongue there and then. Three stitches—three fucking stitches she'd needed at hospital—then like an idiot she'd told the police that she'd bitten her own tongue eating pizza. God, she'd been stupid then, but yeah . . . same old story . . . she'd been in love with the thug . . . she'd believed he'd settle down; he'd change his ways . . . that they'd have kids and everything would be sugar 'n' spice and all things nice. But Joe always said he'd never have kids. ("Can't stand the little turds." He'd spit the words out. "Kids fuck you up.")

Now there he was. Mary Thorp stared in horror. He was going to tear her apart. Hadn't he telephoned her the same day he'd gotten released to tell her just that?

"Mary. Consider yourself fucked," he'd breathed down the phone. "I'm going to come down to Skelbrooke. Then I'm going to fuck your whole life away."

She believed him.

With a shout, she ran up hill through a wilderness of brambles and trees and shadows and headstones. Her feet rapped against the ground hard enough to carry tremors down to the bones in their coffins, startling the rabbits that had nested there. The heat blazed in her face. Her eyes blurred with tears that came out in big glistening gobs.

Oh, God . . . it wasn't as if she didn't know this was going to happen. She should have seen it coming. But she'd ignored that square of paper weighted down beneath a hunk of tombstone outside her front door.

"MARY!"

The voice hit her like the blast from a grenade. Stung by its force, a yelping sound spurting from her throat, she started running.

"Mary . . . you can't run away from me."

She glanced back. Joe Budgen, his face oozing menace, was perhaps a hundred yards behind her. Even though he wasn't running, he surged through the grass like a tank. Her knees turned weak. For a moment she looked down at her legs, convinced they'd buckle, dropping her down in the grass, where all she could do was to lie and wait for him to find her.

In terror she found herself crying out. But she wasn't crying out to him for mercy. She cried out to the source of her misfortune. "I'm sorry . . . I'm sorry. Listen . . . I've been away . . . I never saw your letter. *Look!*" She held up the carrier bag to the trees as if invisible eyes watched her. "Look! I've brought you what you want. But I can't find the gravestone!" Her eyes flashed with hysteria. "It's here! I've got what you want!"

She struggled on, half stumbling, ever conscious of Joe Budgen getting nearer and nearer.

"Please, listen. I'm sorry I ignored your letter. But I've got what—what you want now . . . pl . . . per— leezze . . ." Her voice disintegrated into a stammer. "I— I got it. I—I goddittt!"

At that moment she looked back. Joe Budgen had paused to glare at her through his psychotic eyes. The man should have been laughable there in his faded denim jacket and black turtleneck with a gold Albert chain; his hair flashed blond. He looked more like a rent boy than local hard man. For a second their eyes locked. Nothing moved. A bird sang on the still summer air.

Then suddenly he began to run.

Turning, she ran too.

At that moment a crazy idea struck her. If she could only find the headstone with the crying-boy statue, everything would be OK. Magically she'd be safe like a child crying "Den" during a game of catch. She ran hard. Her eyes scanned the thousands of headstones, looking for that single distinctive statue. All she need do was find that, and to drop the carrier bag onto the slab.

Then she'd be safe. Joe Budgen could do nothing to harm her.

Now she could hear his feet pounding through the grass as he chased her. And as she ran, she found herself crying out over and over, *"No, no, no, no . . ."*

Two

"Miranda?" Paul looked over the ranks of headstones. "Did you hear someone screaming?"

"Screaming?" She shrugged. "There's always someone shouting or carrying on around here. It's nothing but a kids' playground these days."

Paul turned his head to hear the voice again. Although it sounded distant, he could hear real distress running through it.

"Lover's tiff," Miranda said, then pointed with the toe of her sandaled feet. "Look. See that?"

He noticed her toenails were painted a red so luscious that all he could do was stare at them, nothing else.

"See what's written on the back of that headstone? *Peace Be Unto You, Until You Follow Me.*"

He grinned. "In other words, take that smug look off your face, because it won't be long until you're pushing up daisies, too. Where now?"

"Who knows, who cares?" Slipping her arms around his neck, she smiled. "Kiss me."

Paul kissed her. Her lips seemed like vast cushions of velvet. He couldn't imagine anything as soft. Or exciting.

"Mmm . . ." She pulled back her head.

He found himself gazing into her eyes. Wonderful eyes that sent a zillion shivers through him.

"You know, Paul," she whispered, "you can touch me with your hands when we kiss."

This time when they kissed, she took hold of his fingers and guided them down to her breast.

Three

Mary Thorp ran through a tunnel of green as she sped along the path between the bushes. In and out of sunlight she ran. Plunging from deep shade to brilliant light, then back again. She raced through swarms of insects that hung like clouds of gold dust. Ivy snagged her feet. Sweat drenched her.

All the time she could hear *his* feet pounding behind.

The carrier bag swung at the end of her arm. It smacked stone crosses, then rebounded back against her thigh. Jesus . . . where was that headstone . . . she was sure it was close. She could have sworn she remembered that painted Jesus Christ standing with his hand raised like a traffic cop.

But where was that stone with the weeping child? Hell . . . Deep down she knew if she could only slap that bag down onto the stone, all this torture would end. Joe Budgen wouldn't tear her to pieces. He'd go away. He'd leave her and little Liam in peace.

This was only happening because she'd paid no attention to the letter that came in the dead of night a week ago. A folded piece of paper lying there, as if butter wouldn't melt. Damn it. If only she'd done what had been asked of her. Joe Budgen wouldn't be here. He wouldn't be chasing her.

God, if he caught her, he'd really hurt her this time. She cried out as a hand tore at her blond hair. Stopping, she turned to fight him. She wouldn't go down as easy as that. Not submissive, not merely waiting for him to head-butt her, or batter her face against a tombstone. She'd . . .

No . . . a low-hanging branch had snagged her hair. It held her as surely as if it was his fist gripping her. With her free hand she struggled to disentangle the mass of frothy hair from the branch.

Just thirty yards away, Joe rounded the corner. His eyes bored into hers.

"Mary. There's no way you're gonna get away from me. Did you hear me, Mary?"

She raged: *Damn hair, damn hair—I'll shave you off!*

At last she was free. Leaving a few golden strands hanging there, she tore along the path, weaving by tree trunks, leaping over toppled stone crosses. Rabbits scuttled aside. A squirrel raced up a tree trunk.

Behind her she heard his footsteps. Closer . . . closer . . .

Breathing didn't come easy now. Her throat burned. It was closing—the trachea narrowing to little thicker than a drinking straw.

"Where's that grave?" she yelled at the trees. "Where is it?" Then she added in a pleading voice while shaking the carrier bag, "Look. Just like you asked. I've brought it!"

At that moment the sun slipped behind a cloud. Darkness crept out at her. For all the world it could have been creeping from the graves—a graveyard darkness that had all the dead power to seize her and draw her down into one of the coffins, where the lonely dead waited.

"Leave me alone!" she screamed. "Leave me alone!" And for once she wasn't screaming at her pursuer. Because she thought she'd seen a face look through the branches. A stark, white face with veined eyes that bulged obscenely at her.

Footsteps closed behind her.

She ran even more desperately. Now a path cut into the hillside took her into an artificial gully.

The Vale of Tears.

Yes, yes! She recognized this now. The Vale of Tears. A whole labyrinth of channels cut below ground level. Enclosed on three sides, with only the top open to the sky, it formed a complex of individual family crypts; hundreds of them lying behind iron doors. This was the heart of the Necropolis—the city of the dead.

She couldn't be far from the tomb now with its crying boy.

Not far now, not far now . . . the words thudded to the rhythm of her heart. She ran along the stone channels that were narrow enough, if she'd had a mind to, to span with her outstretched arms. Here, roots from trees growing at ground level above her head burst through the walls. Or they forced themselves through the crypt doors. And like scaly tentacles, they reached out at her, tugging her hair and clothes as she brushed by.

Nearly there . . . I'm nearly there. Her heart beat faster.

Now a spark of hope flickered. All she had to do was set the bag down on the grave and cry out in triumph, "There . . . I've done it. I've brought you what you wanted!"

Then everything would be fine again. When she saw little Liam she'd bury her face into his sweet hair. She'd kiss his fingers, his toes . . . *Hell!*

Her feet shot from under her as she took a right-angled bend. She went down hard, sliding on her rear end, skinning her bare elbows. Gritting her teeth, she blinked away the pain, then scrambled up onto her feet. She glanced back. No sign of Joe . . . no visible sign, that is, but she could hear his feet echoing along the labyrinth.

She must be nearly at the grave now. She knew this place. There was a broad pathway that led up a slope. The grave with the crying boy was right at the top of that.

Then she looked at her hands. She stared without understanding for a moment.

Then it hit her. Where's the damned carrier bag? You must have dropped it, you stupid, empty-headed . . .

For a second she planned to run on without it. She was near the crying boy grave. It couldn't be more than a moment away—not if she ran hard.

But what's the fucking point? she asked herself. The reason she was here at all was to leave the contents of that bag on the stone slab. Her eyes scanned the passageway. Yes, there was the bag. She must have dropped it when she fell. But if she ran to retrieve it, there was every chance she'd run straight into Joe as he barreled around the corner.

She listened. The running footsteps grew louder, louder . . . then they stopped. She creased her forehead puzzled. Why had he stopped running?

Maybe she was being given a chance? She took it. Five seconds later the carrier bag was in her hands, the clunky weight in the bottom as welcome as it was reassuring.

Nearly there. She turned back to run the last two hundred yards.

"I said you couldn't run away from me, didn't I, Mary?"

She found herself looking into his blazing eyes. He'd run along one of the parallel channels, then turned to cut her off. Her breath coming in frightened sobs, she backed away from him, the carrier bag held like a shield in front of her chest.

"I told you I'd catch you. And that when I did, I'd make sure you were fucked."

She walked backward until her body hit one of the tomb's iron doors. The clang sounded like the single peal of a bell. Cold air oozed through ventilation holes in the door and onto the back of her neck. Tomb air, which had enveloped a dozen coffins for a hundred years. It stank of death and eternity.

He closed in on her, his hands clenched down by his

side. Despite the fact he'd been running, his face was a bloodless white.

"Please . . ." she panted. "Don't hurt me, Joe, please."

"What is it, Mary?" His face was stiff, unsmiling. "Have you been wondering what I was going to do to you? Maybe have a go at pulling that loose tongue of yours out again? Hmm? Or maybe kick your teeth so far down your throat you can bite toilet paper?"

"Joe—"

"So . . . what do you think it's to be, then?"

"Joe, don't hurt me. It was a long time ago; you don't want—"

"Don't want what, hmm? You were going to wait for me, Mary, but you just got naked for the first guy who came along. You dumped me like I was a piece of shit."

She breathed, deeply, controlling her voice. "Joe. Don't do this, please. I've got a little boy now. I'm all he's got. He'll be put into care if I—"

"If you what? Join those guys in there!" He head-butted the steel door. It rang like a bell. The echoes took forever to die.

"Joe. My little boy needs me."

"What about Stevo?"

"He's no good as a father. He won't look after him."

"How very, very sad." Joe pushed out his bottom lip in mock concern. "Mary, my love, you don't have to worry about a thing."

He raised his clenched fists. She flinched, expecting them to come crashing into her face.

"No, Mary, I'm not going to lay a finger on you. In fact, I came all the way up here to tell you not to worry about little Liam." He opened his fists at eye level, showing her his palms. "I've taken care of him for you."

She saw the palms of his hands. They were covered with dried blood.

Then, as she understood, she began to scream. She screamed long and hard. And the iron doors of the tombs hummed in harmony with her.

Four

"Mmm . . ." Miranda's sigh was as exciting as anything she said; then, giving a regretful shrug, she whispered. "Sorry, Paul."

"Sorry for what?" Paul wondered if he'd tried to cover too much ground too quickly.

"I'm baby-sitting for my sister at four."

She pulled down her T-shirt, hiding her wonderful breasts from his eyes. He felt a pang of loss, wondering if he'd ever see them again; they were such firm handfuls of flesh with a dusting of freckles around the beautifully dark nipples.

For the first time he began to take notice of his surroundings again. They were sitting on a tombstone surrounded by bushes. As he watched her push her hair back from her face, she paused. "I can hear it now."

"Hear what?" He was still all eyes for Miranda; the outside world, and the rest of the cosmos in general, seemed far less interesting than this slender-hipped girl with hair as glossy as fresh chestnut.

"Screaming," she said, frowning slightly while looking down the hill.

"Maybe we should check?"

She shrugged. "Why bother? It's probably kids. This is a mad place." She shot him a grin. "It gets madder after dark. A couple of months ago we built a huge fire and Shaun Richards, oh, you've not met him, have you? Well, Shaun brought in half a dozen cases of beer. Everyone got out of their faces . . . Christ, the hangover . . ."

"Sounds fun." Paul smiled, but felt a stab of jealousy. Just who the hell was Shaun Richards?

"Do you fancy walking me home?"

"I'll be heading that way anyway," he said, deliberately nonchalant (but his heart still thudded outrageously after spending twenty minutes in that tight clinch . . . and, good God, his groin ached; he felt as if he was going to explode).

"Anyway, old screamer's stopped." She spoke lightly. "It'll be kids. Like I say, this is nothing but a big playground these days."

"Little kids by day, big kids by night?"

"Absolutely. You should see what goes on in the crypts."

"Sounds spooky."

"It's damn spooky." She grinned mischievously. "Especially when you're there alone at the dead of night."

"We should try it sometime."

"Yeah, why not," she said surprisingly. "It'll be a thrill."

"I'll bring the stakes. You bring the crucifix."

The mischievous smile came again. "Oh, I'd definitely recommend you bring some protection."

Does she mean what I think she means? His pulse fluttered like butterfly wings beneath his skin.

They headed up a narrow track through the trees. Here, as everywhere, the place was a riot of wildflowers, bushes, nettles. Many a headstone had been toppled; while most were either splashed white with bird crap or dark green and woolly-looking with growths of ivy.

As they crested the hill, Paul noticed a peculiar-looking tomb with a statue of a crying boy.

"Miranda, what on earth goes on here?"

"Oh, that's a famous one."

He waited to hear more, but she didn't offer any elaboration. As they walked by the tomb, she grabbed his hand and gave it a squeeze. "See." She nodded at the tomb. "I told you we get all kinds of crazy people in here after dark."

He frowned at what had been set out in a semicircle at the feet of the statue. "Bars of chocolate? Why on earth would would anyone leave bars of chocolate on a grave?"

She giggled. "Paul! You're so naïve! Haven't you noticed all these soggy bits of spliff around here?"

He looked blank.

She laughed with genuine amusement. "You've never smoked dope, have you?"

He shook his head, feeling awkward and childlike.

Explaining, she squeezed his hand in hers. "Dope makes you ravenous . . . see? Someone's left their munchies behind."

"But all that chocolate?"

She pecked his cheek. "Sweet, innocent Paul . . . I'm going to have to show you the ways of the world, aren't I?"

He was shooting a puzzled glance again at the table-like tomb on which was engraved the name *Jess Bowen*, when Miranda added airily, "Paul Newton, you'll be telling me you're a virgin next."

He laughed as if it was the most ridiculous thing he'd ever heard. Even so, he felt his ears burn as he blushed from head to toe. Despite that, the bizarre image of chocolate bars set out around the feet of the statue glued itself tight in his mind's eye as, hand in hand, they walked down toward Skelbrooke village.

Chapter Six

One

"Dad, can I go on the boat?" Elizabeth looked up at him, her face framed by the bandages.

"Not this afternoon, hon. Your mum and I are busy cutting down nettles."

"I can row it myself now."

Dear God. The idea of Elizabeth taking the boat out onto the lake alone was enough to send floods of ice through John Newton's stomach. Smiling, he diplomatically said, "You can take me out on the boat this evening if it stays fine."

Elizabeth wasn't deflected so easily. "I wanted to show Emma how I used the oars." She looked back at a girl of the same age who stared expectantly at John.

John adopted his calm but firm parental voice. "Why don't you play on the new swing Paul rigged up for you in the orchard?"

To his relief, her face brightened. "I'd forgotten about that. *Come on, Emm!*"

Both girls dashed toward the orchard. Elizabeth's bandage now trailed a loose end like an Arab's turban.

"No falling off the swing, mind." It was only a half joke. He didn't relish a return trip to hospital the same day.

Val hacked the nettles. She gave him one of her twinkling post-lovemaking smiles. "I didn't think you'd have the energy for this."

He smiled back. "I'll manage. Besides, it might give me an appetite for more later."

"You'll be lucky, you monkey, you've had your quota for this week."

"We'll see about that, my dear," he said in a mock Hear Thy Lord and Master kind of voice. "Now get those nettles felled by sundown or I'll put you over my knee."

"You do and I'll bust your ghoulies."

Smiling happily, she swiped the nettles with the scythe. He raked for a while, then asked her if she wanted him to take over.

"Whatever for?" She rubbed the small of her back. "I'm loving every minute of it."

"I thought you might be tired."

"No, I'm imagining these"—she nodded at the nettles—"are the board of directors and I'm cutting off their stupid heads." Swinging the scythe, she hacked through a dozen nettles.

"In that case, I'll leave you to burn off some energy."

"You do that, John Newton, you just do that."

John headed for the toolshed. It was just past four in the afternoon; the sun shone brilliantly. The lake, which sat a good hundred yards uphill from the house, blazed like liquid silver, while another broad thread of silver that was the millstream ran down to disappear under the end wall of the house, before tumbling out the other side.

Despite the morning being pretty much a disaster zone, the afternoon was turning out to be pleasantly relaxing. He still tingled from an hour's lovemaking with Val. Her perfume had insinuated itself into his head, while a delicious sensation persisted that he floated a few inches above the ground. Another bonus was Elizabeth's friend coming around to play (so that now Elizabeth was happily entertained). He walked down the sloping lawn in the direction of the toolshed. In front of him was the house, beyond that the tree line that marked the position of the old Roman road; away to his right were the roofs of Skelbrooke like little tents of red tile. And there, across on the hill a good mile or so away, was the old cemetery, which looked more like virgin forest than the last resting place for a good chunk of Victorian Yorkshire.

He now felt easier thinking of the Water Mill as home. What made him particularly proud was the fact a single book (which took a mere seven months to write) had made this possible. If the follow-up was as successful, they'd be secure here for years to come.

After rooting through the nether regions of the shed, he pulled a tin of grease from behind a jumble of out-grown bikes; then he followed the millrace stream up to the lake.

The stream was still high despite there being little rain for weeks now. But seeing as the lake itself was fed by a dozen or more springs that bled from the hill-side farther up, he figured that it would take a long drought to dent the water flow. After all, the people who built the Water Mill hundreds of years ago weren't stupid. They'd have chosen a site that enjoyed a con-stant supply of water, in order to keep the waterwheel turning and the millstones grinding wheat. Livelihoods depended on it.

A refinement to the Water Mill's lake was a brick-built dam that allowed the miller to control the water flow by virtue of a hefty sluice gate. The mechanism had rusted pretty badly, and John was sure that the thing hadn't been used in decades; nevertheless, he'd taken it upon himself to try to bring the thing back into working order. Every few days he liberally greased the cogs that were as big as bicycle wheels. Maybe one day the grease would soak through the rust; then the handle would turn, allowing him to raise and lower the sluice gate. Of course, Val had inquired why it was important to be able do so.

"So we can control the rate the water flows down to the house."

"Why?"

He'd grinned and replied that it was a boy-thing. In truth there was no real reason. Naturally he had no intention of putting the Water Mill back in working order. The expense would be astronomical. And yet there was something strangely satisfying about tinkering with the century-old mechanism. Maybe it was some unconscious tribute to the ghosts of the craftsmen who'd labored to build the sluice gate. A way of saying, "Look, your work wasn't in vain. See? After a hundred years, someone still cares about what you did."

Smiling to himself, he dipped his fingers deep into the grease. Maybe he was getting sentimental. As he rubbed the grease onto the teeth of the iron cogs, the dog trotted up to investigate, his nose twitching as he caught scent of the rich goo on John's fingers, and and perhaps there was a trace of Val's pheromones mingled with it, too.

"Don't get too close, Sam," he told the dog. "You don't want this stuff up your nostrils." He massaged more lubricant onto the turning rods. "Sticks like poop to a blanket."

The dog wagged his tail.

"And no, you can't eat it."

The dog pricked up his ears, his eyes fixed on John's.

"Go chase mice, boy. There's some under the toolshed."

The dog rolled onto his back for his stomach to be tickled, his pink tongue hanging from the side of his mouth as he panted in the heat.

"No, Sam." He showed the dog his greased fingers. "See, I'm all gunked up?" The dog squirmed on his back, showing his teeth in what had to be a canine grin.

"No way, pooch. Not until I've washed my hands. Go play with Elizabeth."

Even mentioning his daughter's name was enough for him to take a moment to check that she was OK. Val was still decapitating nettles. No doubt, in her imagination, her bosses' heads were tumbling before the blade. Elizabeth and her friend Emma had walked up to the lake. Now they were on their hands and knees at the water's edge, looking, he guessed, at their reflections; then again, it may have been for fish.

Watch out, kids, there's a monster pike in there. Make sure he doesn't steal your noses. . . .

He shook his head. You're getting an anxiety complex about your child, John, he told himself. The kids are safe here. Lighten up . . . nothing bad can happen to them . . . Now, come on, you grease monkey. Back to work.

With a pleasure that verged on sheer eroticism, he worked his well-lubricated fingers into a series of grooves in the sluice gate itself. Hell, maybe he was getting kinky in his old age. To be so satisfyingly pleasured from greasing a heap of old iron cogs and coupling rods couldn't be legal, or moral or godly. He smiled to himself. Why, he was probably carving himself a niche in hell right now. *Stoke up them furnaces Satan, another one coming through!*

As he greased, he found himself tuning into Elizabeth and Emm's conversation.

"Keep looking, Elizabeth."

"For how long?"

"Until I say so."

"My bandage is getting wet."

"Here. I'll tuck it under."

They still gazed into the lake. Studying their reflections or watching for fish or whatever.

Careful of that pike, girls . . . got shark's teeth . . .

See, you can't stop yourself, can you, John? They're safe . . . safe as a whole hill of houses.

Elizabeth was saying, "I'm starting to get frightened, Emm."

"I was frightened when I looked the first time."

"Maybe we should go do something else?"

"No, Elizabeth. You've got to do it. *Got to.*"

"But I'm scared, Emm."

"I'll tell you what to do. You hold my hand. That's what Jenny told me to do when I first did it."

"OK."

"Got it?"

"Yes."

"Now, Elizabeth. You hold onto my hand. It stops you being frightened. And you keep holding my hand as tight as you can, squeeze it so tight I get rug burns. I don't care."

"OK, Emm."

John heard the conversation, but all he did was glance in their direction. It was just some game they were playing. One look at Elizabeth's face told him she wasn't genuinely frightened. Her eyes held that devil-may-care gleam of old. He noticed both girls still stared into the lake, their faces only six inches or so from its surface. So close, in fact, that Emm's pigtail's dipped into the water every now and again. He returned to his greasing, humming to himself now.

"See anything yet?" asked Emm.

"Nothing. Maybe he won't appear?"

"He will, Elizabeth, you've just got to look hard enough."

"What's he look like?"

"Oh . . . really, really awful."

"Yuk."

"His face is the worst thing you'll ever see in your *life.*"

"Maybe we should go do something else? If we go back down to the swing, I'll push you."

"No, Elizabeth. You've got to do this. Now look into the water. Look as hard as you can."

"But all I can see is me."

"Keep looking."

"Why can't we . . . wait. *Emm, I can see him!*"

John jumped, startled by the sudden piercing screams. The muscle spasm sent his finger deep into the sluice gate cogs, nipping the end painfully. Sam jumped to his feet, barking. The girls had startled him, too.

Withdrawing his hand to shake the stinging finger, John watched the girls running away from the lake. Their screams were so high-pitched, it felt like spikes being driven into his ears. He glanced at the dog. Sam watched them with a baffled curiosity. Then the dog looked up at John.

"Don't ask," John said, answering that questioning glance. "Like God, kids move in mysterious ways." He grimaced. "Remind me to buy us a set of earplugs."

Despite his tingling fingertip he smiled. The girls ran shrieking, round and round in circles on the lawn, in a self-induced ecstasy of make-believe terror. Elizabeth's bandage had unraveled yet further to flutter out behind her like a pennant.

In a moment they'd changed direction. Now they tore toward the millrace, still shrieking giddily while shooting looks back at the lake. Almost blindly, they ran straight at the fast-flowing stream.

John scrambled to his feet, holding up his grease-blackened hands. "Whoa! Careful, you two. You'll end up in the stream."

"We saw his face in the water!" Emm squealed.

Elizabeth jumped up and down. "And now he's chasing us!"

"Oh." John nodded, understanding. "The water dragon."

"No!"

"Who, then?"

The two girls yelled in harmony. *"Baby Bones!"*

Then, still giddy with excitement, they raced off down the hill. John wiped his hands on a rag. The dog looked up at him, ears pointing.

"Baby Bones, Sam?" John shrugged. "Who the hell's Baby Bones?"

Two

Round about six, Paul rolled up. John noticed his face was a near cherry red. What's more, he grinned to himself when he thought no one was looking.

"Done much today?" John asked as he returned tools to the shed.

"No." Paul shrugged.

"Where did you get to?"

"Town."

"Anything exciting happen?"

Paul shook his head.

"What did you think of that video last night?"

"OK."

John rolled his eyes skyward. At seventeen Paul was still in the one-word-conversation phase of adolescence. To drag a full sentence out of him took time as well as a full-blooded determination.

"You look happy with yourself, Paul," John said as Paul hung around in the shed doorway. "What's up?"

"Nothing."

"But you keep smiling to yourself. Something funny must have happened. Aren't you going to share it with your old man?"

"I'm not smiling."

"You are."

"How can you tell when I've got my back to you?"

"I can tell, number-one son."

"How?"

"Your ears go up and down."

Paul rubbed his ears. Then added, "It's hot today."

Result! John thought. Without it being levered from him, Paul had spoken a three-word conversational sentence.

"Beautiful, isn't it? Can you pass me the rake? Thanks, son."

"I'm boiling."

"Great barbecue weather, eh?"

"Can I have a beer?"

John glanced across at where Val piled the nettles she'd massacred.

"You know your mother isn't keen on you drinking beer around the house."

"Go on, Dad. I'm dying of thirst."

"On three conditions."

"What are those?" Paul sounded suspicious.

"One. You drink it from your old mouse cup."

"What? It's got a picture of Mickey Mouse on it. I haven't used it in years."

"I know, but it's colored plastic."

"You can't be serious."

"Deadly serious. If you use that, your mother can't see that you're drinking beer."

"If I drink from a bottle across here, she won't see either."

"Believe me, she will. And we'll both spend tonight in hell."

"All right," he relented grudgingly.

"Condition number two. You give me a hand with the boat."

"What's wrong with it?"

"I sunk it in the lake."

"Christ, Dad. What did you do that for?"

"Because it's built out of wooden planks."

"Sounds mad to me."

"If a boat's made out of wood and it's been left to dry out, you need to immerse it in water so the planks tighten up again."

"Otherwise it'll leak?"

"Got it in one."

"OK, deal."

"Are you sure nothing happened to you today?" There I go fussing like a mother hen again, John told himself. But wasn't that the natural way of the parent?

"You look hot and bothered. Has someone chased you?"

"No."

Paul turned away as if nonchalantly watching his mother.

John shook his head. "Paul, your ears are bobbing up and down again."

Well, at least the kid had something to grin about. Better that than looking miserable.

"See you later, Pa."

"Paul. You forgot condition three."

Paul's face turned sullen.

John shot him a smile. "Bring a beer for me, too."

Paul smiled back. It was one of those moments of empathy when John realized that the pair of them were two chips from the same Newton block. There were times John could almost read his son's mind. And he guessed that it worked the other way, too. More than once they'd watched an attractive woman sashay her way along a street. Father and son had then caught one another's eye. They'd known full well what had been sizzling through the other's mind right at that moment.

Three

Emm stayed for sandwiches and ice cream. John helped Val finish heaping nettles into a mound in the orchard. On more than one occasion John caught Paul grinning his secret grin while staring dreamily into space. Sam flopped into a patch of shade. He lay there with his tongue hanging out like a piece of pink ribbon.

Once Elizabeth and Emm had finished their ice cream, they took to kicking a ball about the lawn.

"Keep it away from the roses," Val called. "It'll burst if it catches a thorn."

Elizabeth carefully took the ball out of harm's way into the middle of the lawn. It was a favorite of hers. A Man in the Moon ball she'd bought on a shopping trip with her grandparents a few weeks ago. John had thought at the time it was a bizarre-looking thing. Supposedly a replica of a fairy-tale moon, it wore the Man in the Moon face with his characteristic look of wide-eyed surprise, the mouth open in a big black O. To continue the fairy-tale theme, it was even supposed to smell like green cheese. John had watched Paul sniff it warily, then announce it smelt like puke. At least the stink repelled the dog, who'd enthusiastically burst so many balls with his canines that John had lost count.

As the girls played with the ball, John went to the lake. There, the boat lay on the lake bed where the water was shallowest. Taking off his shoes and socks, John waded out to the boat. With Paul's help he turned it, tipping out the water, then tied it by a line to a tree at the water's edge.

"Wouldn't it be best to leave the boat upside down to drain?" Paul asked.

"If we did that the planks would dry out; they'd start to shrink and we'd spring a leak. This way will keep the wood nice and tight."

"Uh, this mud stinks."

"Don't worry. Wipe your feet on the grass."

Then Paul did one of those things that he was apt to do once in a while. After wiping the mud from his feet by moonwalking backward, he suddenly took off to where the girls were playing. Maybe there was still a good chunk of childlike mischief in him. He wove around Emm, tapping the ball from her with the side of one bare foot.

"And the crowd goes wild," he shouted. "He's taken control of the ball . . . outstanding footwork by Newton. Will the boy score?"

Elizabeth wasn't impressed. "Paul—Pau . . . ullll! Give it back. It's not yours."

Paul dribbled the ball around the girls, his arms out at his sides, while all the time keeping up a commentary. "The opposition don't know what's hit them . . . this boy's so good."

"Paul!" Elizabeth folded her arms. She scowled

through her bandages. "Give that ball back to me. You'll burst it." When that didn't work, Elizabeth appealed to a higher authority. "Mum ... Mum! Paul won't give me my ball back. Tell him."

Paul was, by this time, heading hell-for-leather toward the rosebushes. John frowned. Paul sometimes took real gratification from winding his sister up. The trouble was, she then took some winding down.

"Paul," he called. "Give your sister her ball back."

"I was just about to," he replied, grinning. "Here, Bizzy Lizzie."

He gave the ball a sharp kick. It went sailing over Elizabeth's head.

"Paul, you kicked it too hard."

The ball hit the lawn. It kept on bouncing. Elizabeth chased after it.

Val called across to Paul in her best tone of disapproval. "Paul, that wasn't fair."

"She should have jumped up to catch it."

The ball rolled now, but John saw disaster on its way.

Elizabeth shouted in anger. "It's going into the stream ... quick, get it!"

"Go get the ball, Paul, please," John called.

John walked down toward the stream to check that Paul would make an effort to retrieve the ball. Paul ran toward the stream in a slow lope. By the time he was barely halfway there, the ball had rolled down the bank into the stream.

"Dad!" Elizabeth stamped her foot. "Dad! It's gone in the water."

"Don't worry, hon. Paul will get it."

"He'll get it off *me* if it's ruined."

The current was faster than Paul anticipated. It whisked the yellow moon ball away downhill to the house.

"Get it, you idiot," Elizabeth told him.

"I'm trying, I'm trying."

John watched Paul run after the ball as it bobbed downstream. If anything, he and the two girls were enjoying the chase. All three now ran after the ball, shouting advice to each other on how best to rescue it.

"Get a stick!" Emm shouted.

"No, he can go in for it," Elizabeth countered. "He's not got his shoes on so he's OK."

"I hope he falls in."

Elizabeth sang out with glee, "So do I."

John walked briskly along the stream, following them.

"Paul, you're going to be too late," Emm squealed.

"It's going to get swallowed up," cried Elizabeth.

"I'm trying my best," Paul protested.

John watched as the yellow ball swung out on the current, then back again, as if teasing the three into following. There the stream wasn't at all wide. In fact, in a pinch (and with a slight risk of crotch strain), John could span the stream by standing with one foot on either bank. Only as the channel narrowed did the water's speed quicken. So, it didn't come as any real surprise to John that the ball moved even faster. In no time at all it approached the stone arch in the side of the house. There the millrace ran under the building before it would strike the blades of the waterwheel.

Elizabeth squealed, "Paul . . . *geddittt!*"

But he was too late. The ball plunged into the mouth of the tunnel. A second later it vanished into darkness beneath the house.

"*Paul!*" Both girls were outraged by his failure.

"It was too quick for me," he protested. "I couldn't keep up with it."

"You can buy me another one, Paul."

"Don't worry," John told them, walking up. "The stream comes out at the other side of the house. We'll be able to find the ball there."

Emm shook her head. "That ball's gone forever now."

"You'll get it back, Liz." John smiled. "The stream runs under the house just for a few yards, that's all."

"No." Emm spoke with certainty, her eyes large and

solemn-looking. "The ball's gone forever now. Lost."

With an angry walk, Elizabeth marched around the house to the other side. John followed along with Paul and Emm. The channel broadened again after the stream disgorged from the house, slowing the water right down to a gentle flow.

"I don't see it," Paul said.

"Neither do I," Elizabeth added bitterly. "My moon ball. They only had one left in the supermarket and now it's gone."

"Wait a minute," John suggested. "It might still be working its way through under the house."

All four stared at the archway where the waters tumbled out after traveling the few yards of inky darkness beneath the house.

Val appeared. "Any joy?"

Paul shrugged.

Elizabeth scowled at the water, then at Paul.

Emm said, "Lost."

John tried to sound optimistic. "Give it a little while. It might appear yet."

"It won't." Emm folded her arms. "I knew it wouldn't come out again."

"Why not?" Paul asked with a touch of irritation

"Because," she said in a low voice, "Baby Bones has got it now."

Val raised a questioning eye at John. "Baby Bones?"

John replied with a shrug that said, *Don't ask me*.

"Did you hear that, stupid?" Elizabeth shot a savage look at Paul. "Baby Bones has got it, and he never gives anything back."

"Who the hell's Baby Bones?"

Val shot him a withering look that was a pure clone of Elizabeth's. "Paul? Language."

"Paul, you can buy me another ball." With that, Elizabeth marched away. Emm followed.

Val nodded toward the front door, mentioning to Paul that there was a sink full of dirty dishes. He accepted that he was in the doghouse, and headed off to wash up. Meanwhile, John squatted at the edge of the stream so he could look into the black maw of the tunnel. From its depths he could hear the roar of the water as it ran whatever mysterious course it followed beneath the house. He shielded his eyes, stared harder, but there was nothing to see but complete and utter darkness.

Chapter Seven

One

Stan Price stared out of the window. In his mind he was a boy again. Yet he didn't ask himself why an old man's reflection stared back at him.

Although it was nighttime, the moon was bright enough to reveal the cemetery. Amid the trees, gravestones stood like a battalion of soldiers waiting for the order to attack. He tapped the window. His fingernails, longer than a woman's, but twisted, misshapen, and a bloodless gray color, clicked against the glass. When he spoke, his voice was hoarse from the day's shouting. "Harry . . . Harry? It's Stan Price. Find Mr. Kelly . . . tell him it's started again. Harry? Why don't you come and see me anymore?" He rapped the glass. "Harry. I want to talk to you. I'm frightened."

He stared out, his filmy blue eyes expectant, as if the answering call would come at any moment. Then, shaking his head, he went downstairs where his daughter and son-in-law sat watching television.

"Cynthia. Is it supper time?"

"Oh, Dad. You've only just had your supper."

"I'm hungry."

Robert Gregory gave the old man a bright smile. "You can't be hungry again so soon."

"I am hungry. I haven't had anything to eat all day."

"Dad," Cynthia sighed. "Robert brought some sandwiches up to your room just twenty minutes ago."

"Have you polished them off already, Dad?" Robert beamed. "You must have hollow legs."

"But I feel like I—"

"Now, you get yourself off to bed, Dad." Robert then turned to his wife. "Right, I'm just popping down to the Swan for a swift one."

"All right, dear. I'll get Dad back to bed. Then I'm going to turn in, too. I'm shattered."

"You do that love." Turning on the hearty voice again, he said, "Good night, Dad."

"I—I just wondered if it was supper time yet?"

"Supper time's been and gone, Dad."

Cynthia looked uncertainly at the thin old man. "Maybe I should get him a slice of toast or something?"

Under his breath, Robert said, "Best not." He rubbed his own stomach, imitating someone with indigestion. "Might keep him awake if he overdoes it. Get him off to bed." Then he boomed, "Sleep well, Dad."

As Robert Gregory left the house, he pulled the carrier bag from under a bush. In it were sandwiches and a wedge of cake. When he reached the trash can at the end of the street, he dropped in the bag, pushed it well down out of sight, dusted his hands, then strolled toward the pub lights that shone brightly across the village green.

Two

Mary Thorp had sat on a chair for an hour. She wasn't crying. She didn't speak. Once she had looked at the framed photograph of the blond-haired child on the wall, then shuddered. That was all.

The policewoman assigned to sit with her said gently, "Would you like a drink, Mary, or do you think you might like to sleep now?"

Mary Thorp shook her head.

The policewoman glanced at a clock. It bore the image of Homer Simpson's face. The comic image jarred with the grim atmosphere of the room. And not yet ten. It was going to be a long night.

In the kitchen sat a policeman. "Any joy?" he asked as the policewoman walked in.

"No. She's clammed up."

"I don't suppose it matters now we've got Sonny Jim in custody. Did you see what happened to the chocolate-chip cookies?"

"Believe it or not, Keith, I've got other things on my mind. You'll want another coffee, I suppose?"

"Three sugars."

"Fill the kettle for me, will you?"

"My God, a poor cop's work is never done." He scratched his stomach. "You know, I bet it was that fat hog from forensics that took the last one. That's why he looked so damn smug after he'd finished bagging up the kid. Christ, the pig must have an iron gut. Y' know, he had to use the kid's toy spade to scrape the brains off the window. They'd dried hard as concrete. He also said they found an eyeball in the kid's potty, but if you ask me—"

"*Keith.*" The policewoman caught his eye. Mary Thorp stood in the kitchen doorway.

The policeman wiped a crumb from his chin. "Uh. I'll check if forensics have finished in the garage. Give me a call if you need me, Susan."

The policewoman glared at him. "I'll do that." Then she turned to Mary Thorpe, who stood there somehow detached from the rest of the universe. "Mary, the coffee will be a minute yet. Can I get you anything to eat?" *Pray God, did she hear that insensitive idiot's verbal diar-*

rhea? she thought. *But if Keith Spivey gets decked for unprofessional conduct, I'll wind up hitting the deck with him.*

Mary Thorp looked around the kitchen as if she didn't even know her own home. Then she fastened her eyes on the policewoman. They were strangely glittery. Oh God, here it comes—she'd heard Spivey's tactless drivel.

"Susan?"

"Yes, Mary?"

"They're going to cut him open, aren't they?"

"Mary, sit down, you—"

"They're going to cut my little boy . . ."

"Don't think about that now." The policewoman's voice was soothing. "Look, you go—"

"Autopsy . . . that's what it's called, isn't it?"

Mary Thorpe's voice stayed low, completely controlled. No sobbing. No shaking. No hysterics. Policewoman Susan Derry knew there was a hell of a lot of pentup emotion inside the woman. She sensed it building like a volcano ready to rip its top. The policewoman steeled herself, ready for the outburst of emotion to come. She'd seen it before. But the violence of that release would still be shocking.

"Autopsy . . ." The woman repeated the unfamiliar word. "Autopsy . . . autopsy. It won't hurt him, will it, when they cut?"

The policewoman shook her head.

"No, of course it wouldn't, would it?" Mary Thorp licked her lips. They were chapped and sore-looking. "It can't hurt him, because he'd dead. And it's my fault." She locked her eyes onto those of the policewoman. "Did you know that I could have stopped Liam being killed?"

"It's not your fault, Mary."

"You don't know what really happened? When the letter came . . ."

"What letter?"

"The letter I found under the stone outside." Mary

Thorp nodded toward the door. "I should have done what the letter told me to do."

"This letter was from Joe Budgen?"

"No, of course not." She sounded irritated, as if asked an absurd question. "It was the start of the letters again. It's happened before. Ask anyone. But I ignored it. I thought it was kids playing stupid tricks . . . I just threw it away. And when another came, I did the same. And it wasn't—"

"Mary, sit down," the policewoman said. *Here comes the dam burst.* She checked that the box of tissues were nearby. They were. But if anything, before the tears there might come anger. She also did a quick take of the kitchen to make sure there were no knives or heavy objects Mary might grab.

But Mary Thorp continued in that rapid whisper. "Kids and their tricks. We've seen it all before. Stones thrown at the windows, dog shit through the front door. That's when everyone thought Stevo had snitched on Joe, but that wasn't true. So when the letters started, I thought it was just more of the same. Just kids pissing us about. But what I should have done is take that chocolate straight up to—"

"Chocolate?"

"The letter told me to take chocolate up to the cemetery and leave it on the grave."

"Mary, sorry, I don't understand. What grave?"

"Jess Bowen's. Oh, you're not local, then? Otherwise you'd know. It's famous round here. But if I'd just done what the letter said . . . if I'd left the chocolate up there . . . everything would be all right. None of this would have happened. Liam would still be up in his bed, fast asleep . . . oh, God . . . God, God, God, God." She rocked now, her hand to her mouth. But there were no tears.

"Mary, take it easy. Here, sit down."

Mary did as she was told. But now something had loosened inside her. She continued speaking—words joining seamlessly together. "See, just one lousy bar of chocolate. All I had to do was what the letter said. None of this would have happened. Everything would have been all right; but now he's having that autopsy done to him; they won't hurt him, will they? I couldn't bear it if I thought they were hurting him."

"They'll look after Liam, Mary."

"If you get one of those letters, Susan. And—and it's got those demands. You do everything it asks. Everything. Because it'll tear your life apart if you don't."

The policeman came to the doorway. He caught the policewoman's eye and tilted his head by way of a question. She went across to her colleague.

He whispered, "What's she been saying?"

The policewoman kept her voice low so Mary wouldn't hear. "Nothing that makes sense. If you ask me she's completely out of it."

"Did the Doc give her any knockout drops?"

"He did. Not that they've had any affect."

"Put her to bed anyway."

"Keith, she doesn't look like she's ready to sleep yet, does she?"

"She might, once she's in bed."

"All right then." She sighed, relenting. "But I'll stay near her bedroom where I can keep an eye on her."

"Pizza?"

"Show some respect, Keith. For just once in your life."

"I'll take that as a no, then, shall I?"

Three

"Careful, Val, the garlic bread's hot."

"Oh, I'm ready for this."

"See, I told you that good honest toil on the land would give you an appetite."

"It's toning up my thigh muscles, too."

"Really? Let me feel."

"John Newton, that isn't thigh muscle."

"Nowhere near?"

"No."

"You'll have to give me a conducted tour of your body later."

"John, stop it." She giggled.

"Show me every nook and cranny."

"Shh . . . Paul will hear."

"No, he won't. He's watching something unsavory on television in his bedroom."

"If you don't move your hand, I'll scream."

"Yell your face off, my dear, because here in the Water Mill no one can hear you scream." He'd switched on the Vincent Price impression again. "Now come here. I want to suck your neck."

"You try and I'll chuck your garlic bread out the window."

"All right, then, I surrender. Wine?"

"Need you ask?"

John filled her glass. This was one of his real pleasures of the day. A late supper with Elizabeth asleep in bed and Paul ready to turn in for the night. The time was approaching eleven. Outside, a moon showed its face through the trees, turning the stream into a vein of glittering silver.

As was their habit, they'd taken scatter cushions across to the observation window set in the floor above the millrace. Below them, waters tumbled in a chaotic mix of dazzling whites and glistening blacks. As always, there was something deeply mysterious about that water. How it raced through the tunnel beneath the house to be briefly caught by spotlights set in the tunnel wall. John sat, his upper half supported on one elbow. Although he couldn't hear the roar of the torrent, he could feel its vibration tickle up through his bones. There he made a deal with himself after the hectic (and completely unproductive) day. He'd knuckle down early tomorrow and finish Chapter 1. If inspiration really caught hold, he might crack on with the outline, too. Then he could have the book package to his agent ahead of schedule.

He pushed thoughts of the book aside. Val sat cross-legged on the glass in shorts and a T-shirt. Her hair was still shower-wet, and she looked incredibly desirable to John as he sipped his wine. If it weren't for supper on the plates, he'd be tempted to suggest an early night.

"At least Elizabeth is sleeping," Val said. "I thought her chin would be sore after the fall."

"She's made of tough stuff."

"Mmm, but you should see the graze across her chest, too. She must have been going way too fast."

"Maybe she'll learn from it. I was nearly a basket case after I found her. Tomato?"

"Please."

He speared a slice and slipped it onto her plate. "My nerves can't take any more of Elizabeth's spills... oops."

"Or any of your spills. That red wine better not reach my best new rug."

"Don't worry. I'll mop it up."

As Val sat eating her garlic bread, John pressed a piece of kitchen tissue to the splash of red wine on the millrace glass. Immediately the absorbent tissue sucked the wine from its surface. He finished off by rubbing the glass clean.

"There. Not a mark."

As he rubbed, he happened to look down into the water.

White foam appeared to battle with the dark water for domination of the observation chamber below. As he looked, he saw something solid surge up out of the water. It stood proud of the foam, gleaming beneath the spotlights.

"*Val.*"

"Hmm?"

"You've missed it."

"Missed what?"

He'd only seen it for a second, but now he found his heart beating hard. His palms had grown clammy; his fingers stuck to the glass as perspiration oozed. Which was a ridiculous reaction really. Because all he had seen was a face.

And that face, with the wide eyes, and the mouth stretched into a surprised O, was printed on the side of Elizabeth's ball. The one that had been snatched by the stream earlier in the day and sent plunging under the house. Where no doubt it had been caught in the tunnel before eventually working loose to bob up into the observation chamber right under his nose. He took a swallow of wine. His movements were jerky and the rim of the glass clicked against his teeth.

That was what he had seen—just the ball. It had to be the ball because it couldn't be anything else, could it? OK, so his imagination had exaggerated the image into a face with colossal eyes that bulged at him; the whites of those eyes riddled with purple veins as fat as earthworms . . . yet still his heart hammered against his ribs just as if he'd had the shock of his life.

"Go on then, John, don't keep me in suspense," Val said. "What did you see?"

"Incredible . . . it was Elizabeth's ball. It must have been caught on some obstruction in the tunnel."

Val popped an olive into her mouth. "Then with luck it might turn up downstream in the morning."

"It might," he agreed.

Then once more he found his attention drawn back to the window set in the floor. A window that was like a single great eye that gazed into the heart of some dark and secret place.

Four

After dark the Necropolis becomes a vast and lonely wilderness. Decades of neglect have left it overgrown with hogweed, nettles, hemlock, and grass that reach to your elbows.

Through this wilderness Mary Thorp pushed forward into the depths of the cemetery.

Simon Clark

Monuments to eighty thousand dead marched away beneath the trees with military precision. While a bone white moon revealed the heads of stone angels and cherubs. There were slabs engraved with names, dates, poetry; statements of how the occupants of graves died: *burnt up by fever . . . drowned by accident . . . succumbed to influenza . . .*

To Mary Thorp, the gravestones, the trees, the cemetery, the whole world were nothing but a meaningless blur. She walked in her nightdress, barefoot, her hair tumbling in wild disorder. Her bare legs had been stung a dozen times by nettles. Broken glass littered the ground. A cut that ran from her big toe to heel oozed with blood. She noticed none of that.

Mary walked as if she was asleep. Her eyes glassy. No expression on her face. In one hand she held a carrier bag. One of the few things she was conscious of was the weight of the bar of chocolate in the bottom of it. *I'm here . . . I brought you what you want . . . now make everything right again. Bring my baby back to me . . .*

Trees broke the moonlight, so it looked like a thousand laser beams shone down. They picked out chunks of headstone and crumbling urns. A dog's skull in the grass glowed dazzling white. In one moonbeam her bloody footprint shone a luscious strawberry red.

She cut through the labyrinth that formed the Vale of Tears. The iron doors to the tombs were all locked tight against the outside world. Tonight these ghostly houses of the dead lay in absolute silence. She walked on unafraid. Being alone in the cemetery tonight didn't affect her any more than the nettle stings and gash in her foot. Her baby was all that mattered now. If only she could leave that bar of chocolate on the grave . . . just as the letter demanded . . . she was convinced she could turn back time. She knew in her heart of hearts that she would return home to find the two cops vanished from the kitchen. And she would find Liam asleep in his cot.

There was a power in this cemetery that could do

just that. It had the power to create as well as to destroy.

Hold onto that thought, Mary, she told herself. *Hold it tight.*

She passed beneath the stone archway, and climbed the slope out of the Vale of Tears. Graffiti covered the huge wall that held back the hillside to form a sheer cliff face thirty feet high. On the ground were empty beer cans, broken wine bottles, spent condoms, a syringe or two. Someone had even rigged a swing from a tree. High on beer and marijuana, with sexual excitement crackling in the air, daredevil kids would run, grab the rope, and swing out above the roofs of the tombs thirty feet below. But one slip and they'd be joining the dead beneath them in more ways than one.

Now, even in near-darkness, she had no problem finding the grave of Jess Bowen. Barefoot, leaving bloody footprints, she walked along the path.

There it was. A single slab lying flat on the ground, as large as a tabletop. At one end, as if mourning over the grave, was the statue of the weeping boy. As she approached the stone, a breeze stirred the branches, sending whispering noises through the wood toward her. She glanced to her left, where the ground fell away sheer to the labyrinth of crypts below. Skelbrooke village lay in darkness. Maybe the policewoman had discovered the bed empty by now. Not that it mattered. She was here. She had the chocolate.

Quickly, she went to the grave, brushed away leaves from the stone slab, then as if setting down an offering before an altar, she placed the chocolate beneath the deeply chiseled name: JESS BOWEN.

"There," she whispered. "You've got what you asked for. Now give Liam back to me."

The marble eyes of the weeping boy stared down at the chocolate. Its face blank. A dead silence filled the cemetery.

At that moment Mary felt as if she woke from a dream. With a moan she pressed the heel of her hand to her forehead. "Oh, God, what have I done? He's never coming back . . . oh, God, you stupid bitch, he's dead . . . *he's dead.* . . ."

A breeze rose. For a moment it seemed to rush, cold and loathsome, from some dark void beneath her feet. Branches creaked, leaves rustled. To her ears the sound came as a high giggling that mocked her stupidity.

Suddenly she saw in her mind's eye what she must have looked like. A woman standing in a graveyard at midnight, wearing a cotton nightdress that barely reached the tops of her thighs; her hair a godawful mess; her mind scrambled by grief . . . trying to turn back time by offering chocolate to a statue.

Christ . . . fury erupted. How could she be so fucking stupid? That hideous little statue could do nothing! Absolutely fucking nothing!

Engulfed with rage, with self-pity, with self-hatred, with grief, she howled like a wounded animal. Seconds later, she was swearing, scrambling down on all fours, clawing up handfuls of dirt that she hurled at the statue. Then, crying out in rage, she was on her feet tearing at her hair. She ripped her nightdress open, exposing her breasts.

"Bastard!" she screamed. "I'll break you . . . I'll break you to fucking nothing!"

She kicked at the statue with her bare feet, shattering her toes, bursting open her skin so the boy appeared to weep gobs of blood.

"I'll murder you!" Ranting wildly, she dragged her nails across her own flesh from her left shoulder to her right hip. Blood ran from the furrows in the flesh, smearing her naked breasts.

Still she felt nothing. Even when she clawed her way forward on all fours to swing full-blooded punches at the head of the weeping boy. The crack of a snapping knucklebone didn't even make it through her eardrums to her brain. Inside her, she had become a vortex of rage. Nothing mattered now. Nothing but the overwhelming urge to destroy. And when her blows did no harm to the statue, other than smear it with blood, she realized what must be destroyed. What must be annihilated.

On broken, bleeding feet she sprinted back down the path. Seconds later, she'd reached the edge of the cliff. In one fluid movement she had seized hold of the rope swing that overhung the maze of tombs below; then she noosed the rope around her neck.

She saw the moon. The roofs of Skelbrooke. The glint of the lake across at the Water Mill. She saw a misty face hanging before her. Pray God it was Liam. Her baby was welcoming her across to the other side.

"Wait . . . Mommy's coming!"

Air rushed around her ears; the nightdress rippled about her.

"No!" was the only word she managed to scream as she fell—and before the rope snapped tight. The face wasn't her baby's. The eyes bulged. They glinted with eerie lights. Veins stood out from them as thick as earthworms.

After the echoes of her final cry faded, the cemetery fell silent again, apart from a rushing sound as Mary Thorp swung back and forth, hair streaming from her wide-eyed face. She swung in long, slow sweeps like a vast pendulum. While her blood fell onto the crypts below as lightly as summer rain.

Chapter Eight

One

Friday morning. The day after Elizabeth's fall from the bike. Early morning mist burnt away by the sun promised another sizzling day. John Newton walked Elizabeth to school (she couldn't wait to show off her bandages to her friends). Paul went under his own steam to the bus stop.

Later, John finished washing the breakfast things as Val zipped around the kitchen brushing her hair while picking lint from her business jacket. "Why I had to choose plain black," she said. "It shows every speck of fluff. There. Now, shoes . . . shoes." She slipped them on. The dog interpreting this as a promising sign for a walk wagged his tail. "Not now, Sam. I'm going to work . . . right, John, I'll see you tonight."

"Got everything?"

"As far as I know. Uh, mobile?"

"It's on the hallway table."

"Thanks . . . there go the sirens again."

"It was like that all yesterday afternoon. It sounded more like the Bronx than sleepy old England."

He followed her through the hallway, where she paused to check her reflection in the glass. She looked composed. She was in working-girl mode now. But he still remembered with a thrill how she lay naked on the bed, her hair mussed, murmuring some very provocative, not to say erotic, suggestions, while her eyes sparkled with sheer sex. Christ, why did she have to go to work today? They would have the house to themselves. He could watch her stroll around naked all day.

"Down, boy," John whispered to himself.

"What's that, hon?" she asked back over her shoulder.

"I was just saying have a good day."

"As good as I can. Roll on the weekend."

"We on for that barbecue Saturday?"

"If the weather holds. Oh, nearly forgot." Val slipped her mobile into her purse. "Can you pop round to the Haslems?"

"They're away."

"I know, but I noticed they'd left a window open downstairs. I don't want a burglary on my conscience."

"I'll see to it."

"Thanks."

"See you tonight."

"Ciao!"

After kissing her, he watched her climb into the car, then drive away in a swirl of dust.

John turned to the dog. "There's only me and you now, kidda."

The dog wagged his tail, then went to stand by the closet where his snack treats were kept.

"No, you've just had your breakfast. Why don't you go sit in the sun or chase rodents or something?" John clicked his tongue. "You know, John old buddy," he said to himself, "you've got to stop having conversations with the dog. Or one day they'll take you away to the happy place."

He glanced at his watch. 8:30. He should really be sitting down at the computer to tackle the first chapter of *Without Trace*. But he'd promised Elizabeth he'd take a walk downstream on the off chance that her moon ball had beached itself somewhere. And it was such a perfect day. The great outdoors could have been sweetly calling his name, inviting him to slip on his sunglasses and stroll for a while. What's more, the sirens were now fading into the distance to be replaced by birdsong.

"Come on, then, Sam, just a quick walk. Then it's back to work. If I don't have that chapter done today, smelly stuff starts hitting the fan. . . . God, there I go again. Talking to you."

The dog pricked up his ears, his bright eyes on John's.

"Yup," he said. "I'm on my way to be a fully fledged basket case."

He walked for longer than he intended. Partly he wanted to see the look of delight on his daughter's face if he recovered the ball. Partly because it was such a pleasant day with the sun streaming across the meadow. And partly, yes, goddamnit, he was postponing that moment when he had to switch on the computer and start work on the book. He knew full well now that *Without Trace* wasn't going to be another *Blast His Eyes*. Without a new angle, the book already had the distinct whiff of failure about it. Just for a second he could picture "For Sale" signs appearing outside the Water Mill.

He walked on, following the line of the stream through the field. Cows munched grass. Skylarks sang. A great day to sit by the lake with a beer and a book. Not a great day to sweat in front of a computer screen with the blinds drawn. Sam was ready for a cross-country hike, and only turned back reluctantly when John called him. The Man in the Moon Ball would have to be written off as lost without trace. As Paul was responsible for its loss, the cost of the replacement would be Paul's responsibility, too. Great . . . that would do nothing to enhance domestic harmony tonight.

John cut across the field, heading for the lane that would take him on a more direct route back home. Then he'd check the Haslem place and close the window. At that moment Sam darted into long grass, only to emerge with a mouse gripped in his teeth by its hindquarters. The mouse squealed while twisting from side to side, its black eyes beady with panic. Sam tossed the mouse into the air before catching it in his mouth headfirst.

With a grimace, John looked away as the dog chewed with sheer pleasure, the tiny mouse bones crackling.

"Sam, you are one gross beast."

From past experience, he knew the dog would swallow the mouse whole without spilling so much as a drop of blood. He walked a little faster in the direction of the Haslems' house.

Two

Sam accompanied John into the Haslems' garden. This was unfamiliar territory for the dog, and John watched him run across the lawn, nose to the ground.

John checked that the front door was locked, then headed around the back. The house, a reward for Keith Haslem's years building up a law firm, looked unmolested. Standing back, he shaded his eyes against the sun to look up at the bedroom windows. Everything looked normal. But then, if it wasn't, he still didn't know how he'd get a message to Keith. The family might be up the Amazon for all he knew.

Maybe the law firm wasn't doing as well as was supposed.

John turned over some possibilities in his mind. Perhaps Keith Haslem had indulged in a little embezzlement. These things happen. And it tended to be those that you least suspect. The detective inside him was flexing his muscles. There was a whiff of mystery about the Haslems' abrupt departure.

Sam bounded across what for him was virgin ground. He marked his new territory with a golden splash at every other bush.

"The mystery thickens," John murmured to himself as he went to push the window shut.

Inside, the kitchen was a mess. Someone had broken off preparing a roast. Now a slab of raw beef in an oven tin was alive with crawling flies. The place would be a mass of maggots within days. He could also see breakfast dishes on the table. Cornflakes and milk congealed in bowls. A knife smeared with butter lay beside a loaf of bread that was probably hard as a brick in this heat. The whole house would stink vilely within a day or two. John weighed up the ethics of what amounted to friendly trespass. He'd have trouble squeezing through the window he'd just pushed shut. But maybe Paul could make it through. Then at least he could dump the rotting food safely in the trash. Of course that might trip the alarm. But it was all in a good cause.

The dog by this time had his head in the herbaceous border, snorting loudly. John guessed Sam might have the scent of another mouse.

"Leave it, Sam. Here, boy." John didn't relish listening to the dog crunch up another rodent for a morning snack. The dog snorted noisily, not wanting to quit the delights of the flower bed.

John crossed the lawn. He'd done what he could do for the time being. The house hadn't been ransacked, and although he couldn't lock the window from the outside, at least it didn't present such a blatant invitation to local felons.

Then, once more, John Newton's internal detective showed himself to be on the ball.

"Now there's a thing," he murmured to himself.

In the center of the flower bed was a birdbath. A run-of-the-mill thing, it consisted merely of a concrete post that stood about waist high with a concrete bowl on top.

It was what lay in the concrete bowl that made it special. He stepped up to the edge of the grass to take a closer look-see.

What he saw only added to the mystery. In the birdbath was a layer of ashes. Scattered around the birdbath, on the soil and even resting on the leaves of the plants, were dozens of matches. All but one or two of the matches were used. The empty box lay open on the soil.

"So, Mr. Sherlock Holmes," he murmured to himself, "what do you make of this?"

He picked up one of the matches, then struck it against the box, where it flared brightly. So, the matches weren't duds. Unconsciously, he slipped into the role of detective. A trick he'd practiced since childhood.

"OK," he said. "Give me the scenario." He rose to his feet. "Keith or Audrey Haslem came out of the house, crossed the lawn, placed a piece of paper in the birdbath, and burnt it to ashes. But why not just drop it in the trash?" As was his habit, he answered himself. "Because it was no ordinary piece of paper. They wanted it destroyed completely. Either to hide its contents or because the document became a subject of their hatred. Like a jilted lover burning the photograph of their ex. But why all the unused matches?" He turned the matchbox over in his hand. Again the answer seemed simple. "Because whoever burned the paper had been in a tearing hurry. No. It's more than that. They'd been gripped by sheer panic. So they ran out here, dumped the letter in the birdbath, fumbled with the matchbox, spilt the contents into the flowers, managed to set fire to the paper, then ran back to the house without bothering to pick up the matches."

In his mind's eye, he played out the rest of the scenario. After burning the paper, Keith Haslem had bundled his family into the car (leaving the kitchen like the

Marie Celeste, with half-eaten breakfasts, raw meat exposed to the summer air, the window wide open).

He figured the burner had to be Keith. Yesterday morning the man was certainly the driving force in getting his family into the car and then the hell out of Skelbrooke as if Lucifer himself had gotten a scent of his ass.

"So what were you burning, Keith, old buddy? Check stubs, phony receipts, forged title deeds?"

John stepped closer to the birdbath, then with a finger and thumb delicately removed a fragment of burnt paper. It was fragile enough to turn to dust when he touched it. With even more care he lifted another fragment, which he rested on the palm of his hand so he could study it more closely.

He'd been enjoying himself in his role of detective. But suddenly that sense of enjoyment vanished with a pang that snapped his stomach muscles tight.

On the blackened paper nothing remained of the handwriting but a ghostly trace. Instantly John recognized the looping l's and y's. Then he deciphered two words, *"grief stowne."*

"Damnation." His voice was hushed. "So you got the same letter, too."

Three

"Paul . . . Paul?"

Paul Newton turned to see Miranda catch him up as he walked between the school blocks.

"Miranda? I thought you had Technology this morning."

"I have, but I wanted to catch you before lunch."

He smiled. "You've caught me."

"I can't see you after school tonight."

"Oh, no problem." He sounded cool, but disappointment crashed inside him. Hell, it was over so soon. No more Miranda Bloom. No more of those delicious Spanish eyes looking up into his.

She looked as if she needed to hurry away, and she cast glances back over her shoulder.

Maybe there was someone else, Paul thought morbidly. No doubt she wanted to dash off to meet some stud . . . *oh, crap* . . . *why does it always have to rain on me*. . . . Yesterday he'd felt as if lightning had flickered out of his scalp, sparks out of his fingers and toes. He'd never been that close to a girl before. He'd felt . . . well, he'd felt *transformed.* That memory of her freckled breasts had stayed glued inside his head ever since last night. He was certain the others in class must have realized he looked *different.* Even the security guards must have noticed a difference in him on the CCTV monitors as he zombied his way from class to class, his eyes somehow turned inward-looking. Gazing only at mental images of Miranda, with that lovely smile, her twinkling Spanish eyes, the dark-tipped breasts with their delicious dusting of freckles. God, he was away with the fairies even now as she stood right next to him, telling him the whole deal was off. They were going their separate ways . . . *adios, amigo*. . . .

The thoughts flashed through his head at a million miles an hour. Or so it seemed. And she'd not noticed any change in his expression.

No, there she was, smiling sweetly, holding that Technology file to her breasts (oh, God, that lucky Technology file, pressed so firmly against her body).

"So, that's OK with you, Paul?"

What was OK with him? What had she asked? He smiled a casual smile, but inside his head sheer turmoil reigned. He'd missed some vital words. What had she just asked him?

Paul. Ugly Bob has asked me to dance naked in the school canteen. So is that OK with you, Paul?

"Paul." She glanced over her shoulder, raven black hair swishing luxuriantly. "I'll have to go now. Sheena and Kari are waiting for me. Sorry about not being able to make it to the cinema."

"That's OK." It wasn't OK. It wasn't OK so much it

sucked like the biggest Hoover in Christendom, but what the hell could he do about it?

"Look," she told him, and touched his forearm. "After I get back from my grandmother's I can meet you. That's if you can make it?"

He said that he could. And his heart beat a whole lot faster.

She nodded. "OK. The cemetery gates at seven?"

He smiled easily now. "I'll see you then."

Suddenly she seemed to lunge toward him; her face came up close to his. For one wild moment he thought she'd actually kiss him in full view of the entire school.

Instead, she whispered with a nerve-crackling intensity, "Bring something with you."

The smile he gave her before she darted away was knowing. Inside, his heart thundered against his ribs. He looked around at the others moving like a tide from block to block. Surely he must look different to them now.

What was the word?

Transformed?

Changed?

No, a far more powerful description:

Transfigured.

That was the word . . . transfigured. It's what happens to saints when they've glimpsed Paradise; they glow as if lit up from inside by a whole rack of halogen lamps. Paul Newton felt like that right now. He glanced at his watch. Eight hours until he met Miranda. Then they'd enter the quiet clutches of the cemetery together. Hell. It couldn't come quickly enough.

Four

John Newton returned home. The dog took up a position on the grass bank where he could bask in the sun. Family Haslem's home was secure, if a little untidy. He'd get Paul to tackle the raw meat in the kitchen later; otherwise, the property would become a holiday destination for every fly for miles around.

He made coffee, raided the cake tin, checked his e-mail, and then opened the computer file labeled *Without Trace*. For a whole three minutes he stared at the flashing cursor.

"Well, what are you waiting for? The first chapter and synopsis has to be in the mail on Monday. Tom's going to be pissed with you if you don't do it. Then you won't get the Goldhall contract, then the money stops coming in, then you lose the house, and the poor little doggy and all your children go hungry." He sang the words under his breath; part encouragement, part terror tactics to get his backside in gear so he'd write that first chapter.

But it wasn't coming.

There was no spark. *Without Trace* would be a hash of warmed-over old mystery cases. Tom was right. The book he'd conceived didn't possess a shred of originality. Breathing heavily out through his nostrils, he leaned back in his chair in disgust. As he did so, his eyes took in the shelf where *Blast His Eyes* sat. Now *that* was a book with attitude. So it had started out as a true-life mystery, just as his six preceding books, but it had evolved into a real detective hunt.

He'd begun with the usual book and archive research, blowing the dust off old newspapers (well, the dust off old microfiche files would be more accurate) as he'd unearthed the account of a murder case from 1889. Behind every murder is often a compelling human-interest story. What drove the individual to murder? How did they try to escape justice? Were they caught? How were they punished?

The St. Paxton-Wellman case was no exception. What gave the case an extra splash of glamour was that it told a story of riches to rags—a member of the English aristocracy brought low by all-too-human weakness.

Lord St. Paxton-Wellman, a distant cousin of Queen Victoria, inherited a country mansion in Lincolnshire, just down the road from Lord Byron's estate. With the grand house came a fortune in the form of Indian tea plantations.

The boy was, as they say, set for life.

But instead of doing what the eldest sons of the English aristocracy should have done—that is, acquiring a first-rate commission in the army—he dedicated his life to pleasure. In turn, that led to a pathological addiction to gambling by the time he was twenty-four. There were also rumors that he suffocated his illegitimate child borne by his scullery maid. However, good family connections meant he could pass the buck. A stable lad was convicted at the famous "Bastard Murder" trial of 1879. There were whispers at the time that the boy was a patsy. Even so, he was hanged at Lincoln jail, then buried in lime. As part of the research, John visited the site where the stable lad and other hanged convicts had been interred. Innocently, the burial pit now lay beneath a supermarket car park.

But even though Lord Paxton-Wellman evaded English justice, he didn't slip the grasp of, perhaps, divine justice. His wealth hemorrhaged from him like blood from a severed artery. By the time he was forty the estates were gone, his wife had deserted him and he had lost his manorial home.

Soon his lordship turned to crime. What's more, he had no hesitation in shooting anyone who got in his way. By then, the nineteenth century had become an age when science was beginning to do the miraculous. He must have picked up a snippet of pseudo-scientific research that suggested the eyes of murder victims still preserved the image of the murderer, which, like a photographic plate, could be developed. With the image of the murderer in police hands, an arrest would soon follow.

Well, that was how the theory ran. Of course it was all tosh. But Paxton-Wellman didn't know that. And so that was how the title of the book originated. The wicked lord would literally blast out his victim's eyes with a pistol. Now the story alone would make *Blast*

His Eyes a good commercial proposition for any publisher. But then came a minor miracle. John Newton carried on his book research, picking up tasty nuggets that would add weight to the book, and which eventually led to one of Paxton-Wellman's safe houses, where John found a box that had actually belonged to the man. John had been shrewd enough not to open the box there and then, but opened it live on a TV chat show the day the book was launched. Inside, there had been a monogrammed pistol (without doubt Lord Paxton-Wellman's), china figurines wrapped in newspapers (bearing the date 1889), a Spanish gold ducat, and, perhaps more strangely, diaries that detailed the results of several thousand backgammon games (the lord's obsession for backgammon knew no bounds, it seemed). John had even been able to round off the chat show with a satisfying account of the villainous lord's death by drowning when he tried to escape from the police by swimming across a lake.

Within days *Blast His Eyes* stepped neatly into the top-ten hardback list. John and Val Newton went house hunting. And here they were.

"And here I am," John murmured, turning back to the computer screen. "Hunting for a follow-up."

He stared at the screen for a full five minutes. Then he closed down the computer.

"Damn it." He couldn't settle. As much as anything, it was the events of the last twenty-four hours. Wondering about the origins of that letter he'd found in the garden had been nibbling away in the back of his head. Now he'd just learned that the Haslems had received the same—or a similar—letter. They'd burnt it in what looked like a good deal of panic, then fled the village.

But was there a connection between them running out like that and the letter? Was it just coincidence?

Leaning back in the chair, he stared into the blank eye of the computer screen. That blank glass eye stared right back into his, challenging him to make the connection. He felt a growing edginess. There were questions to be answered. He knew it. But then he should be working.

What was more it was no real business of his how people reacted to letters that were probably, when all was said and done, a prank.

But some weird prank. He poured more coffee. This was going to be a real caffeine bender today, but so what. Restless, he switched on the radio, surfed through the programs, switched it off again, then picked up the letter that had arrived so mysteriously in the dead of night.

Mysteriously?

There you go again, John Newton, he told himself, shaking his head. You've got a weakness for melo-drama—just like old Lord Paxton-Wellman had a pas-sion for backgammon. He stood with the coffee cup in one hand, the letter in the other, and read it through again.

Dear Messr. John Newt'n,
  I should wish yew put me a pound of chock latt on the grief stowne of Jess Bowen by the Sabbath night. Yew will be sorry if yew do not.

Come on, please! Why had the prankster's imagina-tion conked out at the end? Surely he or she could have signed off with some cryptic name—*Mr. X or Miss Y* at least. Then why not something lurid like *Yours Truly, the Skelbrooke Mangler* or *Billy Razor Hands*?

All that for a bar of chocolate?

So why go to all the trouble of using what appeared to be genuine antique paper complete with Gothic handwriting right out of Edgar Allan Poe?

He took a hit of coffee. These questions had gotten under his skin. They itched so much he wanted to scratch them right out of there. His mind went back twenty-four hours. Keith Haslem's ranting as he bun-dled his family into the car was memorable enough. When Audrey Haslem complained to her husband that his language might be a tad colorful for the neighbor-hood, he'd retorted: *"I don't care about the fucking neighbors. If the neighbors had any fucking sense, they'd be clearing out, too."*

There was no doubt that Keith believed his family faced some kind of threat. They had been running away from danger. It was possible that Keith had had dealings with the underworld (OK, it didn't seem *that* likely), in which case he might need to skip town. But then it didn't explain *"If the neighbors had any fucking sense, they'd be clearing out, too."*

Unless, that is, the man had gotten a bunch of terrorists so stinking angry, they were going to nuke the whole village. Admittedly, that was pretty unlikely.

John raised the letter to the window. Enough daylight filtered through to reveal the watermark of a face in profile. Ye gods. An ugly gargoyle face at that. He cast his mind back to when Mr. and Mrs. Gregory were looking for Mrs. Gregory's father. John didn't recall the exact words, Mrs. Gregory's language wasn't as memorably colorful as Keith Haslem's, but John would swear she'd been talking about a letter, too. He looked down at the piece of paper in his hand again, frowning as he tried to remember.

Yes . . . she told her husband that the old man had been upset by the arrival of a letter. But what kind of letter? A credit card statement? A letter from a long-lost lover? A demand for unpaid taxes?

"Not on your life," John murmured. "He'd gotten one of these, too." He laid the letter out on his desk.

Now. If he was to visit the old man at the Gregory home, would he find a letter just like this one? A letter not that dissimilar from the one burned to ashes in the Haslem birdbath?

He felt a tingling in his spine. Accompanying that came a restless excitement. This was exactly the same sensation he'd experienced when he climbed into the attic in Lincoln to find Paxton-Wellman's hidden box of treasures.

He'd caught a mystery by the tail and he knew it. The detective inside him burned to uncover the secret of the letter. Damnit. He should be sitting down to that first chapter of *Without Trace*, but he knew he couldn't settle. OK, he told himself, you've got one hour to get this out of your system. Then you get back to the computer and damn well write.

Moments later he walked through the front door, while calling back at the dog, "I'll only be a few minutes, Sam. You guard the place until I get back."

Then he followed the old Roman road into the village, thinking how he could phrase what might seem a bizarre question—and hoping he wasn't going to make a complete fool of himself.

Chapter Nine

One

John Newton bought the information he required for the price of a couple of postage stamps. Yesterday, he'd seen the old man being followed up the lane by Martin Marcello, and as in most small villages, the prime source of local information was the man or woman behind the counter at the post office. All John needed to do was bide his time until there was no one else waiting to be served, approach the counter, and say, "Morning, Martin. How are you keeping?"

"Fine, John. I'll be even better on Tuesday, once I'm on that beach."

"Oh, Val mentioned you were going away for a couple of weeks."

"I am. And I'm more than ready for it. Are you still busy writing those best-sellers?"

"I'm doing my best." He smiled. "Oh, I saw you up near my house yesterday morning."

"Ah, yes. Our ration of excitement for the day." Martin pushed the change under the security screen toward John. "I was stocking the shelves across there when I saw old Stan Price heading out of the village as fast as his legs could carry him. All he was wearing were pajamas and a ridiculous straw hat. God, I tell you, John. I hope when my time comes I go just like that." He snapped his fingers.

"Stan Price?" John deliberately formed an expression of someone not familiar with the name.

"You won't know old Stan, will you. He used to be a big cheese in Skelbrooke. You see those prints on the wall?"

John looked at a set of framed prints showing Skelbrooke's noted landmarks—the village hall, pub, church, and some of the bigger houses.

"That one right at the end . . . no, to your left, John. The big house painted yellow. That's where Stan lives."

John saw a house name. "Ezy View House, Skelbrooke . . . Ezy?"

"It's pronounced Easy. Ezy View was the name of Stan Price's chain of TV rental stores. You know, he was the first person in Skelbrooke to own a color television set. Kids used to climb onto the garden wall to try and get a look at it through the windows. He knew what we were up to, but he'd never chase us away." Martin rubbed his jaw, remembering. "Stan was a nice guy. He did a lot for Skelbrooke. And they do say that when local people fell on hard times he'd help them out. But there's no justice . . . he's completely senile now."

"You managed to get him safely back home, though?"

"For what it's worth. All that money he's got in the bank and he can't even remember what day of the week it is."

John saw that the conversation was petering out. Martin had turned away to start sticking postage stamps on a parcel.

John tried a little pump-priming. "Doesn't his daughter look after him?"

"Oh, aye. He first started getting confused three or four years ago. He'd go up to the Water Mill asking to see some people who'd long gone from there. In the end his daughter and son-in-law moved in to look after him."

"It must take some doing . . . giving up your home to look after a senile relative."

Martin shot John a worldly glance. "The daughter's OK, a bit on the shy side perhaps, but the son-in-law strikes me as an out-and-out bloodsucker." Martin dropped his voice to a secrets-to-be-told whisper. "By all accounts, the home they gave up was a pokey rented room. When they first got here Robert Gregory—he's the son-in-law—wore baggy-arsed jeans and T-shirts that looked as if rats had been at them. Now he struts around in made-to-measure suits like he's heir to the manor . . . which, in a manner of speaking, he is." The door chimed as another customer entered the post office. Martin touched his nose. "He's just waiting for the old boy to pop his clogs. Now, what's it to be, Mrs. Machen? The usual?"

John stepped back to allow the customer through to the counter.

"Have a good trip if I don't see you before," John said, satisfied with the information he'd gathered. "Pass on my best to Brenda."

"Will do . . . oh, John, don't forget your stamps."

"Thanks." John picked them up, then slipped out of the post office.

Now he knew where to find the old man. But broaching the question of the letter was going to be a bit tricky. So, what should he do? Simply appear at the front door and say, *Mrs. Gregory, I received a bizarre letter the other day. I think you got one, too.*

But then why on earth was he going to all this trouble over a hoax letter? The truth of the matter was that this whole thing had started a tingling in his bloodstream.

He'd felt the same way when he'd visited the county archive office in Lincoln with the intention of checking old newspaper reports about the Paxton-Wellman case. Suddenly it had occurred to him to take a look at the Lincoln census of 1887. Logically, it was a waste of time, but he'd felt that tingle, as if intuitively he knew he would find an important nugget of information. After two hours plowing through lists of property addresses and their occupants, he had turned up one Mr. Zephraim Gordon, which was a known alias of Lord Paxton-Wellman. Hey presto. John Newton had discovered a hitherto unknown safe house of the aristocratic burglar.

Now that same tingle ran through his blood. He instinctively knew he was on to something bigger than a mere hoax perpetrated by a bored schoolkid. After all, a letter that was a mere practical joke wouldn't have provoked that kind of dramatic response in Keith Haslem, would it? Not to the extent that he'd run from the village like the Four Horsemen of the Apocalypse were riding his way.

The yellow house he now knew as Ezy View lay just a minute's walk away. He realized he'd have to concoct some plausible reason why he was going to ask the questions he planned to ask. If he got it wrong, he'd have the door shut in his face. That would be the end of that. Maybe he should play it straight? He'd be the concerned resident of Skelbrooke who'd received a letter. Now he'd heard that the old man had gotten one, too.

Oh, well, he thought, here goes.

Two

The playground vibrated with excitement. Elizabeth's bandage trailed loose again as she ran with a group of boys of her own age. They reached a corner of the playground where a girl from the top year was telling everyone what she had seen. "Then they brought him out on a stretcher."

"What was he like?"

"Did you see any blood?"

The girl shook her head. "He was all covered up. My dad said it was a body bag."

"Then you didn't see his face?"

"No. But I could see the blood from my brother's bedroom. He's got a telescope like they have on *Johnny Quest.* We could even see the murderer's footprints made from blood."

The kids buzzed with excitement.

"Who got killed?" asked a girl from second year, her eyes wide.

"A little kid called Liam Thorp. Now his mother's run away."

Voice roses into a squeal of delicious terror.

"Did his mother kill him?"

"Gross!"

"No," the older girl replied. "His mother didn't kill him." She paused for effect. "It was Baby Bones."

At once the children took up the chant.

"Baby Bones! Baby Bones! Baby Bones!"

Three

From way off in the distance John could hear the chanting coming from Elizabeth's school. He couldn't quite make out the words. They seemed to shimmer on the summer air, growing louder, then softer, before coming back stronger than ever to echo from old cottage walls. Perhaps Elizabeth was one of the chanters. He smiled to himself. She always tended to be in the middle of things.

The yellow house lay ahead of him. It was probably a good couple of centuries old. Tiles dipped here and there with the curve of ancient roof timbers. Cedars stood in the garden, while well-tended lawns rolled up to the house itself. A wall ran at shoulder height around the garden. This must be the very same wall that Martin Marcello and his friends had stood on long ago to catch that first glimpse of color television.

It was certainly a peaceful backwater here. There was little in the way of traffic along this particular street. What cars there were, were expensive enough to reflect the wealth of the neighborhood.

With his opening line carefully rehearsed, he went to the main gate. A sign read: *EZY VIEW*. He turned the handle. Damn. Locked.

Standing back, he looked left and right, wondering if there was another way in. A little way along he saw a door set in the wall. Five seconds later he swore under his breath again. That was also locked. Stan Price had himself a fortress here. Yet, he'd wager, the locked gates were to prevent the old man from wandering away rather than to prevent people from getting in. Frowning, John followed the road looking for another entrance. A footpath ran along the side of the property. He followed it.

At that moment common sense suggested he quit this mission. The computer sat on his desk at home, waiting for him to fire it up and write that first chapter.

You're scared, John Newton, he told himself. Admit you're diarrhea-shit scared of writing the first chapter. This is nothing but a big exercise to postpone the act of sitting down and typing those first few words. You know that *Without Trace* won't be half as good as *Blast His Eyes*, so you're too frightened to even try. Now here you are chasing the proverbial wild goose. Anything to delay the dreadful moment when you have to write.

He pressed the nagging thoughts to the back of his mind and walked on. Here, nettles grew high at either side of him; trees closed overhead. Neglected for years, the path narrowed to a tangle of brambles.

Dead end.

Just like your career, he thought. Unless you can work a miracle in the next few days.

With the way ahead closed off to him, he turned

back. But the detective inside him nagged like a personal devil. *Newton. Are you going to give up so easily? You've got to make the effort. You've got to take risks. Remember? You followed that hunch at the archive office. You turned a so-so book into a best-seller. You can do it again. But only if you follow your heart, not your head. . . .*

Yeah, he told himself sourly as he sidestepped a fistful of dog poop on the path: *Yield to the Force, Luke Skywalker. . . .*

That was the moment when he stopped dead in his tracks and did something that came as a complete surprise.

He jabbed his toe into a hole in the weathered brick, then climbed onto the wall. *Great. Now you're a housebreaker.* He found himself grinning despite it all. *C'mon, for heaven's sake, you have a way with words. If you're challenged, come up with some plausible excuse . . . the gates were locked. You needed to see Mr. Gregory. You thought you saw smoke coming from the toolshed.*

"Yeah, and you're on a mission from God," he added flippantly under his breath.

He swung his legs over the wall. Below him, a lawn ran up to the house. At this height he couldn't even break a leg if he tried. He eased himself forward and dropped down onto the grass. Then, as nonchalantly as he could, he strolled toward the house.

He'd just cleared the ornamental bushes when he heard a shout.

"Oh, damn," he murmured, his heart sinking.

Chapter Ten

The cry came again. John turned to its source, a "plausible" excuse for his climb over the garden wall already forming in his mind. But John wasn't ready for what he did see.

It was old Stan Price, this time dressed in trousers and a white shirt open at the neck, straw hat perched on his head. The man's face was incandescent; the eyes blazed with what seemed to be sheer ferocity.

"What kept you?" the old man cried. "I've been waiting for days to see you!" Stan Price beckoned John.

John recovered his composure. "You wanted to see me?"

"Yes, of course, of course. Come over here." The old man waved John across to him, as if he were bursting with news.

When John got closer, the man reached out to grab him by the wrist. Even though Stan Price was incredibly thin, with fingers like twigs, he was surprisingly strong. But then he was so fired up with emotion, he looked ready to go a couple of rounds in the boxing ring.

John started speaking. "Good morning, Mr.—"

"Harry!" Stan Price's eyes sparkled with delight. "Harry, thank God you've come."

"Mr. Price . . . I think you've got the wrong—"

"Harry. Where on earth have you been? Oh, never mind that now. You're back, that's all that matters . . . it's so good to see you. I've been calling you night and day, but I couldn't make you hear. Wouldn't your mother let you out? Oh? Did she find those cigars? I said we should have hidden them in the barn." Stan Price shook John's wrist, his eyes glistening. "Oh, God, it's good to see you again."

"Stan, I wonder if you're daughter's at home. Mrs. Gregory?"

But Stan Price continued speaking as if he'd not heard. "If we get time we'll go down to the river. I've found a pool there where the carp are like this!" Releasing his grip, Stan held his hands apart to show the size of the fish. "I'll get my bike out and the rods. Did you bring your rods, Harry?"

"Mr. Price. I'm not here to go fishing. There was—"

"Of course, of course." The old man suddenly became thoughtful. "Harry. There was something else I had to tell you. It was important. Very important." He rubbed his forehead with the bent arthritic hand, the liver spots covering the skin like oil stains. "So important. Now what was it?" He noticed his own ancient hands, and stared at them in surprise. "I don't know what's happening to me, Harry." He shot John a searching look. "I keep forgetting things. Silly little things and ffftt!" He tapped his head. "They go just like that. And I get stupid ideas . . . yes . . . I could have sworn someone told me you were dead, Harry. Who'd tell me a ridiculous thing like that? Especially when there are so many televisions in the world today. Televisions? Now why did I say that?"

The excitement that had briefly energized the old man passed. John saw confusion cloud the old man's eyes. Suddenly he seemed physically smaller, as if some evil spell was shrinking him, causing his face to shrivel into a sad landscape of deeply etched valleys and gullies that reached toward his eyes, which had become a faded blue.

"Harry. You're not dead. Why did they say that?"

Now it seemed cruel to John to deny that he was Harry—whoever he was. "Why don't you sit down?" John suggested, and nodded to a garden bench.

"But I've a consignment of television sets due at any minute. New ones from Japan . . . color . . . they make them to show programs in color these days, Harry. Can you believe that?" His blue eyes fixed on John's face.

John nodded. "Color televisions will be in big demand, Stan. Now, sit down, please. It's too hot to stand in the sun."

"The summer's are in color these days, too. Just look at all that green." He nodded in the direction of the cemetery, where trees ran riot across the hillside.

"They certainly are," John agreed. He shot a glance up at the yellow house. Surely Mr. and Mrs. Gregory would have noticed the old man wasn't alone now.

"You haven't brought any cake, have you, Harry? Or an apple?"

"No, sorry, Stan."

"I'm so hungry these days. I don't seem to get enough to eat. But I know why you're here, you know."

"You do?"

"Yes. You're here about the letter."

"The letter?" Despite the heat, a cold trickling sensation ran down John's spine. "Did you receive a letter, too, Stan?"

"Oh, yes."

John leaned forward. "What did the letter say, Stan?"

"Oh, the usual."

"The usual?"

The old man looked around as if suddenly agitated. "That's why I was shouting for you night and day. For some reason I can't go up there anymore. I don't know why . . . so you've got to go."

"Go where, Stan?"

"To the Water Mill, Harry. You must warn Mr. Kelly that it's starting all over again."

Gently John asked, "What's starting again?"

"All that trouble . . . all that horrible trouble that happened before. You remember, Harry? It was a proper nightmare. All those people got hurt, and Ben and old Mrs. Stokes died." His forehead wrinkled, as he shook his head. "She got took that night when . . ." He sighed as if the memories were suddenly too powerful to allow him to speak.

"Stan. This letter that came. What did it say?"

"Oh . . . Harry. I'm frightened. It's just like last time . . . just like it . . . I thought you'd been frightened away. That's why you wouldn't come."

"Stan . . ." For a moment John was going to ask about the letter. Then something prompted him to ask a different question. "Stan. Who's Baby Bones?"

The old man drew breath like he'd been plunged in ice water. His frightened eyes locked on John's.

"Harry? Why did you ask that? For pity's sake . . . you know all about Baby Bones. *It was you who saw his face!*"

"Eh, excuse me . . . excuse me?"

John looked up to see Mrs. Gregory walking down the path toward them. She ducked her head as timid as a frightened bird. "Can I help you at all?"

"Cynthia," the old man said, excited. "Look, it's Harry. He's come back!"

"Dad." She gave an embarrassed smile in John's direction. "This gentleman isn't Harry. Harry's—" She shrugged. "This is Mr. Newton. He's an author."

So my fame precedes me, John thought. Quickly he climbed to his feet and held out his hand. Cynthia Gregory shook it, but it was such a faint, ghostlike shake of the hand, he hardly felt her touch at all. "Call me John. Pleased to meet you."

"It's Harry . . ." the old man said, looking from one to the other as if he were a lost child.

"Now, Dad, you sit there. I'll bring you a glass of orange juice in a minute." Then, turning to John, she whispered, "I'm sorry about that. I hope he didn't trouble you. He gets a bit confused."

"No, no not at all. In fact we were having quite a conversation."

Stan Price looked up. "Mother. Is it all right if Harry and I go fishing?"

"I'm not your mother, Dad. I'm Cynthia."

Inwardly John winced. He hated seeing the poor woman squirm with embarrassment like this. But it wasn't her fault, or the old man's. John gave a friendly smile. "Stan was telling some of the history of the village."

"Oh?"

"I've only lived here a few months, so it's quite something to hear about what happened in the past."

"Oh." Her cheeks pinked. "Nothing exciting ever happened here. It's all a bit of a backwater."

"The letter," the old man said.

"Don't you start about that silly letter again, Dad, please. I've had enough of it."

"I got a letter," the old man insisted.

Cynthia smiled apologetically at John. "You'll have to excuse him, sorry."

John maintained his smile. "A letter?"

"Oh, it's nothing. Some kids have been playing a practical joke on Dad. Which is criminal really, considering he's . . . well, you know."

John gave a sympathetic nod.

The old man stood up. "Harry's going to take the letter up to the Water Mill. Mr. Kelly will know what to do."

Cynthia spoke more loudly at her father. "Dad. John Newton here lives up at the Water Mill now. He's a famous writer."

John turned to the woman. "This Mr. Kelly. Did he live at the Water Mill once?"

"Yes. He was the local schoolteacher, but it's going

back some time now. Let's see, Dad's eighty-two next, so it must have been more than seventy years ago when Mr. Kelly lived up there. But I expect your home's changed a lot since then."

"I imagine so. I think there are some photographs of the place from around then. I'll have to dig them out."

"Color televisions," the old man was saying. "That's the future. People won't go to the cinema anymore. Not when they can sit in the comfort of their homes and—"

"Oh, Dad, here's Robert. He's brought you your paper."

John looked up to see Robert Gregory walk quickly across the lawn. He didn't look like one happy bunny. He was pocketing the gate key while stabbing John with suspicious glances. Nevertheless, he boomed out a hearty greeting. "Hello there. John Newton. How are you?"

"Fine, thanks. And you?"

"Can't complain." The handshake was as hearty as the voice. "Do anything for you?"

Here comes reason-for-being-here time. John smiled. "As you know, I saw Mr. Price yesterday. I found myself walking by here this morning and thought I'd drop in and see how he was . . . just for my own peace of mind if anything."

John was surprised (but didn't show it) by Robert Gregory's reaction. An expression of pure suspicion flitted across the man's face. But he recovered quickly. "Well, thank you. That's most decent of you, John. Most decent."

"Color televisions," Stan Price told them. "Color televisions in every home."

"There's your paper, Dad," Robert boomed.

"Is it time for supper? I'm hungry."

"Hungry?" Robert awarded John a glassy smile. "You've only just had breakfast, Dad. Now, John. Can we get you a drink of something?"

"No, thanks. I just called by to see if Mr. Price was all right."

"Any reason why he shouldn't be?" Suddenly Robert Gregory's voice adopted a prickly edge.

"No, not at all. But I felt guilty after rushing off like that yesterday when you were looking for him."

"Oh, of course," Cynthia said remembering. "How's your daughter? You were taking her to hospital, weren't you?"

"She'd taken a tumble of her bike. She's fine now." He smiled. "In fact, she's so proud of the bandage round her head, I don't think she'll ever take it off."

Robert Gregory had returned to his best-of-buddies voice. "I'll walk you to the gate. We have to keep it locked these days." He glanced at Stan. "Better safe than sorry."

"Of course. Good-bye, Mrs. Gregory."

"Tea for two," the old man was saying. He looked so tired, it was a struggle to support his head on that pencil-thin neck of his. "Tea for two and chocolate cake. Harry's hungry, too, Mother."

"I'll get Dad a cold drink," Cynthia said, relieved she could return to the house. Clearly, she was acutely embarrassed by her father's senility.

John made a point of saying good-bye to the old man. Although he must have been a ghost of his former self, John didn't see why he should be ignored.

"Nice weather we've been having," Robert Gregory said conversationally as he accompanied John to the main gate a moment later.

"Let's hope it stays like this. We're having a barbecue this weekend." John noticed how the man shot glances at the main gate, then at the door in the wall, no doubt wondering how John had entered the garden if they were locked. That would be Mr. Gregory's very own mystery for today. Figuring out how John Newton walked through walls.

John found himself not liking Gregory very much. He was too hearty, too familiar. And there was something shifty and secretive about him.

*Let's hope the mystery of my arrival keeps you awake in
the small hours, you little creep.*

"Here we go," boomed the man, pulling a key from
his pocket like a jailer.

John squinted against the sunlight, then reached into
his pocket "Uh . . . trust me, I'd forget my own head if
it wasn't screwed on tight."

"What's that, John?"

"I left my sunglasses on the bench. I'll just get them."

Before Robert Gregory could respond, John jogged
back across the lawn to where old Stan Price sat on the
bench beneath the shady branches. John was conscious
of Robert-the-creep-Gregory's searching stare in his
back. There were no sunglasses, of course; even so, he
mimed picking them from the bench, then slipping
them into his pocket.

John had intended to talk to Stan Price one last time
(he doubted he would get another chance to speak directly to him). He planned to simply ask what was in
the letter, getting confirmation that the letter was similar to the one he, John Newton, had received—and
Keith Haslem, too.

Stan looked up into John's face. "You're not Harry,
are you?" he said softly.

"No, I'm not, Stan."

"And I'm not young anymore, am I?"

How could John answer that one?

Stan continued. "I live here with my daughter and
son-in-law."

John tilted his head in surprise. Before, when he'd
talked to the man, it had been like talking to a ghost.
As if only a splinter of the man's personality still survived in his softening brain. Now he sounded rational.

"I'm sorry." The blue eyes fixed steadily on John's.
"I didn't catch your name?"

"John Newton."

"Pleased to meet you, John Newton . . . call me Stan.
I apologize if I got you confused with someone else. I
get so forgetful these days. My God . . . I hate what I've

127

become, you know. I really wish I could kill myself."

"Stan, I'm sure your family wouldn't be happy to hear you saying that."

"Oh, wouldn't they, John?"

"Stan," John said gently, "I received a letter a few days ago. I think it's similar to one you received."

"You found it under a stone in the garden?"

"Yes."

"Oh, John." Stan spoke with an aching sincerity. "I'm so sorry for you, son. Really, I am. You've done nothing to deserve it. . . ."

The blue eyes clouded a little, but he kept on shaking his head as if he'd heard bad news.

"Stan. Who was the letter from? Why do the letters frighten people so much?"

Stan looked up into John's face. A breeze disturbed the branches, sending a dappling of sunlight streaming across the old face. It looked as if spirit hands ran across the man's head, trying to steal away what was left of his mind.

"Stan? Why do the letters scare people?"

"John, I'm . . ." The breeze gave a ghostly whisper to the trees. Stan's voice became a croak. "I'm hungry. Harry, I haven't eaten for days. Harry, ask them to bring me my supper . . . please . . . please . . ."

As John stepped back, Robert Gregory's voice echoed from the garden walls. "Did you find them, John?"

John looked across to the man, nodded, and patted his pocket. Then, under his breath, he said to Stan Price, "Take care of yourself, Pop."

With that, he crossed the lawn. Robert Gregory told him to have a good day, then shut the gate behind John. The key turned loudly in the lock.

John walked along the street. The sun shone. Open spaces were flooded with light. But, as if noticing for the first time, John saw that shadows were darkest on a summer's day. They seemed to hide beneath bushes, in corners, below cars. They seemed to watch him walk by. They seemed . . . he tilted his head, looking . . . they seemed different. Altered somehow.

That night John Newton got another letter.

Chapter Eleven

One

"Is it deep?"

"Fairly deep."

"Deep enough to drown?"

"Easily. That's why you must treat the lake with respect."

"Does that mean we shouldn't call it rude names?"

"You know what 'respect' means, Elizabeth. Don't go messing around at the water's edge. Don't go out on the boat unless I or your mother is with you."

"Or Paul?"

"Possibly."

"Dad? Have people drowned in our lake?"

"Not that I know of. *Elizabeth!* Be careful when you move about the boat."

"I won't tip it up, Dad."

They were out on the lake in the row boat. The evening sun drenched the Water Mill with amber lights, turning the walls into a mottling of warm flesh tints.

Elizabeth had been keen to row the boat herself. In fact, she'd been keen to play in the boat alone, but that was tempting fate too much, so John had agreed to be the passenger. Now he sat in the stern, trailing his fingers in the water.

There wasn't any real destination to head for in the boat. The lake, roughly circular in shape, covered an area of maybe four tennis courts and that was it. Long ago its purpose was to serve as a reservoir for the mill, providing a permanent and controllable flow of water to the turbine that drove the millstones. It also served as a fishing pond and swimming pool. No doubt fish still lurked beneath the reeds, but as John had never found the idea of fishing at all appealing, the denizens of the lake would be safe from him.

"Try and pull the oars together at the same time," he told Elizabeth. "We're going round in circles."

"Like this?"

"That's better ... pull harder on the left one ... no, that's your right ... pull harder with this one." He tapped her left hand with his finger. "That's it. We're going in a straight line now."

"What time will Mum be home?"

"Soon, I hope."

"She's not usually this late."

"Perhaps she got held up in the traffic or had to work ... whoa, watch out for the island."

The boat's underside scraped over a submerged stone.

"We've hit an iceberg!" Elizabeth grinned, her eyes bright. "Send an SOS to the *Carpathia*."

He laughed. "Women and children first."

Elizabeth effortlessly slipped into a game. John saw that in her imagination the boat was holed below the waterline, that they were sinking fast. He trailed his hand in the water, watching his daughter row frantically for shore, her hair flying out, laughter bubbling from her lips. "She's going down by the head. SOS!" she called. "Women and children first."

"And writers . . . don't forget the poor old writers."

He looked down in the direction of the house. Val appeared on the path. In one hand she carried her briefcase, in the other her jacket. She looked frazzled and more than ready to unwind after what he guessed must have been a trying day at the office. He waved, she returned the wave with her briefcase, and although dead beat, she flashed a warm smile at him.

"Mum's home," he said. "No . . . Elizabeth, don't stand up in the boat."

"I'm only waving."

"You're best sitting down to wave." He smiled. "We don't want to find ourselves swimming home, do we?"

Elizabeth continued circling the island. Her energy seemed inexhaustible. She'd bounded in from school, the bandages trailing to her knees. They were grubby enough to be nearer to black than white. John had removed them, leaving only the sticking plaster on her chin like some funny little goatee. As always, Elizabeth had been full of news. She'd told him over juice and chocolate-chip cookies that a child had been murdered in the village. He'd already caught that on the lunchtime news when he'd returned from calling on old Stan Price. That probably accounted for the wail of sirens the previous evening. He gathered it was one of those sordid domestic incidents. A guy had murdered the child of his ex-lover in revenge for being dumped. Thank God the bastard hadn't got far before the cops caught up him. With luck, he would rot in jail.

As was typical with news that had flashed mouth-to-mouth around school, the murder had been embellished with all kinds of unlikely details. It had taken John some time to divert Elizabeth's attention off the subject. At least now she was thrashing away with the oars happily enough. She hadn't mentioned the murder in the last hour or so.

After indulging her fantasies that she was on board the sinking *Titanic,* she allowed the boat to drift while she gazed down into the water. John found himself relaxing. Here, the peace and quiet was incredible. Dragonflies skimmed the water in flashes of brilliant turquoise. A kingfisher dove into the lake in search of minnows. Water dripped from the oars, sounding like notes played on some exotic musical instrument. Elizabeth hummed lightly to herself.

By now Val had emerged, freshly showered, changed into cutoffs and a T-shirt. She sat on a patio chair with a cup in her hand. John found his mind turning to squeezing a great pile of oranges, then mixing the juice with crushed ice. The more he thought about the iced drink sliding down his throat, the more appealing it became. To paraphrase one old song, it was summertime and the living was easy. He looked back at Elizabeth. She still stared into the water.

He leaned sideward a little to see into the lake. He saw reflected sky, a strand or two of weed. Nothing else.

"See any fish, hon?"

He waited for a reply, only she was too mesmerized by the water.

"Elizabeth. See any fish?"

"No," she said at last. "I'm looking for Baby Bones."

Two

Ten minutes later John sat down beside Val. He asked her if she'd heard of anyone by the name of Baby Bones.

"Baby Bones?" She shrugged. "Sounds like a cartoon character to me. Why?"

"I've heard Elizabeth talking about this Baby Bones over the last couple of days. She seems obsessed with him . . . or it."

"Don't worry. She tends to get fixated on people or things every so often. Remember how she used to go on endlessly about the *Titanic*?"

"It's just how she talks about this Baby Bones. She seems excited and frightened all at the same time."

"Baby Bones?" Val sipped from her cup, thinking. "Isn't that the one from the *Rugrats* cartoon?"

"That's Chucky, Lill, Phil, Tommy, and Angelica."

She smiled. "You know your cartoon characters, Mr. Newton."

"It rubs off when you've sat through hundreds of the things while the kids watch them."

"Are you sure you're the hardworking writer that you seem to be?" Her eyes twinkled. "It sounds as if you sit in front of the cartoon channels all day."

"I wish." He smiled. "At least that way I'd know if this Baby Bones was a cartoon character or not."

"Or Elizabeth might have picked something up from a book?"

"Might have," he allowed. "But I was up on the lake with her just now. She was staring down into the water, and when I asked if she was looking for fish, she said, no, she was looking for Baby Bones."

"She obviously gets the strange imagination from you, John."

"She told me that if you saw Baby Bones looking back at you, then you would soon die."

"And you think she was genuinely frightening herself doing this?"

"As I said, it's a mixture of excitement and fear. You know." He shrugged. "The same as how she gets riding a ghost train."

"I wouldn't worry about it, John. It sounds like one of these schoolyard myths that children frighten each other with. You know the sort, step on a crack in the pavement and you'll die, or hold your breath when an ambulance goes by, otherwise you'll catch a disease."

He nodded. "Or the plant Mother Dye. When I was a kid, local legend had it that if you picked the plant your mother would *die*." He grinned. "Steve and I used to tease our mother no end by telling her we picked huge armfuls of the stuff."

"And as she's still alive and kicking, it's obviously just another of those half-baked superstitions." She leaned across and squeezed John's knee. "See, Baby Bones is just one of those stories that kids tell each other. Elizabeth'll have forgotten all about it in a few days."

"And no more Baby Bones."

"Right . . . now, what are we going to cook for supper, handsome? Pork chops? Steak? Quiche?"

"Quiche with salad. It's too hot to stand over a stove." He stood up, stretching. "I'll make a start on it."

"Will Paul be back to eat with us?"

"No, he's meeting some friends this evening. He said he'd make himself a sandwich later."

"I'll come and do the salad."

"No. You look bushed. I can manage."

"Come here." She touched her lips.

He kissed her.

"Thank you. You're a good man."

Smiling, he walked back into the house. Elizabeth sat cross-legged on the observation glass while gazing down into the waters rushing through the millrace below. She was lost in her own world. John, not wishing to disturb her, went into the kitchen to make a start on the meal.

Three

The evening sun sliced through the trees in the cemetery, glinting from headstones, warming the faces of stone angels. Already, shadows had begun to pour into the Vale of Tears, filling the labyrinth of passages with a shade so dark and so thick it looked as if liquid darkness leaked from the vaults.

Paul walked with Miranda Bloom along one of the passageways. The walls of the crypts flanked them above head height. You couldn't see backward or forward more than fifteen paces, due to the sharp turns of the passageways. Only the roof was open to the evening air. Yet the branches of trees lidded even that.

They walked hand in hand, enjoying the silence and

privacy after a day spent with a thousand students at school. Here they could be alone, say anything, do anything, knowing they wouldn't be seen or overheard.

In the shadowed gullies Miranda moved with a dreamlike beauty, her Spanish eyes glinting provocatively, her hair black as raven's feathers, spilling over one bare shoulder. Paul Newton's heart beat hard. He glanced at Miranda. She smiled, and as she walked she reached out, allowing her fingertips to brush the walls and the steel doors of the crypts.

Thousands and thousands of bodies interred in those tombs, Paul told himself. *Did a single one of those dead people ever feel like me? Yes, they must have. Millions of men and women must have experienced the same emotions shooting through their bodies like fire . . . like electricity . . . but how come it feels as if I've discovered something completely new? Here is Miranda Bloom. In a short skirt. In a sleeveless top . . . come to that, a shoulderless top. All I can see are acres of smooth olive skin. She's smiling at me. We're no longer talking. Because we don't have to talk. Everything's happening through smiles, eye contact, a raise of the eyebrow. God . . . how come her teeth are so white? It doesn't seem possible that anyone has felt like this before. . . .*

Behind iron doors caskets lay stacked one on top of another. Layer upon layer of dead men and women stretching back 150 years or more. They were bones now. Fleshless skulls. Lipless, bloodless. Leering mouths full of rotted teeth. Skeletons housing cobwebs and rodents' nests. But once they had hearts that must have pounded like his. Bellies with fire inside them that burnt like almighty furnaces.

The heat shot out from the center of his stomach to his fingertips.

Once those long-skirted Victorian ladies had slipped beneath the sheets and smiled at their menfolk, flashed those come-to-bed eyes, then sighed with pleasure as flesh met flesh, as nipples rose hard, as mouths pressed against mouths in kisses of overwhelming, superheated passion. Electric thrills surged up his spine.

Those people in their tombs were bone dust now. But once they'd ridden that surging wave of erotic excitement he felt now.

"Nearly there," she murmured. Her hand squeezed his.

Yes, oh, my God. Nearly there. To many this was a journey of just a few hundred yards from the village. For Paul Newton it was a journey of many years. Ever since he'd been twelve years old he'd wondered what it would be like to lie naked with a girl. Now, in a few minutes time . . .

His lips were dry. His heart thundered.

Now the passageway broadened out. Ahead was the cliff face, through which a path ran on a rising rampway, passing beneath a stone arch. Inscribed on that, the words *GONE TO GLORY*.

Leaves sang as the breeze caught them.

Jesus . . . he was going to explode . . . he couldn't wait any longer.

"Yo!"

Shit.

Sitting on top of a wall were three teenagers. One he recognized from the school football team. "Paul Newton. My man. How's it going?"

Damn, why did they have to be here?

A weight sank through his chest into the pit of his stomach. "Not bad, Al, how are you?"

"Fair to middling. Evening, Miranda."

"Evening, Al."

The heftily built Al looked down at them, legs dangling, the muscles clearly bulging through his jeans. The three passed a joint between them. The other two were hitting the giggling stage. Al seemed unaffected. But then there must be a hell of a lot of flesh to saturate with the weed before it started to tickle his brain.

"So, you've come to the scene of the crime?"

Casually, Paul shrugged, making sure he didn't arouse the three's curiosity by openly resenting their presence (and signaling as clear as horse piss that he'd had what promised to be an evening of electrifying sex shattered to friggin' smithereens . . . *hell and damnation*). "What crime scene?"

"Murder." Al pulled on the joint. Held it for a second, then spoke using the lung full of smoke, each word appearing as a ball of blue. "There was . . . a little kid . . . murdered yesterday. Poor devil."

"We heard," Miranda said. "But it happened down in the village, not up here."

"That's true. But didn't you hear about the kid's mother?"

"No."

"She came up here . . . last night." Al pulled on the joint again before passing it on. "She hanged herself from that tree across there. But she'd mutilated herself first." He pointed. "Hands. Feet. Face. She was hanging there like a rag doll, dripping blood all over the place." Then he pointed to his face, his fingers open like a fork. "Eyes staring . . . just staring like she'd seen something that had terrified her."

Miranda gave a shake of her head. "You know how to decorate a story, Al. I bet you'd do a really good job with our Christmas tree."

He looked down, his lips forming a twitchy smile. "I found her, Miranda," he said, his, voice light as a whisper. "I found her hanging there. Wearing nothing but a little nightdress. Blood all over her legs." Taking the joint back in his fingers, he shook his head at it. "They don't grow stuff like they used to, Paul. This isn't having any effect." He looked across at the tree; its branch still projected out above the Vale of Tears. What was left of the rope, with a fresh cut mark at the bottom where they'd brought her down, swayed in the breeze. "She won't go away, Paul. I can still see her there. I can see her eyes." Al shook his head savagely, trying to dislodge the memory. Then, failing, he wedged the end of the joint into his mouth. He sucked so hard that the fiery tip glowed white.

Four

"I thought there'd have been some cops here," Miranda said later as they cut across the cemetery, away from where Al sat, trying to fog the memory in clouds of marijuana smoke.

Paul shook his head. "I suppose once they've removed the body and checked the area, there's nothing to stay around for."

"And why didn't they take the whole rope away, not just the end with the noose? It's ghoulish."

He looked at her. Her eyes were bright in the dusk. She looked cold.

"Are you all right, Miranda?"

"Fine."

"I could walk you home?"

"No. I'm OK, Paul."

"Uh, here come the ghouls. It's show time." He nodded down the hillside where clumps of people were moving up the hillside to where the tree with the rope stood. "I imagine this'll become something of a tourist destination. I only hope they washed the poor woman's blood away. Come on." She took his hand. "Let's find somewhere quiet."

Five

In the thickening gloom Stan Price looked out of the window. Hunger burned fiercely inside him.

"Harry . . . Harry. Stan's a hungry boy, Harry. Bring me some of your Ma's cake. Harry?"

In the distance, the hillside cemetery swelled from the ground like a pregnant belly.

"Baby Bones is coming today. Baby Bones is coming to play." The old rhyme came back to him. They'd sung it in the schoolyard once. His grandmother knew it, too, from when she was a child. *"Baby Bones, Baby Bones. Down on your knees and pray. Baby Bones is coming today. . . ."*

139

How did the rhyme end? He frowned.
Now he remembered. It had no end.

Six

At the far side of the cemetery Paul and Miranda found a quiet corner where they could be alone. Here there was little in the way of footpaths. Compared to the trees, the tombstones were black dwarfish figures. There was no noise apart from the breathlike sounds of leaves disturbed by a slight shift in the evening air.

"Alone at last," Paul said.

"Amen to that."

As if ropes had been released, they suddenly moved together, kissing each other hard on the lips.

Paul's heart surged. "God, I've waited for this."

"Paul?"

"Yes."

"I've got to be back by nine."

"Damn . . . no, I'm not angry with you. I'm just annoyed that we haven't had longer together."

"It's only half past eight." Then she said something that almost stopped his heart. "We've got time . . . if you want to?"

She sat down on a bank of grass between two mattresslike tombstones. Her skirt slipped upward, showing a breathtaking stretch of the thigh. She loosened her top from the waistband of the skirt. In a moment he was beside her, kissing her lips. Her wash of dark hair across the grass was so beautiful it winded him. Golden dandelions encircled her head like a halo. For a while all he could do was watch her in wonder. Then:

"Here," he whispered, slipping off his T-shirt. "Put this under your head."

She smiled up at him. "I feel so excited I could burst."

He kissed her. "I've been like that all day. God, you look amazing." Her hands closed behind his neck. She pulled him down onto her, kissing him hungrily.

Within seconds he'd slipped off her top. Her bare breasts rose up in two beautifully pointed mounds. The nipples were dark, enticing. Freckles dusted her skin. She was breathing hard now. White-hot lightning seemed to sear through him from head to toe.

"Paul. Paul?"

Her eyes twinkled at him in the gloom.

"Did you bring anything?"

Good God. He could have punched his own forehead. He'd even been to the bus station rest rooms where there were condom machines. Without a problem he'd bought a pack as easily as buying gum. But the moment when she asked him *Did you bring anything?* he saw his bag lying at the foot of his bed. In the side compartment safe and sound—but not here—were the rubbers.

Damn. He let out a sigh. "Miranda . . . you're not going to believe this."

"Oh, no, don't tell me. . . ." She screwed up her face as if someone had just stood on her bare toe. "You haven't forgotten to buy some."

"No. That's just it. I bought them. But I was in such a rush to see you tonight. I . . ."

"Oh," she groaned with disappointment.

"Sorry." He felt the biggest fool known to humanity.

Good-naturedly she smiled up at him, then sighed. "You idiot."

"I second that."

She kissed him. "I'll never survive the weekend now."

"But we could see each other tomorrow."

"I'm going away to London. It's Dad's birthday and he's taking us to see a show."

"Oh, shit."

"Oh, shit and the rest. I'll be sitting through a horrendous musical feeling so hot I could erupt."

He looked down at her breasts. Once more they'd disappear. For how long this time?

She lightly scratched his back. His skin goosed. "You

141

know, Paul. I've just finished my period."

"Yeah?" His mouth dried.

"We could still see this through to the end."

"Are you sure?"

"Sure I'm sure."

"I mean, will it be safe?"

"I'm punctual as the town hall clock."

He looked down into her sparkling eyes. Her mouth was parted in a smile that made him want to melt. But . . .

"Miranda?"

"Mmm."

"It will be . . . you know . . . unprotected."

"I haven't any dark secrets, have you?"

"No. But—"

"Shh . . . now help me take off my skirt."

Chapter Twelve

One

That Friday evening the clock in the hallway hadn't struck nine before Paul came in through the front door.

John Newton noticed his son's face glowed red; he'd been running.

"You're back early, Paul," John said from the kitchen.

"Yeah . . . you know . . ."

"Fancy a beer?"

"No."

"No? Wait, I'll get my diary and make a note of that." John smiled. "Paul Newton refuses beer. U.N. to call emergency meeting."

That should have brought at least a weak oh-no-Dad's-trying-to-be-witty smile to Paul's face, but he looked flustered. There'd been some trouble with a bunch of kids in the village when they'd first moved there. Paul had been hassled just because he was new. John hoped it all wasn't flaring up again. He gave another broad smile, aiming to put Paul at his ease.

"The beer's nice and cold," he said. "Red Stripe."

"Red Stripe?" *Result.* "Oh, all right. Thanks."

"It's a bit on the warm side to be running."

"I was just hurrying to get back."

"Oh?"

"There's something I want to watch at nine. Anything wrong, Dad?"

"No . . . it's just you look as if you've run a marathon or something."

"I'll have a shower later. The beer's in the refrigerator?"

"Yeah, top shelf. There's some kabanos sausage wants eating too."

Paul shrugged, looking distracted. He seemed to have his mind on other things. "I might later."

"Are you all right, Paul?"

Suddenly, he looked defensive. "Fine. Why?"

"You look as if you've lost something."

Paul appeared uncomfortable. "I don't see any beer."

"Top shelf, Paul."

"Right."

Paul crossed the kitchen. John watched him and gave a little shake of his head. Maybe he himself had been just as edgy and preoccupied as a teenager. Adolescence should carry a government health warning. John poured a glass of milk for Elizabeth, then went through into the living room where Val watched television.

"Everything OK?" she asked with a sleepy smile.

"Everything's fine."

Outside, the sun at last slipped behind the hill, and darkness rolled down over them like a cloud.

Two

"Is it supper time?"

"You've had it earlier, Dad. About half an hour ago."

"I'm hungry."

"There's no more until breakfast. There . . . have you done your teeth?"

The old man sat on the edge of his bed, dressed in pajamas. "Is there any cake?"

"Well, I could do him a slice of toast," Cynthia told her husband as he folded Stan's clothes.

"Cynthia, he'll give himself a stomachache if he eats before bedtime. Then if he can't sleep, we'll be up half the night with him."

"But—"

"Cynthia. He'll be right as rain."

"If you say so, Robert," she said meekly. "Now, Dad. Time for bed."

Robert Gregory glanced at his watch in a bored way, then added. "Oh, I might as well slip to the pub for the last one. Fancy a walk down with me?"

"Oh, not me, Robert. You know I don't like going into bars late at night."

He kissed her on the cheek. "Right-oh, dear. You help yourself to a glass or two of sherry. I'll be half an hour tops."

"Bye, dear."

"Good night, Dad," he boomed.

Five minutes later Robert Gregory stooped down by the bush near the garden gate, picked up the carrier bag of sandwiches, cake, and unopened bag of bacon snacks, and carried them down the street as far as the trash can. Casually he dropped in the bag, then pushed it down with his fist. Cynthia wouldn't have seen. The walls around the garden were far too high to see into the road. And she'd never come outside after dark by herself. Whistling, his hands in his pocket running loose coins through his fingers, he headed in the direction of the inn's lights that shone across the green.

In his bedroom at Ezy View, Stan Price waited until his daughter had returned downstairs to her sherry and the Friday night movie. Then he picked up the toilet roll that stood on his bedside table—the one that they used to wipe his chin after his drinks and medicine.

He tore off one square. Fed it into his mouth.

Chewed. Swallowed. Then tore off another piece of

toilet tissue. As he ate, his mind, no longer distracted by the ache of hunger, cleared a little.

"John Newton," he murmured, remembering the name. "John Newton ... I've something to tell you."

Three

Paul lay on his bed. His fingers were knitted behind the back of his head (that still felt hot enough to scorch the pillowcase). He gazed up at the ceiling, not seeing the posters blue-tacked there but picturing Miranda's smiling eyes.

Smiling eyes ... he liked the phrase, and rolled it round inside his head. Smiling Spanish eyes she had. Those breasts, too, all dusted with freckles. Nipples. Dark. Deliciously dark. His mind swam, dizzy as a kitten chasing its tail.

Time had stopped obeying the rules of physics. Forget relativity, Einstein. Paul found himself slipping back in time to when Miranda lay as near naked as you could possibly get.

Her skirt slipped higher. She wanted him as much as he wanted her. Forget the laws of gravity, too, Newton. There was an irresistible gravitational pull between them. That welded them tighter than glue. God ... her eyes ... those sparkling, erotic, sex-charged eyes ...

But just as he was getting to break through one of those key boundaries of his life, a bunch of kids had appeared, mooching amongst the headstones not more than thirty paces away. Armed with air rifles, they were more interested in birds in the treetops than what was happening on the ground.

Luckily, the naked pair hadn't been seen. They'd gathered up their clothes and run like soldiers moving through sniper territory. Laughing with excitement and incredulity, they'd found themselves at the old railway station that had once served the Necropolis. Time had raced by. Miranda was due home in fifteen minutes.

"God," she said out of the blue. "I really wanted you back there, Paul."

"Me, too." He smiled. "It looks as if we're going to have to hit the pause button until next week."

"Not quite," she said. Then she did something for him that made Paul realize she'd lived a little longer in the adult world than he had.

Paul gazed up at the ceiling, certain the grin on his face would never disappear in a million years.

Four

At a little after midnight, John Newton opened the back door of the house. The dog had an urgent need for the yard by this time. He ran sniffing amongst tree trunks. Soon he'd disappeared into darkness, where John heard liquid splashes as Sam relieved himself.

Clouds slipped across the sky, leaving the moon a nebulous smudge of white above Skelbrooke. Even so, he could still make out the path leading up the hillside toward the lake, and although pleasantly drowsy, strolled up there, enjoying the cooler evening air. As Val got ready for bed, he'd spend a few minutes out here, while the dog did what a dog's gotta do.

On the lake, which was as smooth as a vast dark mirror, the boat stood motionless. To his right he heard the hiss of the water running down its channel to the millrace beneath the house. This was a nice time of day. Paul and Elizabeth were asleep. The house, with the exception of a single light, lay in darkness. There was a sense it was ready to slumber, too. He yawned. Tomorrow he'd write a few pages of the first chapter of *Without Trace*. Then later he'd fire up the big barbecue on the patio and sizzle up some hamburgers and pork chops. In the back of the refrigerator there was the bottle of barbecue sauce he'd brought back from his book promotion tour in Australia. That stuff was to die for—rich, dark, savory . . . maybe he'd ask Paul to pick some fresh strawberries from the market garden down the road, too.

Sam snuffled by, his nose Hoovering the grass, as he followed the trail of some mouse or hedgehog.

John stretched, enjoying a mighty yawn. After he'd finished, he moved downhill toward the house. There the bedroom light burned. He caught a glimpse of Val's naked silhouette cast against the curtain.

"Sam . . . Sam?" he called softly. Then listened. He couldn't hear the dog. No panting. No scrape of his claws against the grass as he marked his territory. No nothing.

"Sam? Where are you, boy?"

Like a cannonball Sam shot out of the darkness, his tail tucked in tight between his back legs, the way he did when he was frightened or hurt.

"Sam," John said gently. "Come here. What on earth's the matter?" He stroked the dog, who gave a twitchy shake of the tail. "Has something given you a fright, then? Come on, boy. Let's go inside."

In the dead center of the patio, in the light spilled from the bedroom window, John saw a chunk of stone. He watched as the dog went forward to sniff at the unfamiliar object. Sam was still a good three paces from it when his body locked up like a statue, the hair on his back bristled. Then he shuffled backward away from it, ears flattening.

"Don't worry, Sam. It can't hurt us." He picked up the stone. His eye caught something that had been beneath it. "Oh, no . . ."

Inexplicably, his heart sank. And for a second it seemed more like winter than summer . . . he shivered.

"Sam. It looks as if we've got another one."

He bent down, his fingers hovering over the oblong of folded paper on the patio, momentarily reluctant to pick it up. The thing could have oozed some contamination the way he was suddenly repelled by it.

"Come on, Newton . . . it won't bite you."

As if plucking it from a fire, he grabbed the letter, his teeth gritted. Sam watched him.

"You didn't want me to pick up it either, did you, boy? Don't worry, it's only a letter."

He looked from the folded paper to the hunk of stone in his other hand. Like the first time, it was a piece of smashed tombstone. Engraved on it, a single word, *suffer*, that had probably been chiseled there a hundred years before. It certainly wasn't new. But he didn't doubt that whoever had chosen it as a paperweight had also made sure it bore a suitably resonant message. All part of the sick little game.

The pathetic freak. Whoever it was needed therapy. Or (even better) a good hard kick in the backside. He leaned over the patio wall, then dropped the stone behind a line of bedding plants where it wouldn't be noticed. The last thing he wanted was to upset the rest of the family needlessly. This was the kind of thing that would prey on Val's mind. So with her up to her eyeballs in work, he intended keeping this secret. Walking toward the door, he unfolded the letter. Same heavy paper. Same antique feel to it. As if it had been torn from a two-hundred-year-old ledger. He turned it to the light. Same handwriting, too. An old-fashioned Gothic style.

Dear Messr. John Newt'n,
I should—

"Christ!" He jerked backward. "Val. I didn't see you. Hell, you scared me half to death."

She stood in the doorway. He saw the glint of her eyes. He sensed she was smiling. "I was just beginning to wonder if some man-hungry goblins had spirited you away."

He took a deep breath and patted his chest as if to encourage his heart to keep beating. "I took a walk up to the lake."

She was wearing a T-shirt that barely reached her thighs. Across the breasts were the words *Oh, you know what I want you to do.*

"What have you got there?" she asked, nodding at the letter in John's hand.

"Oh, nothing. Just a chocolate wrapper or something."

"Well, get rid of it quickly, then come to bed." She smiled back at him as they crossed the kitchen. "It's the start of the weekend, you know?"

"Coming . . . you go to bed, too, Sam."

The dog stepped onto his bean bag in the corner of the kitchen, turned around a couple of times, then curled himself down onto it, his tail covering his nose but his eyes still bright and watchful as John stepped on the pedal of the trash.

"All done?" She waited for him at the kitchen door.

He smiled, nodded, and mimed dropping something into the trash, then let the lid drop down. Without Val noticing, he slipped the letter into the back pocket of his jeans.

And just what would the letter say this time?

He knew he would have to read it, driven by the same impulse that makes you look at a car wreck as you drive by, but he couldn't do so now without Val seeing. It would have to wait till morning. Good God, the world of secrets. But, he told himself, his motives were pure. There was no point in worrying the family unnecessarily.

A moment later he killed the lights and darkness claimed the ancient house.

Five

Elizabeth lay in bed. Wide-awake, she picked at the scab beneath her chin. The thing itched now like spiders burrowing under her skin. No way could she sleep with this pricking and itching.

Shit, she thought with a wicked grin. Shit. It's itchy shit.

Switching on her flashlight that she kept by the bed, she shone it at her wall clock. Three o'clock. That's three in the morning, she told herself. She'd never seen what the outside world looked like at this time. She went to the window, pulled the roller blind away from the glass at the bottom (in a way she had been forbidden to do)—but who would see her now?

Shit could see me now. She grinned at her reflection. *Shit could see me.*

Outside, the lawn was as black as deep water. The sky was dark, too. She could only see the lumpy silhouette of a bush.

"Shit dark," she murmured. "Dark as shit."

Everyone was asleep. Mum, Dad, Paul. Down in the kitchen Sam would be curled up in his bed. The world slept, too. She couldn't see any birds flying in the night sky. Everything lay still.

Elizabeth was about to return to bed when she saw a face looking up from the patio at her. She couldn't make out a mouth or a nose, but the eyes were huge and dark, and they stared straight up at her. Maybe it was Emma? They'd talked about going out on a secret adventure one night. Maybe Emm had come now. Elizabeth rolled up the blind, then pushed open the window. Instantly the smell of damp slithered up her nostrils.

It wasn't Emm, but it was a girl of around her own age. Eight or nine perhaps. She'd fixed her eyes on Elizabeth's. They were intense, serious-looking eyes. For some reason Elizabeth found it hard to break away. And there were times when they didn't look like dark eyes at all . . . only holes that ran deep inside her head.

Then the girl spoke. "Elizabeth. Do you want to see where I live?" The girl held out her hand.

Elizabeth shook her head. "I'm not allowed out by myself at night."

"Me neither. I'll get into trouble if he finds I've gone."

The girl held up her hands as if ready to catch Elizabeth if she jumped from the window. "I'm bored, Elizabeth. I want to show you where I live."

"Sorry. I'm going back to bed now."

"No. Please don't . . . I'll wait until you come down. We'll only be a few minutes and it would be so nice to talk with you for a while."

"Where do you come from?"

"Near here."

"No," Elizabeth said. "Where did you first come from?"

"Sorry. I don't understand what you mean."

"Your accent's different."

"I was born here. I've always lived here." The accent was the same as those in old black and white movies. Then the girl paused. She gazed up with those eyes that looked like holes bored deep into a slab of wood. "Please spend some time with me."

Now this was a strange thing. Elizabeth didn't remember leaving the house. Only, all of a sudden she found herself walking down the lane with the white-faced girl.

Whiteface stared at her. The eyes were round and dark. Even though Elizabeth was this close now, the girl's eyes still looked like holes. Just holes in white wood.

It was cold out here, despite it being a summer's night. Cold. Dark. And not a happy place to be. The lane ran ahead of them, a pale strip lying between monstrous growths of trees that reached up and over them with dark, ragged arms.

Ready to pounce, Elizabeth.

She shook her head. She shouldn't be out. Not with this white-faced girl with black holes for eyes.

"Not far now," whispered the girl.

"I don't want to go any farther. I want to go home."

"Hold my hands, Elizabeth, if you're frightened. We'll soon be there."

"But I—"

"You want to see where I live, don't you?"

No, I do not, Elizabeth told herself. I don't want to see where you live at all.

Above her darkness swirled in twisting vortices. Whirlpools of shadows veined with purple. They reached out to her, enveloping her. And even those shadows possessed wide, staring eyes that bore into her as she walked by.

Then Elizabeth giggled.

"What's so funny?" Whiteface asked.

"I know what this is now."

"What is it?"

"It's a dream," Elizabeth told her. "I'm dreaming."

A slit appeared in the skin beneath the twin holes in the girl's face. "You're dreaming?" The slit became a smile. "Yes. That's exactly what it is, Elizabeth. You're lying in bed at home with your bear in the red jacket and you're dreaming your head off."

Elizabeth saw the smile was only as real as the eyes. And the eyes were only holes in a hard, white face.

"Come on, slow coach," sang the girl. "Come and see where I live."

"You live in dreamland." Elizabeth allowed the girl to take her hand. It squeezed tight as a metal band around hers. "You live in dreamland and use dream telephones and sit on dream chairs."

"Of course we do, and I'll show you . . . but hurry!"

This was a dream, Elizabeth told herself. She couldn't be harmed. They walked quickly through the darkness, sometimes half running as if late for a bus. Whiteface urged her on.

The main road that skirted the village was a silent, dead river of tar this time of night. No traffic ran now. But would it in a dream anyway? Any second whales might break through the blacktop to blow vapor into the air.

This was a dream, Elizabeth insisted. Anything could happen. Anything . . .

The girl moved faster, pulling Elizabeth along. The hand around hers shrank into a tight iron ring. Whiteface looked eagerly forward, the eyes fathomless pits.

The Necropolis, we're going to the Necropolis. . . . Elizabeth looked up at the hill swathed in dark, lumbering trees. Now they moved faster, Whiteface even more eager.

"Nearly there, Elizabeth. We're nearly there!"

An iron fence loomed. Whiteface rushed toward the gap in the palings. Beyond, there were the graves, bursting like scabs from the grass. A stone Christ with no face towered over the nettles, his hands reaching out at Elizabeth, fingers hooked into lethal claws.

Suddenly Elizabeth was appalled. "This is a dream . . . *this is a dream!*" Only, now a clear note of uncertainty sounded in her voice.

"Of course it's a dream, Elizabeth. Come with me. Hold my hand. I'll stop you being frightened."

"Where are we going?"

"To where I live."

"I . . . I've seen enough. I want to go . . . h-home." Her eyes streamed as a dark and terrible fear squirmed into her stomach and forced its scaly passage up through her throat. "I want to go h-h-home!"

"But it's only a dream, Elizabeth." The black slit in the girl's face widened, aping a smile. But there were no lips. No tongue behind it. Only darkness that echoed the darkness where the eyes should be.

"Come and get some chocolate with me, Elizabeth. I know where there's plenty. People came and left it at little Jess Bowen's grave."

They were running through the cemetery by now. Elizabeth didn't have the strength to resist. The iron grip on her hand, so bone-achingly tight, did not slip; she was dragged between the massed ranks of tombstones.

"We'll get you a lovely big piece of chocolate, Elizabeth." Then Whiteface added in a voice that sounded closer to thunder on a winter's night, "Yum. Yum."

Gravestones loomed out at her; great, dark guardians of the underworld. Sometimes stones loomed close to her face. In a daze she found herself reading snatches of verse:

Darkness Demands

Weep not for me parents dear
Weep not for me in vain
I am not dead but sleepeth here. . . .

Breathless, with a stitch digging deep into her side, she moved between evil-looking stone buildings with iron doors behind which wordless mumbling pleaded for release. She shook her head trying *not* to hear; they grew louder and she shut her eyes. No, no, no, no. . . . *No!*

When she opened her eyes, she found herself standing by a grave with a statue of a weeping boy. Her breath came in ragged sobs.

The white-faced girl bent down to pick up one of the chocolate bars that lay there. She didn't seem to hold it in her hands . . . instead, she gripped it between two strangely bunched fists. "Here's a beautiful bar of chocolate, Elizabeth. Here. Hold it tight."

"I—I want to go home."

"But you are home, Elizabeth, dear."

"I'm dreaming . . . I'm dreaming . . ."

"If you wish."

"Please, I want to wake up."

"No! You're coming with me." The hand gripped Elizabeth's wrist. A grip so crushing that Elizabeth cried out. Then she was being dragged forward. She lost her balance. The stone slab of Jess Bowen's grave rushed up at her. She flinched, expecting a blow against her face.

But there was no blow. Even though she fell onto the slab, she did not strike it. In fact, she did not stop—she fell right through.

And still the hand pulled her cruelly down. Now she fell through the earth as if she'd fallen into a lake. Its surface crust rose above her head. Everywhere the roots of trees snaked through the soil like arteries through flesh. Meanwhile, the soil formed a pale brown mist all around her. She was floating through it, being dragged by the white-faced girl. They were divers swimming through a subterranean ocean. While at either side of them, hanging like some grim-looking fruit in Jell-O, were narrow boxes.

Some were intact. Some were so rotted they collapsed under the weight of dirt bearing down from above. From one, a skeleton hand had forced its way through a gap between lid and coffin. He'd been buried alive a hundred years ago to scream and claw at his tiny wooden prison before he choked on his own poison air. Now, eyeless bone stared from the crevice as she passed by.

Then came multiple family burials; coffin stood on coffin until they formed weird underground totems that towered gloomily in brown mist.

"Welcome to my home, Elizabeth."

"Let me go!"

At the sound of her cry, bones in their coffins stirred restlessly. From infant burials came the wail of babies, left neglected in the cold and dark for all these years. Hungry, pitiful cries sent cataracts of ice water flooding her veins.

Suddenly a thunderous pounding came from a coffin bound in chains.

"OUT! LET ME OUT!"

Elizabeth's heart rolled in horror. From everywhere came the sound of bone pounding on wood, as skeleton fists fought their way out.

"Please! I want to go home!"

"Calm down, Elizabeth." Words oozed from the slit in the white face. "You'll drop the chocolate."

"I don't want the chocolate. I want to go home!"

"Elizabeth, stay near to me. It's not safe to go too close to them. They get angry . . . Elizabeth, keep away from them!"

Elizabeth managed to slip from the girl's crushing grip. She swam through the brown, swirling mist, trying to escape. And as she struggled back toward the crust of the surface that sprouted a fuzz of grass and nettle roots, she blundered against a great block of a coffin that rested like a fallen monolith on the shattered bones of pauper burials.

With a roar the lid opened, the sound crashing against her head. Two pus-wet eyes glared into hers from the darkness within the tomb. Then arms swam at her from the gloom, fingers clenching like the mouths of serpents eager to bite the life out of her.

Screaming, she tried to pull away.

It did no good. Hands gripped her by the shoulders. The white-faced girl sounded far away now. "I warned you . . . I told you not to get too close!"

Elizabeth screamed again. The grip on her shoulders was agonizing. She felt herself being drawn toward the rupture in the coffin. Inside was an abyss as dark as the far side of the moon. Still she struggled, pleading for help. But there was no help to be had. She looked down to see a forehead of broad bones that had all the hard white gleam of dinner plates. Now the blazing eyes had become part of a face.

Or what passed for a face after years underground . . . *Teeth swathed in sick-looking moss. A mouth running with worms slowly opening. Within that a black tongue, rotted and slippery as leech flesh.*

She wanted to close her eyes . . . she wanted to die right then . . . die and see nothing more . . . but her eyes had locked wide . . . they fixed onto the eyes in front of hers that blazed with a cold and dreadful triumph. She could no longer scream. But she would feel everything that happened next.

Cold hands drew her into the coffin. It engulfed her like a cave. And at last she was alone with its occupant.

Six

"Christ, Elizabeth. What're you making that noise for?"

She squinted up against the light. Paul stood looking down at her. He shook his head. "I can even hear you in my bedroom."

She sat up with a stuttering kind of cry. Her heart thudded.

"Elizabeth? Are you all right? Do you feel sick?"

Now her brother's face changed from irritation at being wakened at what must have been an ungodly hour, to a look of concern.

She was shaking. When she did try to speak, her throat felt as if it had wound itself up into knots.

"Hey, Lizzie." Her brother's voice was gentle. "Take it easy." He rubbed her back through her pajamas. "You've had a bad dream, haven't you?"

The words still refused to pass through her throat. All she managed was a nod.

"I'll get you a drink of water," he told her, smiling. "You lay back and relax. Big bro's taking care of business now."

She managed a smile in return. What was more, the knots were leaving her throat.

His smile broadened. "And don't worry about bad dreams. They can't hurt you—remember that."

Paul had started to walk away when he noticed something by the bed. He picked it up. "Hey, Liz, you don't want to go leaving this on the floor, otherwise Sam'll end up having it." He held up a dark slab and whistled. "Now that's a formidable-looking bar of chocolate, Elizabeth. Where did you get it from?"

Chapter Thirteen

One

"I need green."

"Uh ..."

"I want to finish a picture for Sam's birthday card and I haven't got a green for the grass. Paul?"

"Hmm?"

"Wake up. I want a green. Can I get one?"

"Uh ... whatever."

Paul lay with the sheet over his head. He'd returned to bed after being wakened early by his sister's cry. Luckily, he'd gone straight back to sleep and had dreamt about Miranda. Jesus H., would he ever be able to get the girl out of his head? It was as if her face had been tattooed in fire across his brain. All he could do was think about her. Now she'd be in the car with her family. Heading south for London. She'd have risen early to shower ... oh, Christ ... Elizabeth, get out of my bedroom ... I want to imagine Miranda Bloom working away at that smooth skin with the soap. ...

"Which compartment are your pens in?"

"I don't know, Elizabeth," he murmured, not wanting to be fully awake. "Just look. You'll find them."

"Have you got a green one?"

"Yes."

"I can't find them ... are you sure they're in here? What's this, then? Bubble gum?"

"God knows, Elizabeth ... it's early ... I wanna sleep."

"I've not seen any gum like this before."

Find the pen and go. Miranda's in the shower ... it's just getting interesting.

"Can I have a piece?"

"Piece of what?"

"Gum."

"I haven't got any."

"What's this, then?"

Hell.

He exploded from the bedclothes to grab the packet of condoms from Elizabeth as she tried to tear open the cellophane with her teeth.

"Ouch, Paul! Don't snatch."

"It's not yours, Elizabeth."

Oh, my God, he thought, his face burning, can you imagine what his parents would say if Elizabeth had gone downstairs with *those* in her hands?

"I only wanted one piece." She scowled. "Greedy guts."

"It isn't gum." Sweating hard, he rolled out of bed and slid the condom packet high on a shelf where Elizabeth couldn't reach.

She went to bounce on his bed, her hair flying up and down. "What were they, then? Cigarettes?"

"No. You know they weren't cigarettes."

"Might be little ones."

"Why aren't you out playing?"

"I'm going to help make breakfast. What's in the packet?"

"Nosy."

"I'll tell Dad."

"They're just staples for the stapler. I've run out."

"Why have you gone so red?" She licked her finger and held it out as if touching hot metal. "Sss!" she hissed. "I know what they are." A grin spread across her face. "You bought them from the drugstore."

This time his entire body blazed hotly. "It's just a pack of staples."

"I don't believe you. You've got a girlfriend."

The heat spread through every vein of his body. She was sure to snitch.

"You went to the drugstore because you've got a girl-friend."

"Elizabeth—"

"You've gone and got some cream for your zits, haven't you?"

"I haven't got any zits, Elizabeth. Now, if you don't mind, I'm going to get dressed."

Elizabeth gave the shelf where he'd left the condoms an appraising look, then before she grudgingly left the room, said, "I'd buy another packet." She grinned. "You're going to need lots and lots now you've got a girlfriend."

"Like I'm going to be covered with a million zits. Yeah, whatever, Elizabeth. Whatever."

Giving a knowing smile, she echoed, "Yeah, whatever, Paul. Whatever."

Once she'd left the room, he quickly moved the condoms from the shelf to a box beneath his bed.

The next time he met Miranda, those little beauties would be in his pocket.

Two

Reading the letter wasn't easy. With it being Saturday morning, Val, Paul, and Elizabeth were at home. Short of sneaking the letter into the bathroom to read as if it was from a secret lover, John Newton realized it might be some time before he could be alone.

Simon Clark

By nine, the day was already warm enough to sit out on the patio for breakfast. Sam showed no sign of his scare from the night before. He lay in the shade, only glancing up as Elizabeth, then Paul came out to join them for toast and fruit juice. The meal was relaxed. Everyone seemed to be in good spirits. John did, however, find his eyes drawn to where the letter had made its mysterious appearance beneath the fragment of headstone. For some reason he expected there to be a stain or something on the stone slab where the letter had rested. Of course, that didn't make a lot of sense, John told himself. But there was some quality about the letter . . . as if it swarmed with bacteria or some unidentifiable contamination. Touching the letter with his bare fingers made him uneasy.

Again he found himself asking who would go to the trouble of finding sheets of antique paper—blank antique paper at that—then writing a message in it in a Gothic hand? And why had the hoaxer sent letters to such a disparate bunch of people? As far as John knew the recipients had been himself, a writer; Keith Haslem, the lawyer; and Stan Price, an elderly and senile man. If it was someone's idea of a joke, then it wasn't a particularly hilarious one.

A thought struck John all of a sudden. It was an uncomfortable thought at that. Maybe this was some perverse experiment? Maybe the letter sender intended to study the recipients' reactions. That put a different spin on things. He found himself scanning the hedges, then the meadows beyond, for a staring face, or the flash of reflected sunlight on a telescope lens. Was his family being watched as they sat out here eating toast?

Hell, now he did feel vulnerable. And all too exposed. After all, last night a man or woman had left the letter on that very paving slab in front of him. If nothing else, weren't they guilty of trespass? Come to that, they could easily have slipped into the house through the back door as he walked up by the lake with Sam. What might they have done then?

"Anything on your mind, John?" Val looked at him over the rim of her orange juice glass.

"Nothing much." He smiled. "I wondered if we had enough pork chops for the barbecue."

"There's a full bag in the freezer. We could do with more mayonnaise, though."

"I'm going down to the supermarket later. I'll grab some then."

"Don't forget the beer."

He grinned. "Don't worry. I won't."

Paul heaped marmalade onto his toast. "Bud for me, Dad. And plenty of it."

"John, have you been giving our son beer again?" Val pretended disapproval, but she couldn't help but smile.

"Just the occasional one." John returned the smile. "To educate him as a responsible social drinker."

"I'll wash the car for you this morning, Mum," Paul said quickly.

"Why, thank you very much," she said, surprised. "It could certainly do with it."

"White shows dirt," Elizabeth told her. "You should have a black one ... Emm's Dad's got two black cars. One has a roof that comes right down."

"BMWs," Paul added. "Top of the range. Her dad's got a Harley as well. Goes like a bat out of hell."

Val smiled at John. "Maybe we should have inherited rich grandparents."

"Oh, hon. Think of the satisfaction we get slaving away all week for our crust of bread at the weekend."

"Hmm, John, I always guessed you had a puritanical streak running through you."

"Just a good honest work ethic."

"All right, dear heart, you might as well exercise it right now by making me a cup of coffee."

"I'll do it," Paul said.

"Then one for me as well, please," John said, surprised.

After he'd gone, Val said, "Something tells me that Paul will be asking for a favor before long."

After breakfast, the family went their separate ways for a while. Paul finished a homework assignment. Elizabeth threw a ball for Sam. Val caught up with telephone calls to friends. John grabbed the opportunity. He went to his study, where he pulled the letter from his back pocket. *Maybe I should have worn latex gloves . . . there's something about the feel of the paper . . . like skin . . . Cold, dead skin . . .*

Holding the letter to the light that fell through the window, he read it in full.

Dear Messr. John Newt'n,
   I should wish that yew pore a pinte of porter onto the grief stowne of Jess Bowen by the Sabbath night. Yew will be sorry if yew do not.

Immediately he went cold. He shivered, dropping the letter onto the desk as he did so.

Straightaway he felt ashamed of his reaction to the letter. Come on, Newton, it's just a letter. A sick letter from some sick bozo. Did it chill him so much that the letter writer knew his name (and probably a damn sight more about him)? Was it because he sensed he was under surveillance? That some stranger watched him? They knew his movements. They'd sneaked onto his property to leave the letter there.

He had to nail the bastard who was doing this. . . .

He found himself seething with anger. This was nothing less than an invasion. An invasion of property. An invasion of his life. An invasion of his right to privacy. Fists clenched, he glared at the letter.

Pore a pinte of porter onto the grief stowne . . .

For one thing, what the hell was a pint of porter? He all but snatched the dictionary from its shelf. "Porter, porter, porter," he growled under his breath. Finger stabbing down on the page, he scanned down the list of words.

Portage.
Portal.

Portend (Despite himself, a little of the definition leapt at him. *Portend: an omen, especially of evil*). Oh, no, you don't, he told his insidious imagination.

Porter: door or gatekeeper.

No, not that one. He skipped to the next definition. *Porter: one employed to carry baggage.* No. Next. *Porter: a dark brown, bitter beer.*

A pint of porter? So that's what the letter writer wanted. A pint of beer. Why not a gallon? A bucket full? Or a whole hogshead? Why just a miserly little pint?

"And why use the old name for beer, you pretentious little jerk?"

He picked up the letter again, his eyes burning at the handwriting. It didn't flow in the elegant style he would have associated with archaic writing. There was something spiky about it. A neurotic's handwriting, he decided. Someone with a monkey on his back . . . someone eaten up with—

"Yo, Dad! Can you move the cars?"

"What?"

"Sorry, Dad."

"Paul," he snapped. "Jesus, don't you ever think to knock!"

"Dad, I'm sorry. I didn't realize you were working."

Shit. This letter was poison. He was brooding so much over it he'd wound up biting his son's head off. The thing was making him cranky as hell.

"Don't worry, Dad, I'll ask my mother."

"Paul . . . Paul?"

But Paul had gone. John sighed. He felt like a real mean son of a bitch now. Paul didn't deserve that. He picked up the letter and glared at it. "This is your fault, you little bastard." Anger burned in his voice. "You're not getting anything out of me. Nothing."

Three

Paul scrubbed the white paintwork of Val's car hard. After that, he hurled bucket after bucket of cold water to shift the foam. Then he went to work with the wash cloth.

Val looked up from her newspaper as John crossed the patio. He saw her knowing smile.

"Mystery solved," she said.

"Pardon?"

She knew about the letter?

"Mystery solved," she said again, nodding toward Paul, who was attacking the car's lights with what to John looked like sublimated fury. No doubt he was still angry at John's chewing him out a few minutes ago.

"Paul?" The cogs inside John's head whirled furiously, trying to engage. Val knew about the letters? She was saying that Paul was responsible? He gave a puzzled shake of his head.

She smiled. "I know why Paul's so eager to wash the car."

"Well?" He made a point of smiling casually.

"He wants me to teach him to drive."

"Oh." His muscles unclenched. "I see." Now his smile was one of relief. "He did seem suddenly eager to start washing the cars. At least we can be guaranteed the shiniest paintwork in the village for the next few months anyway."

They sat for a while in the sun. John watched Paul at work (detecting one or two reproachful glances from his son). *I admit it, OK. I snapped when I shouldn't have. I sounded like an irritable old whiner. It's the letters. They made me lose my sense of proportion. Look, John Newton, the sun is shining, life goes on . . . so don't dwell on stupid letters written by some loser with nothing better to do. Now, you go across there and make up with your son.*

He strolled across to the car. Paul'd certainly lavished some care and energy on Val's car, which was guaranteed to get into her good books. The Golf was her pride and joy. She'd saved hard for it from her own salary for over two years. When she first bought it, he'd hardly seen her for days on end. She found endless reasons to buy a newspaper, or carton of mushrooms, or got a sudden urge to visit a friend—any excuse to simply get into the car, turn the ignition key, then surge away down the road. He suspected she'd followed some weirdly Byzantine routes for those mushrooms or newspapers. But why not? She'd earned the right to savor the pleasures of driving what was one sexy set of wheels.

"You've done a good job, Paul."

John noticed the way his son's eyes flicked up suspiciously into his, probably wondering if this was a subtle buildup to another ear-bashing.

"Got any plans for today, Paul?"

"Why?"

Again, suspicion.

"I wondered if you fancied lighting the barbecue for me later."

"I'm going with Mum to the library first. Some books need to go back."

"There's no rush. Don't worry."

Paul twisted the water from the washcloth as if he was ringing an enemy's neck.

"Paul. I apologize for snapping at you like that a few minutes ago. I didn't mean it."

"Then why do it?"

"Call it first-chapter blues. I've just started on a new book . . . it gets me all tense and on edge, which I know is a rotten excuse . . . so if you want to tip that bucket of water over my head, be my guest."

It broke the ice. Paul smiled. "All right, Dad. No worries."

"See, even we saints get bad-tempered sometimes."

"Some saint. Oh, Dad?"

"Yep?"

"OK, if I have my allowance before I go into town?"

John felt a grin steal onto his own face. "You'll go far, Paul, won't you, son?"

"Just a chip off the old block, Dad. Now, what was that about a bucket of water and your head?"

"I'll get my wallet." John made for the house.

Simon Clark

Four

Stan Price knew what he must do. As he stood looking out of the window, he experienced one of those all too rare moments of lucidity. There, in the sunlight, the mass of trees that crowned the old Necropolis on the hill moved in the breeze. For a while it looked as if the whole cemetery was breathing—some colossal beast that inhaled, exhaled, then shook itself as a stronger breeze ran through the branches.

"Telephone Dianne Kelly. She's the only one left who knows what to do . . . she's the only one left." Murmuring the same words over to himself, he crossed the bedroom to the door. As he did so, he happened to glance into the mirror. "Oh, Dear Lord, that's you, Stan. You're old . . . you're old." Stan couldn't take his eyes from the reflection. The neck appeared too thin to support the head. The fingers looked like bird's claws, mere talons of hands with precious little flesh. "Oh, dear, Stan. What happened to you?" He looked to the window. "Harry." His voice croaked. "Harry. Where are you?"

Harry's dead, he told himself. He died years ago. Only you're too far gone to remember.

But he did remember now. He remembered Ezy View, his chain of TV stores. He remembered Cynthia and Robert's move into his house—they weren't invited, he remembered that. But then he'd become so forgetful . . . he'd cook breakfast at midnight . . . he'd walk miles to one of his stores . . . but it wasn't an Ezy View TV rental store anymore. He remembered his confusion standing there at the dead of night, key in his hand, looking at the Chinese restaurant and wondering why the new color TVs weren't displayed in the window. More flashes of memory came to him. Walking through the village in his pajamas. Wetting the bed. Always hungry. Yes, always hungry these days . . . Robert Gregory . . . color TVs by the score . . .

He clenched his fists. There was an oily quality to his

mind now. All too easily it slipped away into a dream world. Then he believed he was ten years old again. A ten-year-old who didn't know why his best friend didn't call for him anymore. Oh . . . the times they'd caught fish in the Ebeck. Roach. Perch. Once a massive pike that had been the size of a whale. They'd fought the monster until . . .

His mind began to slide again. No, he couldn't let go yet. "Dianne Kelly. Phone her. She's the only one left."

He went downstairs to the telephone in the hall. There was his telephone book. Nine tenths of the people listed there were dead now. But not Dianne Kelly. No, sir. He was sure she was still alive. Made of tough stuff . . .

Willing his fingers to move, he flicked through he pages.

From the living room came the sound of the television. Robert Gregory and Cynthia were watching comedy. He heard bursts of canned laughter; then a deep voice made some comment about the show. Robert Gregory was master of the house now.

Didn't Robert once slap Stan? Images flickered in his mind. Slaps across the side of the head where the marks wouldn't show. When he asked Robert for food. Many, many slaps.

Kelly, Dianne. There . . . the telephone number. With an effort he held onto a splinter of rationality. He knew what he had to do. He must telephone Dianne Kelly, then tell her the letters had started again. She was there the first time. Only fourteen years old, though. But her mind was clear as glass. She'd know what to do. She was their only hope. . . .

Yes, yes . . . his heart beat faster. The telephone was ringing. Suddenly, he felt younger, his veins tingled. He hadn't spoken to Dianne in years.

"Hello," came the familiar voice in his ear. She sounded so bright. You wouldn't have guessed she was in her eighties.

"Hello?" she said again.

"Dianne. This is Stan Price. Dianne, listen, the—" Suddenly, he realized he was hearing the dial tone. Puzzled, he went to redial. Then he saw a finger resting on the cradle. His eyes went from the finger to the face beside his.

"Now, Dad. What are you playing with the telephone for?"

Robert's face loomed forward. The eyes bulged into his. Stan saw his own face reflected in the man's pupils.

"I was calling a friend."

"You don't have friends anymore. They're all dead."

"I need to speak to Dianne."

"Don't you realize, you stupid old man? Everyone you knew died years, fucking years ago."

Robert's hand closed around Stan's elbow in a crushing grip. "Now, Dad. Get up those stairs before I lose my temper with you."

"Dad? Did you want anything?"

Robert released his cruel grip when Cynthia appeared. "I caught him messing around with the telephone."

"Dad, you know you're not allowed to touch it," she scolded affectionately. "Now come through into the kitchen. I'll pour you a glass of milk."

"Don't give him anything else to eat," Robert said quickly. "He ate a huge breakfast. He'll make himself ill if he keeps stuffing himself."

"I need to telephone Dianne Kelly."

"Yes, Dad, plenty of time for that later. Come on, we'll get you a nice drink."

Stan allowed himself to be led away. With Robert standing by the telephone, he knew there would be no chance to make the call yet—that all-important call that burned in his veins so much it hurt. No . . . he'd have to wait . . . be patient . . . but how long could he hold onto his sanity before dementia rose up like a tsunami to engulf him in confusion once more?

Behind him, he heard the telephone ring. Robert answered in that hearty voice of his. "Hello? Oh, Stan

Price? No, sorry, he can't come to the telephone. No . . .
Dr. Dianne Kelly? Oh, I'm sorry he bothered you, Dr.
Kelly. . . . To be honest with you, he's become very confused these days . . . yes. Dementia, I'm afraid. Yes, it is
very sad. He's not suffering at all. You know how it is
with these things; it's the carers who have the tough
time of it. His daughter's at her wits' end. . . . Yes, I'll
pass on your regards to Stan. Sorry that he disturbed
you. Good-bye."

Stan Price sat at the kitchen table as Cynthia poured
the milk. He tried to remember something he should
do . . . it was important. He tried so hard to remember
that his shoulders started shaking uncontrollably. They
were still shaking when his son-in-law came into the
room.

Chapter Fourteen

One

Two letters lay on the table in front of him. The paper? Creamy. The ink? More of a brown than black. It looked watery, too. Clearly the letter writer had used a fountain pen. Or, mused John Newton, a goose feather cut into a quill. Now he could not look at the letters without a smoldering anger. He had even begun to envisage who the sender might be. At first he'd pictured a couple of giggling kids concocting the hoax letters over glasses of orange soda and potato chips one boring Sunday afternoon. Now he had a different image. In his mind's eye he saw a middle-aged man obsessively laboring over the letters with, yes, maybe even a quill, which he'd dip into watery ink.

But God knows what the ink was made of. Urine and blood? Toad blood? Bile from a stolen cat?

The more John Newton thought about it, the more bizarre the letters seemed.

He read the first letter in full again.

Dear Messr. John Newt'n,
  I should wish yew put me a pound of chock latt on the grief stowne of Jess Bowen by the Sabbath night. Yew will be sorry if yew do not.

Once more he'd slipped into the detective role. Quickly he reprised the facts. The letters arrived by an unknown hand at the dead of night. They were undated, unsigned. They were addressed to John Newton in person (although they did favor the quaint spelling of *Newt'n*). The letters demanded payment in the form of goods—the first was chocolate, the second porter, an archaic term for a dark beer. They stipulated a deadline when payment had to be made. Then came a threat if he did not comply. Although, so far the threats were undefined, merely an ambiguous *"Yew will be sorry if yew do not."* And yes, note the cute "olde worlde" spelling of "you."

But why me? Why had he been selected for this lunatic's attention? Maybe there was no reason. Most victims of crime asked the same question. Why had they been singled out to be mugged or burgled? The truth of the matter is, as police confirm, there is nothing personal about crime in ninety-nine out of a hundred cases. Thieves tend to be opportunists. They don't know their victims. They see a chance to steal a car and take it. It's as impersonal as that. Even so, he harbored the lingering thought that the letter writer was engaged in some personal vendetta; after all, the letters were addressed to him personally.

John pulled aside the blind. Val and Paul had gone to the library about an hour ago, with Val promising to be only twenty minutes, because they planned an early barbecue. He glanced at his watch. Dead on twelve. Maybe he should make a start. He wanted the charcoal good and hot before cooking the chops.

Maybe it would be a good idea to light the barbecue with these two letters? Already, he felt annoyed with himself for brooding over them. But the way they were addressed to him personally with a *demand* for the chocolate and the beer . . . hell, it made him seethe. Yes, the demands were trivial. But there was something goading about them. In short, some stranger had set out to invade his life. They were deliberately attempting to take control of him to a certain degree by demanding that he perform *certain* actions by a *certain* time. Damn it. They weren't going to do that.

And Keith Haslem? Had he really bundled his family into the car and driven them away from letters like these? Once more John glared at the spiky handwriting.

"No way, you creep. You are not getting anything from me. Nothing!" His fury surprised him by its intensity. For a moment he wanted nothing more than to throw open the window, wave the letters in the air, and yell: *"Did you hear that, whoever you are? I've got your letters! I've read them! But you won't get even the time of day from me! You're getting nothing. So, go ahead. Do your worst! I dare you!"*

A breeze swung back the window with a bang. The blind fluttered. Instantly, the letters scuttled like eager vermin across the table.

So, go ahead. Do your worst! I dare you! His imagined challenge reverberated back at him. Would he really do anything as foolhardy as inviting the letter writer to execute the threat? He thought of Elizabeth playing out in the meadow alone. If there really was some creep watching the property. Then they might . . .

"Dad . . . *Dad!*" Elizabeth's voice brought him to his feet. There was something shocking about the tone of it. "Dad! Come here! Quickly!"

"Coming." He ran across the landing, then took the stairs two at time.

"Dad, quick! It's our car!"

Two

He walked into the lounge to find Elizabeth staring at the television.

"Dad," she said pointing. "That's Mum's car."

This didn't make sense. At least for a moment it didn't. He found himself looking at a car on the TV screen. It lay on its side spanning a road. The commentary stated, "Rose Way is backed up by at least two miles. So if you want to get into town by way of Junction 18, forget it."

That was the moment when he felt as if his internal organs had detached themselves from their anchor points and slipped down through his body. He wasn't breathing. And he knew it. But somehow, breathing no longer seemed important. Terror, pure terror, rolled through him in a cold, blue fog.

"Dad, it's Mum's car. It's all smashed up . . . the firemen can't get her out."

The commentary came in again. "This's Mac Nugent, your eye in the sky. If you've just joined us, you're seeing one of the worst RTAs I've ever seen in this job. A white car . . . what looks like a white VW Golf has been top-sliced when it ran under a jackknifed trailer before turning on its side. Rescue services are on the scene. But it's an awful, awful mess. Traffic into town from Junction 18 is completely static. Nothing's going to move down there for hours."

"Oh, my God," John breathed. His eyes locked onto the screen with an intensity that shut him off from the rest of Creation. Fluids leaked from the car as if it was some slaughtered beast. But the liquids weren't purely oil or water or brake fluid.

The camera in the hovering helicopter zoomed into a brutal close-up that winded him.

"Yes," the commentator was saying. "I am afraid what you are seeing is blood. You can see surgical dressing down there, too. Paramedics have crawled into that wreck. They are fighting to save those poor unfortunate people in there. I've been told we're going to stay with this until we get word on the condition of the passengers. This is truly awful. . . ."

Elizabeth sat as if she'd been set as tight as glue. Her

eyes glistened as she stared. "Mum and Paul have been hurt, haven't they?" She looked at him. Her eyes were round enough to be shocking. "Will they be all right?"

His eye roved over the scene filmed from the helicopter. In the corner of the screen were the words *EYE IN THE SKY—LIVE!*

"Paul's dead," Elizabeth said.

If sound could be dark, then those words were as dark as grave soil.

On the screen, there lay the torn body of the car. Ambulance lights flashed. Police, paramedics, firefighters ran around the car in a dance of life and death.

This isn't happening to me . . .

"Dad . . . Dad? What are you doing?"

"I'm phoning your mother's mobile number."

"You can't."

"Elizabeth, shh, please."

"Dad?" Emotion distorted her voice.

"Hon, I want to be able to hear her voice. I thought . . ." Abruptly, he put the phone down. What was he doing? Trying to phone what might be a corpse locked in that tangle of scrap metal? He shook his head. But the thought echoed inside his skull: What if he telephoned Val? If she could answer the mobile, he might get a chance to say good-bye.

Christ . . . he was shaking. He felt as if his body was going to tear itself apart.

"There is a passenger . . . one passenger free of the car. One free of the car." The TV commentary cut through the room.

John knelt in front of the TV as paramedics eased a woman through a windshield now devoid of glass; it looked like an eye torn from a living face. Within moments the woman lay on a gurney, her neck in a brace. Paramedics fastened belts around her blood-drenched body.

"Is she still alive?" Elizabeth asked in a small voice.

John crouched almost on top of the screen, now so

close he could see the lines that formed the picture. *Get a close-up of her face; come on, get a close-up of her face.*

The rotors of the helicopter were close enough to blow dust across the road along with the bloodstained dressings discarded by the medics. There was the car again. Filling the screen. A mess of bent metal, shredded tires. A motor exposed and naked now that the hood had been torn clear. That was the moment he saw it.

A red line painted down the side of the car. No, in fact, two narrow lines running in parallel along the body of the car. They were so fine that he didn't notice them before.

"Hon," John whispered. "Hon. That isn't your mother's car."

"It is . . . look."

"No. It's the same make, the same color. But her car doesn't have red lines painted down the side."

"Then it's not Mum and Paul in there?"

"No. It's someone else." He was trembling, and his throat burned so hotly he found it hard to speak. "Haven't we been a pair of idiots scaring each other like that?"

"But it looks the same."

"I know, hon. It's a coincidence, that's all."

He dialed Val's mobile.

"Hello."

"Val?"

"Hi, John. I'm in the supermarket. I've got the mayonnaise. Do you want any more of that tomato ketchup they do here?"

He held out the phone so Elizabeth could hear. She was wiping away tears, but grinning all over her face.

"Hello, John? Did you catch that? Do you want any more ketchup?"

"No, thanks, love."

"I'm in the queue. I'm just about to be served. Did you want anything else?"

"Only for you to be home soon, hon."

His insides were water, but he was grinning, too. Elizabeth came to him, encircled his neck with her arms, and hugged him. They stayed like that for a long time.

Chapter Fifteen

"Do you have any porter?"

"Any what?"

"Porter." John Newton had been testing the man's reaction as much as anything. But the manager of the local Rhythm & Booze looked puzzled. *That rules you out as a mystery letter recipient as well as the mystery letter writer.*

The man scratched his head. "Porter? Oh, you mean port? We've ruby, tawny, and white. It's over there by the sherry."

"No," John said. "Porter's a beer."

"Sorry, that's a new one on me."

The afternoon sun burst through the plate-glass windows of the store with a dazzling intensity. Ceiling fans stirred the air, but it was still searing. John felt pearls of sweat roll down inside his shirt. He'd anticipated the storekeeper wouldn't know what porter was, so John had consulted the encyclopedia for a modern alternative.

"I'll take a couple of bottles of Guinness, then, please," John reached into his pocket.

Simon Clark

"Sorry, we're out of bottles . . . there should be some cans across there next to . . . no, wait. My apologies, we're out of cans, too."

"You're out of Guinness?"

"I can't understand it, either," the man said, looking genuinely puzzled. "We had a real run on it this morning."

"It must be the hot weather." John smiled, but his gut reaction told him exactly what had happened. The mystery mailman had visited other people in Skelbrooke, too.

"Do you have any other stout?"

The guy didn't want to commit himself. "I'll just check. That stuff's been selling fast, too." He craned his neck so he could see to the back of the store. "There's none left on the shelf, but there are a few bottles in the refrigerator."

John fetched the bottles himself. They were metric half-liter bottles. He bought two to be on the safe side.

Christ, just listen to himself. He was buying the beer as if lives depended on it. But then maybe . . . he closed off the train of thought. All this was veering close to the delusional, if not out and out insanity. After John handed over the cash, the guy slipped the bottles into a lilac carrier.

"Phew. Feel that heat. I'll be ready for a cold one myself tonight." He handed John the bag. "There you go, sir."

John thanked him. Once he'd left the store, he walked by the village pond, where Robert Gregory was throwing whole sandwiches to the ducks.

Robert Gregory? He'd certainly taken a dislike to the man when he'd visited old Mr. Price. Could Gregory be the letter writer? *Christ, you are getting paranoid, John. Come to that, you're going soft in the head.* These letters were like insect bites on the back of his neck. Tiny, insignificant things, but God how they itched. They dominated your day. You couldn't sleep at night for them. He followed the road uphill, the sun hot on his back. It was a little after three. The barbecued food he'd eaten lay heavy and undigested in his stomach. He'd eaten it to show there was nothing amiss. But the scare a few hours ago had left him badly shaken. If anything, Elizabeth had recovered faster than he had when she realized it really wasn't her mother's car lying mangled on the road.

For a few minutes as they'd watched the live TV coverage, he'd really believed that it was Val's car. And that his wife and his son were lying crushed inside. Of course, it was a mistake anyone could make. Your wife or husband has a car of the same color, the same make, and you see it smashed to pieces on the road. You might jump to the same terrifying, albeit wrong, conclusion. But you'd recover quickly enough. Perhaps you'd feel an idiot for frightening yourself in such as way. Then that would be that. An anecdote you'd tell over dinner . . . nothing more.

But hell . . . he'd still been shaking twenty minutes later. The worst of it was, he knew why he was still shaking. The letters. Those damned awful letters. With their demands and their threats. He remembered full well how he'd wanted to shout from the window earlier, *Go on, do your worst! I dare you!*

Now this was the crazy part. After he'd seen the car wreck on TV, and then realized it wasn't Val's car after all, he had told himself: *That was a warning. You challenged the letter writer to do his worst. Even if you'd only thought that challenge. Five minutes later you saw the car wreck on TV. You believed your wife and son were dead. What you've just had is what they call a Scarborough warning, a shot across the bow, a promise of what's to come if you don't yield to the demands.*

Which was madness.

But was it? He'd received the first letter demanding he leave chocolate on the grave of a Jess Bowen. He'd ignored it. Elizabeth had fallen from her bike, slashing open her chin in the process. For a moment he'd thought someone had cut her throat. That she'd been lying dead on the grass. Now he'd seen the car wreck.

But wait a minute, he told himself . . . just wait a minute here . . .

So wrapped up in his own thoughts, he stepped out into the road without looking. A car horn blasted him. Quickly he stepped back, checked the road was clear, then crossed to where the gates of the Necropolis stood like the bones of a gigantic bird against the sky. They were locked. Figuring there'd be another way in, he followed the fence uphill. The lilac carrier bag containing the bottles of beer swung in his hand.

So overgrown was the cemetery, he couldn't see more than a few yards into its interior. Nevertheless, he could make out rows of headstones marching away into shadow. A bird screeched in a treetop.

He was thankful there were no other people around, for the simple reason he didn't want anyone seeing what he was going to do. Because already he'd picked up the train of thought from a moment ago, when a car had nearly broken him like an egg over the hood. Was he really attributing some supernatural power to the mystery letter writer? If he ignored the demands could *he*, or some great diabolical *IT*, really have the ability to pitch Elizabeth from her bike, or cause some stranger's car to crash? Simply to serve as a warning to one John Newton?

But then the Haslems had fled in terror. Think about it, John. Two hundred years ago your ancestors wouldn't have doubted it for a moment. For them dark forces prowled the night like ravenous panthers, just waiting for someone to let down their guard . . . With a deliberate effort, he closed off the thought. He made a pact with himself. He'd do what he had to do, then he would forget all about it. He'd force the memory into some back closet in his head and seal it there for good.

He continued up the hill. It had grown hotter than ever. The white path bounced sunlight back into his face. Behind him, Skelbrooke slumbered in the heat. Across the valley he could see the roof of the Water

Mill. Val, Paul, and Elizabeth would be there; no doubt Sam would be lying in the shade, his tongue hanging like a strip of pink plastic from his mouth.

Moments later, John reached a gap in the fence where it had been broken down. As he entered the cemetery, he saw a man of around fifty walking down the hill. Immediately the man saw John, and quickly turned off on another path to avoid passing him. John noticed a lilac carrier bag in the man's hand.

"Snap, mister," John murmured, then strode on up the hill.

He soon realized this was going to be no easy task. The cemetery was vast. Tombstones must have numbered in their tens of thousands. Most graves contained more than one person, some contained whole families. He plowed on up the hill.

It was the first time he'd been in the place. Soon he found himself taking paths at random. One took him into what appeared to be a whole forest. Tree trunks had toppled stone angels. Roots had burst open grave slabs like wafers. He found it impossible to read the inscription on every single stone. He scanned them as if he was speed-reading a book.

He came across a mattress-sized stone surrounded by an iron fence. Tied around the palings were a host of multicolored condoms. Elsewhere he saw hypodermic needles in the dirt. While wedged in the crook of an angel's arm was a homemade bong, consisting of a plastic soda bottle with a plastic bag taped to the bottom, so the same lungful of smoke could be re-breathed several times. Crack heads could be thrifty, too.

Seconds later, he exchanged cool shade for brilliant sunlight. The intensity of the light was like a blow across his forehead. Turning left, he forded a swathe of fern. A large angel blocked his way. Aerosoled across her stone wings were the words *FLYING CUNT*.

This was getting crazier by the moment. Here he was wandering around a cemetery with bottles of beer in a bag. Anyone noticing would figure him an alcoholic in search of a quiet corner to get juiced.

Headstones bristled from the earth in dizzying profusion. How could he find the one that bore the name Jess Bowen? Earlier, he had wondered if the Jess Bowen headstone really had been here, but after seeing the middle-aged guy with the lilac carrier bag, he knew with a gut certainty the "grief stowne," to use the quaint words in the letter, was here. But where?

After a while, the trail that had been a winding affair with nothing but dirt underfoot joined a broad path of stone slabs the size of tabletops.

The stones were a funereal black. Perfect for the Necropolis. Following them, he wiped the sweat from his eyes. Already he was getting a little taste of hell himself. The endless maze of paths, the acres of grim headstones, the searing heat, the silence, with everything overhung by the most evil-looking trees he'd ever seen. And not forgetting, either, that he walked over the ribs and skulls of the dead.

The path ran downhill, then entered a channel. Walls rose at either side of him; soon he found himself in a labyrinth of alleyways. The surrounding buildings stood a good dozen feet high, with the walls almost closing off the sky above him into a narrow strip of dazzling blue. In some places trees had sprouted from the roofs, to seal the alley entirely, creating a dark tunnel. On both sides of him were dozens of iron doors. In these were holes just large enough to insert a finger.

Not that the idea appealed to him. These were the crypts. They were probably stuffed to the rafters with caskets containing what remained of the neighboring cities' richest and finest. But they were rotting down to meat paste in their silk shrouds now, just like the poorest man that ever walked. What was this place called? He'd heard the name once. . . . Valley of Tears? No, he realized . . . Vale of Tears. An appropriate name. He could well imagine weeping mourners passing this way with a black-draped coffin that would be sealed behind one of these many doors. Wealthy Victorians—ostentatious even in death.

He kept up the mind chatter. It was deliberate. He was excluding any questioning thoughts about why he was really here. After making lefts and rights, either at random, or according to how the layout of the labyrinth dictated, he found himself following a broad ramp that ran upward into a gully that split a cliff in two. The cliff was man-made, with a retaining wall of huge blocks of stone. These were topped with plump little winged babies in stone. A few had fallen (or perhaps, more likely been pushed) from the wall to plunge the thirty or so feet down into the Vale of Tears below.

Sweating in the heat, he toiled up the hill. Still, he checked the names on the stones. No Jess Bowen. This was hopeless. Maybe he should simply forget the whole thing?

But what were the consequences? It didn't seem rational, but a gut feeling sang out loud and clear that he'd been issued a warning that morning. He'd been awarded a glimpse of the consequences if he ignored the letter's demands. Vividly, he still saw in his mind's eye the TV image of blood running from the car onto the road. *You've got to do this, John. You've got to. For your family's sake.*

Thirty minutes later he had to admit he was getting nowhere fast. He'd seen graves of all shapes and sizes. Some were the size of houses; some were shaped like pyramids, or mock chapels. Others were tiny headstones the size of a paperback book, marked with merely the occupants' initials—*TP 1901 . . . SLWS 1910.* If it were one of the microstones, he could easily miss it in the long grass.

He passed a clump of bushes that looked as if they were wrestling a plaster Christ to the earth. Ahead was a stretch of ground scabbed black with tombstones. After scanning a dozen of these for the name Jess Bowen, he happened to glance back down into the Vale of Tears. There, a woman walked along one of the alleyways below. She had long blond hair and strode purposefully toward the ramp. Despite her purposeful walk, she did seem uneasy, glancing backward once or twice. It was what was in her hand that gave it away. A lilac carrier bag.

And don't I know what you've got nestled there in the bottom, John told himself, crouching out of sight. A can or two of Guinness. Or were you late going to the store like me? In that case, it'll be bottles of Samuel Smith's stout. A strong ale as black as the shadows that oozed amongst the crypts.

John saw that he didn't have to look for the Bowen grave himself now. The blonde would show him. He hung back behind the bushes, knowing he must look like a stalker if anyone caught sight of him. Well, hard cheese, as they say. If lurking here in the vegetation saved him endlessly walking around the cemetery, then that suited him fine.

The woman walked swiftly up the ramp. Now the lilac carrier bag was in her two hands. She was scared. There was no doubt about that.

Discreetly, he followed so she wouldn't see him. But he didn't have to follow far. Just fifty paces or so from the top of the ramp, she stopped on the cliff top. Then, looking around, furtive as a burglar, she pulled two cans from the carrier bag.

Ah, the early bird . . . she got the Guinness.

Urgently now, she pulled the ring opener on the can. It squirted out at her, shaken by the walk uphill. She didn't make a fuss about it messing her clothes. Instead, she tipped the beer onto a grave. When one can was empty, she pushed it back into the bag, then opened another. She shook this one to get the beer out faster; instead of a black trickle, it spurted a creamy white all over the grave. When she'd done, she bagged the second empty can. Then, with a backward glance at the grave, as if fearing something would burst from it to drag her screaming into the earth, she returned the way

He stretched out his legs. Elizabeth sat watching home video clips on TV. The kind where children tumbled from swings, adults fell into streams, and athletes tripped over hurdles. Now she laughed out loud as a mountain biker slithered down a muddy hill into a ditch. As usual, she sat cross-legged on the observation window, with the millrace running beneath her bottom.

Through the living room window, John caught sight of Paul coming across the lawn after taking the dog for a walk. With the evening air warm and sticky, the dog plodded, his tongue almost trailing in the grass.

"It's going to thunder," Elizabeth announced without [tak]ing her eyes from the screen, where a tipsy best man [fell] into the wedding cake.

["A]nd probably rain," Val added. "I best get those [g]as chairs inside from the patio."

["I'l]l see to that," John said. Val smiled her thanks, [p]atted his rear as he stood up. "Good man."

[In tr]uth, he felt too restless to sit and watch TV. What [he'd do]ne that afternoon left him oozing with guilt. [As if he'd do]ne something unpleasant, dirty, unwholesome, [wron]g...but what had he done? He'd simply [tipped tw]o bottles of beer over a gravestone.

[T]he feeling came to him that it was like having [sex with a] stranger. Some sordid little act in the bushes. [After]ward he and the stranger emerged red-[faced, pers]piring, grubby, then went their separate [ways witho]ut mak[in]g eye contact. He knew he [shouldn't feel] guilty or sordid about simply tipping [beer on a] gravestone, but there it was—the feeling [wouldn't l]eave him. The emotion was still raw, un-

[...] he told himself. In a day or two he [would all] but forgotten about it. Certainly this [sens]ation would have left him. He waved [and wal]ked toward the house. Sam ran for-[ward w]agging his tail, despite the poor dog [feeling] the heat.

["Tea r]eady," John called. Paul gave a

---

she came. Soon, all John could see was a spot of blond hair moving down the hillside.

So, John asked himself, how many other people have received the letters? How many of those have met the demands? Perhaps this made what he had to do a little easier. Others had come here today to carry out the furtive little ritual. Now here comes another, he told himself as he crossed over to the grave.

There it was. A slab of granite the size of a child's bed. Although reddish in color, it was mottled with black, lending it the same noxious hue as ground beef when left out of the refrigerator on a warm day. Engraved deeply in the center was a name: *JESS BOWEN*.

No dates. No rhymes. No epitaph. Nothing but a name.

At one end of the slab stood the statue of a crying boy. He'd been carved to show him weeping over the tomb, broken-hearted by the death of whoever lay six feet below the sod. What did strike John forcibly enough was the smell of beer. It hung in the warm air. There was something cloying, almost treacly about it. The stonework itself was sticky. Beer had even pooled in the chiseled words of the name.

Now what did the letter say? *I should wish that yew pore a pinte of porter onto the grief stowne of Jess Bowen....*

The deadline was the "Sabbath night," which would be tomorrow, Sunday night.

"Well, I'm ahead of schedule," he murmured, pulling the bottle from the bag. "Come here and fill your fucking boots."

He glanced around, not wanting to be seen by a passerby. But as he did so, he wondered if someone—namely, the mysterious letter writer—lurked in the bushes watching him. No doubt spanking his filthy little monkey as he ogled yet another victim carrying out the bizarre ritual.

But then he wasn't going to rationalize this, John told himself. The detonation of absolute terror he'd experienced when he'd seen the wrecked car on TV had knocked the flippancy from him. OK, so it didn't make a whole lot of sense. But it was like throwing spilt salt over your shoulder, or not walking under a ladder. This was nothing more than one of those glitches in the modern world. Another little superstition that instinct told you to observe.

"Come on, you little beauty, drink up . . . drink up," he murmured, hearing the sarcastic sneer in his voice. Twisting the cap from the bottle, he poured the dark liquid over the head of the statue. It coursed down the statue's weeping face in great, black tears. They dripped from its nose and chin onto the blood red tomb itself. John poured more beer across the stone slab, splashing the letters; it streamed in black rivulets to the ground, where it was swallowed by the thirsty soil.

In his mind's eye he saw the beer flowing down underground, filtering through stones and dirt to gush into the coffin six feet down, where an accumulation of the black liquid would pool there, soaking what bones and shreds of skin remained of Jess Bowen.

When he had tipped the last drops of the second bottle onto the statue, he stuffed the bottles into the bag, then walked away down the hillside. He didn't look back. The sensation he experienced now wasn't what he had expected. He thought he'd feel foolish for yielding to the demands in the letter. He didn't. Instead he felt grubby and guilty. As if he'd been forced into some perverse sexual act with a stranger. What's more, he'd thought this ritual would have been the end of it all. Now he felt as if it was just the beginning.

Chapter Sixt

One

They say a good English su followed by a thunderstor proverb, thunderheads gr the horizon, and that Sa Shadows ran from the bleeding.

"Anything on you around his neck as

"The book," he chapter. Tom's

"Don't wor problems bef

He smile switch off

"Well in the Relax."

"I will."

thumb's-up sign, then mimed drinking from a bottle.

"Ok, get me a can as well . . . and ask your mother if she wants one."

Again, Paul gave the thumbs-up.

John stacked the chairs inside the garage. The rain hadn't come yet, but clouds slid over the sky like a colossal gray roof. He felt the heat rise. After leaving the garage, he returned to the house, going straight upstairs to wash the salt from his face left by a sheen of perspiration. Even the cold-water faucet was lukewarm. He splashed his face, then rubbed it dry on the towel. As he did so, he realized he hadn't checked his e-mail since yesterday. He walked into his study, switched on the computer, logged on, and hit the *Send* and *Receive* icon.

There were two items of mail. One was headed:
You've been warned!

Hell. The mystery letter writer had his e-mail address. He hit *Read Mail*. The message filled the box on screen. It wasn't what he expected. A message warned of a new computer virus marauding across the World Wide Web. He deleted it, then checked the next message. This one was headed *Champagne Time*. It was from his agent, and sent, coincidentally enough, the same time he'd poured beer onto the Bowen gravestone. Tom must be catching up on some overtime at the office, but then the guy was a workaholic.

> *Hi John,*
> *You're not going to believe this. Just in from Thailand is an offer for the Mandarin translation rights of* Blast His Eyes. *They will pay $20,000 on signature of contract. Well, my old buddy in crime, do we accept?*
> > *Best wishes,*
> > *Tom*

That was good news. Tremendous news. But why did he feel so emotionally flat about it? The e-mail could have been nothing more than a circular about health insurance. Not an offer to put thousands of bucks into his bank account. He checked the time of the e-mail. 3:57. Yep. Posted just as he shook the last few drips of beer from the bottle onto the head of the weeping statue.

Again he felt a surge of superstitious dread. Christ, all that stuff—omens, superstitions, hexes, good-luck charms, the whole stinking pile should be dead and buried. But why did he feel as if a toxic chunk of rotting flesh had just crawled over his grave? Before he could even suppress the thoughts, they spat into his head, like pus erupting from some boil buried deep inside his head.

This is a two-way street, John. The letter demands chocolate and beer—with menaces—but the little old letter writer tucked away in his tomb up there in the Necropolis gives you a reward in return. Fair exchange is no robbery. The little sobbing statue got the nice cold beer, while you, John Newton, are going to get a nice fat check. Why, John . . . you've got the best deal, haven't you? You've got yourself an idiot demon who dishes out more than he takes . . . you want to go up there and give that old grave stone a big, sloppy kiss. . . .

"Stop it." He clenched his fists, surprised he'd spoken out loud. "You're going crazy . . . it's just coincidence."

Yeah, like the Titanic *ploughed through the same chunk of ocean* coincidentally *occupied by a dirty great iceberg . . . like JFK's head just* happened *to occupy the same airspace that a rifle bullet would rocket through at six hundred miles an hour . . . like Christ by mere* chance *strolled through a garden where the bad guys lay in wait. And what was it he said when arrested? "But this is your hour, and the power of darkness."*

Somehow the words seemed apt. John shut down the computer and went downstairs. Through the windows, the clouds had turned black. Across at the Necropolis, the swollen mass of trees reached upward to mate with the darkened sky. Even from here he could see those trees in the cemetery roll and shake as trunks shifted, flexing before the force of a sudden breeze. In John Newton's dark and haunted mood, he didn't doubt for a moment that the roots writhed like tentacles in the earth, and where they broke through the rotting walls of the coffins, they curled, twisted, uncoiled like fingers stirring the bones of the dead into new and hellish configurations that no human mind could fathom.

Two

Paul had finished the pizza when the telephone rang. "I'll get it," he said. He left the living room, where they'd been sat round the coffee table, sharing a pair of vast pizzas. In bowls were the remains of coleslaw, potato salad, cherry tomatoes, and hunks of cucumber made shiny by a splash of virgin olive oil.

"No, me!" Elizabeth shouted.

"Let Paul get it, Liz," John said. "It'll be for him."

Val grinned. "Mr. Popularity seems to get all the telephone calls anyway."

"Thank heaven for e-mail." He made himself smile. *Funny how you can have a problem that eats away inside like tuberculosis of the bone, but as far as everyone else is concerned, you're still the happy-go-lucky guy or gal. But then, by the time you're ten years old, society expects you to be able to mask your emotions.*

Val asked, "Any e-mail messages? I heard you logging on earlier."

"Just a couple."

"Oh?"

"Yep. One warning about a new computer virus."

"Oh those—they're regular as the mailman. And?"

"One from Tom. A Thai publisher has made an offer on the Mandarin-language rights to *Blast His Eyes.*"

"Can you say how much, or is it one of these times where we have to tickle your feet until you crack?"

"I'll crack . . . twenty thousand dollars." Now a

pleased grin did reach his face. Twenty thousand dollars. Those were three good words.

"Twenty thousand!"

"Are we rich, Dad?" Elizabeth piped up from the millrace glass. "Can we buy a pony?"

"John . . . I'm shocked . . . no, that isn't the right word. Stunned? Gob-smacked. My God, congratulations." Val's eyes glittered. "We must celebrate this one, John!"

"You're right." His grin broadened. "I'll go buy a bottle of champagne."

"Don't get wet."

"Get the glasses out. I'll be back in ten minutes."

Val's sheer joy at the rights sale genuinely pleased him. Now, as he slipped out the front door for the five-minute walk down to Rhythm & Booze in the village, his emotions were mixed. The letters troubled him. What he did at the grave troubled him, too. But this hefty injection of cash into his bank account was good news indeed.

He walked into the growing gloom. His luck was holding out. It hadn't started raining yet. Even so, in the distance thunder announced its appearance with its first grumble. The second grumble was louder. The third sounded like approaching hooves.

Three

"Paul?" The voice was familiar.

"Miranda? I thought you'd be at the theater?"

"I am. I'm on my mobile in the ladies' room. Hear the echo?"

"Are you having a good time?"

"Not bad. But I wish I was with you."

"I wish you were here, too."

"I've missed you. . . ."

There was a breathy pause. Paul could hear voices echoing dimly through the earpiece from a theater in faraway London. He pictured Miranda's Spanish eyes. The chestnut hair.

"I missed you, too," he whispered, feeling a tingle. "When are you back home? Monday?"

"No, that's why I'm phoning. Dad's going for a birthday drink with his brothers tomorrow night. I could meet you tomorrow evening."

Paul's father waved as he left the house. Paul paused, not wanting to speak until he was out of the way.

"Paul? You still there?"

"Where shall we meet?"

"Same place, of course. Cemetery gates."

"It might be raining. It's just started to thunder here."

"No problem. I know somewhere that's dry and private."

"I'll be there."

"Oh, I've got to go, Paul. I wish I hadn't. Bye."

"Whoa, what time tomorrow?"

"Eight. And this time don't forget to bring *you know what*."

With electric thrills running through him, he replaced the telephone receiver and looked at the hallway clock. Five minutes past eight. That meant less than twenty-four hours until he saw Miranda. He thought about the cellophane-wrapped packet upstairs. God, he wished he could made those hours fly.

Four

The girl looked at John defensively from behind the counter as he walked in.

"There isn't any Guinness left." She sounded as if she was trying to answer him before he asked the question. "There isn't any stout left at all."

Why aren't I surprised about that?

He smiled. "No. I'm looking for a bottle of champagne."

"Oh. We've got plenty of that."

"Any already chilled?" He smiled again at the girl.

She looked frazzled. She'd clearly had a swine of a day.

"There's some in the refrigerator . . . next to the white wine."

"Got it." He chose two bottles. "Have you had a run on Guinness today?"

"You can say that again. The shelves had been stripped by the time I started my shift." She relaxed now, sounding chattier, as she realized he wasn't demanding that particular brand of beer.

He said, "It must be the heat. People have worked up a thirst."

"But we haven't sold more of the other beers than usual. If you ask me, the whole village has gone stupid or something. Do you know, when I told people all the Guinness had gone, they started getting really nasty? One woman threatened to report me because we'd run out of all the stouts. As if it's my flipping fault." The girl was really getting it off her chest. "I told them that there'd be plenty of Guinness in the supermarkets over Leeds way. But no, they wanted it there and then . . . that'll be forty-five, please. Thank you." She punched the till keys.

"I expect everyone'll be back to normal in a day or two."

"That's if the aliens haven't sucked out what's left of their brains," she said obliquely, perhaps referring to some movie she'd seen recently. At last the scowl left her face; suddenly she looked warm and even quite pretty. "Or it might have been the weather making them cranky. Listen to that thunder."

He picked up the carrier bag—the same lilac color that he'd carried through the Necropolis earlier in the day.

"Enjoy your celebration." She smiled at the bag containing the champagne.

"Thank you. I hope you don't get anyone else hounding you for Guinness."

She shrugged. "The night's still young, unfortunately."

He left the store as thunder crashed against the village. Still, there was no rain. But it couldn't be far away now. Walking quickly, he headed through the village in the direction of the Back Lane. The old Roman road would have weathered many a fierce storm in its two-thousand-year history. Plenty of storm water must have run off its stone blocks, to swirl along the grooves worn by chariot wheels. It would have witnessed storms of an altogether different nature, too. It had seen guerrilla wars fought by rebellious Britons against occupying Roman legions. Then there were countless invasions, civil wars, plus feudal strife, assorted banditry, and even Nazi bombing raids. He didn't doubt that those grooves had, from time to time, run with more than water.

Now they were weathering an altogether stranger storm. What he'd taken at first to be an isolated incident with just two or three people receiving the mystery letters had become something of an epidemic. Many villagers had received letters with identical demands. Today a steady stream of men and women, clutching their lilac carrier bags, had climbed the hill to the cemetery. They'd found the Jess Bowen grave. Then they'd made their payment in beer, pouring it over the stone figure of the weeping boy. The whole area around the tomb squelched underfoot in a sticky, tarry mess of stout.

Now it was dark enough for the pub's lights to blaze out across the green, sending shimmering ghost lights across the waters of the pond.

For a moment he thought the pub was deserted, but as he passed he looked in through the windows. There were plenty of people in there. A surprising number, in fact. They sat with their drinks on the tables in front of them. But the usual animated conversations, bursts of laughter, and lighthearted banter over the pool table were absent.

Who's died?

The thought was flippant. And he regretted it. Just

the day before a child had been murdered in the village. The child's mother had hanged herself. Exactly where, he didn't know, but he'd heard about the deaths on the radio.

Then he did something so out of character, it caught him by complete surprise. Without any hesitation he walked into largest of the Swan's bars. Tobacco smoke and beer odors hung densely in the air. There was something else, too, in the atmosphere. Something pungent that he couldn't readily identify.

Instead of heading to the bar, he walked to the far wall where there was a dartboard. Beside that hung a blackboard to record the scores. He set down the bag containing the champagne. Then he wiped a set of old scores from the board.

By this time, he sensed all heads turning to watch what he was doing. The tension in the air rose. Voices stopped.

Selecting a piece of chalk from the shelf beneath the blackboard, he wrote in large letters:

Porter
Jess Bowen

On the point of returning the chalk to the shelf, he changed his mind. Of course there was another important name here. One that didn't appear in the anonymous letters.

In huge, stark letters he spelt out the second name:

Baby Bones

Then he turned to see the reaction of the crowded bar.

Chapter Seventeen

One

Thunder crashed over the house. Stan Price opened his eyes. "Harry," he whispered. "Harry, we've got to do something." Lightning sent splashes of white against the wall, creating the pattern of a shifting face. A face with bulging eyes. And a leering mouth that looked as raw as an ax wound.

"Harry, it's back."

So weak was he with hunger that he fell instantly asleep once more. He dreamed he was lost in a forest. But instead of trees, televisions had been piled one on top of another; weird totems with dozens of staring glass eyes. Power cables hung like creepers; aerial wires were strangling vines. In the dream thunder sounded, too. A titanic groaning sound, like a trapped man trying to break out through a nailed coffin. Instead of lightning, TV screens flashed white; each one showed a face with eyes that bulged out . . . staring at him with wormy veins that ran thick and dark from fierce black irises to pouched sockets. Thunder became a monstrous heartbeat. The earth shook . . . a million faces leered.

He ran faster through swaying cables. The totems of TV set upon TV set creaked, swayed, threatening to topple and crush him. With thunder battering his ears, Stan Price ran faster. But he was lost. The faces, all identical, in a million TV screens watched him go by.

Thunder roared.

Stan scrambled through the swaying forest. "You're lost, you foolish old man. Lost."

No way out . . . no way . . . no way . . .

Two

In the bar of the Swan Inn, John Newton turned to face the thirty or so faces that looked back at him. Still there was no sound. Come to that, no reaction either. John cleared his throat. He could have been a teacher facing his first class.

"I'm sorry to interrupt your evening." He looked around at the unsmiling, watchful faces. Behind the bar the landlord and his wife watched, too, without moving so much as a muscle.

He indicated the words chalked on the blackboard. . . . *Porter, Jess Bowen. Baby Bones.*

His voice sounded calm in his ears. Inside he trembled.

"Do these words mean anything to anyone?"

He scanned the faces. There wasn't a flicker. People had locked up tight; the shutters were down—no one home. Silence.

"Or," he continued, "has anyone has seen these words recently?"

No reaction.

He nodded back at the blackboard, then read off what he'd written there. "Porter. Jess Bowen. Baby Bones."

Nothing.

He gave a dry laugh. There was precious little humor

in it. "You know, there's been a hell of a run on Guinness and stout at the store. Not a bottle left . . . I wonder what anyone makes of that?"

Now he saw two or three people give tiny shakes of their heads. He knew they weren't so much responding to his questions as shaking their heads in disbelief.

Why was the idiot saying *those* words? Why doesn't he shut up? Why doesn't he keep quiet about it? We always have, so why should he make a song and dance of it?

John was no mind reader. But those were the questions going through their minds right there and then. He knew it.

He gave it one last try. "Has anyone been to the graveyard today?"

"Mr. Newton." It was the landlord's voice. It sounded strained. "John . . . you might not have heard, but a little boy died in the village recently . . . I don't think anyone's in the mood for games tonight."

John looked back at the words on the blackboard, then nodded. It was nothing to do with the death. These people were going to keep mum. And they were going to keep mum because they were frightened.

He picked up the carrier bag containing the champagne. "I'm sorry. I didn't mean to disturb you."

With that he left the pub. Thunder sounded like a massive door slamming behind him.

These people knew all right. They knew plenty.

Three

The clock struck two in the hallway downstairs. Stan Price opened his eyes. The ceiling flickered blue-white. Lightning's noisy twin sounded off just seconds later. If it rained, his mother wouldn't let him go fishing tomorrow. Harry had a new rod, and it would be great to try get the carp down by the . . .

No. Stan shook his ancient, wrinkled head. He raised his hand in front of his eyes. In the flicker of lightning he saw brown liver spots, the fingers that were so thin as to be nearer to bird's talons, not the muscular fingers with good square nails he'd known in the past. No. His mother had been dead seventy years. It was after the third letter had arrived. She'd been traveling back from Leeds by train. For some reason she'd leaned against the carriage door. No one saw it happen, but she fell out onto the embankment. The train was going very slow. She should have survived the fall. But she'd rolled back down the slope and under the wheels of the train . . . the poor woman. Not yet forty.

Yes, he remembered it all clearly now as he lay there watching reflected lightning flashes play like ghosts across the ceiling. They darted toward the bathroom door, then back again, to swirl around the light fixture in a whirling vortex of electric blue.

Harry was dead, too. There'd be no more fishing trips. Then, as happened so infrequently these days, his mind swung into focus. He remembered the letter arriving during the night last week. He'd read it where Cynthia had left it on the kitchen table. She knew nothing about what it meant . . . ignorance is blissful indeed, he thought, as he pulled himself out of bed onto shaky legs. His stomach burned with hunger. He was getting weaker by the day.

For a moment he pictured going to the refrigerator to help himself to sausage, bacon, mushrooms, eggs. Beautiful big white eggs, he'd eat them raw if he had to. But no. Prioritize. *Prioritize!* He'd used this word often enough in business long ago. Decide what's really important, then do that first.

He shuffled to the door, then clinging to the banister rail, took one step at a time . . . if he fell now everything would be ruined. There was only one person who knew what to do. Stan would have been the one to act once, but his days of being fit and able were long gone. Why, at any moment his mind could go again, clouds of unreason would roll in and he'd be a babbling shell of a man once more, crying out for his best friend that had lain dead in the ground these last five years. . . .

No, he was an old man who was regularly slapped by his son-in-law. One Robert Gregory, who waited impatiently for his inheritance.

Stan Price wiped his face with a trembling hand. The exertion soaked his skin with perspiration. Now across the hall . . . ahead, stood the table with the telephone. He made a point of not switching on any lights. Don't wake Robert . . . you'll not get another chance to make this call. The next time you slip into dementia you might never emerge again. Time is running out. . . . Lightning flickered. Shadows leapt from the walls. He flinched, afraid the darkness would seize him.

Then, steeling himself, he walked on.

He found the telephone number in his address book. Talon fingers prodded the buttons. Thunder rumbled. It might wake Robert. Robert might find him. Stan could almost hear the sneering voice: *Telephoning people in the middle of the night, Dad? Why do you have to embarrass us so much, you filthy old man?* Then a full-blooded slap to the back of his head, sending him staggering, with pains shooting down his neck so ferociously he'd wonder whether the vertebrae had shattered. But that's what Robert Gregory wanted. He'd tell everyone that poor old Stan Price (with fog for brains and withered legs) had slipped on the staircase, or fallen into the bath, or tripped over a rug and broken his skull like an egg.

Thunder hit the door with the sound of a savage kick. Something out there wanted *in!* It wanted to stop Stan Price from making the telephone call . . . he could feel it in his brittle old bones. Air currents rattled the door handle. Through the window bulging eyes stared in. . . .

Harry . . . Ha—reeeee . . . No. He was losing his grip on reality again. It was all starting to slip from him . . . why was he in the hallway in the middle of the night?

"Hello . . . Hello?"

The female voice in his ear brought him back into focus as it continued with an irritable: "Hello. Who in damnation is phoning me at this time of the night?" Static crackled on the line. "Hello . . . who's there? Oh! Suit yourself . . . only I don't appreciate being woken by your silly games. I'm going to hang up now. Good-bye."

Frantic, he forced his wits together with an effort that made him shudder from head to toe. *"Dianne Kelly."*

"Yes, speaking. Who—"

"Dianne. Listen." With a sense that time was running out he spoke quickly, his voice little more than a whisper. "This is Stan."

"Stan Price?"

"Yes."

"Stan? They told me that you'd gone soft in the head." It was the old Dianne Kelly, sharp witted, straight to the point. "You sound OK to me, but you do realize what time it is?"

"Yes, Dianne, please listen. I'll have to be quick—"

"Why, what's wrong, Stan? You sound rattled."

A light came on upstairs. Robert's voice sounded muffled but annoyed. "Stay in bed, Cynthia. I'll go see to him."

Stan held the phone close to his mouth. "Dianne. It's started again. A letter came last week."

"Sorry, Stan. There's a lot of interference on the line. The angels must be frying bacon tonight. What was that you just said?"

"Dianne—"

"Now, now, Dad." Robert's tread sounded heavy on the stair. "Put that phone down. It's not a toy, you know?"

Closing his eyes, Stan concentrated on speaking clearly. "Dianne. Listen. It's starting again. A letter appeared last week."

"Stan, speak up . . . the static's awful."

"Dianne. Cynthia found the letter under a stone in the yard. She doesn't know what it is. But there's a man living up at the Water Mill; he—"

"All right, Dad. Give me the telephone."

"Newton, they call him, John Newton. I don't know how much he knows, but he must—"

Lightning and thunder mated—blue light burst through the hallway. The sound of cathedrals collapsing crashed through the house.

Stan saw the trail of sparks through the door glass. They spurted down the outside of the house, following the telephone line like a fuse to dynamite. Then a fist of fire struck the ear that touched the telephone. The floor rose up to strike him a second blow.

For a full second he stared at the rug, so close he could see individual fibers. Then his eyes closed. If it thundered again, he never heard it.

Chapter Eighteen

One

Dead of night. John Newton lay on his back, gazing at the ceiling. Lightning flashes were few and far between now. Thunder sounded muted, damped down by rain that drummed like a thousand skeleton fingers on the roof tiles. Val lay on her side, her back to him. He felt the rounded form of her naked bottom against his hip. She slept soundly after more than an hour's lovemaking.

For John, the champagne had only worked its magic for a couple of hours at most. Then the warm, contented envelope that surrounded him had evaporated. And now the time was coming up to three. He'd been brought awake by the terrific crash of thunder a little after two. Now sleep seemed as far away as the dark side of the moon. He listened to the rain along with the sound of his own thoughts.

Did he really walk into the bar and chalk those words on the board? Then stand there challenging people to tell him more? Yes, he had, and in the coming days he knew he'd attract some reproachful looks from his neighbors. But they were scared. They were scared to answer him tonight when they saw that blackboard bearing what looked like an incantation.

Porter
Jess Bowen
Baby Bones

He understood the first two on the list. The third, Baby Bones, was still a mystery. He'd heard Elizabeth use the name when she and Emma were frightening themselves in that game. Later, Elizabeth claimed that if you saw the face of Baby Bones in the lake, then you'd die. It all sounded like some local spook story that kids scared one another with.

Val murmured in her sleep. He rested his hand on her hip. The skin ran smooth and deliciously warm over the curves of her body. Turning over, he moved in close to her back so the contours of her body followed the front of his. He had everything to feel good about. The book sale to Thailand. The champagne. The pleasant evening in front of the TV with his family. Then coming upstairs at bedtime and realizing that Val was in one of her sexy moods, her eyes giving him the come-on; the way her hands caressed him as they slid together across the bed. The way she'd teased him with her tongue to the point of explosion. Life didn't get better than that.

And several thousand dollars will soon be slipping into your bank account. Now that is sweet. Twenty thousand dollars . . .

Dirty money. The words weren't rational. He'd earned the money through writing a best-selling book. But the e-mail was dispatched the very same moment he'd poured beer onto the Jess Bowen grave. The money made him feel as if he'd gone a-whoring for it. As if he'd rented his body for perverted sex acts. Dirty money, for a dirty boy.

That didn't make a hatful of sense, did it now? There could be no connection.

But there is, Johnny boy. There is a connection. You know there is. You know that because you ignored the demand for chocolate. That's why Elizabeth fell from her bike, and tore open her chin, and—

He blocked the thoughts.

The thunder died to nothing. Rain tapped at the roof and windows; it was the sound of fleshless fingers rapping maddeningly. Not wanting just to enter the house, but to get into his head, too.

Christ. Suddenly, he felt hot. There was no air in the room. He slipped out of bed, crossed to the door by touch alone in the darkness, then went down to the lounge.

It was a little cooler downstairs, and he felt the air caress his naked body. After switching on a table lamp, he went to the window. Peering through his reflected face as if it belonged to a ghost, he looked outside. There was nothing but absolute darkness. All he could see beyond the glass were rolling beads of rainwater.

Hell, he felt so wide awake, he could have been shot full of cocaine. Restless, he prowled the big room, looking at the blocks of stone that formed the wall. Not one was the same size or shape. Some looked like the heads of statues from which the faces had been slashed. Lowering his gaze from the stone wall, he looked down into the millrace.

The glass lay there, just a step away from his bare feet. Now he felt the vibration of those subterranean waters running up through the stone. He sensed the tremendous power there. A surging, gushing elemental force. The glass screened out the sound. Nor could he see anything. The observation chamber existed only as a black, fathomless pit.

After all this rain, the stream was in turmoil. It rushed down from the lake, then under the house. He'd never felt the vibration as strong as this before.

As much to distract him from his own troubled

thoughts, he switched on the spotlights under the mill-race glass. At first the light dazzled him. All he could see was a block of white light beneath the glass set there in the floor. Soon, however, his eyes adjusted to the brilliant glare.

It was quite a sight. Certainly enough to take his mind away from the mystery letters. Water swirled in a boiling vortex, surging, whirling, exploding upward, spattering the glass. The sense of power there was breathtaking. How many thousands of gallons a minute were coursing through the channel? He couldn't even begin to guess a figure. But the volume must be tremendous. The sight of it was nothing less than awe-inspiring.

To the house, the millrace must be like a main artery in the body. A conduit for liquid under pressure. He felt its beat through the soles of his feet. He pictured Elizabeth sitting here cross-legged to watch TV. Dear God . . . if the glass should break when the millrace was in flood? He tried to stop his imagination forming pictures, but the force of his thoughts was too great.

Screaming, hair streaming out, eyes terrified. "Dad!" Then vanishing down into the pit of swirling water. She becomes the piston in a cylinder driven by brutal force . . . rammed through the tunnel beneath; grating against stone walls; stripping skin from muscle, then muscle from bone, before being spat out the other side in a froth of blood . . .

No. The glass would not break. Strong enough for an elephant, the agent had said. Even so, the images lingered.

John stood there, watching water cascade along its course. Every so often it erupted in a blaze of white froth as if creatures writhed beneath its surface. He knew that long ago men and women would stare for hours on end into fast-flowing streams. It was a way of inducing hypnotic trances. Then they might commune with dead ancestors or hear the commands of their gods. The stream thrashing its way across the bottom of the pit held his attention in the same way. He felt his *self* detach from his body.

And at that moment he found himself in the Necropolis again, walking through the maze of crypts that formed the Vale of Tears. It was night. The darkness near absolute. The doors of the vaults were closed tight on their sleeping occupants. He walked up the ramp to the top of the cliff. A few yards away lay the grief stowne. (Grief stowne? Yeah, why not.) The grief stowne of Jess Bowen.

There a man did something by the grave. Tears ran down his face. He was working at an object with a knife.

In his dream, John stood at the man's side. He looked down. Blood ran down the face of the little sobbing statue, just as the beer had yesterday. John turned to the man. It was the landlord of the Swan. He was cutting the throat of a rabbit that belonged to his young son, and he was crying as he did so, sick with fright and self-disgust, and he let the dying rabbit kick and scream and bleed over the tomb.

"You've got what you want," the landlord cried. "You've got what you want! You're not having anymore . . ."

John threw out his elbow . . . it struck the cushions that formed the back of the sofa. Light came in a gray wash through the curtains. He hauled himself into a sitting position. How long had he been sleeping there naked on the sofa?

Shivering, he stood up. He couldn't believe how cold he'd become. He felt as if he'd been swimming in the ocean in winter. Cold to the roots of his bones, he made his way upstairs before slipping into the warm envelope of sheets beside his wife.

Two

Keith Haslem, holed up in a motel three hundred miles from Skelbrooke, couldn't sleep either.

His muscles ached with tension. When he looked at his bare back in the bathroom mirror, ridges appeared to twitch, then squirm beneath the skin. Fuck. The muscles in his goddamn back were alive—yeah, but not alive in a human-biology sense, but alive like a nest of snakes—twisting, writhing, coiling, uncoiling like crazy. They were going into spasm every couple of hours. Just yesterday his leg had gotten the cramp. He'd watched agonized, yet with a terrible kind of fascination, as calf muscle rose against skin. Almost the size of a baby's fist, knots strained against the underside of his skin. It looked like a face straining through from the other side. And trying its darnedest to burst out. God Almighty, it hurt! A sickening hurt that made him want to pound the wall of the motel, yelling at the top of his voice.

Now his wife and daughters were sleeping in the bedroom. And Keith Haslem felt like a caged animal. Maybe he should have stayed home. He could have confronted the demands in the letter head-on rather than running away like that. Shit, his back hurt. He looked again at the skin with its covering of black hairs. Then he looked back at his eyes—they were tired, yet they had a burning look to them. Tired, frightened eyes. Hell, he wanted to go home.

But he knew that he daren't. Not yet. There might be another letter waiting for him. Just like the last one. Lying under a shard of tombstone outside the back door.

Rubbing his sore back, he looked at the shower. It might ease the ache. And in the absence of acupuncturists, or masseurs, or even fucking morphine, he might as well give it a go. He turned the shower full on hot. There was a trick to these motel showers. You had to twist the lever as deep into the hot mark as it would go. Once it came through boiling hot, you gradually nudged the shower control over toward cold until it was just right.

He stood watching the shower. Soon steam billowed as the water temperature soared.

Groaning, tired to the bone, he rolled his shoulders. His neck muscles had stiffened, and he felt the makings of a headache in the back of his head. He rested his face against the glass shower door, watching the water as, not far from boiling, it blasted down into the ceramic trough. Jesus. This stress was really getting him down. He ached; dizzy spells turned his brain ass-over-tip. Maybe this was the makings of flu.

The water looked hot enough now. He opened the door, then carefully leaned in, his arm snaking around outside the flow of water. Even tiny droplets hitting his arm stung like fury.

His fingers had almost reached the shower control lever when something popped inside his head. *I heard that*, he thought, surprised.

The artery running through the segment of brain that controlled motor function within his body had ruptured. Blood flowed out into the brain, crushing delicate tissues, destroying whole bundles of nerves.

Keith Haslem felt nothing of this. He simply froze there. A naked man reaching into the shower. Something was happening to him, but he didn't know what. Only, he couldn't move his limbs anymore. He was conscious. Completely conscious. He saw the jets of boiling water. He saw the tiles beyond through the stream. He saw the kids' shampoo bottle on the shelf in the shower.

Another thousand or so neurons died inside his brain.

Keith Haslem slowly collapsed forward into the shower. He turned as he slipped downward, his one good hand clutching the edge of the door. A moment later the top half of his body lay in the ceramic trough. He looked up at the jets of water driving down into his face. The water also struck his throat and chest and genitals.

He'd never known such pain. The water was only a

few degrees short of boiling. His flesh turned red, skin began to peel.

He couldn't bear the agony. Yet he could not move. With all his heart he wanted to scream for help. For someone to save him from this living hellfire.

But he couldn't utter so much as a groan. All he could do was lie there, his mind clear, his senses acute, his nerves raw, his skin nearer purple than red. And all the time the near-boiling water blazed down upon his naked body.

Three

That Sunday afternoon, Val took Paul and Elizabeth on a duty visit to their old neighbors in Leeds. John had said he needed to work on the first chapter of the book. Val had smiled understandingly. "In that case, I'll stretch the visit out to a couple of hours."

As he suspected, he couldn't settle to work on the book. Instead, he found himself taking the two letters from the envelope and brooding over them, looking for some clue hidden, perhaps, in the handwriting. He held them up to the glass again, looking for words that had been erased or some faint mark that would point to the identity of the writer. Both pieces of paper bore the watermark that could just be made out when held to the light. An ugly face in profile that was little more than smoky marks in the fabric of the paper. He tried tearing a corner of it. It was tough, but did tear when he applied greater pressure.

He was still examining it when he heard Sam bark. In a blur of black, the dog sped around the house and onto the driveway. John looked down to see an old lady walk through the gate, then breeze up the path. She was looking the Water Mill over with interest. He watched with a sinking sensation. Dear God, the dog would bark furiously at the woman and probably frighten her silly. Sam did stand there with his front paws splayed, his eyes on her, obviously ready to deliver a series of machine-gun-rapid barks.

The old lady, however, crisply gestured for Sam to come to her.

To John's surprise the dog obeyed, tail wagging, his head down as if shy to meet the stranger. She made a fuss of the dog. He lapped it up, sniffing her hand, and swishing his tail so hard it swept gravel from the driveway.

John didn't recognize the visitor. She was tall, with no sign of a stoop despite her age, her long gray hair was tied back, and she wore a summer dress of pale pink, with a set of pearls around her neck. Even from this distance she cut a distinguished figure. Dropping the letters onto the table, he went down to her.

"Hello," he said, exiting by the front door as the old lady walked up the path with Sam following.

"Good afternoon."

John noticed the way her bright blue eyes looked him over, assessing him from his shoes to his hair. She held out her hand.

As he shook it, she said, "I'm Dianne Kelly." She looked up at the house. "I used to live here. My bedroom was the one over the front door."

"Oh?"

"Now. Let me explain why I am here. I had a telephone call from an old friend last night. Stan Price. I understand you've met him?"

"Yes, just a couple of days ago."

"Good. I suspect you went to his house to ask him some questions. As you will have seen, Stan is a little far gone to be able to answer them as coherently as one would wish." She looked John in the eye. "Perhaps tea is in order, because we've a long conversation ahead of us, Mr. Newton."

Chapter Nineteen

One

This is where I found out everything. The words went through John's head as he showed Dianne Kelly into the living room. *The letters, The Bowen grave—everything.*

He saw her sharp eyes absorb every detail. She took a particular interest in the observation window that exposed the millrace. Still in flood, it surged through the stone tunnel beneath the house in a white fury.

"That's new," she said. "When I lived here the stone floor was covered with an assortment of rugs. We didn't have central heating, either." She smiled. "Or television. We did have a wireless in a big brown Bakelite case over there beneath the window. My father used to love to listen to opera from Vienna. At night it came through on long wave with such beautiful clarity. My father always used to say that Germany had the most beautiful music but the most diabolical politics." She smiled again. "You must forgive me if I wander.

We oldies are inclined to do that, you know, Mr. Newton."

"John, please. Take a seat, Mrs. Kelly."

"Ah, thank you. It is Miss Kelly. I never married." She chose the sofa, then sat down. "I carry too much personal baggage to make an agreeable wife for a man. Besides, I became too wrapped up in my career. I trained as a doctor, and ended up serving thirty years here in Skelbrooke as a general practitioner. Oh, what a lovely view of the garden. I'm pleased you haven't torn down the orchard . . . you don't plan to do away with it, do you?"

"No, not at all, Dr. Kelly. I've always wanted to live in a house with an orchard."

"Then you have your wish. And please dispense with that fussy title. Call me Dianne."

"All right, Dianne." He smiled. "Do you have milk in your tea?"

"Just a drop, please."

He found himself rushing to make the drink. Once more he found himself eager to hear what she had to tell him. When he set the cups down on the table by the sofa, he expected more small talk. But Dianne got straight to the point.

"John. You have received an anonymous letter."

"It's two letters now."

"I see. Will you show them to me?"

He returned with the letters. She didn't take them from him, but touched the tabletop . . . *leave them there*. His heart was beating hard. This is what it feels like when you break down the doors of a tomb to see what lies inside, he told himself. As much as curiosity, he felt a hefty dose of trepidation. He was leaving the familiar to venture into unknown territory.

Choosing the armchair facing the sofa, he sat down, then leaned forward so he could see the letters. He watched her study them. Her blue eyes burned. The color went from her high-cheekboned face. This wasn't a pleasant experience for her. Hand trembling, she raised the cup to sip the liquid.

When she spoke, she didn't mention the letters. Sitting back in the sofa, she said, "Stan Price telephoned me last night. As soon as I heard what he had to say, I knew I had to come here. Because the rest of the Skelbrooke sheep won't so much as bleat."

Skelbrooke sheep? He figured she wasn't being complimentary about his fellow villagers. But then in the pub last night, they did look like a bunch of sheep. Frightened sheep at that.

He said, "What did Stan tell you exactly?"

"Not much. An awful and freakish thing happened. As he was speaking to me the telephone line was struck by lightning."

John's skin crawled. "Is he badly hurt?"

"Fortunately, no. Most of the charge earthed through the telephone cable, although he was knocked to the floor, and he has a burn to the fleshy part of his ear."

"You've seen him today?"

"Oh, yes. I've just come from the house, in fact. He still looks shaken, but the most distressing aspect is that he's as confused as ever. Senile dementia is a wicked thing, isn't it? It's a cancer of the personality rather than the body. And Stan Price was such a perfect gentleman. Honest, hardworking, generous, compassionate. He was a very good friend to me for years and years." She sighed. "I spoke to Cynthia, his daughter, you know? As painfully shy as ever. She does genuinely care for her father, but I have to say I'm not taken with the son-in-law, Robert." Then she added surprisingly. "To me, he looks a bastard."

John felt himself warm to Dianne Kelly. So she got the same vibes from Robert Gregory, too? John nodded. "I can't say I was taken with Robert either. He seemed a bit too full of himself."

"Of course he's only looking after Stan so he can get his hands on the money once Stan goes. He's probably dipping into Stan's accounts even now. After all, I don't see an idler like Gregory being able to afford handmade Italian shoes, do you?"

"I see your point." Dianne Kelly would have made a formidable detective with that attention to detail.

"Which is very sad, John, but it's not why I am here." She clasped her hands together on her lap. Once more he thought she'd begin to talk about the letters. But she didn't. Not at first anyway. She said, "I'm going to relate certain events that happened here in Skelbrooke. It was a long time ago now. More than seventy years, in fact. The place was lot different then. Roads quieter. You'd see horse-drawn carts. The Necropolis up there on the hill was still a working cemetery. Special funeral trains brought mourners and their dear departed in black carriages. Sometimes there would be a dozen funerals a day, especially after a cold snap. And, of course, whole families would arrive by the same trains to visit graves. It was a bustling place in those days. As well as a full timetable of funerals, there were teams of gardeners keeping the place trim.

"You'd be surprised to see the cemetery in those days, John. There was a tearoom staffed by girls in black uniforms with black-lace pinnies. There were even black-lace tablecloths on the tables. Stan Price was a real joker as a child; he told me that there was even black sugar in the bowls, and milk dyed a funereal purple." She smiled. "Children actually believed him, too. The Necropolis brought prosperity to the village—it employed dozens of people. Of course, it was a hangover from the Victorians—they were death-obsessed. They saw funerals as being glamorous, romantic rituals that had all the pomp and display of a society wedding." She looked up at John, her eyes wise but sad. "See how easy it is for us old folk to wander off the subject?" Her eyes rested on the letters. "Now, John. I have things to tell you. . . ."

Two

John didn't interrupt. He sat back, allowing the old woman to tell her story as she needed to tell it. Outside, it was warm, if overcast. Clouds piled layer upon layer until the sky wasn't just dark, but had become a deep reptilian green. As it grew darker still, the floodwaters running along the channel to the house darkened with the sky. John Newton's mood mirrored the morbid weather. To him the stream had taken on the ugly aspect of fluid discharging from some vast necrotic ulcer. One that rotted in the once-beautiful face of this little rural village.

As he listened to the calm voice, he grew colder and colder. But it was nothing to do with the temperature. The story was taking him to a dark place—a place he was afraid to visit. . . .

"I was born in this house eighty-four years ago. My father, Herbert Kelly, was head teacher at Skelbrooke School. He was tall, slim, had a sharply trimmed beard, and wherever he went he wore a Panama hat. You could see him walking across the fields from miles away. That white hat of his was a beacon. And he had a good heart, John. He believed every child had a spark of greatness in them, and he loved the village where he lived. Many a night he would sit at the typewriter, working on his newspaper column, *Aspects of Skelbrooke*, where he wrote about local characters and trumpeted the achievements of ordinary people who lived here. And he loved his family. He made time to be with us, and to listen to what we had to say. He often said that his children taught him far more than he taught them. He adored my mother, Beatrice—you know, she was the first woman to graduate from Leeds University with a civil engineering degree. . . . Oh. I'm making this sound so rosy, aren't I? Happy families 1930s-style. When ice cream tasted like ice cream; when you got more bang for your buck."

She smiled. "In retrospect it does seem like that. I

remember playing in the lake. I'd paddle in the water with my little sister, Mary. We'd catch fish with a string and a worm. The sun always seemed to shine. Butterflies of every color you could think of flew through the orchard. We had a lovely big brown dog called Teddy. We ate well; we were so healthy, we glowed. Then, one morning in October, my father told me he was going to pick mushrooms from the meadow. He put on his Panama hat, picked up the basket, and left the house. He was back two minutes later. He didn't have any mushrooms, but he was carrying a piece of paper. He was smiling and saying that it was a funny way to send a letter. That's the last time I can remember him smiling in such a genuine and carefree way.

"Anyway. He laid the paper down on the table." Her eyes grew faraway. She was replaying the memory before her mind's eye. Every detail as clear as the day it happened. John pictured a scholarly-looking man, smoothing down the letter with his hands. The big brown dog would be wagging its tail, wondering what all the excitement was about. The two girls would be clustering around to see the paper. A grandfather clock would tick in the corner, while on the stove a stew would be simmering in a pan the size of a baby's bath.

She continued. "First of all, he asked us which one had been playing the joke. Of course Mary and I didn't have a clue what he was talking about. Then he read the letter to us." The old woman closed her eyes, reciting from memory. "*Dear Mister Kelly, I should wish yew put me a pound of chock latt on the grief stowne of Jess Bowen by the Sabbath night. Yew will be sorry if yew do not.* Naturally, he thought it was a prank. In fact, he was amused by the inventiveness of what he guessed was one of his pupils trying to get their hands on a bar of chocolate. My father put the letter away. He ignored it. The Sabbath came and went. A few days later I climbed over the fence to the field. I was in a hurry, coming home from school. My cousins were coming from Leeds and I wanted to change into a new dress.

Anyway, as I climbed the fence, I swore someone caught hold of my foot and tipped me over it. I came down with such a bump. My head split open from my right eyebrow to my left temple." She touched her forehead, where a scar ran across the wrinkled skin. "Good grief, what a mess. My father was convinced I'd been hit by an ax. I finished the evening lying on the sofa looking like an Egyptian mummy with bandages swathed all around here." She made a circling motion around her entire head.

John thought about Elizabeth. The fall from the bike . . . *her throat's been cut.* . . . The words from his initial reaction swam round his head. After returning from hospital, Elizabeth sat on the observation glass, her head festooned in bandages.

Water in the millrace boomed, sending tremors up through the stone floor.

Dianne Kelly had fallen silent for a moment, too, her fingers once more going to the scar that must have once been a raw and agonizing slash. "Poor Dad. He was beside himself with fright . . ." She took a breath before continuing matter-of-factly. "My father commented on the letter in his *Aspects of Skelbrooke* column, but . . . and he remarked about it to us at the time, no one in the village mentioned the mystery letter, even though they chatted to my father about other incidents in his column. We didn't know then that an outbreak of such letters was one of those 'subjects' not to be discussed. Like madness in the family or if an uncle had died of syphilis. Local people clammed up tight about it. So, life went on in the Kelly family. Dad taught his students. Mother worked on her civil engineering papers. Mary and I went to school, and we played in the meadow in the evenings." She paused as a rumble sounded through the house. It was one of those sounds that were so deep they were felt rather than heard. Straightaway, John realized it wasn't thunder. It sounded as if a solid object was being dragged through the millrace tunnel, scraping against the stone walls, buffeting against joists and pillars. The scraping sound came again. Claws scraping against stonework . . . John closed off the thought. He turned to Dianne. "Then more letters came?" he asked.

"Yes. One that demanded porter—that's an old-fashioned name for—"

"Beer. Yes." He nodded toward the letters on the coffee table. "I got one of those, too."

"And other people were receiving the letters. Although the rest of the village kept their mouths shut tight. But I found out from Stan Price that his father had received one, then a second."

"Stan's father ignored them, too?"

"Yes. A week after receiving the second, Mrs. Price fell from a train and was killed."

"But it was an accident?"

"Let's say it appeared to be an accident. But with hindsight . . ." She didn't complete the sentence. From the tunnel beneath the house the scratching grew louder. Demanding attention. With an effort she drew her gaze from the observation window to look John in the eye. "My father ignored the second letter as well. A week later the school governors summoned him to a meeting. They suspended him from his teaching duties . . . he never told us why. He was a proud man. What they did wounded him more than words can say." Her eyes rolled down to the letters as if fingers had somehow gripped her eyeballs and twisted them down to stare at the letters against her will. John saw she hated them.

"The mood in the house became terrible," she said. "From sunlight and happiness to a dark, depressing place. Hardly anyone spoke. But, like a disease, this gloom spread through the village. People started to leave. Oh, they never said they were leaving because of the letters . . . only, suddenly families were taking trips to the coast, or visiting friends. But they left in a hurry. Which, of course, was foolhardy, because you can't run from this thing. It follows you. Then when it finds you, it cuts you down."

"I don't understand. What followed them?"

"Not a person. Let's say that bad luck followed them. Very bad luck at that. The Markham family went all the way to France, but they were badly injured when the hotel elevator they were in suddenly plunged three floors into the basement. Ill luck picked up their scent and followed them . . . it happened to others, too. Mr. Ventor's youngest boy drowned in ditch water just eight inches deep. No one knew how it happened. And although the Ventors might not have known the exact circumstances of the death, they knew full well what caused it."

"You mean they ignored the letters that arrived just like these?"

"Yes. These came in the dead of night, didn't they? Weighted down with a piece of gravestone?"

John nodded as Dianne Kelly continued. "Today I saw Mrs. Booth from the house at the end. She told me about Keith Haslem."

"I saw him leaving in the village, too." John gave a humorless smile. "In fact, he was in such a hurry he nearly ran me down."

"He received the letters, I imagine?"

"I found burnt paper in the birdbath. He'd obviously set fire to them, then he'd run for it."

"Foolish man." She looked at John. "You haven't heard what happened to him?"

"No. The last I saw of Keith he was tearing out of here like something was chasing him."

"Something was." She shook her head. "From what I gather, Keith Haslem stayed in a motel a good way from here. He was taking a shower when he suffered a stroke. Apparently, he was also badly scalded."

"He's alive?"

"But in something of a mess, I hear. He spent a long time in the hot water before he was discovered. He's going to need extensive skin grafts."

"Dear God," John whispered. The scraping noises grew louder, more frenzied beneath his feet. Something wanted out. He shivered.

"And it was no coincidence that poor Stan Price was struck down. And I use the phrase deliberately. *Something* sensed he was trying to warn me about its return. It directed that lightning bolt at the house as an assassin might direct a bullet from a gun."

"What happened to your father?"

"Three weeks after the first letter arrived came the third one. Asking—no, demanding would be a better word—demanding that a red ball be left at the grave of Jess Bowen."

"Your father still ignored the letter?"

"No. This time natural instinct overrode his usual rational self. You must remember, he was still in a state of depression after being suspended from his duties. As well as depression, perhaps desperation came to the fore. He didn't show me the letter, John. I never saw it, but I overheard him talking to Mother about it. He kept repeating that a red ball must be left at the grave. One morning I saw him leave the house with a red ball. Later, I visited the cemetery with Stan Price. And . . ." The smile that twitched her mouth was grim. "Red balls. Dozens of red balls all clustered round the head-stone." Her voice grew stronger, and she laid so much emphasis on every syllable, it was as if she pushed rock solid words through her lips: "John Newton, believe me. When the letters come with their demands, do not ignore them. You obey. You obey them to the word."

The scraping and scratching came again from the tunnel beneath the house. *Talons raking furrows through the stone, clawing in fury. Something raging at the two for daring to speak about the letters* . . . John fought the image from his mind. No, that was to be sucked into a pit of superstition . . . what next? Slit the throat of a lamb? Daub its blood on the stupid, sobbing statute at the Bowen's grave?

KREEEEEE!

The scream came up through the floor. A huge object must have been forced along the tunnel by the pressure of floodwater. John resisted the impulse to look through the observation glass to see what was passing beneath the house. He gave Dianne a colorless smile. "The stream's in flood . . . debris's being flushed through."

She didn't give the impression of agreeing or disagreeing. Instead she merely said. "I've heard the sound before, John."

Now he knew he had to hear the end of Dianne's story. "After the letter demanding the red ball . . . that was the end of it?"

"That was the end of the letters. At least my father didn't admit that any more had arrived. He'd given what the letter writer had demanded. A day later the school governors announced he was reinstated. But . . ." She shook her head. "Life wasn't the same. I think something had broken in my father's heart. He became very quiet, very unhappy. Once I saw him in the orchard. He was weeping."

"The letters had stopped arriving in the village?"

"I believe so. Everything returned to normal. But one morning I awoke to find my father and sister gone."

"Gone?"

"Vanished. My father had packed a case with his and Mary's clothes without Mother or I knowing. Then the pair of them crept out in the middle of the night and . . ." She shrugged. Her eyes were dull with pain, recalling that morning seven decades ago.

John said, "I don't understand. The letters had stopped; why should your father leave like that?"

"I think the whole incident had poisoned my parents' marriage. My father's orderly twentieth-century world had been turned upside down. I believe he decided to make a clean break."

"It's not unusual for a husband to leave home. But isn't it unusual for the husband to take one of the children with him?"

Again Dianne gave a little shrug. "Mary was his favorite. Perhaps leaving his youngest daughter behind was too much to bear."

"Where did they go?"

"We heard nothing for three days. Then a letter arrived from Liverpool. It was from my father, clearly it was his handwriting. It simply said he and Mary were leaving for a new life overseas. A little later we received a telegram from Canada. One terse sentence stating Father and Mary were well, that Canada was beautiful and God Bless." Her voice had taken on a bitter edge. "That was the last we heard of him and Mary."

"You believe he really went to Canada?"

"Yes, I do. I guess he remarried as well. Of course that would be bigamous, but by then he'd have adopted a new identity and probably had begun teaching again." She sighed. "In my imagination I picture him living in a wooden house, painted a nice gleaming white. He listens to his opera on the radio. His new life continues nicely. He doesn't forget us, but his memories grow dim. And he grows older. Mary marries. She has children. And although my father must have died years ago, his grandchildren are still alive and well with families of their own in Toronto or Calgary or wherever. He'd even taken a photograph with him, one of us all together—Mother, Mary, the dog, and myself. We're standing by the front door of the house . . . my sister holding a doll I made her from—but that isn't important. Not anymore."

John saw a bitter well of rejection in the old woman. She masked it well. But he imagined she asked herself time and time again: Why had her father deserted them? Why had he chosen to take eight-year-old Mary—not Dianne?

John spoke with a real sympathy. "I'm sorry. It must be painful to talk about it."

"It is. Time will fade your clothes and the color of your hair, but it doesn't fade memories like that." Her eyes glittered. "You know, John, you can't begin to know how angry I feel. We were such a happy family. Then all those ties were torn apart just like that." She clicked her fingers. "My mother died ten years later of a broken heart, I'm sure. She's buried in the old Necropolis, up in the Vale of Tears . . . isn't that a romantic name for what in effect is a dumping ground for our dead?" She finished her tea. The scraping sound continued beneath the floor. Every so often it became frenzied, as if something fought its way to the surface. She chose to ignore it.

"So, there you have it, John," she told him. "Periodically, like an epidemic of some vile disease, Skelbrooke suffers an outbreak of these letters. They make trivial demands for chocolate, beer, and children's toys. The repercussions, however, if you chose to ignore the demands, are anything but trivial. Stan Price lost his mother. Our family disintegrated. Today Keith Haslem lies paralyzed in a hospital bed."

"But seventy years separate the letters your father received and the ones that arrived just a few days ago." John picked up one of the letters. "Are you telling me that the same person wrote them? Whoever it is must be a hundred years old."

"John?" She sounded surprised, as if he'd misunderstood some fundamental fact about the whole matter. "John. No human being wrote these letters."

"Then what did? Are you telling me it was a ghost?" Something like a grin appeared on his face, but it was closer to a spasm, a reflex action over which he had no control. "I don't believe in ghosts, Dianne."

"No, neither do I."

"I'm sorry, I don't understand."

"I don't understand either, John. None of us can. We can only *feel*. Do you follow? We *feel* what's happening at the level of animal instinct. Deep, deep down here." She pressed a hand to her heart. "These letters appear in cycles of every seventy years or so. They make their demands. The foolish ignore the demands, then suffer the consequences. Those who are wise obey. As I said before, it only requires the recipient of the letter to offer up some sacrifice of chocolate, beer, something trivial. In return they are spared heartache."

"But you're telling me that some supernatural force is creating these letters, then somehow delivering them? All in return for confectionery and beer. Its strikes me—"

"John—"

He found himself angrily spitting out the words, "It strikes me you have some idiot demons round here."

"*John*—"

Down in the millrace the furious scratching soared to a crescendo. *Goddamnit, it wanted out....*

"John, please. It is difficult to explain," she said calmly despite the noise. "No, I'll go further than that. It is impossible to explain. Any more than you could explain the scientific cause of an eclipse or an earthquake to a Stone Age man. All I can suggest is suspend your disbelief for a moment, so we can use our imagination."

"But I—"

"No, bear with me. Darwin formulated the theory of evolution at an early age. It came to him in a flash of inspiration. But before he could go public he had to find proof to support his hypothesis. So he spent years collecting evidence for his theory to make it credible to the scientific community. Now, over the last seventy years, I've thought long and hard about these letters, and about the ill fortune that befell not just the Kelly family but others who chose to ignore them. But like Darwin when he couldn't immediately prove his theory of evolution, I can't *prove* what I tell you now. Call it an exercise in imagination, John. But at that animal-instinct level I believe, given a split hair or two, it is near as damnit true."

The demonic scratching and scraping continued as she spoke—dark music to her words. She said, "I have a medical degree, I trained as a doctor to become one of society's warriors, if you will allow the conceit, to fight disease. And it is a strange battleground, I can tell you. I have seen things that simply refuse to be explained by science. I have spoken to a healthy man in the street on a Saturday and have signed his death certificate on the Sunday. Killed by a virus that we can't even name. Maybe it had lain dormant in the dust of his attic for three hundred years. Maybe it floated down through the atmosphere from outer space. Who knows? On the other hand, I've seen a child close to death with cancer, one who's had the last rites because our drugs and radiotherapy don't work anymore. I've even had the child's death certificate ready in my bag, but instead of being called to a dead child, I find one that is rallying, whose eyes are brighter, who can ask for a drink of water. Then a month later I've seen the same child playing in the park. What has happened there?" Her voice was earnest, the words rapid, almost hypnotic.

"Remission?"

"Yes, we give it a scientific name: remission. But the bottom line is, we don't understand what happened. *Something*, whether it's the child's guardian angel, Almighty God, or some natural biological defense system, has acted. The cancer withers; the patient recovers. And I, and the whole damned medical profession, haven't a clue what has really happened. All we do know is that the cancer has had its backside kicked." She knitted her fingers together. "Now. Five thousand years ago men and women watched the sun rise into the sky. They didn't know what was happening, so to somehow ease the pain of their ignorance, they invented stories about gods riding a fiery horse through the sky by day, then stabling it at night. Believe me, John, there is something in Skelbrooke. A *something* no one can understand or even name. *But it is here.* It's more deeply rooted into the earth than those trees across there. In fact, *IT* is probably older than the bedrock on which the village stands. In my imagination I see it living under the Necropolis hill. Maybe it can harness what remains of those thousands of dead minds for its own purposes.

Who knows? But I see it there in my mind's eye: way, way underground, buried far below the deepest coffin. A formless mass of purple light that has grown like a cancer, spreading its roots out through the earth and into the foundations of our homes. For reasons best known to itself it forms letters—perhaps out of thin air, for all we know. They arrive at night, they make demands. If the demands aren't met, it has the power to turn lives into a living hell. Or it can even snuff them out completely."

"You mean it's some old god that still demands its tribute in sacrifice?"

"I wouldn't pretend that I know that much. Only that there is some *essence* or entity that has the power to demand gifts from us, and can inflict punishment if we ignore it."

"But why such trivial demands? Chocolate? Beer?"

"Perhaps what it demands isn't important. It might only crave that we acknowledge its power. Like a humble soldier saluting a general or an employee calling the boss 'Sir.' The gift might merely be a symbolic gesture that we recognize this thing's power over us."

He considered for a moment. "Does this *thing* have any connection with Baby Bones?"

"Baby Bones?" She gave a weak smile. "I haven't heard the name for while. That's what local children call it. I've often wondered how the name originated. Whether it was simply invented by a child or if it derived from something else. After all, there are the remains of a five-thousand-year-old settlement down by the village pond. I daresay this sinister little *thing* exerted its influence even then, and those Stone Age men and women had a name for it that might have even sounded like Baby Bones to our ears. Only, the name became corrupted down through the centuries. Just as the Egyptian name for Set became corrupted to Satan." She looked at her watch. "Five o'clock. Is that the time? I must be away, otherwise I'll miss my train."

"Can I give you a lift to the station?"

"That's very generous, but no. I'm going to have a last look around the village." She sounded tired. "I don't intend coming back here. Too many memories. And these days they have a way of intruding on reality." She nodded toward the window. "When I look out now I can still see Mary on the garden swing, and the dog chasing butterflies." She glanced out, and John saw her shiver. "And I can see my father up there in the orchard . . . with his head pressed to the tree, hiding his face the way he did when—oh, dear, John. There I go again." A tear formed in her eye. "Too many memories, young man. And they get harder to bear the older I get, so—" She took a breath. "So, last year I bought an apartment on a cliff top with a lovely view of the sea. And that's where I'll stay until they carry me out."

"Thank you for coming all this way. And for telling me—"

"Telling you what, John? That an evil spirit lives under the Necropolis? That it writes menacing letters?" She shot him an appraising look. "Do you believe me, John?" A grim smile stretched her thin, old mouth. "No, don't answer that. You'll find some diplomatic answer for the old woman . . . but deep down you believe me, even though you'd deny it a hundred times. At least this week you will. But next week, who knows?"

Beneath the floor the scraping reached a wild frenzy. "If it is true, Dianne . . ." He spoke carefully. "What do you suggest I do about the letters?"

The grim smile widened. "Well, for the sake of argument pretend what I have said is true. Then I suggest you do exactly as the letters ask. Meet their demands. If the letter asks for a shiny red ball, then leave a shiny red ball on the Bowen grave. If it demands a new pair of shoes leave those, too. Don't worry, John. The letters never ask for very much, our demon of the graveyard has modest tastes, but whatever you do, don't ignore the letters. The repercussions will be terrible. Trust me on that, John." She stood up. "And soon the letters will

231

stop. Oh, they'll return again in seventy years, but you won't have to worry about that, will you?" She picked up her purse. "Thank you for the tea, young man. I'll say good-bye now." Before leaving, she looked down at the letters. He realized she'd never once touched them. She nodded. "Same handwriting, too. Good-bye, John. Good luck."

A moment later she walked through the garden gate, then turned left down the lane. He stood on the path to watch her go. She never looked back at her former home. And a few seconds later she had vanished from sight.

Chapter Twenty

What John Newton did next nearly cost him his life.

After watching Dianne Kelly walk away down the hill, he turned back toward the house. The old woman had certainly given him something to think about. His reason rebelled at the idea of something—a demon, or spirit, or some malign intelligence under the hill—that had the power to create those letters from thin air, then drop them into gardens. That was a difficult concept to swallow. But then some strange stuff was going down in Skelbrooke. Villagers had become withdrawn. Keith Haslem had fled as if he'd had Lucifer himself on his heels.

Okay, so Kelly received a number of mystery letters seventy years ago. And now similar mystery letters had arrived. They would be easy enough to forge, wouldn't they? He gazed at where the stream poured from the tunnel beneath the house. Hell, he should have been smarter. He should have asked the old lady if she still had the original letters addressed to her father. Also, suspicion had begun to nag. Why did such an apparently loving father suddenly run out on the family *after* the letters *stopped* arriving? Sure, the man had been stunned by the suspension from his teaching job for heaven knows what reason. But he'd been reinstated. Surely Kelly knew that he was over the worst. That life would soon return to sunshine and roses.

Unless, that is . . .

John gazed at the water tumbling from the tunnel mouth as a tingling sense of revelation ran through him. Unless, that is, Herbert Kelly had something else to hide?

The water surged with such energy, it turned to foam. John's heart beat faster as he sensed its absolute power. Tons of the stuff must be driving through there in a matter of seconds. At an animal level he experienced sheer awe at its force.

It sounded far away now, but he could still hear the scratching and scraping as if claws dragged along the underside of the tunnel. He walked down to the stone archway set into the bottom of the house. The millrace foamed from it, then tumbled into the stream before running downhill to feed the village pond.

The sights and sounds of the water exploding from the wall were hypnotic. He not only found himself gazing at the torrent, but leaning toward the stone mouth from where the water exited in such a spectacular, heart quickening display.

Oddly, in that state his mind became clear. *Dianne Kelly hasn't told you the whole story. Either she doesn't know it all. Or she held back. Herbert Kelly grew more withdrawn, more depressed when the letters stopped. Had a secret love affair ended? One of the women to leave the village had been his mistress? Or had he never been reinstated as schoolmaster? Only, he couldn't bear to lose face by admitting he'd been fired.*

His eyes were drawn to the maw of the tunnel. The stream had stopped foaming. Now it became gel-like. A deep green so clear he could see through the water to where stones lined the tunnel. It must be a turbulent water hell in there, with thousands of gallons of water fighting through too narrow a channel. It was a wonder the sheer force of it didn't rip up the floor of the house.

The stones blurred through the distorting lens of water. He leaned forward to see deeper into the tunnel, his face nearly touching the yard-thick jet of water. Spray tingled his face; draughts generated by the torrent's passing ruffled his hair, tugged his shirt. Its full-blooded roar punched deep his ears.

The water hypnotized him, drew him closer. He wondered what it would be like to slip his face inside the cool, green jet. . . .

He looked into the rock artery that ran through the depths of his home. He saw the regular slabs through the water getting smaller and smaller as they receded into the distance. The liquid turned from green to a swirling darkness that was as enticing as it was awe-inspiring.

That was the instant it came. A dark shape, sleek as a crocodile, fast as a torpedo, shot from the darkness. A distorted face locked on his, blurred by speed.

In one convulsive movement he jerked backward from it. A split second later it burst from the tunnel.

A long, dark neck, a body pitted with age, frayed serpent skin.

Water splashed into his eyes, his heart rammed against his chest.

Then, as he threw himself back, he recognized what it was. A huge old fence post, three hundred pounds of timber at the very least, had been drawn by the floodwater under the house. What he took to be a face was only the frostbitten end of it. But it exploded from the millrace tunnel with the ferocity of a bomb. If that thing had struck him in the face, it would have smashed his skull to splinters.

The post had a sting in its tail, too.

The end of it cleared the tunnel, dragging behind it a mad tangle of barbed wire, coiling into a dozen hangman's nooses. Once more he ducked as a noose of barbed wire threatened to slice off his head. The barbs on one loop raked the side of his head. As the timber post crashed back down into the water, John saw a tuft of his hair on the wire.

"Damn you," he panted as he dropped down onto the grass. "Damn you."

Only he knew he wasn't damning that piece of water-bloated timber.

Trembling, he returned to the house. He touched the side of his head. When he looked at his fingers, they were tipped with blood.

Still catching his breath, he went to the bathroom to clean the wound. It must have been that balk of timber, scraping its way through the gullet of stone, driven on by the pressure of the water, that had created the hellish noise. But how did a post of that size get into the stream? The millpond was fed only by springs from the hillside farther up. Either the fence post had lain at the bottom of the lake and the storm had loosened it, or someone had dumped the three-hundred-pound monster into the stream.

But who would do a thing like that?

Baby Bones.

The answer came automatically.

He pushed the name aside. The rational part of him could do just that. But there was an older, primeval self buried deep inside his head. One that operated by instinct. Yes, he could laugh at what the woman had told him. But that older *self* showed him a picture as he might be in the future, of him weeping pitifully against an apple tree in the orchard just as Herbert Kelly had wept all those years ago. Yes, he could ignore it if he chose. Yet the great and dark and terrible picture of him weeping heartbroken tears was there, nonetheless. A resonant omen.

Chapter Twenty-one

Dianne Kelly walked through the broken fence into the vast cemetery known as the Necropolis. She remembered when its lawns were neat, bushes well pruned. Once, brass bands played in the bandstand. Now it reeked of urine.

She would keep the pledge she'd made. She wouldn't return to Skelbrooke. Yes, her career as a general practitioner there had been long and satisfying. But without the work to divert her, she had come to dwell too much on that dreadful time seventy years ago when her father had seemed to lose his mind with despair. So, this was one last visit. She would pay her respects at the family tomb, where her mother had been interred after the leukemia had turned her blood to water.

Dianne walked on beneath the dark ceiling of trees. It was silent. No one else was in sight. The smell of rain-sodden soil hung thickly in the air. Nettles swayed and danced on either side of her. In the depths of the wood, branches groaned. Overhead, clouds nearer to green than black warned of a coming storm. Already the place oozed deep shadow as daylight faded. The sound of dripping trees became a spectral hiss.

She didn't want to be here when the rain came, but she'd decided to stand before the family crypt, say her good-byes. Then it would close a long chapter in her life. She might only have a few years left to her at most. She was determined to spend them looking over the ocean far away from the Skelbrooke. And far away from the nameless *thing* that ran through the earth beneath her feet like a stain.

Stone angels watched her pass by. She stepped over the shattered head of a cherub. A Jesus leaned over her, so distorted by erosion, his face had become a leper's face of holes and rotting eyes.

John Newton would now be struggling to accept what she had told him. She knew that. He would want to dismiss her idea of a malignant power beneath this very hill. Yet some deep buried instinct wouldn't allow him to reject it out of hand. For the sake of his family he must accept what she had told him. The demands in the letters would be trivial. All he need do was take a little away time from his civilized self and offer up those sacrifices . . . as his ancestors had done without so much as a quibble for thousands of years. They would have understood. And in a little time he would understand too. Then the letters would stop. He could go on with his life.

But don't ignore them, John Newton. Don't ignore them. Otherwise things will happen that'll eat into you for the rest of your life.

Dianne Kelly made her way into the Vale of Tears, its grim stone walls rising up until only a narrow ribbon of greenish sky remained above. Shadows were cold—and somehow seemed like liquid. Damp found its way fast through her skin into her old bones. She scanned the names above the iron doors that sealed the crypts—*BYERS, REDWAY, MORCHANT, LEBERVILLE. . . .*

The Vale of Tears had become a playground for children, just as the rest of the graveyard had. Broken glass littered the ground; it flickered with spectral lights like so many eyes staring up at her as she passed. Walls were covered with graffiti: names, curses, statements of love and hate. A child's bike had been broken against a wall. Some way ahead up the ramp to the cliff top was the Bowen grave, but she didn't have time to see it now, not that she wanted to. She would always feel a skin-crawling revulsion whenever she set eyes on it.

Passing along the narrow man-made gullies from where tree roots hung like dead tentacles, she scanned the names above the doors once more—*SNEYMAN, PARKES-LOWE, SPURLOCK.* She wasn't looking for *KELLY*, but for her mother's maiden name. A moment later she saw it. *HAYLING.* Her eyes swept down from the carved block above the lintel. The iron door of the crypt lay open.

The wretches . . . couldn't they leave anything alone?

This had happened before to other crypts. Vandals had broken in. Often they smashed open coffins out of ghoulish curiosity. Skulls wound up under some adolescent's bed as grisly trophies, no doubt. Experiencing sadness as much as anything, she entered the vault. Darkness sucked her in, like a snake swallowing an egg.

The coffins, she saw to her relief, were untouched. Stacked on shelves, they were still draped in what remained of sheets—one or two bore the skeletons of floral tributes that were more than a century old. Here she was in the presence of her ancestors. Prosperous businessmen and once elegantly beautiful women.

Perhaps, even with her eighty-four years, she might have the strength to close the crypt door to keep out the rats and vandals?

But a moment later she realized she wouldn't have to. For the door swung shut with the ringing sound of a titanic funeral bell. That was the moment, too, when she knew that she wouldn't be saying good-bye to Skelbrooke after all.

Chapter Twenty-two

"I did warn you."

"And you were right. This place is a swamp."

"How was it?"

"The show? Well, let's say my dad enjoyed it."

"Enough said. Watch out for the puddle."

Miranda held out her hand. Paul took it and helped her step over a pool of water that stretched across the cemetery path.

Well, he thought, it's here at last: Sunday evening. He'd counted the minutes away. Now Miranda was close, her Spanish eyes darting sexily around his face. Her chestnut hair fell in thick coils down her back. *God, she looks good. There's a perfume in her hair . . . the sway of her hips . . . Jesus . . .*

"How was the hotel?"

"OK." She smiled at him, amused. And when she spoke again, he realized she'd heard enough small talk. "Paul. Did you bring the you-know-whats?"

He smiled back, his heart beating faster. "Yes, I've got the you-know-whats." He patted his back pocket.

"We are talking about the same thing? Rubbers? Durex? Condoms? Sheaths?"

"Yes. Definitely here."

"Good." Grinning, she led the way along the avenue of crypts. He sensed her rising excitement as she rapped on the doors with her knuckles. "Rise and shine. It's time to come out and play!" She tapped the iron doors again before running lightly ahead of him, her hair swinging from side to side.

He laughed. "You'll get the shock of your life if they knock back from the other side."

"Who cares! Let them come to the party!"

She rapped on a door; it chimed like a bell. Now, in the depths of the shadows, she was a flitting shadow herself, as light as a ghost, her eyes flashing with an eerie light.

Overhead, trees loomed over the walls, all but sealing Paul and Miranda in and blocking what little light filtered through the heavy clouds.

At one point she stopped at a door. Ventilation holes had been set into the door at around shoulder height. They were large enough to allow you to insert your little finger, although Paul wouldn't have cared to do that. His imagination only too quickly supplied the sensation of dead teeth clamping around his finger at the other side of the door.

Miranda put her mouth to the one of the holes and called, "Great Grandma, Great Grandpa, it's time to pull on your dancing shoes and come outside." She knocked on the metal door. The sound went booming into the depths of the vault; then the echo came like the sound of hysterical shouting. She put her eye to the ventilation hole. "That's it, Great Grandma, kick off the lid and come out here. I want you to meet my boyfriend." She shot him a wild grin, her teeth flashing like neon in the gloom. "Take a look, Paul." She invited him to put his eye to the hole. "The family are dying to meet you."

Paul marveled. "My God, Miranda, what are you on?"

"Quick, Grandma's pressing her ear to the other side of the hole. Come here and whisper a few words into her head bone."

He laughed. Then his eyes strayed to the lintel above the door where a name had been carved.

BLOOM.

His eyes widened. "This really is your family grave?"

"Well, tomb or crypt would be a more accurate description. But yes, there's a vault in there full of dead Blooms. Boxes and boxes of them."

"You've been in there?"

"No. Once when I was little, I was so curious that I came up here with a flashlight. I shone it through one hole while I looked through the other hole."

"What did you see?"

"Oh, awful . . . this big, watery eye looking back at me."

Her face was so serious that he did a double take. Then she laughed and grabbed his arm. "Idiot," she said happily, squeezing him so her breast pressed against his elbow. "You swallowed that one, didn't you?"

"Hook, line, and sinker."

"Come on." She pulled his arm. "I've missed you. I want to make up for lost time, don't you?"

"I was just thinking the same thing."

They made their way through the narrow alleyways, with their iron doors that sealed the dead from the living. Darkness oozed thickly around them; dusk was early tonight. The earth beneath their feet smelled damp, with spiky scents of nettles and hemlock. When a light breeze touched the trees, unsettling them into swirls of muttering whispers, water would drip down. Fingers without skin tapped on coffin lids. At least, that was what it sounded like to Paul. Fingers tapping.

He shook his head. This cemetery had a habit of leaking into your skin to fool around with your brain. He caught up with Miranda, who danced lightly ahead of him, elfinlike, and somehow otherworldly.

He ran, leaping over the puddles. At the corner of one alley, he saw rainwater had coursed down there like a stream to leave a smooth layer of silt across the path, right up to one of the doors. Floodwater had even run into the crypt, perhaps stirring a few old bones in the process.

With care he avoided the fresh deposit of earth, choosing the opposite side of the path, where it was firmer and where he'd seen Miranda skip lightly across.

As he edged by the expanse of mud, he saw a set of footprints.

"Hey, Miranda," he called. "Look at this."

"Look at what?"

"There's some footprints . . . they lead into one of the crypts but they don't come back out again." He looked at the door, implacably shut against the outside world, sealing tight whatever decayed within. Above the door was a name plaque: *HAYLING.*

"Miranda. Someone's gone into the crypt, but they never came out."

"Likely story, Paul."

Surprised, he looked up. She was already on top of the man-made cliff looking down at him; she was smiling. "Are we going to have some time alone today or what?"

He looked down at the footprints—they were small, ladylike ones—they did appear to lead into the crypt. Only now the door was shut.

He took a step forward, his foot sinking with a *squish* into moist dirt. In the door were ventilation holes. Curiosity drew him to them. He couldn't resist just one peek through a hole into the crypt.

Breeze stirred the trees above, raising a whispering sound while water droplets fell around him, making him think of fingers tapping on wood faster and faster.

"Paul . . ." Miranda's voice was deliciously teasing. "Paul . . . orrrl . . ."

Gently he tapped a knuckle on the door. The echo came back so sharply he wondered for a moment if someone inside the crypt had given the door a loud answering knock.

He listened. A dry whispery silence. Nothing more.

From above, Miranda's voice came teasingly again, but this time with a hungry edge. "Paul. Oh, Paul? Miranda's so cold and lonely."

With a shake of his head he said under his breath, "OK, you dirty rotten vampires. Stay put, Paul Newton's got business to attend to."

With that he turned, jumped across to firmer ground, and walked to where Miranda stood waiting for him.

As he jumped his heel must have caught the tomb door, because it boomed behind with a thunderous sound.

Two

"And you say you were cut by the barbed wire? Don't move . . . there, that should do it."

"I was in the orchard; there was a loose strand of barbed wire in the hedge."

"Does it sting?"

"Not much."

"What were you doing prowling about in the bushes anyway?"

"Sam was in there, going crazy. I thought he'd got hold of a hedgehog or something."

"So, you wound up the injured hero, hmm?"

"I'll live."

Smiling, Val shook her head at the dog that sat there, his tail swishing back and forth across the carpet. He'd got the grinning look on his face. Sam knows the truth, John told himself. He knows I nearly had my head sliced off when the fence post burst out like a torpedo. He knows we had a visit from a stranger, too, with a dark tale to tell. But, thank God, dogs don't speaka da

English. Val wouldn't be the wiser. He could hide this from her.

But why hide it? Why not tell her everything as she dabs antiseptic cream on my head? But . . .

But what? She'd worry. Yes. She would. A trouble shared isn't a trouble halved. It's trouble just spread a bit further, troubling people who don't need to be troubled.

He felt sudden heart-warming burst of love for his wife. She'd certainly gone through a whole potty full of shit when he first tried to cut it as a writer. When manuscripts came bouncing back in the mail with rejection slips that were so damn depressing, he had to reach for the whiskey bottle. Times were tough five years ago. They'd had to sell the car to keep the roof over their heads. Even when his first books hit the stores, they paid so damn little. That old saying really was true: *Crime doesn't pay.*

Or at least it didn't pay *him.* He'd spend a year writing a crime book, only to be paid what amounted to nickels and dimes. Come Christmas he'd wind up working nights in a mail depot to ensure that there'd be turkey on the table and presents in the Santa sacks.

Of course he and Val would argue, then endure the stony silences that followed. This wasn't some poverty paradise where they'd laughingly boil up a supper of potatoes and cabbage. But Val had stuck with him. She'd weathered the rough times. Now life was good. *Blast His Eyes* sold like hotcakes. He didn't want to go upsetting things now. No, he'd see this plague of mystery letters through to the end himself.

Then, as Dianne Kelly said, that would be an end to it for a while. A long while. So he shouldn't try to get all logical and reason it out. He'd go with the flow. He'd meet the demands of the letters. Then he'd forget them.

Outside, clouds had drawn a dark sheet over the face of the earth. Raindrops fell on the roof. A branch, or maybe a piece of timber, passed through the millrace.

The sound of huge talons scraped furiously at the stone beneath their feet.

Three

"And this was the Necropolis station?"

"Cool, isn't it?"

Paul stood beside Miranda in the abandoned ticket office. With the windows boarded, it was a velvety dark until she lit a candle. "It's something of an after-school clubhouse," she told him. "There's candles all over the building. You might even find a few cushions, too."

"I thought it would have been wrecked." He looked around. There was no graffiti, with the exception of a few names scribbled in pencil on the wall. He noticed a timetable on the wall printed in heavy Gothic type.

"See that one?" Miranda pointed at the timetable. "19:00. The Last Train." She smiled. "For lots of people who came here, it really was the last train."

Paul looked around. Light fittings an inch thick with dust hung from the ceiling. The remains of heavy velvet drapes in still-rich, dark funereal purple covered the windows. On an upholstered bench against the wall, someone had spread a modern checked blanket.

"Are you sure we're alone?" he asked.

"Are you sure you've got the goodies?"

He looked down at her. In the candlelight she was breathtaking. Her eyes sparkled, her hair was luxurious, while the curve of her slender waist was something else. Once more he found his eyes drawn to her breasts molding a white T-shirt.

He thought about them. The freckles. The dark nipples.

God, this was a long time coming.

She kissed him on the mouth. "Paul, I asked if you've brought them with you."

Them. The delicious way she charged the word with emphasis was enough for his blood to run hot.

He slipped his hand into his back pocket, found the packet, then drew it out.

"Oh, hell, no," he breathed.

"What's wrong?"

"I've picked up Elizabeth's gum by mistake. That means she must have—"

"Paul! I don't believe it."

He showed her the packet. "I got you that time."

"You did, Paul." She smiled, then kissed him again, her lips soft, open, wonderfully warm and as wonderfully moist. "Hook, line, and stinking sinker."

When he kissed her now, he felt as if he was on a huge slide. A dizzying ride that caught hold and took him whether he wanted to ride it or not. His head swam, his heart beat faster, his breathing came in gasps, and—great God in heaven—he'd never been this hot before. He thought he could explode with such force it would tear the roof off the place.

Another force took him over now. His hands moved over her body as hers moved over his. Their kiss was seamless, powerful, passionate.

Ninety-five percent of his being strained to merge with her so completely, they fused into a single entity.

Yet, that five percent of him hung back, thinking with a quiet surprise, *Yes, Paul. It's really happening. This is going to be the first time. If only the others could see you now. With one of the most beautiful girls in the school— Miranda Bloom with the long suntanned legs, Spanish eyes, lashings of hair that swathe her breasts when she walks, hips swaying.*

Rain fell on the roof with the sound of dry lungs beginning to breathe after a century's pause. It rose and fell with a sizzling hiss. Shadows inflated from dwarf silhouettes to those of giants in the candlelight.

Miranda slid out of her clothes. Then, gripping his shoulders, she straightened her arms, pushing him back. She looked up at him, inviting him to gaze on her naked body.

Her voice dropped to a whisper. "What you see is what you get."

Gooseflesh rose her breasts into points, the tips darkening. Her perfume rose into his nose, engulfing his head. His body crackled with an excitement that was nothing less than electric.

Like dance steps he'd learned long ago, then forgotten, it came to him. He knew what to do. It was straightforward now. There was nothing complicated about the process at all.

Soon they lay together on the blanket. Her bare skin pressed against his. There was a sense of resistance. As if he'd reached a sealed door that couldn't be opened— not in a million, billion years. The sound of falling rain ran through the room and through his head like the labored breathing of a thousand souls. He'd gotten this far. The door was closed. He lifted his head dizzily: his eyes opened to see a pair of eyes looking back into his . . . distorted misty globes, burning with primeval fires.

The door isn't opening. You're shut out. You're not going in. You're not entering. You're not penetrating. His back muscles quivered, his knees trembled. Then he felt Miranda's hands circling his behind, gripping him, then pulling him down.

He moaned with pleasure the same moment this beautiful girl beneath him released a cry that sounded like pleasure, pain, bliss seamlessly joined.

"Paul . . . Paul . . ." Her breath rushed in his ear.

The impossible happened. The door opened. . . .

He found himself slipping deeply inside her; the pressure of her encircling him was enormous. Shooting stars streamed through his body. Now his hips moved like a motor as he thrust into her, eliciting gasps and tiny, kittenish cries from her lips.

There was music running through the universe. And this was its rhythm. He beat down with his body. The rhythm ran through him, an eternal life-creating rhythm.

He thought about nothing now. He was nothing but the rhythm and the beat that went on and on until he heard a panting cry rising up through his throat, growing louder and louder until he couldn't hear the rain. He'd have heard nothing if all the iron doors in the Necropolis tomb had crashed open at once.

At that moment he cried out. As the explosion tore through him—through bone, blood, and skin—leaving him gasping for air and his heart pounding like thunder.

Chapter Twenty-three

One

Monday. Noon. Clouds were breaking after a night's rain. With the rim of the cup of coffee touching his lip, John Newton dreamily gazed at the computer screen. Once more he read the opening lines to his new book, *Without Trace*.

One day you might disappear.

It might be just another everyday kind of morning. You get out of bed, you dress, you eat toast, and drink some coffee. Then you leave the house.

And you never return. As simple as that. You vanish. You're history. No body is found. No clues. No nothing. Gone.

It had been there under his very nose all along. Only he'd not known it—at least not on a conscious level—but he'd actually begun writing the book he was born to write. *Without Trace* wasn't meant to be a collection of individual cases about Mrs. Y disappearing over the side of a car ferry, or Mr. Z going out to buy a packet of cigarettes never to be seen again. Those cases had been covered. Good Lord, he had them in books right there on the bookshelf. No. What hadn't been recorded at all were the Skelbrooke disappearances. Of course, he'd play down the supernatural elements. He could leave that side of it to the reader's discretion in a "Now make up your own mind what really happened" chapter at the end. But the naked truth was that certain people in the village seventy years ago did vanish without trace. His blood tingled in his veins. This was it. He felt like a gold prospector who'd just seen that yellow glint in the dirt. He could furnish the book with photographs of the missing Mr. Kelly and his daughter. He could track down police records, sift through newspaper archives, maybe even find passenger lists of Liverpool-Canada crossings seventy years ago.

What would really hit the jackpot was to track down the descendants of Herbert Kelly in Canada. What's more, Mary Kelly might still be alive, even if she was only just the right side of eighty.

"The game's afoot, Watson," he murmured, gazing at the screen. "The game is most definitely afoot."

Last night he'd dreamt he'd been in the old engine room of the Water Mill. For some reason he'd dreamt he'd wept over the rusted mechanism. It hadn't worked for a century, but he was desperate to get the thing back in use. He longed to see the great cogs go around as the waterwheel turned the axle. Then the massive millstones would grind again. If he could do that, everything would be all right.

But the damn lever wouldn't budge. Everything was frozen. Everything was rusted. That heap of junk was locked solid. He wept like a brokenhearted child.

Then, in the dream, Herbert Kelly had walked into the room. John had recognized the schoolteacher instantly from Dianne Kelly's description. Tall, thin, bearded; a white Panama hat that was so bright, it dazzled John and he had to close his eyes against the glare.

"I can make it work, John," Kelly had told him. "I can make it all work like clockwork."

John tried to watch him work the controls. As far as John knew, there was only one lever that set the monster machine in motion, yet Herbert Kelly made numerous delicate adjustments to controls John couldn't see because the hat was so dazzling.

Then the cogs started to turn, the axles spun, the millstones grated round and round like old gramophone records.

Kelly, in his shining hat, walked across to him, then pinched John's stomach so hard that he cried out.

Kelly whispered in his ear, "And if you work it all wrong, Newton, I'll make you cry again."

John Newton had woken to find himself lying facedown with his hand under his stomach. It felt like rock pressing into his flesh. But as he groaned himself fully awake, that was when he knew what *Without Trace* would be about.

The dream about Kelly—weird and incomprehensible as it was—triggered the necessary inspiration . . . or maybe the ghost of the old schoolteacher had really come padding upstairs to whisper in John's ear as he slept. Anyway, he, John Newton, had the makings of a book.

"OK, Tommy, it's over to you."

With a click of a button he e-mailed his agent the chapter he'd revised that morning, along with a brand-new outline that set out the skeleton of the book—an exclusive investigation into real-life disappearances.

Now he could play detective again. He'd hunt down clues. From them he'd piece together a detailed description of what happened seventy years ago in this village and in this very house. And today he had the house to himself. Val had left early for work; Paul and Lizzie were at school. He looked around his room. Maybe Kelly had used this as *his* study all those years ago. There was even an ancient cast-iron peg behind the door where he might have hung his white Panama hat. So, where to start?

Two

The neon strip lit the attic brilliantly. There were no funky Gothic cobwebs and no mannequins clothed in dust. Instead there were neatly painted ceilings, carpeted boards, varnished cupboards. The only glitch in the sterility, a cluster of packing cases left over from when the Newtons had moved in. Mainly they were Paul's childhood toys, which he'd never bother to unpack anyway.

John crawled into the eaves of the roof, but there was nothing there, apart from a couple of ancient computer games on cassette, which made them look positively Cretaceous. After the attic, he worked his way downstairs floor by floor. Again, he told himself that the old lady yesterday hadn't revealed everything. He had a gut feeling that Herbert Kelly had hidden a number of facts from his family. Maybe he'd kept secret some of the letters he'd received? If he had, he would have needed to hide them. And letters were small enough to be slipped under skirting boards or in cracks behind cupboards.

John mentally stepped into Herbert Kelly's shoes. Now, he asked himself, if I had something to hide, where would I hide it? It had to be in the house. He wouldn't risk burying letters in a jar in the garden, say, because there'd be a chance damp would find its way in to ruin them. But would Kelly preserve the letters? Maybe he'd burnt them?

No. That didn't ring true. Schoolmaster Kelly was a meticulous man. He'd keep the letters in good condition.

John went through room after a room. Paul's was a mess. What looked like a collection of yogurt cartons (still smeared with the stuff) stood on the windowsill.

The cupboards and closet in Paul's room were all modern. There was little point looking there.

Elizabeth's room was far tidier. She'd even laid out her pajamas on the bed with a paper drawing of her own head pushed into the neck of the pajama top, so at first glance it seemed she still lay on the bed—or at least a rolled-flat version of her. Here, the cupboards set into the wall were probably as old as the house. A quick inspection told him that unless he took a hammer to them, there was no obvious place where the letters could be hidden. The same state of affairs presented itself in every room of the house. Where possible, he tugged aside furniture and lifted carpets. The boards were nailed down. He'd need a crowbar to lever them up.

In the living room he stood in the center of the floor and said out loud, "Mr. Kelly. Tell me where you put the letters . . . please!" His voice sounded small.

There was no answer. At that moment, however, the dog started to bark. John looked out of the window in the direction of the meadow. There, by the back gate, stood a figure.

Tall. Thin. It wore a brilliant white hat.

John started, and his blood thundered in his ears.

"Idiot, John Newton," he breathed. "Great prize idiot." As he watched the figure, the hat detached itself from the head to fly away on a large pair of wings. It had been a gull on the gatepost. His imagination had completed the trick.

No, he told himself. Herbert Kelly's too far away from the Water Mill to help you now. Not only many thousands of miles away; more significantly, he was six feet down in God's own earth.

The ghostly illusion created by the post and gull did give him pause for thought. This harem-scarem escapade of him playing the detective was, he realized, his attempt to blunt the deep unease he felt about the whole situation. The fact was, he was receiving bizarre letters that demanded chocolate, beer, or whatever, and that were rounded off with a threat if he did not comply. Even if he mentally got the proverbial dust pan and brush and swept up all the supernatural elements and dumped them in the trash, that still left the mysterious appearance of the letters, coupled with the suspicion that he and his family were being spied upon.

As a writer he controlled the information at his disposal. That control extended to how he wrote his books; what slant he put on the story; how and when he chose to mystify the reader; and when he supplied solutions to the crime. By taking the Skelbrooke disappearances as the subject of his next book, he didn't have to be a detective to figure out he was aiming to control what was happening around him. In truth, however, he'd be deluding himself if he thought he could control events.

No. The letter writer was in control—whether it was some bony-kneed phantom or a human being with a grudge. Val could take the dog out tonight, find a letter on the patio, then when she bent down to pick it up, an intruder might lunge out. . . .

He killed the conclusion to the scenario.

No, he told himself. . . . we're not out of the dark woods yet. . . .

Three

"Look, Dad. Someone's left a ball on that grave." Elizabeth skipped forward. "And another . . . and another, *and another!*" She laughed in amazement. "There's loads. Can I take one home with me?"

"Best not."

"Aw, go on. Just one."

"No, Lizzie, they don't belong to us. Besides—"

"Aw, Dad."

"We don't know where they've been."

"We do, they've been in the graveyard, haven't they?"

"And what do you think your mother would say if we came back with a big pile of balls we'd found in a graveyard? I'd wind up locked in the toolshed for a week."

"Just one. *Please.*"

"No, not on your Nellie. Are you going to eat that chocolate before it melts or what?"

"I'll give a piece to Sam . . . if I can find him." She looked around the overgrown cemetery. "Did you see where he went, Dad?"

"He's probably hunting mice."

"He should have been a cat, not a dog. Where do you think they all came from, Dad?"

"The balls . . ." He shrugged. "Someone might have stolen them, then dumped them here."

"They're all different sizes. Look, there's one with Homer's face."

"Don't touch it, Elizabeth."

"I just wanted to—"

"*Don't.*" Then gently he added, "It's not too savory up here."

"How come?"

"There aren't any toilets nearby. Someone might have—"

"Whizzed on the balls? *Gross!*" Deterred from looking at the balls any closer, she went in search of the dog.

"Don't wander too far," he warned. "It's like a jungle around here."

"Any tigers?" Her eyes were serious, but he knew she was kidding.

"No tigers. But there's a cliff down that way; it's a sheer drop, so be careful."

"Yes, Dad."

"And don't pick up anything off the floor."

"*Dad. I am nine years old—not four!*"

Shaking her head, she walked away through the long grass.

John hadn't intended to bring Elizabeth, but she'd insisted. She'd heard about the Necropolis from the kids at school. Now she wanted to see it for herself.

Which made things difficult for John. Another letter had arrived during the night of Tuesday/Wednesday. Now, on the evening of Wednesday, he was here to deliver what the letter demanded.

Just a red ball—a stupid red ball. No size or type of ball was stipulated, only that it should be a red one. Yes, it was so trivial as to border on the absurd, but once more he felt his veins flush with ice. Who had come silently as a ghost in the middle of the night to leave the letter?

Baby Bones? That local boogeyman that had supposedly haunted the neighborhood for the last ten thousand years?

No, he promised himself not to think about that. He'd meet the demands in the letter, then forget it. Clearly, his neighbors had done likewise. As Elizabeth had pointed out, there were dozens of red balls clustered around the tomb of Jess Bowen. The weeping-boy statue gazed down on them.

Counting trophies for your master? Suddenly he had a savage need to kick the head right off the shoulders of the idiot statue. This surrendering to the demands of the letters made him feel so weak and useless. It was like being at school again when a bully takes your candy away and you can't do squat about it, except feel hurt and humiliation.

"Elizabeth!" He spoke more sharply than he intended.

"What?" Her surprised face appeared over the long grass. From here, the scab on her chin had all the look of a big black spider clinging to her skin.

He smiled to show he wasn't angry with her. "I just wondered where you were, that's all."

"I found Sam. But I don't think he wants to stay here. He won't walk any farther."

"Don't worry. We'll be going in a minute."

"What did we come up here for anyway, Dad?" Obviously the big old cemetery held no allure for her.

"I needed to do some research for my new book."

"About graves?"

"A little."

"Is it going to be a frightening book?"

"I hope not . . . more suspenseful."

She stroked the dog's head. He sat with his ears flat to his head, looking unhappy.

"How long will you be now, Dad?"

"Not long. I'm just going to make a few notes." As he slipped his holdall from his shoulder, he turned his back on Elizabeth.

He'd intended to walk up here alone this evening, leave the red ball on the grave, then go. Elizabeth's insistence that she tag along made it a little more difficult. But he'd agreed that Elizabeth could come along for the walk. Now, with his daughter busy stroking the dog, she wouldn't notice what he did next.

He opened the holdall, pulled out a red ball, and wedged it between the shin of the statue and the slab of the Bowen tomb. *There. Done. I've paid my dues . . .*

He fastened the bag. "All done, Lizze. Ready for home?"

The dog responded first. In a dark blur he raced down the hill. If anything, the animal appeared to be displaying a real burning need to get out of the place.

They walked along the paths between swaths of shoulder-high weeds that in turn were overhung by clumps of yew, alder, and birch. John noticed Elizabeth's thoughtful expression as she looked at the headstones.

She slipped her hand into his.

"What's it like to be dead?"

"I don't know, Elizabeth."

"Do you think it's a nice feeling?"

"It's probably like being asleep."

She allowed her fingers to run over the smooth granite slab of a whole family who'd died of cholera a century ago.

"Do you think people know when they're dead?"

"I can't say, Lizzie."

"It won't hurt, though. Those people in there"—she nodded at the graves—"won't feel cold, and it won't be uncomfortable to lie in a coffin?"

He always felt uneasy when she talked about death. "I hope Sam hasn't run too far," he said, aiming to change the subject.

"At least people won't bug you when you're dead, will they?"

"I guess not." He gave her hand a gentle squeeze.

A little while later, they reached the break in the cemetery fence. Sam was there, waiting for them. His tail wagged, swishing the grass as they walked up.

After her morbid meditation, Elizabeth suddenly seemed brighter. "Can I hold the leash, Dad?"

"Why not. Careful at the main road, though."

John clicked the leash onto the collar and handed Elizabeth the loop to hold.

She walked a little ahead of him. The gravestones stared down at her like so many dark, fathomless eyes. And suddenly, to John, she seemed so fragile in a world crowded with so much danger.

Chapter Twenty-four

One

"Baby Bones . . ."

"Don't start all that again, Dad. It's not nice. Here, hold my hand as you get in." Under his breath, Robert Gregory whispered, "We wouldn't want you to slip, would we now?"

His wife called from the bedroom, "Are you all right in there, Robert?"

"Fine, Cynthia."

"You don't need any help?"

"No, dear. We can manage perfectly well." He maintained the cheerful boom for her benefit. "We're doing all right, aren't we, Dad?"

"Baby Bones." The old man's voice was whispery. "Has Dianne Kelly told him about Baby Bones?"

"I'm sure she did, Dad."

Cynthia tapped on the door. It was so fainthearted as to be barely audible over the slop of water in the bathtub. "Robert? Do you know where the towels are?"

"Got them right here, dear, they're warming nicely over the hot rail." The towel lay on the floor where he'd kicked it under the toilet bowl. He sat the old man down hard into the bathtub, the bones in his ancient butt clicking loudly against the enamel as if there was no flesh covering them. But that was about the size of it anyway, Robert thought sourly; the old man's buttocks looked like a pair of Savoy cabbage leaves; you couldn't find anything more wrinkled if you tried.

"Harry, there's a briefcase in—"

"I'm not Harry, Dad. I'm Robert."

"Harry, there's a briefcase in the workshop. At the back of the cupboard. Mr. Kelly gave it me the night he left. Make sure John Newton gets it up at the Water Mill. There are important papers in there. They'll help John Newton to—*ah!*"

Robert poured a jug full of cold water over Stan's head, making him gasp.

That shut you up, you old snatch.

Cynthia must have been hovering outside the bathroom door. Robert heard her voice again with that frightened trembling quality he hated so much. "Robert. Dad likes to have his hair dried straight after it's washed. Would you—"

"*Cynthia.*" With an effort he softened his voice. "Cynthia, why don't you go downstairs and put your feet up. I can manage."

Yes, I can manage to bathe the old wretch. I've been doing it God knows how many months now. I've soaped that old cabbage leaf skin of his, washed his hair until it looked like a bunch of rats' tails, dried it, combed it, powdered the old man's ass. And I'm sick of it.

"All right, Robert," came Cynthia's watery voice. "I'll go downstairs, then."

"Yes, you do that. I'll make us all a coffee when I come down."

"B-b-berr . . . ber . . ."

Robert didn't know if the old man was trying to speak or just blowing water from his lips.

"Soon have you done and dusted," he boomed at Stan. Then he turned on both bath faucets. The water came out in fat glistening jets, swirling round the old man's legs, rising up along the tub sides, covering the old man's genitals. The penis was large and thick, not at all shriveled as he would have expected. But it was unusually white and looked more like a stick of celery lying there in the bath.

Robert gazed at the rising water. The shock of the cold dousing had shut Stan up nicely. No more babble about Baby Bones or Harry, or whatever else obsessed that senile brain.

The old man's ear must have been sore still from the lightning strike. A blister swelled from the skin like a black grape.

Robert shook his head. What had happened to *his* luck? Here he was living with his rich father-in-law, waiting for the bastard to die. The man gets an ear full of electricity when lightning strikes the telephone lines, but all he suffers is a single blister on his ear. God Almighty. The old bastard's indestructible.

A rage that was bitter and dark swept through Robert Gregory, searing him from head to toe. Where was the justice? What had happened to his—Robert Gregory's—luck? Had he broken a mirror, or shot a freaking albatross or something?

Eyes glazing, he watched water rush into the tub, climbing up the sides, swirling round Stan's chicken-bone chest. A few minutes ago Robert had been running his eyes over the man's bankbooks. There was the money. Tens of thousands. Like rows of bloody telephone numbers. But Robert Gregory couldn't touch a penny of it. Then there were the great bundles of title deeds to Price's dozens of properties. The wily old beggar had not just run a chain of TV rental stores; he'd bought the land on which they stood, and the buildings that housed the stores might be as much as four or five stories high. The upper floors he'd let as offices. Although the Ezy-View TV business had gone, the money river still flowed. Only Stan Price was too addled to spend it. And the accountant Stan had hired years ago merely allowed a niggardly amount through to cover the running of the house, food, and taxes.

Dear God . . . again that dark wave of bitterness ran through Robert. The money was so close he could almost taste it. . . .

Now all that Stan needed to do was something that thousands of men and women did the world over every day.

DIE.

It couldn't be simpler for the old man, could it? He didn't need what was left of his brains to figure out how to expire. All he need do was breathe his last breath. For his blood to curdle in his heart. Then all that lovely, lovely liquid money would come gushing Robert's way. Dear Lord. The things he could do . . .

Robert gazed down at the water bubbling over the old man's chest.

The money . . . that was what Robert wanted. He could do so much. So many wonderful things. Dear God . . . in Leeds he'd seen a beautiful little prostitute doing her rounds in black leather trousers; they'd been so tight she—

"Bath's full. Bath's full."

The words were a slap in his face. In a white-hot fury he glared down at the man. "What's wrong with you?" he snapped. "I don't give you enough food to keep a rat alive, and still you keep spouting your fucking gibberish." He mimicked a whiny voice. "Baby Bones, Harry, Mr. Kelly, letters, scary letters . . . *shit, you can't be indestructible! You can't!*"

With that, he put both hands on Stan's shoulders and pushed him down hard. The man's rump skittered along the bath; his head went under with hardly a splash.

From underwater the man's blue eyes gazed up into Robert's. They were so shot full of surprise that Robert wanted to laugh viciously at them. Bubbles streamed from the ancient mouth.

Robert bore down on the man. The only sound, the water streaming from the faucets into the bath.

Robert Gregory pictured the smiling face of the pretty little prostitute. Oh, he knew she'd be so hot, so charged with sex—not like that rag-doll wife of his. The money would be—

"Robert. I've brought a clean pair of pajamas."

Robert's eyes snapped into focus. He saw the old man's face beneath the water. Blue eyes gazed limply up into his.

Robert snapped his head around. With her father naked, Cynthia wouldn't come into the bathroom. Even so, she held her arm through the door, dangling the pajamas.

Dear God! This wasn't the way!

Robert thrust his hands down under the old man's shoulders and pulled him up clear of the water. The head rolled. Stan coughed out the water, then breathed deeply.

No, he couldn't drown the old man . . . the police would realize that he hadn't died of natural causes. No, there had to be another way. Subtle, think subtle, he told himself as he watched Stan wipe his face with those liver-spotted claws of his.

Hell's teeth, the old man had the lungs and heart of a Marine. It would need a bullet to finish him.

Outside the door, Cynthia sounded agitated, as if she guessed all wasn't well in the bathroom. "Robert. Is Dad all right? Why's he making that noise?"

Still she didn't come into the bathroom. Robert found himself talking to the hand that held the pajamas. "Dad's got some shampoo in his eye. We're taking care of it now." Robert sounded as hearty as ever. God, when it came to keeping up a pretense, he was good. "We'll soon have you right as rain, won't we, Dad?"

Stan Price looked up. For a second there was just a

hint of reproach in his eyes. But the man had the memory retention of a goldfish.

Confusion seeped back into his expression. He ran a hand through rat-tails of hair. "I'm hungry," he cried plaintively. "Is it supper time?"

Two

Heaven is an abandoned railway station in a cemetery. The thought ran through Paul Newton's head as he held Miranda. This was the third visit to the old building. A dozen candles burned, sending wisps of smoke to the ceiling; a hundred shadows danced on the walls.

How many times had he made love to her now? Seven? Eight?

Eight, it must be eight. Condom factories would be forced to work overtime at this rate. Smiling, he nuzzled her fragrant hair. They should really put on their clothes again. There was a chance someone might slip into the ticket hall through the window with the loose board, just as Paul and Miranda had. And just like them, it might be another teenage couple looking for a piece of private heaven.

But it was so good lying here beside her on the upholstered bench. Her naked body was a whole landscape of curves, crests, hill, valleys. A place for his stroking fingers to explore, leave for new territories, then return a few moments later.

"Mmm . . . that feels good," she breathed. "Are you sure you haven't done this before?" She kissed his chest.

"What makes you say that?" He smiled.

"Paul, don't kid me. You were a virgin until Sunday evening, weren't you?"

"Me? No way."

Her voice continued in a gentle sleepy purr. "Miranda knows . . . Miranda knows. But I think you're well up the learning curve now."

"Practice makes perfect."

"Is there one left in that packet?"

He smiled. "Well, I do believe there is."

"Good," she said firmly, then held him tight. "Use it."

Chapter Twenty-five

Wednesday evening. At the same time as Paul lay with Miranda in the Necropolis station, and while old Stan Price coughed bathwater from his throat, John Newton sat gazing down through the glass into the millrace. The floodwaters were falling, but the bottom of the chamber still churned white, as if beasts writhed beneath the surface. If he could have lifted the observation window like a trapdoor, no doubt he'd have been struck by spray, along with an updraft of icy air and the roar of water.

Despite the fact that he sat there without moving a muscle, his thoughts mirrored the turbulent waters below. The result of searching the house was a great fat zero. This time he'd found no convenient tin trunk full of the letters Kelly received seventy years ago. Maybe he'd burned them. Maybe he'd dumped the whole lot over the ship's rail as it chugged across the great, wide Atlantic to Canada. John wouldn't have blamed the man.

Again he wrestled with his own dilemma.

So, he told himself, you could jump two ways with this. You could go with the scenario that there's some freak writing the letters, leaving them in the garden at night, then no doubt exulting in the perverse thrill of watching all those poor saps (including one John Newton) trekking shamefaced up to the Bowen grave with gifts of chocolate, beer, and red balls.

But then he could jump in the other direction. The direction pointed out by old Miss Kelly. That all this was the product of some monstrosity that had haunted these hills and valleys long before the Romans had even driven their highway through the place two thousand years ago.

He strained to accept the first scenario: the control freak forging letters. Then said freak laughing himself into a sweat while he watched all those jerked-around fools rushing to pour beer over the grave. But John's instincts were pushing him to the second scenario. He wished to hell they weren't. It bordered on madness. Yet deep inside, a primeval sliver of his brain insisted, "Yes. What the old woman told you is true." It was the same cluster of brain cells that prompted you to throw spilt salt over your left shoulder, or not to walk under a ladder, or that gave you that momentary twinge of unease when you realized you had to take a flight on Friday the thirteenth.

Yes, of course, it's a heap of crappola; it's all solid sterling-silver bollocks . . . or so you tell yourself. But doesn't a knot of unease appear in your stomach when that magazine horoscope catches your eye? The one that warns you a spell of bad luck is coming your way? He remembered as a child when he lived at Number 11 Hadrian Close. He'd always been amused by the fact that the house numbers skipped from 11 to 15. Hey, these were rational people in Hadrian Close—schoolteachers, lawyers, hardheaded salespeople. But were any of them happy to move into a house with 13 on the door?

Were they? Hell.

Superstition isn't a one-off peculiarity of Hadrian Close either. When he became a paperboy he never did find a house numbered 13 on his rounds. The house after number 11 either was 11A, or nimbly skipped ahead to 15.

He stared dreamily through the glass into tumbling waters now flecked green with pond slime carried down from the lake. All the time the gluttonous throat of the tunnel gorged on the water, sucking it down into the roaring darkness beneath the house. Driftwood raked stonework like fleshless fingers. It hammered against archways. The sound worked its way into his brain. He clenched his fists and shut his eyes because at that moment it seemed as if it would continue for an eternity.

Chapter Twenty-six

One

The June sun returned. That Thursday morning the heat hit the moist ground, raising a mist that buried Skelbrooke as deep as the rooftops.

Robert Gregory wiped the sweat from his forehead with a hunk of kitchen roll. His hands shook; his stomach twisted as though a hundred little hands plaited the muscles.

Big day . . . it's a big day, Robert. A big day . . . He tried to stop the same thought shooting round and round his head. He couldn't. It was all he could do to stop saying it out loud. *It's a big day, a big, big day. They don't come any bigger. It's a—*

"Robert, have you seen Dad?" Cynthia walked into the kitchen with an armful of washing.

"Upstairs in his room as far as I know, dear." Robert sweated hard. He leaned forward, resting his hands on the worktop, making a show of staring out the window, so she wouldn't notice the way balls of perspiration stood out on his forehead. "Will you take a look at that mist? I haven't seen anything as bad as that in years."

She looked. "Good heavens. You can't even see as far as the gate." With a sigh, she began to push laundry into the washing machine. "I hope it clears soon. I want to get this onto the line." Pausing, she frowned. "Are you sure Dad's still in his room? I thought I heard him coming downstairs about half an hour ago."

"Positive, dear. He was listening to his radio."

"I can't hear anything. I best check."

"No, dear. I'll do that." The muscle knots had reached into his throat. "I'll check in a minute. I was going to make some coffee first."

"Thank you, love. I'll make a start on the ironing."

Robert Gregory stood with his hands bunched into fists on the worktop. He stared out into the mist that swirled like a lake of milk around the house, hiding the gates in the garden wall.

A gleeful horror blazed inside him. Cynthia could have stood beside him, stared into the mist—stared until her eyes bulged—but she wouldn't have seen that the gate was open.

Just a few minutes ago Stan Price had shuffled downstairs wearing a business suit over his pajamas. Robert had opened the kitchen door, then gone down through the mist to the gate and unlocked it. When he'd returned to the house, the old man was walking out of the outhouse with that dotty old straw hat on his head. For some reason, he also clutched a briefcase to his chest like it was a sickly child. The briefcase had seen better days. The leather sides were cracked and wormy-looking. Cobwebs clung to it in dusty white clots.

"I'm going to the office," he'd told Robert. "There's a consignment of color televisions due today . . . you know, this time next year there will be a color television in every house." He adjusted the straw hat. "I'll be back around five."

Robert shot a sweaty look at the house. Cynthia wasn't in sight.

"OK, Dad," he whispered. "I'd look sharp if I were you. You're running late."

"Oh, mustn't be late. It would set a bad example. Cheerio."

With that, the man had hobbled away; the business suit pants not quite meeting the jacket exposed a backside of striped pajama.

Robert had stood, not daring to breathe in case Cynthia appeared. If she saw her father it would ruin everything. But no. Stan moved off down the garden to be swallowed whole by the mist.

Now, twenty minutes after Stan's departure, Robert still looked out the window. His eyes burned into the mist. Even though he couldn't see more than thirty paces, his mind's eye flew like a missile through the fog.

He pictured the man, shuffling in that rapid little step of his, straw hat on his head, filthy briefcase clutched in both hands. Stan Price was making for the Ezy-View office in Leeds. An office that hadn't existed for the last ten years.

But that didn't matter to Robert Gregory. His heart hammered. He was frightened, elated, excited, and sickened all at the same time. Because it took no effort on his part to imagine the old man walking through the misty streets. He'd be heading for the long-unused railway station up by the Necropolis.

It was dangerous enough for a feeble old man up there. Even more dangerous was the main road he must cross. Through the thick mist trucks, buses, cars, motorbikes, and vans would come ripping through the countryside. Of course, they always drove too fast. Visibility was poor. A doddering oldster would be putting his life in his hands crossing a road like that.

Especially one as confused as Stan Price.

Robert Gregory's luck was changing. He could feel it. The blood roared through his head. *It's a big day . . . it's a very big day. . . .*

Darkness Demands

Two

Tom phoned early. John Newton heard sheer triumph in the voice. "John . . . John? I haven't woken you, have I?"

"Writers have to get up early, too, Tom. To get kids off to school and partners to their day jobs."

"And here I was, thinking all you authors lay around in bed all day, downing absinthe and sucking on cigarette holders."

His agent's laughter rattled the earpiece so powerfully, John had to jerk the phone from his head.

"Now listen, John." Tom spoke as if it had been John laughing like a loon. Not the other way around. "I had lunch with the Goldhall editor. I presented him with *Without Trace*. Of course he told me that the market is flooded with real-life crime stories. That he'd have trouble convincing the reps, that bookstores would say it's all old hat, dee-dee-dah-dee-dah. . . ." Tom's idiosyncratic way of saying *etc.* "But I knew he was simply trying to talk down the advance. So I said to him, 'Jim, we've both been in this game long enough to know that you're simply serving up bullshit. Now, here's a napkin. You write down the advance you're prepared to pay. I'll laugh in your face. Then I'll cross it out and write something a little more realistic. I told him: John Newton is big now. I'm closing overseas deals on *Blast His Eyes* every other day."

This was a typical Tom telephone conversation. The man loved to reenact business deals down to every detail. John could even picture Tom walking around his office, the phone scrunched between his shoulder and the side of his neck so he could gesture with both hands. But then Tom was good. He didn't merely pitch book offers at publishers, he gave them a performance. Once, so the legend went, he'd pulled a tablecloth from a table in a restaurant, wrapped it around himself toga-style, then acted out a scene from a movie script he was selling. The producer had sat there in awe, then simply pulled out a checkbook and bought the script there and then.

Tom now replayed the meeting with Goldhall's editor. "Of course he wrote down a piffling amount on the napkin, John. I crossed it out. I wrote in another figure. He laughed and crossed it out. Then I said, 'Look, Jim, it's ten to three. I've another appointment in ten minutes with the biggest publisher in London. They're going to make an offer on *Without Trace*. So it's over to you, Jim. Either you write a sensible figure on that napkin and make me cancel the appointment, or I'll pay for the meal now and we won't waste any more of our time."

At last John broke in. "Tom, you're making me sweat now. This suspense is getting a little intense."

Tom's laugh rattled the earpiece again. "Well, he did write a figure down on the napkin."

"And?"

"And then I picked up my mobile and canceled my next appointment."

After closing the conversation with Tom, John went out onto the lawn for a breath of fresh air. He still carried the cordless phone, holding it tight in one hand like it was a lucky charm.

He breathed in the morning air. Here the ground was clear of mist, but down in the village it lingered to form a milky lake. House roofs poked through like strange-looking boats in a fairy tale. Up on the hill, mist rolled amongst the trees in the Necropolis. It looked like a land outside time.

He rubbed his face. What Tom had told him continued to roll around his head. He even wondered if he should put the back of his hand between his teeth, then give a good hard bite to make sure he wasn't dreaming. With a deep breath he thumbed the cordless phone's keypad.

He stood listening to the ringing tone as he gazed over Skelbrooke. "Hello, Val. Tom's just telephoned. Goldhall have made an offer on the new book. Wait a minute, Val, you're not driving are you? No? Good." He felt a smile reach his face. "They're offering an advance of one hundred thousand." He grinned at Val's scream of disbelief. "At this rate you're going to be sick of champagne."

It's all too good to be true. The thought sneaked into his head. As quickly he shut it out again. No, this was good news. Maybe even that old Baby Bones had something to do with it? You made your sacrificial offering, then you got something good in return. His grin widened. Maybe he should tip a whole barrel full of beer over the Bowen grave. Then, who knows? A million-dollar movie deal?

He was grinning like an idiot now. So what if he did look smug as hell. He felt pleased with himself. No, scratch that—he felt nothing less than euphoric. That little village down there had just handed him one wonderful peach of a story. And now he'd write a best-selling book. *So bite me!*

He was on the point of returning to the house to begin work on the book when he saw a figure coming through the mist. It wore a funny hat, moved in a funny way, and, oh, my, it wore funny clothes.

"Good God," John told himself, half amused, half surprised. "It's old Mr. Price."

Three

The first time John Newton had seen Stan Price walk up the lane, the old man had hurried by as if he'd had the hounds of hell on his trail. This time, however, the old man turned into the driveway of the Water Mill. In his arms, held tightly as if it were a baby, was a leather case. John went to meet him.

The old man looked in distress. Sweat ran down his neck, staining the pajama jacket beneath the business suit. On one foot he wore a bathroom slipper; the other was bare. Probably one of the slippers had fallen off in his hurry to get here. John noticed the end of the old man's bare big toe was bloodied where he must have stubbed it. The straw hat sat on his head at what would have been a laughable angle if the old man hadn't made such a pitiful sight.

John Newton's euphoria vanished.

He quickly walked toward Stan Price, taking the man's elbow as he moved unsteadily toward the house, his eyes burning on the front door as if it was the finishing line at the end of a grueling marathon.

"Mr. Kelly..." The voice came as a dry whisper. "Mr. Kelly. I've brought your bag...I kept it safe all these years...."

"Mr. Price," John said, steadying the man as his balance gave out. "Mr. Price...Stan. Careful, you'll fall if you don't slow down."

The man at last noticed John. He looked up at him from beneath the brim of the cockeyed hat. "Mr. Kelly. I'm sorry it took so long to get here."

"Stan," John said gently. "I'm not Herbert Kelly."

"I need to see Mr. Kelly. It's important." Stan's blue eyes fixed on John's. They were the very picture of fright. "Will you fetch Mr. Kelly, please?" Then he called out toward the house, *"Mr. Kelly? Mr. Kelly! It's Stan Price. I've brought the bag!"*

The effort of shouting toppled the old man. John caught him as he fell forward, then helped him toward a bench on the lawn. "Sit down, Mr. Price...here, that's it. I'll hold onto the bag for you."

"No." The man sat, but wouldn't relinquish the bag.

John watched the old boy sit there for a moment. His head was hanging down until his chin touched his chest. The walk up here to the Water Mill had squeezed out every drop of stamina.

"I'll get you a glass of water, Mr. Price...no, please, sit here and get your breath back."

John returned a moment later with iced water. Stan drank deeply, so deeply it overflowed the rim of the glass at the sides to run down his chin.

"It's OK, Stan. Take your time." John crouched down

on the lawn beside him. "Don't rush. You're OK. Rest here a minute, then I'll run you back home in the car."

"*No! He's trying to kill me!*"

"Sorry? I thought you said—"

"Yes, you heard right, John."

John smiled. "You remember my name?"

Stan Price turned his head to look directly at John. "Yes . . . I do, don't I?" For a moment he looked pleased with himself and smiled. Then confusion darkened his face again. "But I won't find Mr. Kelly here, will I?"

John shook his head. "Sorry. Mr. Kelly hasn't lived here for seventy years."

"Seventy?"

John watched a war taking place behind the man's eyes. Confusion, allied with senile dementia, battled with lucidity. It didn't take a medical genius to know which force must ultimately win. The man's eyes cleared, briefly sharpening to how they must have appeared when he was a younger man; then moments later they'd become misted, unfocused, flicking around at his surroundings. What he saw of the world either baffled or frightened him.

Stan Price stared at the front door. "It's white now. It was brown. Harry would always run ahead of me so he could pull the handle. He loved to ring the doorbell. He used to . . ." Confusion flooded the eyes again. He looked down at the briefcase. "Mr. Kelly gave Harry one of these as well. 'Look after them, boys,' he told us that day he went. 'Look after them, boys. And don't tell a soul you've got them. They might be needed one day.' Then he walked through that door. He started to wave at the two of us; then he turned away and he was touching his eyes like this." Stan rubbed his thumb against his eye. "John," he said hushed. "Mr. Kelly was crying. Can you imagine that? Mr. Kelly was crying."

John knew he should get Stan into the car, then back home as quickly as possible. But the man seemed to be in one of his all-too-rare phases of mental clarity.

John said, "Stan. You told me that someone was trying to kill you."

The man's eyes widened. "Did I?"

John nodded.

"Who's trying to kill me?"

"I don't know, Stan, you didn't say."

Stan shook his head. "Oh . . . I get so forgetful . . . these days I can't tell if I'm dreaming or awake, Mr. Kelly."

John gave a sympathetic smile. This wasn't going to be easy. "Do you remember who I am, Stan?"

"Oh, yes . . . you're—you're . . ."

"John."

"Yes, yes. John Newton. Writer. Uhm, letters . . . you asked me about letters. Yes, I remember now. I remember!" The smile lit up his entire face. "You came to my house, Mr. Newton. You sat beside me in the garden. You met my daughter, Cynthia. Yes, yes."

"Stan." He smiled warmly. "Call me John."

"John. Yes. Yes. Will do, John." Words bubbled from the man's mouth as he became suddenly animated. "Ah, the old Water Mill. Harry and me swam in the lake. Of course the door was brown then, not white. You pulled a cord to ring the bell inside. It wasn't electric, of course, you—"

"Stan. Did you come up here to see me?" John touched his own chest. "John Newton?"

"Yes, of course. But I had to tell my son-in-law I was going to the office; otherwise he wouldn't have let me come. He's Adolf Hitler, that one. A right Adolf Hitler . . . he takes the plates away . . . he takes the plates and the tray . . ." Confusion caught him again. His voice faltered as he lost the conversational thread. "Cynthia puts the plate in front of me. *Wheesh*. Robert takes it away."

"The empty plate? You must be happy to have your family living with you."

"Cynthia, yes. Not Adolf Hitler . . . they should have

278

killed him years ago when we won the war. I can't imagine why they let the swine out."

"Stan." God, John's own head spun as he tried to understand the man. "No, Adolf Hitler doesn't live with you, it's Robert, your son-in-law."

"Ahm, Robert. Yes. Yes. I tricked him this morning." Suddenly bright again, Stan tapped his head with his finger, pleased. "I fooled him. I pulled these clothes over my pajamas and pretended I'd gone all cloth-headed again. I got this briefcase from the workshop in the garden; then I told him I was going to my old office."

"So you intended to bring the briefcase up to me all along?"

"Of course. Dianne Kelly said that you might find it useful. After all, we know what you're going through. The letters . . . the threats . . . it must be a difficult time."

"Tell me, Stan. Other people are getting similar letters in the village?"

"They are that."

"Did you get one?"

"I think so. I can't remember properly now, and I'm pretty sure I tried to run away, but *he*, Adolf Hitler, brought me back."

"You don't like your son-in-law much, do you?"

"Him? Not in a thousand years."

"But you said that you told him you were going to the office?"

"Yes, I fooled him, didn't I?"

"But why did he allow you to leave the house?"

"I—I'm not sure."

"Didn't he try and stop you?"

"No. Told me I was late, as a matter of fact." Stan fixed a sharp eye on John. "Here. Take this."

He handed John the briefcase. Even though it was cracked and covered with dust and cobwebs, John could read a name stenciled in white along its side: KELLY.

"I've never seen inside of it," Stan told him. "Mr.

Kelly told me I should hide it until it was needed again."

"And Dianne Kelly asked you to pass it on to me?"

"Yes."

John looked at the briefcase. The leather had hardened to the texture of wood. Its weight alone told him it wasn't empty. Maybe this was what he'd been searching the house for? Across the fields the mist was thinning now. Houses materialized as if a ghost village was appearing down in the valley. Only the Necropolis managed to hold onto the mist. It lurked among the trees. Ghost forms, forced back into shade by the sun.

"Thank you, Stan," he said sincerely. "My God, I'm shaking all over . . . I'm actually frightened to look inside here."

"Afraid of what you might find?"

"I guess so." Even though his teeth chattered, a smile reached his face. "Is this an eerie experience or what?"

Stan Price reached forward and squeezed John's arm. "I wish I could make this all right for you, John. Trouble is, I've lost just about all the brains I ever had. I know in an hour, or even five minutes from now, I'm going to be a senile old fool again." He sighed. "Just one of nature's tricks, I'm afraid."

At that moment a car tore up the Back Lane. It swung directly through the gates and powered along the driveway toward them.

"Don't let him take the bag," Stan said, panicked. "Don't let him take it. It's yours. You need it. Hide it, hide it!"

John slipped the ancient briefcase beneath a bush.

Robert Gregory kicked open the car door. His face burned a blood red.

"We've been going mad with worry," Robert Gregory barked at John. "Couldn't you have had the common decency to telephone and let us know where he was?"

"I'm sorry," John said. "Your father-in-law wasn't in

a fit state to be left alone. I was going to bring him down in—"

"Dad. In the car!" the man shouted at Stan as if he was a runaway dog. "Come on. Cynthia's in a heck of a state." He opened the passenger door for Stan, then jabbed a finger at the seat.

"Just a moment, Stan. I'll give you a hand." John gently helped the old man to his feet.

"Why do you do it, Dad?" Robert boomed. "Why do you try and run away?"

"I was looking for Harry. We're going fishing."

"God help us. Harry died years ago. It's OK." He snapped this at John. "I'll take him now."

Robert grabbed the old man, and then with barely a pretense of gentleness, shoved him into the passenger seat.

"Harry wanted to go fishing."

"I bet he did," Robert snarled. "Put your legs in so I don't slam the door on them."

John's patience evaporated. "Take it easy with him. He can't move that quickly."

Robert rounded on John. "What do you know what he can or can't do?"

"Stan's exhausted. Show a bit of consideration, can't you?"

Robert tapped his nose. "You, Newton! Keep this out!"

With that he climbed into the passenger seat. Then he raised his hand. It was to draw the seat belt across the Stan's chest, but the old man raised his hands in fear as if to protect his face from a blow. Robert Gregory saw what the man had done, and hurriedly pulled Stan's arms down, then fastened the seat belt.

John felt as if he'd been slapped himself. He looked from Stan to the ugly brute of a son-in-law.

So, that's it, Gregory, John told himself as the truth crept home. *That's why the old man thinks you're Adolf Hitler. You bastard, Gregory. You miserable, abusive, bullying bastard.*

281

Chapter Twenty-seven

One

Robert Gregory crushed the gas pedal to the floor, sending the car roaring down the old Roman road. Anger seared him. He managed to keep the rage bottled until he was well out of sight of the Water Mill; then he released it in a rush.

"I don't believe it. I don't fucking believe it. You must lead a charmed fucking life!"

"I was looking for Harry," Stan Price said, frightened. "I wanted to go fishing."

"Harry's fucking dead. And so should fucking you be!"

Unable to stop himself now, he leaned toward Stan, then snapped his elbow back into the old man's chicken-bone chest.

"*Uh!*"

The flow of traffic at the main road stopped him driving farther. He shook his head, marveling at the unbroken stream of trucks and cars. "How do you do it?

How do you walk through this without so much as turning a hair?"

Stan rubbed his sore chest. "Baby Bones."

"Yeah, I'll Baby Bones you, you old dog."

He raised his elbow again. Instead of flinching, the old man began to laugh.

Surprised, Robert didn't follow through. "Jesus Christ, what on earth does a pile of skin and bone like you find so funny?"

Stan reached down into the storage compartment in the door and pulled out two sheets of paper. On each one were a few lines of Gothic-looking handwriting.

Robert Gregory snapped angrily, "What have you got there?"

Stan laughed until his eyes watered. "You—you've been getting them, too . . . *you've been getting them, too!*"

Robert Gregory snatched the letters. "I meant to throw these out. Some stupid brats have been playing a prank."

"You've ignored them?"

"Of course I bloody well have."

The old man laughed again. A loud, braying laugh, so raw with emotion that it unsettled Robert.

"He's ignored them." Stan shook his head. Tears of laughter rolled down his cheeks. *"He's ignored them!"*

At last a break appeared in the traffic. As Robert Gregory pointed the car's nose homeward, he hissed through clenched teeth, "Go on, laugh. Because I haven't finished with you yet."

Two

Thirty minutes after Robert Gregory drove Stan Price away, John Newton still smoldered with anger. *He makes my blood boil* . . . an old phrase but an apt one. John paced the lawn, his blood running hot in his veins. John kicked the head off a dandelion. *So help me, I should have grabbed Robert by the shirt collar and chucked him into the pond.*

283

There was no doubt in his mind that Robert Gregory ill-treated the old man. To what extent, however, he couldn't say. Stan had certainly expected to be slapped when Robert had raised his hand to get a hold of the seat-belt buckle just over Stan's shoulder.

Now John remembered with a biting clarity that Stan had claimed someone was trying to kill him. John had written that off as a delusion cooked up by dementia. Now he wasn't one-hundred-percent sure. But what could he do about it? He'd needed a damn sight more proof if he was to telephone the police. Should he talk to Stan's daughter, Cynthia Gregory? But she was so timid she'd probably back up any cock-and-bull story Robert Gregory came out with.

John walked toward the orchard. From the shade of the trees, Sam watched him. He paused to rub the dog's head. "It's a cruel world," John murmured. "Sometimes you find yourself standing by, watching shit happen and knowing you can't do a damn thing about it." The dog licked his hand. John smiled. "Well, if you get a chance, boy, you tear a bloody big lump out of Gregory's ass."

For a while John did a few pointless chores to take his mind off what had happened; he made coffee, scratched out weeds from between the cracks in paving slabs, worked more grease into the sluice gate clogs up at the pond. The thing hadn't been opened in years. Now it had become a personal quest to free the mechanism. Pick the bones out of that one, Freud, he told himself, wiping the grease from his hands.

He then went to weed the flower bed. Hell's teeth. He should be writing. He knew that. But Stan's visit had unsettled him. Especially the ugly scene with Gregory yelling at the old man like he was a dog. Now he didn't think he could settle to do anything productive— or meaningful. That is, until he saw the briefcase.

Gregory's stormy arrival had wiped the briefcase from his memory. Now it sat there under the holly bush. Cobweb-smeared, cracked—oozing with questions.

He paused with a bunch of bindweed in each hand. So what was in there?

A pile of baby bones . . .

Despite himself, he smiled as his runaway imagination slipped in the macabre answer.

No. Unlikely. More likely it contained the letters that Schoolmaster Kelly received in this very house seventy years ago. No sooner had he thought this, then his curiosity ignited again. He wanted to open up that case, pull out the letters, then run upstairs to compare them with the ones that had arrived over the last couple of weeks.

Would the demands be the same? Would they be phrased the same? And more importantly—goddamnit, the hairs rose on his neck—would the handwriting be the same? He dropped the weeds, then sat down on the bench with the briefcase on his knee.

KELLY stenciled on the leather blazed at him. The thing might have been broadcasting, *OPEN ME! FIND OUT WHAT'S INSIDE!*

He fumbled with the lock, which secured a hefty leather strap over the case, before noticing a key tied by a cord to the handle. The key had oxidized to a dull orange. Immediately the rust came off onto his fingers as he forced his now-shaking fingers to grip the key, push it into the keyhole, and turn it.

C'mon, c'mon, c'mon . . .

The key went in. No problem.

It would not turn. Big problem.

Damn it.

He wanted it open now. He wanted to see what the case contained. There were answers in there. He wanted to get them together with the questions whirling around his head.

Getting sweaty in the hot sun, he twisted the key in the lock. His fingertips tingled under the pressure. Kelly's briefcase didn't aim to yield its treasures easily.

Grunting, John turned the key as hard as he could. Movement.

Damn. The key wasn't turning in the lock. It was the metal barrel of the key that was twisting under the pressure.

"Christ, John, you don't know your own strength . . . c'mon, apply a little science to the problem here."

He blew into the lock, then examined what he could see of the mechanism. After seventy years in the garage or wherever, the metal parts had rusted tight as glue. Experimentally, as if prizing apart the jaws of a crocodile, he attempted to pull open the briefcase, hoping the leather strap that held it shut would simply snap. Five minutes of sweating and cursing proved that the strap still held good and strong.

Now it really was time to apply a modicum of intellect rather than a truckload of brute force. He carried the bag to the toolshed, where he laid it on the workbench. After that, he aerosoled oil into the lock. For a moment the oil pooled, glistening, in the lock; then, as if thirstily sucked from within, it vanished into the lock. Now he'd have to stomp down his impatience for a while as he hunched over the bag, staring at it, willing the oil to run into the lock mechanism—lubricating, dissolving old grease, working into little levers and springs so he could unlock it. But this was going to take time.

After spraying the lock again with oil, he went indoors.

Now he felt fired up. He'd start work on *Without Trace*. What was more, he sensed an urgency now. It was more than just writing a new book. The Skelbrooke disappearances had knitted themselves into his life now. This was personal involvement. The more he learned, the more he could deal with what faced him.

As he walked into the house, the dog, for no accountable reason, threw up his head and gave a long howl that somehow wrenched at his heart. The howl echoed across the valley to the cemetery on the hill, where the sounds faded and died amongst the gravestones.

Three

"Miranda's not here!"

Paul rocked back on his heels. He hadn't expected that kind of reaction simply for knocking on the Bloom family's front door. But there was Miranda's mother, white-faced, with two staring eyes that looked like balls of black glass set in her head. Jesus, he'd never seen such an expression on someone's face before.

It made his skin crawl.

"I'm sorry to have disturbed you, Mrs. Bloom," he continued politely. "But Miranda wasn't in school this morning so I thought I'd call to find out how . . ." His voice began to falter as those ball-like eyes stared at him as if he'd just disemboweled himself on her doorstep. "I wondered if she's . . . that she might have been ill or she'd . . ." He shrugged, finding it difficult to finish the sentence under a stare that rolled wildness, madness, and terror all into one.

What the hell's going on here?

He'd only met Mrs. Bloom a couple of times, but she'd always been friendly, even a little flirtatious. She had the same dark Spanish looks as Miranda, with neat short hair that was an attractive feathery black. Now she stood there at midday in a white bathrobe, her hair spiky, unpleasantly oily-looking, and shooting those eyeball-rolling looks first at him, then along the street. She looked as if she expected Death himself to dance around the corner, swishing his scythe this way and that.

"Mrs. Bloom?"

"Yes . . . *what?*"

Her eyeballs rolled from him to the street. Again that look of distraction.

"Mrs. Bloom, I wondered if I could speak to Miranda?"

"No."

"Is she out?"

She rolled the eyeballs at him—they flared with absolute dread—then she looked away, this time over the rooftops, as if she couldn't bear to look him in the eye.

"She's not here. She's gone."

"She's gone?"

"Yes. Didn't you hear me! She's left home." The woman took a deep breath. "So don't bother coming back because you won't find her here."

Paul was thunderstruck. "Did Miranda say where she was going?"

"Of course not! She's just packed her things and gone."

"Mrs. Bloom, I'm sorry. I don't know what to say. If she—"

"Now go. Please go away." Her face twisted as she struggled not to cry. "Can't you see how upset I am?"

A split second later John found himself staring at a closed door. From inside came the sound of the woman sobbing. For a moment he stood there stunned. He looked up at the windows, hoping to see Miranda's face, but the drapes were drawn, giving the appearance of a house in mourning.

At last he walked away. Part of his world had been taken from him. For now shock numbed him, but he'd start hurting soon enough.

Chapter Twenty-eight

One

The cursor pulsed on the screen in front of him. In that disconnected state he entered after working for a while, he wrote, lost in the words that appeared on the screen. He was no longer conscious of the world around him. The hot sun on the blind. The dog asleep beneath the desk. A wasp buzzing against the windowpane.

Every now and again a sense came strongly to him that the laws of time had melted. As his fingers hit the keys, he could picture Herbert Kelly typing in this room seventy years ago. Both he and Kelly had the same thing on their minds. Letters that arrived at the dead of night. Kelly must have asked himself the same questions that John Newton asked now. Where did the letters come from? How were they delivered? Who wrote them?

Did Kelly wrestle with the concept that no human being was their author?

He must have. And Herbert Kelly must have paused

typing, too, to stare at the wall, lost in thought. No doubt as the same sun struck the blinds, as a wasp murmured against the windowpane, and as another dog in another decade dozed by his master's feet.

John wrote, conscious that he'd become a near echo of Herbert Kelly. Both were the same age when the letters arrived. Both must have reacted the same way initially. Surprise, even amusement, followed by a degree of outrage that an intruder had crept onto their property. Then outrage giving way to unease and fear. Probably Kelly had gone the same route as John, hunting out others who'd received anonymous letters with demands for trivial gifts, yet uttering threats for noncompliance.

John had been sitting at the desk two hours now, devouring books on British myths and legends, then typing with machine-gun speed, filling the screen with black print.

Someone once said, "The past is another country." That may be, but humanity had arrived at this country of the present still carrying baggage from "the old country" of long ago. And that old country of the past was awash with superstition. No one could escape it. It governed lives as much as the laws of government today. Similarly, to break any of those laws of superstition, either deliberately or accidentally, could land you in a whole heap of trouble. He ran through a list he'd written.

It's bad luck to point at the sun. Bad luck, also, to walk counterclockwise around a church. And bad luck for all the following, too: not to bow to a new moon; to put shoes on a table; to open an umbrella indoors; to bring elder branches into the house; and most definitely it's bad luck to cut the fingernails of a child under the age of twelve months (the child would become a thief). Omens of death included seeing a butterfly at night, seeing a cricket leaving the house. Or if sunlight fell on a mourner at a funeral, it meant that person's imminent death. On the other hand, you might encourage good luck to come your way by stirring your pans clockwise or nailing a horseshoe to your door.

Even hardheaded lawyers couldn't shrug off the idea that the sun and the moon had supernatural powers over people. The Lunatic Act of 1842 coolly defined a lunatic as "a person afflicted with a period of fatuity [fancy lawyer-speak for idiocy or lunacy] in the period following the full moon." In short, lawyers were even prepared to accept that seeing a full moon might drive you nuts.

Smart people not only learned to recognize bad omens, but also learned measures to protect themselves from evil. Horseshoes were a favorite. If you were really smart, you could tap into the occult powers. A girl curious to know the identity of the guy she'd marry would peel an apple, then throw the peel back over her shoulder. If it formed a letter, then that was the initial of the man she'd get hitched to. And just because the calendar had scrolled on a few years, that didn't drain superstition of its potency.

John recalled a physics teacher at school, a practical man to the very marrow of his bones. Once he'd talked about the leukemia treatment he'd received as a child. The teacher had finished off by saying, "I'm healthy enough now, touch wood." And he'd actually looked for a piece of wood to touch. That had meant walking a dozen paces to press his finger against a door frame.

Someone had piped up, "Are you superstitious, sir?"

The teacher had replied, "No, of course not."

"Then why did you touch the wood, sir?"

"Because I'd be a fool if I didn't."

Which just about summed up modern humanity's attitude to superstition, John told himself. Deep down we feel we must protect ourselves from some entity that has the power to inflict bad luck. So we still throw salt over our shoulder into the eye of the Devil, or we touch wood, or we avoid walking under ladders. Superstition in its many forms continues to leak into our lives. John scanned the list on the computer screen again.

If you suffer from warts, rub the wart with a potato, then put the potato in a dry place. As the potato shrivels, the wart shrivels with it.

To cure an alcoholic, give him a drink from a cup made of ivy wood.

To bring good luck to a new home, bury a cockerel in the foundations.

To protect your home from evil, plant hedges of holly.

On impulse he went to the window.

"Just look at that, Sam," he murmured. "in every garden a holly bush. But we'll be all right, won't we, boy? Touch wood."

Two

By midday, the sun had taken the shadows. Temperatures climbed remorselessly now, drying the soil into scales. John fed the dog, then returned to the briefcase in the shed. The key wouldn't turn in the lock. He sprayed more oil through the keyhole. Damn. The contents could have been sitting in a valley on Mars for all he could get his hands on them.

He realized he could cut the leather strap, but it that would be like desecrating one of Herbert Kelly's cherished possessions. He could imagine the young schoolmaster of more than seventy years ago, setting the white Panama hat on his head, kissing his wife and daughters, then walking to the village school, whistling as he went while proudly swinging the briefcase.

No, there wouldn't be much left that Kelly held dear. He'd not damage the briefcase.

John was making a sandwich when Paul walked through the door. John noticed the time stood a little before two; then he shot a questioning look at his son, whose expression was stonelike.

"You're home early, Paul."

"I don't feel well."

"What's wrong?"

Paul hung his bag on the back of a kitchen chair, then kicked off his shoes. One struck the dog's bowl, splashing water against a cupboard.

"OK, I'll wipe it up," Paul snapped before John could open his mouth. Angrily, he dragged a bundle of kitchen tissue from the roll.

As casually as he could, John asked, "Can I get you anything?"

"How do you mean?"

"Aspirin or a drink."

"No, I just feel sick, that's all."

"Oh."

John sensed he walked on eggshells now. Paul looked tense. Something had happened at school. But just what was anyone's guess.

John finished making the sandwich, then said, "Is anything bothering you?"

"What do you mean?" Again that defensive rise in his voice. "Nothing's bothering me."

"Paul, if there's a problem, you can always—"

"There isn't a problem. Why do you always have to ask that? Like I'm a mental case or something!"

"Paul, if you give me chance to—"

"OK! I smoke dope and fuck the Pope, what more do you want to know?"

"Paul. There's no need to kick off like that. I only asked—"

"You only ask this, you only ask that. What's wrong? Can't you write the fucking book!" His face flushed red. *"Jeez . . . I hate this!"*

John had never seen his son like this before. Paul looked a step away from totally freaking out. He glared around the kitchen, his fists clinched. He seemed to be looking for something to hit.

Then he snatched his bag, sending the chair skittering across the tiles with a teeth-jagging screech. Without saying another word, he marched out of the room. A moment later, John heard Paul's bedroom door bang. After that, John sat with the uneaten sandwich in front of him. He felt like an idiot, knowing he should say something to his son. But what? And what had brought on that near-epileptic outburst?

Is that you, Baby Bones?

Did you make this happen?

I've given you what you want. So why are you screwing around with my family? I've yielded to your demands . . . I don't ignore your letters anymore. Baby Bones? Do you hear? Give us a break. I don't ignore your letters. . . .

I'm missing a letter.

The thought hit him hard enough to make him sit up straight. No—that wasn't possible. He'd found each letter out there on the patio. With the exception of the first one, he'd quickly complied with whatever was demanded—the beer, the red ball. So, the demands were trivial, but he'd played by the rules of the letter writer's game.

He went out onto the patio, his eyes scanning the stone slabs. They were clear. No chunks of gravestone. No letters waiting there as insidious as drops of poison.

He shielded his eyes against the burning sun. No. This was ridiculous; he was turning frigging paranoid. He'd gotten like those poor saps who daren't get out of bed on Friday the thirteenth, or slept with a row of onions on their window to stop the boogeyman from climbing in. He wouldn't let superstition eat into him like some mental cancer. That was nothing less than fucking schizophrenia.

The heat bore down on him; his shirt burned against his skin, making him itch uncomfortably. The dog paced nervously some way off, eyeing him as if he'd turned rabid.

Yeah, man bites dog. That's a headline.

Shit . . . think straight, Newton.

Paul's been stung with some shit that teenagers get stung with every now and again. Now he's come home to piss pure liquid anger over everyone. That's all! You can't blame this on the big bad spook that lives under the hill.

But no. He felt it in his guts. Once more he searched

the patio. This time, right under the patio table, he saw that one of the shadows had acquired a lump. Skin crawling, he dived down at it. He grabbed the black lump as if he was grabbing a live rat, and pulled it out.

There in his hand, a little larger than a paperback book, sat a shard of tombstone shaped like a heart. On it was one word: *taken.*

His mouth dried. He'd not seen this stone before. He'd swear.

A moment later, he confirmed the fact when he counted the pieces of tombstone that had arrived with the letters. He'd received three letters. But now he had four lumps of dead stone.

How's your arithmetic, John? Four pieces of stone? Three letters?

One of the letters is missing.

Chapter Twenty-nine

One

That afternoon John, by turns, looked for the missing letter or fumed over the recalcitrant lock. He sprayed more oil into the keyhole, then left the bag on the workbench to allow the lubricant to seep into the mechanism.

By now, he couldn't look at the briefcase without his heart beating faster. There was crucial information in there, he knew it—a treasure chest of answers.

Next he went through the trash. As he slipped a pair of polythene freezer bags onto his hands to serve as mittens to keep the festering goo off him, he wondered if Val had gone onto the patio that morning, seen the letter, and simply dumped it. Alternatively, Paul or Elizabeth might have moved it.

Flies attacked the trash as eagerly as he did. They clamored around junked food that had been sweated good and hard by the sun. He plunged his hands down through layers of cans, paper bags all soggy and brown, empty coleslaw cartons, garlic dip, salsa, and cottage cheese. Hell, this was a witches' brew and a half.

At first the dog came, his nose high, sniffing, as the fresher food smells rolled out of the trash can. But as John excavated deeper, turning up a full carton of cream that oozed green pus, the dog backed away, sneezing.

No joy. Queasy from the stench, he peeled the plastic bags from his hands.

John Newton was convinced a letter had arrived. He realized the repercussions if he failed to meet the demands. Bad things would happen. To his family. To him. Simple as that.

Look at Keith Haslem. He believed he could escape the influence of the letters simply by leaving the village. He'd thought wrong. Now he lay in a hospital bed, paralyzed by a stroke; his face melted by a boiling shower.

After scrubbing his hands, John went upstairs.

Paul lay on his bed, fingers knitted behind his head, staring up at the ceiling.

"Paul?"

"Yeah."

"How're you feeling?"

"Great," he grunted.

"Can I get you anything?"

"I'm trying to sleep, Dad."

"Sorry . . . just one thing, though?"

"What?"

"You didn't find anything on the patio this morning?"

"Like what?"

"A piece of paper."

"Oh, Christ, Dad. What on earth are you talking about?"

"Never mind. Sorry to have disturbed you, Paul."

John heard the sarcasm slip into his voice. He didn't intend it, but Paul's moodiness had started to irritate him.

"Door, Dad."

Biting his tongue, John banged the door shut behind him.

Two

Paul glared at the ceiling. Why had Miranda left home? He couldn't believe she'd do a thing like that. She'd always lived harmoniously with her parents. And if she had left, why hadn't she told Paul she was going? He'd gone head over heels for Miranda; now she'd simply upped and left. And if Miranda was a runaway, as her mother had implied, would the police be involved? Miranda was almost seventeen. It wasn't as if she was a child. She'd be able to find a job and a place of her own to live.

But, and he found the truth as hard to swallow as a rock, she'd abandoned him; dropped him like a shitty bit of rag. When it came down to it, he didn't know what hurt most: Miranda vanishing or the rejection. Gritting his teeth, he rolled over and pushed his face against the pillow. He'd never experienced anything like this before. This was sheer fucking agony. He'd fallen in love for the first time and lost the girl all in the space of a week. Christ, this was torture. But the worst thing was, he knew he couldn't do a damn thing about it.

Three

The sun burned ferociously. Sam slunk off into the shade in the orchard. All John could see of him was a dog-shaped shadow glued to a pink tongue. The mill-pond mirrored the sky. Butterflies streamed across the meadow, psychedelic splashes of color on the wing.

John still drew a blank on the fourth letter. He was certain one had arrived. He was equally certain a member of his family had moved it. But where?

By three-thirty Elizabeth was home. She changed into

a swimming costume. At first she wanted to paddle in the lake. John told her that was a definite no-no. The sides of the lake were steep; in no time at all she'd be in too deep. Elizabeth compromised, playing with the garden hose, watering the trees, then herself, then the dog.

Paul stayed in his room. John found the silence ominous. Any moment he expected to hear the crash of furniture against the walls.

The lock on the briefcase wouldn't budge. Like its big-brother mechanism up at the sluice gate, what should be moving parts stolidly refused to move. Whatever secrets the case contained weren't going to be revealed yet.

A little after five, Val turned the car into the driveway.

He greeted her with a kiss. "Had a good day?"

She unbuttoned the top of her blouse. "A hot one. I'm going to peel these clothes off and have a cold shower."

"Want any company?"

"A cold shower. Where I cool down and become calm and composed. Not all fired up and raunchy." She laughed. "And congratulations on the new book deal. You deserve it." For a while they talked about the book, and whether it would be tempting fate too much to book an overseas trip on the strength of the advance. Then, as they walked to the house, John told her about Paul.

"I haven't seen him lose it like that before," John said. "I thought he was going to kick the kitchen to pieces."

"He's growing up, John. He's having to learn how to handle new experiences."

"But he's seventeen. I'd have thought he'd be growing out of adolescence."

"John, not everyone keeps such a tight grip on their emotions as you, you know."

John shot her a double take. "Are you saying I'm repressed or something?"

"No, just controlled. Goodness, it's hot." Pulling a Coke from the refrigerator, she rolled it against her forehead. Perspiration rolled down her throat, to moisten the neck of her blouse. "Maybe I should shave off all my hair," she breathed.

"Maybe you should."

"John?" She looked stung by his response. "What's wrong?"

"Sorry. I didn't mean that." He smiled, shrugging. "Just one of those days, I suppose."

"*One of those days?* You are joking?" Her eyes widened in surprise. "Your agent closes your biggest book deal so far, and you say you've had a lousy day?"

"Well, maybe not lousy *per se*." He forced a smile. "But eventful . . . certainly eventful."

"We're going to celebrate."

"Of course we are."

"How about a trip to London. Bright lights, big restaurants?"

"Now you talk my language."

"All right. When?

"How about next weekend?"

"A bad time of the month."

"Oh."

"And we do want to celebrate every way we can, don't we?"

"Absolutely."

She kissed him. He tasted salt on her skin from the perspiration. "And I'm glad the book deal worked out, John." She kissed him again. "You know something?"

"What?"

"I think all our good luck's come at once."

"Touch wood." He reached out and squeezed the back of the kitchen chair as hard as he could.

Four

An observer watching from a place of safety might have described it as the calm before the storm. That

Thursday evening they ordered pizza in order to escape the heat of the kitchen. Paul ate his in the sanctuary of his bedroom. John, Val, and Elizabeth ate outside in the shade of the house. At seven in the evening the sun was still pretty brutal.

He and Val eased the pizza on its way with iced beers. Elizabeth sucked on a carton of black-currant juice. Sam sat under the table. His tongue dripped saliva onto the stone slabs. But the heat did nothing to dissuade him from munching any crust that came his way.

"John, if we're going to be in for a heat wave, we should have some decent air-conditioning."

"And a swimming pool," Elizabeth added. "With a diving board."

John smiled. "Whoa. I haven't even signed the contracts yet."

"In the meantime, we'll have melted into sticky puddles on the ground."

His smiled widened. "OK, I'll make some inquiries about air-conditioning. Right, I'll shift these. Otherwise we'll have ants all over us." He collected the pizza cartons with their cargo of dead crusts, then went to dump them in the trash. After that, he took another shot at unlocking the briefcase. Still no joy. He squirted more oil through the lock.

"John. Where did you get that monstrosity?"

He squinted back at where Val stood in the doorway, silhouetted by the setting sun. "Somebody from the village gave it me this morning."

"What is it, an old Gladstone bag?"

"Something like that. It's a bit too boxy for a briefcase. Little beauty, isn't she?"

"If beauty's in the eye of the beholder."

"It is old."

"You're not thinking of using it, are you?"

"No. The lock's rusted to buggery." He gave the keyhole another squirt. "I'm hoping it might contain some information for my the next book."

"Ah, the disappeared of Skelbrooke."

He nodded at the briefcase. "It belonged to Herbert Kelly, who lived here when it all happened."

"Do you think you've another *Blast His Eyes* on your hands?"

"That's what I'm hoping, hon."

"Do you suspect our Mr. Kelly of murdering the people who vanished?"

"No. He wasn't the type."

"Is there a murderous type? Remember, it's always supposed to be the person you least suspect."

Grinning, he wiped his hands on a cloth, "Ah, you astound me, Holmes."

"Sarcastic swine." She grinned back. "I've a good mind to chuck you in the pond."

"You'll have to catch me first!"

That was the last carefree evening.

Five

Even the sunset didn't bring relief from the heat. As John splashed cold water on his face in the bathroom, he heard Val scolding Elizabeth in his daughter's bedroom. The voices echoed across the landing.

"Lizzie, how many times have I told you to put your videos away on the shelf when you've finished with them?"

"I did. Paul must have—"

"Paul's not touched them. Now where's *The King and I* tape?"

"I don't know."

"But the box is empty."

"Uh, it's here under the pillow."

"It'll wind up broken. Put it away properly."

"Mum—"

"And I had to tidy up after you on the patio this morning. I nearly broke my neck tripping over the things you'd left out there."

"But I didn't—"

"Now come on, time for bed."

"I'm sleeping on top of the bed." This time Elizabeth sounded sulky.

"All right. Now lay still; try and keep cool."

"I won't be able to sleep. I'm too hot."

"Just try. Give me a kiss good night."

Their voices dropped into muffled sounds now. As he toweled his face, he heard Val call, "John, Elizabeth's ready for her good-night kiss."

He walked into the bedroom. "Ugh, I have to kiss this monster?"

"Dad!" She giggled.

"Now, John, don't be getting Elizabeth giddy. I've had to scold her for being so untidy."

"Then I'll bite the monster's head off." He bent down as she lay in bed and pretended to gnaw at her neck. She squirmed, giggling louder.

"Dad! I'm red hot as it is . . . Mum, he's making me hotter!"

"John." Val suppressed a smile. "Leave her to cool down."

"Aye, aye, Skipper."

Then he kissed his daughter. "Love you, Lizzie."

"Love you, Dad. Don't forget the swimming pool."

"I won't. I'll start digging this very minute."

"Isn't he an idiot, Mum?"

"He's a world-class idiot, but we love him to bits, don't we?"

"Another hug." Elizabeth held out her arms. He leaned over the bed again as she gave his neck a firm squeeze.

"Sleep well," he said.

"I will."

"Don't let the bedbugs bite."

"I won't."

"Have sweet dreams."

"I will."

"OK, you two," Val intervened. "Don't take all night about it."

A moment later, the lights were out and he followed Val down to the lounge. There, the millrace sighed beneath the glass. Outside, bats darted by the windows where insects were lured by the light.

"Peace at last," Val whispered.

"It'd be all happy families if it wasn't for Paul." He flicked a switch on the wall. Instantly light filled the observation chamber. Below the glass, water foamed a dazzling white. "I wish I knew what was eating him up. If there's some trouble at school, we should—"

"John. I know what it is."

John blinked, surprised. "You do?"

"Yes."

"Since when?"

"He told me about an hour ago."

He shook his head, puzzled. "Why didn't he tell me?"

"You know what teenagers are like."

"But I'm easygoing. I always figured I was the kind of guy people could confide in when—"

"John—"

"Especially my son." He felt irked. No two ways about it. He'd been kept in the dark.

"Well, it was one of those personal matters, John. He wanted to keep it private."

"He's not got the clap, has he?" The words raced ahead of common sense. From the stung look on his wife's face, he wished he could reel them back in again. Too late.

"No, he has not got the clap. What the hell made you say a thing like that?"

"I don't know . . . well, yes I do. He was acting so bizarre, I thought it had to be something out of the ordinary."

"It is out of the ordinary." Val folded her arms. "And keep your voice down. I'm not supposed to be telling you."

"But I'm his—"

"John—"

"After all, I—"

"John. Shh!" She glared at him. "It's all about a girl . . . Paul's girlfriend."

Again John felt a prickle of surprise. "I didn't even know he was seeing someone."

"He's not a little boy, John. It's only natural, you know?"

"I know . . . but . . ." He shrugged. "This thing with your kids growing up just sort of creeps up on you." In a calmer voice he said, "So what happened? She dumped him?"

"Don't ever become an ambassador, John. You don't score well in areas of tact or diplomacy."

He sighed, out of his depth. "So what did happen?"

The girlfriend's pregnant. This time he did manage to keep those three little words from slipping out.

Val sat down on the sofa. "Apparently, he's been seeing a girl called Miranda Bloom. They were close."

"He never mentioned anything about a Miranda Bloom."

"I imagine he was a little shy. It was his first real love."

"Oh."

"Well the long and short of it is, Paul went to call on her this lunchtime, only to be told that she'd upped and gone."

"She's left home?"

"For good as far as Paul can make out."

"Why?"

"Paul didn't get all the details. It looks all very sudden. The girl's mother was too upset to talk about it much."

John let out a breath. "No wonder Paul was cranky."

"Cranky isn't a good word, John. He's shattered. He feels like the rug's been pulled from under his feet. That he's been rejected. Emotionally he's going to be pretty raw for a while."

John nodded in agreement.

"So," Val said firmly. "Go easy on him. It's not like

305

he was ten when a hug and a chocolate bar could solve all his woes. OK?"

"OK." John rubbed his jaw. "I don't know," he said. "When you're five, you're taught how to cross roads, how you're not to stick your finger in the electric socket or mess with matches. But there's not a lot of guidance about dating or relationships. You have to make it up as you go along."

"And sometimes you do get your fingers burnt."

"Perhaps there really should be a college for life skills." He brushed his hand across the air in front of him as if reading from a poster. "Curriculum: loving and dumping; how to make friends in high places; how to brown-nose when the time is right; how to give someone a verbal kick up the rear when they take you for granted."

Val gave a tired smile. "Add parenting skills to that. And while you're about it, why not put the patience of saints into easy-to-swallow capsules?"

"It could go on the same shelf as Mother's Love. . . ."

"And we'll buy you a family pack of Tact and Diplomacy, dear."

"Ouch." He smiled at her. "I don't suppose we are truly awful parents, are we?"

"We don't do badly. But I could do with a shot of that Patience of a Saint potion. Elizabeth's going through one of her untidy phases again. There's so many cake crumbs on her carpet, it's like walking on gravel."

"Yuk."

"She leaves her tennis rackets on the lawn. I found her bike up by the pond this morning. And when I put that away I nearly fell over a piece of stone she'd been playing with on the patio."

"Oh?" The blood suddenly thudded in his ears. He sat up, alert. "Lizzie had left a stone there."

"Yes. Well, it must have been Lizzie. Who else would leave a slab of rock there, right in the middle of the patio?"

His throat tightened. "Why would she do a thing like that?"

"Some game, I suppose. She still plays that prince-and-princess thing with invitations to royal balls and whatnot. There was even a piece of paper folded up under the stone."

"Oh? Did you throw it away?"

"The paper? Why, what's so important about it?"

"Nothing. It's just she likes to keep everything she writes."

"More fool me, I should have thrown it away, but like a soft mumsie I put it in her box."

They talked for a few more minutes. The time was almost eleven when John made an excuse to go upstairs.

Seeing by the landing light alone, he crept into Elizabeth's bedroom. Despite her predictions otherwise, she was now fast asleep. She lay on her side, her face pressed against a stuffed bear. From the next room came the sound of Paul's TV.

He allowed his eyes to adjust to the gloom, and then he saw the box in the corner on which Elizabeth had written *Miss Lenny*. For a long time he thought that was the name of a character she'd invented. Suddenly, it clicked. With a blend of smart vocabulary and a youthful inability to spell, she'd attempted to use the word *Miscellany*; after all, the box contained a jumble of odds and ends. Silently, he went on his hands and knees to look into the box. The first thing he saw was the scab she'd picked from her chin: it sat in the bottom of a glass jar like a black spider.

But there, right on top of oddments of toys, comics, pencils, and notepads, lay a folded piece of paper.

For a moment he felt himself become detached from the world. The night was hot, but where he found himself was suddenly cold.

Already an aura of unease had formed around him like a dead hand. He didn't want to touch the paper with his naked fingertips. But here it was: letter number four. No doubt about it. The paper had that waxy antique texture. It wasn't white, but had the creamy yellow of old bone.

OK, what is it you want this time? A pound of nice ripe plumbs? A quart of rum? A pretty picture of a cat? Or a slice of cake crumbled over the grave of little Jess Bowen?

To the sound of his daughter's breathing, he angled the paper to what little light fell through the doorway. Then he read the letter:

Dear Messr. John Newt'n,

No soul should exist alone. And I, like all people, desire companionship. Therefore, I will take little Elizabeth Newt'n away with me as a friend. Yew will leave her in the graveyard by the sepulchre of Posthumous Ellerby on Saturday night. If yew do not, yew will be very sorry.

Chapter Thirty

The strip-light sizzled into life, filling the shed with light.

There on the workbench lay Herbert Kelly's brief-case—a boxy, dwarf coffin that held the secrets of people long dead. John Newton had come down here immediately after the meaning of the letter had sunk in, the paper still gripped in his fist.

It wants Elizabeth . . . it wants Elizabeth. . . .

The words roared through his head.

No, he told himself, it wasn't supposed to be like this. Dianne Kelly maintained the demands were always trivial—beer, chocolate, a ball. Not this . . . this didn't make sense. The old woman insisted that the letters her father had received seventy years ago hadn't asked for anything more. Unless, that is, Kelly hadn't told his family everything.

John shoved the key in the briefcase lock. Or at least he tried, only his hands shook as anger and fear convulsed him.

Fuck you!

He tore the ax from the wall, knocking aside cans of paint as he did so. They rattled onto the concrete floor. From the house came barking as Sam reacted to the noise.

"Damn you!" he snarled, directing his hatred at the letter writer—whoever, whatever it was. *"Damn you!"*

He attacked the briefcase with the ax. The bastard lock wasn't going to keep him out anymore. The big ax blade bit deep into the leather, opening great wounds in its sides. Another ax blow struck the lock a glancing blow; sparks spat across the benchtop. Another blow crushed the handle. Burning with rage, cursing, grunting, he rained down ax blows. The name *KELLY* exploded below the furious strikes.

The bag slid off the bench onto the floor, where John struck it with all the fury of a warrior beheading monsters.

At last the bag burst open, bleeding papers onto the floor. He stood, glaring down, panting, and sweating so hard, droplets fell onto the paper, loosening the ink into a series of Rorschach patterns. The inkblots looked like naked skulls with gouged sockets.

Shit. He'd never felt anger like this. He wanted to find the old Kelly woman, grab her by her thin shoulders, shake her. Yell in her face: *Why didn't you tell me! Why didn't you tell me!*

"John, what the hell's going on?"

He looked up to see Val through sweat-blurred eyes. Still gripping the ax, he dragged his forearm across his face to wipe away the perspiration.

"What's going on?" she said again. "Have you gone insane or what?"

"I needed to open the bag."

"At this time? It's nearly midnight, for heaven sakes."

Once more he found himself on the verge of telling Val everything. But as if Kelly's secretive nature had leaked into his own soul as he slept in the schoolteacher's old bedroom, he knew he couldn't.

310

"I needed to get this bag open." He spoke woodenly—and admit it, he told himself sourly, not altogether rationally.

"Couldn't it wait until morning?"

"I've wasted enough time. I need to start work on the book."

She stared at him. He saw the searching look in her eyes, as if she was hunting for some early symptom of insanity.

"John, it's nearly midnight."

He attempted a smile. It felt like a crazed leer twitching across his face. "Well, hon . . . that's writers for you. We're a wild breed. Tearing up the rule books, acting on impulse, kicking out the nine-to-five."

"John." She laughed, but it was brim full of unease. "Stop doing this. I don't like it. And put the ax down . . . I don't want you chopping off my head or anything as impulsive as that."

He realized he held the ax like a weapon. He laid it down.

"Sorry," he said. "Not being able to open the bag was really pissing me off." He brushed back his perspiration-soaked fringe of hair. "Maybe it's the heat."

"Come to bed, John. You can work on the book in the morning."

"OK." To his ears, his voice sounded calm now. He attempted another smile. It came easier this time. "You go on up. I'll just tidy up here."

With another nervous laugh, she nodded at the ax. "But leave your friend behind, won't you?"

"Sure. Now you get off to bed. It's late."

Looking a little more reassured, she smiled, then walked across the patio to the house that rose darkly against a starry sky. He saw Paul's light still burned. His son wrestled with his own torments tonight as well.

When Val had closed the door, he picked up the butchered remains of Kelly's case and put them on the bench. Then he scooped up the papers that had fallen out onto the floor. Wiping the sweat from his eyes, he pulled up a stool and sat down to read.

He saw straightaway these were carbon copies of typewritten documents. They'd been carefully bound into files backed with stiff card covers. One file was titled *The Skelbrooke Mystery*, another simply *Five Letters*. A third bore the word *Cuttings*. All the titles were in the neat hand, John surmised, of Herbert Kelly himself.

John glanced out through the open door. Moths danced like snowflakes in the shed's hard white light. The house now lay in darkness. Val must have persuaded Paul to go to sleep. Maybe she, too, now lay on the bed, too hot to lie beneath the covers. He imagined her gazing up into the dark, puzzled by her husband's suddenly weird behavior. Maybe she even wondered if he would climb the stairs with the ax in his hands.

More moths swarmed over the window, drawn by some insectile passion to reach the light. Did the letter writer operate on that same instinctive level as the moths? Or was there intelligence there? Was the letter writer exquisitely conscious of the alarm and dread instilled into those men and women who were on the receiving end of the demands? Mouth dry, veins pulsing in his head, he pulled the file marked *Five Letters* toward him. He glanced at the letter he'd taken from Elizabeth's *Miss Lenny* box. He read it again. Once more he winced at the line that seemed to launch itself from the page right into his heart: *Therefore, I will take little Elizabeth Newt'n away with me as a friend.*

Dear God. His stomach muscles knotted. The meaning was all too clear. The letter writer expected John to deliver his daughter to the cemetery. Then to walk away, leaving her there.

He'd already gone through dozens of scenarios centering on the idea (even the hope!) that the letters were a hoax. But gut instinct yelled loudly that they were not. A few days ago he'd made a pact with himself to simply do what the letters demanded. To hand over the beer or chocolate or whatever as the other villagers had done. But that was all before this letter arrived. This piece of poison changed everything.

This letter demanded his daughter. No way would he do that.

He broke away from staring at the window, which now seethed with a hundred or more moths. He shook his head. What was it with this village? The place became more otherworldly by the minute. Stars shone bright with witch fire in the night sky, brighter than he'd ever seen them before. A plague of moths had descended on his home. Bats whirled soundlessly around the shed, faster, faster, faster. Frogs croaked in the stream. An owl hooted three times. A meteor slashed through the constellation of Cancer.

These were omens of death. He found himself battening onto the notion with a strange and terrible ferocity. As if the truth had been dangled in front of him for days, only he'd been too blind to see.

Across the patio crawled three hedgehogs. Three bristling lumps in the darkness.

Another meteor flashed across Cancer like a knife cut, opening up a rent in heaven through which the god of all dark places, all bottomless pits, all poison wells, all open graves, could look down on one John Newton. Sweating there in the same shed where the long-dead Herbert Kelly had sweated, too. Whatever bulbous eye stared down at John from the darkness of outer space must have seen Kelly reading the letters, gnawing his knuckles, wondering what to do. John sat on the stool, hardly breathing the hot night air, feeling himself cocooned in the aura of his own bleak fear. A fear that seemed to leak from his skin like perspiration. He knew he was following in Kelly's footsteps—history repeating itself.

He thought back. Dianne Kelly had described her father weeping against a tree in the orchard. The letters had eaten into him, too. He'd gotten unpredictable. Even to the point of packing his bags and slipping away with his daughter at the dead of night.

Now John sat up, the blood buzzing in his ears. Wait a minute, wait one damn minute... Kelly's sudden personality change, leading the normally loving husband and father to suddenly skip the country with his daughter, had puzzled him.

Quickly, John put his hand on the file in front of him. His heart bumped hard against his chest, his fingers tingled. When he opened this file, would he see those sinister letters written in the same hand on the same waxy antique paper?

Moments ago he couldn't bring himself to open the files; now he couldn't move fast enough.

He snapped back the cover.

Hell...

He'd not anticipated this. Not one bit. Instead of letters written in a weird, spiky hand, he saw sheets of flimsy paper bearing a few blurry words. They weren't the original letters. They were carbon copies of typewritten versions.

Overcoming the pang of disappointment. John quickly read began to read.

Dear Messr. Kelly,
   I should wish yew put me a pound of chock latt on the grief stowne of Jess Bowen by the Sabbath night. Yew will be sorry if yew do not.

Yes, same style. Same archaic spellings. Same demand.

But would the handwriting have been the same? Once more his whole being strained to believe these letters were the work of a lunatic hoaxer. Some sadistic son of a bitch who got his kicks watching the villagers of Skelbrooke make fools of themselves.

Yeah, well, maybe a week ago, he might have believed the hoax premise. Not now. A few days had left him a whole lot smarter, hadn't they?

With the pulse thudding in his neck with all the dark power of a funeral drum, he turned the pages. Yeah, there was the *pinte of porter* one. The next letter demanded one red ball. The third a quarter of cake. (Oh, that one's a variation on my collection, John thought sourly. You wanted something different for a change, you filthy little bastard.) The sourness threatened to become bitter rage again.

He closed his eyes, breathed deeply, steadied himself, then opened his eyes to read the fifth letter.

Dear Messr. Kelly,

No soul should exist alone. And I, like all people, desire companionship. Therefore, I will take little Mary Kelly away with me as a friend. You will leave her in the graveyard by the sepulchre of Posthumous Ellerby on Saturday night. If yew do not, yew will be very sorry.

See, John? All your winning lottery numbers have come up at once. Herbert Kelly kept the last letter secret from his family. Kelly received a letter demanding that he leave his daughter in the Necropolis.

The mental strain had nearly broken Kelly. But he'd come up with a plan. Before the deadline in the letter expired, he'd taken his youngest daughter, Mary, as far away from Skelbrooke as possible. But what about Keith Haslem? He'd tried to outrun the evil influence of the letters, but he'd failed, winding up felled by a brain hemorrhage. *Maybe you didn't run far enough, old buddy. Maybe if you put a whole ocean the size of the Atlantic between yourself and Skelbrooke, you'd be beyond the reach of Baby Bones or whatever the malevolent little tumor full of pus called itself.*

John imagined Kelly's dilemma as he struggled to find a solution. At times, it had gotten so bad he'd broken down. Dianne Kelly had seen her father weeping in the orchard. The man had truly gone to hell and back as he weighed up the options. Stay here, ignore the letter, hoping that ill luck wouldn't visit the Water Mill in spades. Or maybe he'd considered the unthinkable.

Lead his daughter by the hand to the cemetery at midnight, and then leave her for whatever waited there. But no. Kelly had taken a tough option: He'd abandoned his wife and eldest daughter for a new life in Canada with Mary.

John looked up from the file. A vibrating rug of moths pressed against the window, straining to get through the glass to the light.

I'm walking in Kelly's shoes now, he told himself. The letter has arrived demanding I leave Elizabeth in the cemetery at midnight on Saturday. That's just two days away.

Do I ignore this?

Do I take Elizabeth away?

Come on, Newton: think. Think!

What the hell do I do?

Chapter Thirty-one

One

The night was hell. John slept in short nightmare-haunted snatches. His mind seemed intent on recapping the last few days. He dreamt of Elizabeth cycling down the lane, where she'd fall and gash her chin. But in this dream version of events, a dark phantom shape pursued her before seizing her and throwing her to the ground. He dreamt of letters being borne into the garden by shadows. Then he was standing by Jess Bowen's grave, surrounded by a million red balls that became a million staring eyes. The weeping statue leered at him with a goblin face.

He'd woken, panting in the airless bedroom, hair matted against his head in a sopping cap. Outside, an owl hooted. A fox gave a snapping bark like a demon laughing out on the lawn.

At last he slid away into restless, churning sleep. The nightmares returned; he was back in the Necropolis. The ground curled up round him in waves; tombstones became teeth ready to grind his bones to a milky paste. And behind it all, behind every tombstone, behind every sinister cherub, behind every rotted Christ, he sensed the dark unchanging intelligence that had sent out its insidious demands for the last five thousand years. The fear it generated in men and women in the village became a vast, wet wound from which it sucked with all the gluttonous hunger of a vampire.

Moments later his mind broke through into consciousness again. He lay twisting the sheet in his hands, thinking about the letter that demanded he leave Elizabeth in the Necropolis. How long would it take to get flights to Australia or Thailand or Chile? Any damn place provided it was far enough away from Skelbrooke and whatever sucked on the wound that bled a bright red terror.

"You were late getting to bed last night," Val said on the Friday morning.

"I read the documents in the briefcase."

"Anything of use?"

"There might be."

The conversation over breakfast was tight. Val repeatedly eyed him as if another head had sprung out of the side of his neck. He guessed she was still perplexed, if not downright alarmed, by the way he'd attacked the briefcase with an ax. But he'd had to know what was inside.

And now you do know. Kelly received letters just like yours.

Paul had left early for school, his face still dark and thunderous. Elizabeth had made her bed. Now she walked the dog around the meadow on his leash.

"It's going to be a hot one today," Val said, striving to be conversational.

With the letter preying on his mind, he was in no mood for small talk; he nodded, however.

"John, is there something troubling you?"

"Nothing out of the ordinary," he lied, then immediately wondered why he shouldn't tell her the truth.

In case you have to leave with Elizabeth in a hurry, he told himself. He looked at Val, his lips pressed together as if holding back what he really wanted to say.

I love you, Val. But I can't bring myself to tell you what I know. That there's something out there we can't understand. And that something has demanded that I hand over our daughter. At best you'd laugh in my face; at worst you'd have me committed. I need to be free to act in our family's best interests. Good God, I might even have to flee the country.

The surge of love for his wife grew so intense, he had to look away.

Minutes later, Val drove out through the gates with Elizabeth in the passenger seat bound for school. Now John sat in the house with only his worries for company.

The temperature climbed fast. The sun came crunching through the windows like some Martian heat-ray. Even closing the blinds didn't help. With the heat oppressing him on the outside and pure dread chilling him from within, he spread the documents from Herbert Kelly's briefcase onto the desk.

This time he opened the file marked *The Skelbrooke Mystery*. On flimsy paper was what might have been a chapter of a book. Again he was acutely conscious of the fact that Herbert Kelly might have typed these pages in this very room. More than once he looked back, half expecting to see a tall figure standing there. John dragged the sweat from his eyes with the back of his hand, then began to read.

THE SKELBROOKE PHANTOM
BY HERBERT C. KELLY

A coroner's report of 1787 records matter-of-factly that "George Spurlock poisoned himself on account of him seeing the face of Baby Bones looking at him through the parlor window glass." Delving deeper into church records and other archive material, we find earlier references to a shadowy figure known as Baby Bones. Although more ancient documents refer to the character with variations of the name, such as "Baby Bowne," "Bonnie Bones," or "Jack-Of-Bones." A Norman manorial indenture of 1190 names an evil spirit "that sorely troubled aldermen, yeomen, and peasant alike" as "Father Bones."

Like many English villages, Skelbrooke attracted the attention of supernatural entities. What is so unusual is that whereas the dragon, wyrm, hobgoblin, knucker, cockatrice, and other fabulous beasts of legend dwindled into obscurity in neighboring villages, the myth of Baby Bones never lost its grip in Skelbrooke. At intervals of between fifty and eighty years, it would issue demands of tithes or payments from certain villagers chosen at random. How it delivered these demands is rather mysterious in its own right.

Legends tell that a child or "an idiot" would vanish from the village, only to return within days talking "at first in tongues," then issuing demands for beer and food in a "voice that wasn't his own." Baby Bones required that loaves, cakes, and flagons of beer be left on the splendidly named Crackling Hill, which is now the site of the large cemetery known as the Necropolis.

John paused. Kelly had written a background to the Baby Bones myth. John guessed from its reader-friendly style that it was intended for publication in his regular newspaper column; also, the *lightness* of tone suggested that it was written before Kelly received the letters. He read on.

Failure to comply with the demands that came via the mediumistic children or village idiots resulted in the village suffering months of ill fortune. Letters written by a parish priest in the fourteenth century lamented "a grievous conflagration that reduc'd the village households by half and claim'd the eldest son of the feudal

Lord Geoffrey Thomas D'Montaine." On most occasions, it must be stressed, Skelbrooke met the demands with good humor in an ancient festival that greatly predates, yet anticipates, the modern Halloween "trick or treat."

After a while, Baby Bones began to issue its demands via letters delivered during the witching hour. These, written in an archaic hand, are always anonymous, always request some petty trifle such as cake or chocolate, yet are concluded with a threat if the demands are not met. However, on occasion our local neighborhood phantom would revert to employing a human messenger. The last recorded instance was in 1850, when an orphan child by the name of Jess Bowen returned after apparently "wandering off into the woods for some long days." True to form, the young child marched into the village speaking nonsense. Then one night he made his rounds, knocking on a door here, a window there, before demanding that the householder leave a freshly killed goose on Crackling Hill. The voice that came from the child's mouth held such a deep timbre, "as the bass notes of a great cathedral organ," it struck terror into all that heard it. However, upon the boy knocking at the door of Benjamin Greensmith of Skelbrooke's Water Mill, events took a brutal turn.

On hearing the deep voice thundering its demand from the lips of the half-starved orphan child, Greensmith seized a shovel and struck the boy a "frightful blow" to the head, killing him instantly.

In a spirit of rebellion the villagers refused to "pay their dues" to Baby Bones; not a single goose was left on Crackling Hill. Within twenty-four hours, however, Greensmith's infant daughter had drowned in the Water Mill pond. The village priest fell from his horse and lay paralyzed until the day he died. A month later an epidemic of cholera struck Skelbrooke (but not touching any neighboring village or town). By Christmas, forty-three of its inhabitants had died and were buried in pits filled with burning lime at the crossroads. Benjamin Green-

*smith left Skelbrooke on New Year's Day, 1851, an emo-
tionally broken and financially bankrupt man. He would
die a year to the day after he killed the orphan boy, by
swallowing acid.*

*In order to make amends, little Jess Bowen was ex-
humed from a pauper's grave and reburied at the village's expense in the Necropolis. The grave was adorned
with a formidable granite slab and a rather sentimental
statue of a weeping boy. But this charitable act begs the
question, were the villagers "closing the stable door after
the horse had bolted"?*

*Even today, the myth of Baby Bones endures as a
children's spook story to be told at night around a crackling fire when the moon rides high and the owl hoots.
But, with the exception of the youngest children, who
believes that dark forces can reach out, demand "treats"
from us, then, if we should ignore the demands, punish
us with "bad luck"?*

The last paragraph had been crossed out, and in the
margin was a single fiercely scribbled word: *Wrong!*

So, Herbert Kelly had learned the hard way, too. Like
the doomed Benjamin Greensmith in 1850, who'd killed
the orphan boy Jess Bowen. Now the ghosts of these
former residents of the Water Mill who'd received the
sinister demands were beginning to line up behind the
present owner, John Newton.

Perspiration stuck his hands to the paper. He needed
a drink like crazy, but he knew he had to go through
the files from beginning to end. All this made a terrible
sense now. But a bleak foreboding hung over him, as
if a storm was building over the house that would soon
break with devastating results.

Inside the study, the temperature rose as the sun
climbed higher, subjecting Skelbrooke to its naked heat.
John read the seventy-year-old files, searching, he
hoped, for an answer to his own dilemma.

Most of the files consisted of carbon copies of typewritten notes. (Clearly written in a hurry. John imag-

ined Kelly furiously hammering at the typewriter keys; sometimes with a force so great that the typeface had punched right through the paper, leaving holes through which daylight passed.) The notes revealed Kelly's sudden obsession for researching superstition. They echoed John's own notes of just a day ago. Likewise, Kelly devoted pages on how to protect yourself from ill luck. John scanned the list:

> *Planting holly bushes.*
> *Burying a cockerel in the foundations of a house.*
> *Throwing salt over your left shoulder into the eyes of the Devil.*
> *Cold iron is a powerful defense against witches and demons, particularly in the form of horseshoes.*

Good God. Herbert Kelly had been laboring to find a weapon to use against whatever force had sent the letters! He'd also made sure that his work would be preserved so that people who came after him could pick up where he left off.

The overwhelming conclusion John reached was that Kelly had run out of time. He'd tried to discover some supernatural protection for his family, and perhaps Skelbrooke in general, but he'd failed. Beaten by the ticking clock, he must have packed up his notes into a variety of bags before handing them to people he could trust to preserve them. Ten-year-old Stan Price had been one such person. Now Stan had passed Kelly's notes to John to continue the work.

As John flicked through a bulky file, a piece of paper slipped out, a pencil drawing made by a child. At the top of the picture stood a house. The perspectives and proportions were skewed, but he recognized it as the Water Mill in which he now sat. The distinctive roof shape was there, while a series of straggling lines depicted the millstream running beneath the house itself. In the foreground were four figures. The tallest wore a hat, the next wore a long skirt, the third had pigtails, and the fourth was the smallest, holding a doll. In a child's hand beneath the figures were the words *PLEASE LORD, PROTECT OUR HOME AND OUR FAMILY. AMEN.* Then a drawing of a sad face with tears forming pear shapes on the cheeks. A note on the reverse of the drawing ran:

> *I write this in haste. Mummy and Dianne. I will miss you very much, but Daddy says we must leave at this very moment. If we do not, bad things will happen to our family and our neighbors. Please hug Teddy for me. I love you all. Mother, I always tried to be a good girl and make my bed every morning and keep the sink clean. I am crying now. Daddy promises we are leaving for a finer place.*
>
> *Mary Kelly, aged nine*

To try to ease some of the sting of leaving in secret, Herbert Kelly had suggested that Mary write a farewell letter to her mother and sister. She had, only for some reason he'd never posted the letter to the family he'd left behind in Skelbrooke. Now here it was: in the hands of the wrong person, seventy years too late.

John glanced at his watch. It was now noon, Friday. The latest letter demanded that he leave Elizabeth in the graveyard at midnight on Saturday.

That didn't give him long. It didn't give him long at all.

Two

Stan Price sat in the shade of a tree.

Robert Gregory glared at him from across the lawn. Why wouldn't the old man die? This heat alone should be enough to kill him. But no, Stan Price sat lost in his senile daydreams, smiling to himself—*actually smiling damnit!* Gregory hated everything about his father-in-law. The old-man hands that were liver-spotted claws, the ridiculous straw hat, that scrawny turkey neck.

Robert Gregory hoed the soil, yet all the time his eyes burned into the man. He was still furious about how Stan had laughed at him yesterday. It was all over those stupid letters that had been left in the garden. Clearly they were a windup by some kids. The letters had been addressed to Robert personally, but they'd deliberately misspelt his name in a juvenile attempt to bug him.

Dear Robert Greg'ry,
I should wish yew put me a pound of chock latt on the grief stowne of Jess Bowen.

Yeah, and pigs might fly. OK, so the letters had been mildly irritating, but it was the old man's reaction to them, the way he'd laughed and laughed, that had boiled the blood in his veins.

No, it would be Robert Gregory who'd have the last laugh. *I've got plans for you, my dear old dad. Just you wait and see.*

All he needed was luck, lots of lovely luck, to be on his side.

Robert watched a butterfly settle on a leaf, its powder-blue wings trembling in the sun. With a surge of savage excitement he plunged the hoe blade down at the insect, cutting it neatly in two.

Chapter Thirty-two

John walked the dog. He intended going only as far as the village pond. But as if he'd been drawn there by invisible wires, he found himself walking up to the Necropolis.

The sun beat down, cracking the soil into the pattern of reptile scales. Big bloated cemetery flies sat on path. Trees were motionless. No one was about. Nothing moved. The houses in the village were sealed boxes. It was a world holding its breath, waiting to see what happened next. In his pocket was the latest letter. He knew it by heart. Its words went round his head like an evil chant:

No soul should exist alone. . . .
And I, like all people, desire companionship. . . .
Therefore, I will take little Elizabeth Newt'n away. . . .
Yew will leave her in the graveyard. . . .
By the sepulchre of Posthumous Ellerby . . .

Where was the grave of Posthumous Ellerby?

Hell, why should he want to know? It wasn't as if he was going to find it and—then what? Chain his nine-

326

year-old daughter to it as midnight approached?

Yeah, smelly old Baby Bones . . . in your dreams.

As he crossed the grass to the gap in the broken fence, Sam suddenly stopped, then lay down on his stomach, his head lifted up, watching John as he entered the cemetery.

John looked at the dog. "You're not coming in, are you, boy?"

The dog watched him, his black fur glossy as polished coal in the sun, his tongue hanging down as he panted.

"But it's not too hot in here, is it?" John gave a grim smile. "It's too cold. Way too cold." As he stepped over the threshold into the Necropolis, a shiver ran through him, and for a second he did feel cold. Uncannily cold.

"You stay here, boy. I won't be long." The dog remained alert, his ears up sharp. He reminded John of the sacred black jackal Anubis that guarded the tomb of Tutankhamen. If only Sam did have the power to guard their home; to keep away the bad things that circled with all the dark ferocity of sharks circling a sinking ship.

"Wait for me, boy." He flashed a grin that weirdly felt wild and dangerous. "But come running if I howl."

Taking a deep breath, he plunged into the shoulder-high weeds that swamped the cemetery in a green ocean. From it sprang thousands of tiny black islands— the stones of the dead. He walked up the hill, stepping over broken vodka bottles, syringes, a bloodied tampon that had been torn out in the passion of the moment.

From his waist up it was hot as hell. But it was cold at his feet, where the grass held in the shade, and a little of the night. A rotted face peered at him from above the grass, the gouged eyes locked onto his. Erosion had made a meal of the stone angel. Disfiguring it. Reworking the face into something that oozed sourness. Frost had taken away its wings, too.

Moments later he entered the shadowed world of the Vale of Tears. Doors of cold iron ran ahead of him at either side of the passageway. He walked faster. The tomb walls nearly met overhead. In fact, he'd swear they were closer than the first time he'd come here. All he could see now was a narrow blue cut of sky. Tree roots that sprang from the roofs of the vaults snaked above him, while all the time the smell of old coffins leaked through holes in the iron doors to worm its way into his nose, then into his throat, lodging there as tightly as a fish bone.

Far away a dog howled. Sam, maybe, mourning the disappearance of his master into this world of rotten wood and moldering bone.

He turned through the maze at random. Straight ahead stood a tomb that was larger than the rest. Moss covered the walls in a greenish goblin fur. This time twin iron doors held fast the dead inside. Above the doors, two words were cut deep into the stone.

POSTHUMOUS ELLERBY

"Oh, Christ," John murmured. "Why did I have to see that?"

I don't have to know where Ellerby's tomb is. There's no need at all. But a voice inside his head disagreed: *You must know where to bring little Elizabeth tomorrow night . . . when you leave her here. She will be the companion of the demon forever and ever. Amen.*

"No, she will not," he grunted as he toiled through the airless world of the tomb complex. "Even if I have to take her to Canada, too. I'll not abandon her here."

Panting, sopping with perspiration, he ran up through the gully in the cliff. Soon he found himself standing before the tomb of Jess Bowen, the orphan boy whose skull was shattered on the doorstep of the Water Mill. Little Jess Bowen, who'd returned from the woods to speak with the deep, rumbling voice of a man.

The grave still bore traces of beer. The red balls were here, untouched; along with chocolate bars, melted into shit-brown pools in the dirt.

John glared down at the statue of the crying boy.

Then it became too much. Like Herbert Kelly before

him, who'd wept into the trunk of the apple tree, and Greensmith, who'd shattered the head of the orphan boy, a wild emotion fueled by fear and bitter frustration exploded inside John Newton.

With his left foot he stamped hard into the face of the crying boy. The stone shattered beneath his heel, sending fragments skittering across the gravestone.

Panting, John hissed, "You've met your match this time. I'm not going to give you what you want." Anger seared a fiery path right through him from head to toe. *"I'm going to fight you. Just you wait and see."*

Chapter Thirty-three

Later that Friday afternoon, the Newton family returned home one by one. The dog greeted each one, wagging his tail, making as much fuss as the heat allowed.

If you stood on the lawn, listening, you could hear the onslaught of the sun cracking the earth beneath your feet.

John worked on until evening, reading every book and website on folklore and superstition he could find. After that, he returned to Kelly's typewritten notes. Kelly had searched for a weapon of sorts to fight whatever had sent the demanding letters. Now John aimed to finish the job. At six, Val tried to cajole him into taking a cold drink in the garden, and with the words becoming spinning black dots before his tired eyes, he did need a break.

"You're going at the new book hard," she told him as they sat in the shade of a tree with a cold beer apiece.

"I made a flying start," he replied. "I wanted to keep the momentum going."

"Well, you should see the black rings under your eyes, John. Take it easy, OK?"

They sat for a while. Even talking, in this heat, required physical effort. Paul lay in the shade near where the millrace disappeared under the house. Elizabeth was the only one braving the direct glare of the sun. In shorts and T-shirt she practiced tapping a tennis ball into the air with a racquet. The sound of ball against catgut echoed like a hollow-sounding heartbeat.

John's mind gravitated back to the letter. He couldn't think of anything else now but finding some kind of solution. Naturally, he could not obey the demand this time and leave Elizabeth in the cemetery tomorrow night. But to refuse would immediately invite retribution. Just what that retribution might be, he didn't know. But it would come, he knew that. He'd been given a taste of it before when he'd ignored the first letter and Elizabeth had inexplicably fallen from her bike. Just a couple hours ago in a fit of rage, he'd kicked the crying-boy statue to pieces. No doubt about it. He'd sent a powerful signal to the demonic force known as Baby Bones that he, John Newton, was no longer going to yield to its demands.

Already he felt uneasy, however. Even with thirty hours to the deadline, he wondered if he'd trigger some early response. He found himself looking around the garden, then at the sky.

What are you expecting, John? A plane falling out of the great wide blue yonder to crush the house? But misfortune's coming, Johnny, boy. It's coming soon. You can feel it, can't you? It's clotting the air. You can even breathe it into your lungs. A formless dread that clings to your skin like slime.

You shouldn't have wrecked the grave of the little orphan boy, lying there in the ground with his skull all broken like a dropped egg. You shouldn't have desecrated the statue.

That's like sending a big fat e-mail to that smudge of darkness there in the heart of the hill that oozes its poison all over the village. You told it plain that it's not getting its paws on your daughter. That it can go to hell. I'd wager no one's rejected its evil little letters as firmly as that before.

The sweat rolled into John's eyes. It burned where it touched like acid. All he could see were blurred greens of trees, and the dissolving outline of Elizabeth as she played with the ball.

So, how're you going to defeat the thing, John? What's it going to take? A cross of iron planted up on the cemetery? Or maybe a sack full of salt—isn't that a sure way to kick the Devil's ass?

He took a mouthful of beer, but found it hard to swallow. His throat muscles were knotting with tension. Perspiration still burned his own eyes. He could barely see a damn thing. And the heat squeezed his lungs so hard, it was all he could do to draw breath.

"I'm going back to work on the book," he said suddenly. "I've a lot to do."

"John, can't you just take it easy for this evening?"

"I can't." He found himself snapping the words. Val looked stung.

"Sorry, Val, it's something that can't wait."

He returned to the house. He'd reached the top of the stairs when the telephone rang. Before he could reach it, the ringing stopped; someone had answered the extension in the kitchen.

Paul's voice shimmered along the walls. The tone stopped John in midstep. His son's voice rose in surprise, even astonishment.

"Miranda!" he heard his son exclaim. "Where are you? I thought that . . . No, no. OK, I'm listening."

John didn't mean to eavesdrop, but as he began to climb the stairs he heard Paul's surprised voice. "Let me get this straight. Your mother received a letter that said what?" A pause. "But that's insane . . . it must be from some nut."

A letter? John stopped and listened hard. Paul said something he couldn't make out. Then his voice rose as if he'd just heard something that astounded him. "So, because of that your mother sent you to London? When will you be back?" Another pause, then Paul said, "Miranda, if there's some weirdo sending letters, then your mother should call the police."

The blood tingled in John's veins.

So he wasn't alone. That was why Miranda Bloom had left home. Mrs. Bloom had received the same sinister letters. Only she'd chosen to send her daughter on an extended trip to London. Hopefully, out of harm's way until it blew over. But did it work like that? Look what happened to Keith Haslem. Maybe you had to cross a whole ocean to escape its malign influence.

At that moment John decided to book two airline tickets as soon as he possibly could. This time tomorrow he and Elizabeth could be on the other side of the world. If it had worked for Kelly and his daughter Mary, then it would work for John and Elizabeth Newton. Crossing that volume of saltwater did break the thing's hold.

"Dad, what are you doing?"

Paul stood at the bottom of the stairs glaring up at him. His face had a dark, angry look to it. "Did you hear enough of my telephone call? Or do you want a tape so you don't miss anything?"

Stung, John said, "I wasn't listening . . . at least not deliberately."

"Oh, you just happened to overhear as you stood there on the stairs? Dad, I could see your reflection in the oven door. You were gulping down every single word."

"Paul. I'm sorry. I didn't mean . . . Paul?" He ran downstairs as his son walked away. "Paul, listen. This is important. Was that Miranda?"

"You're not wrong, Sherlock."

"Paul, wait a minute. Am I right in thinking that Miranda hasn't really run away from home, but she's staying in London?"

"Right, and her mother made her."

"And this is to do with some letter that Mrs. Bloom received? Did she say—"

"Dad. Her mother made her go—she wanted Miranda to stop seeing me."

"But did Miranda say that?"

"It doesn't take a genius to figure it. All this about some fucking letter arriving in the fucking dead of night is a crappy excuse to get Miranda away from Skelbrooke."

Paul seethed with anger. John could see it in the way his son walked, fists clenched. He followed Paul through the back door.

Val sat under the tree, while Elizabeth still played ball beside the stream. The heat was incredible.

"Paul. Did Miranda tell you what was in the letter?"

"No, Dad." He turned and glared right into John's eyes. "Don't you get it? There probably isn't even a fucking stupid letter."

"John, I'm sorry you're angry. This has got to be a shitty—"

"You're damn right it's shitty. But all you can do is bang on about it, Dad. *What's in the letter, Paul? What does it say? Did it come in a purple envelope, Paul?*"

"Paul—"

"*Paul, Paul, Paul.*" His son mimicked him cruelly, squinting his eyes. "*I'm a famous writer, Paul. I want to scoop out your brains and put them in my shitty book, Paul.*" His voice rose to a yell. "Just leave me alone, Dad! It's none of your business. Got that? None of your friggin' business!"

Elizabeth looked around, startled by the shout. The ball she'd been bouncing clipped the edge of the racquet and shot across the lawn. She saw it would roll into the stream. Obviously mindful that she'd already lost a ball that way, she raced after it as fast as she could, her bare feet blurring at an incredible speed as she ran downhill to reach the ball before the water carried it under the house.

Val realized what would happen next. John did, too. "Leave it, Elizabeth. I'll get it . . . Elizabeth!"

In the Necropolis hill something dark was grinning

there. John saw it in his mind's eye as he watched with horror as his daughter tried to stop suddenly at the water's edge. She was too fast now. On bare feet she skidded across the grass. With a burst of spray she hit the water.

In seconds the stream carried her down to the house. Even though it hadn't rained for days, the flow of water was still remorseless.

Crying out, thrashing her arms and legs, she tried to stand. And she would have been able to stand easily with the water coming barely to her waist if the current hadn't been so strong—so uncannily strong.

"You bastard." The words escaped John's lips, directed at whatever lurked beneath the Necropolis, but it was Paul who turned around with an expression of shocked amazement.

"It's not my fault," Paul retorted. "She slipped!"

The look on his son's face as he glared back contained nothing less than hatred.

By now Elizabeth had been carried to within twenty yards of where the water disappeared with a rumble into the stone throat that ran beneath the house.

"Dad . . ." she cried. *"Dad, I can't get out!"*

John ran toward the stream. Paul was closer. With an athletic leap, Paul jumped into the stream between Elizabeth and the tunnel entrance.

Now all he had to do was stand there and catch her. The width of the stream was no more than five feet. In theory, it would be hard for her to slip by his long arms.

But then there was another factor in this.

An ancient driving power that made demands. That had the power to punish anyone that refused those demands.

And it's all your fault, John Newton. Dispelling the irrational accusation from his mind, he ran forward, aiming to catch Elizabeth if she was swept past Paul. Her hair matted across her face, she tried to swim, her T-shirt inflating around her in a soggy mass. At that moment she cannoned into Paul. He slipped backward, but still managed to grab her sopping T-shirt with one hand while reaching out to steady himself against the bank with the other. Muscles stood out like cables in his arm as he raised his sister from the water. Then he twisted around to hand her over to John. By this time Val had reached them, and together they lifted Elizabeth out onto dry ground.

Paul saw that his sister was shaken by the fall. He gave her a reassuring smile. "That was a close one, Lizzer." He grinned. "At least you won't have to wash behind your ears tonight."

The second Elizabeth was out of his hands, his center of gravity shifted; his feet seemed to slide forward from under him and he fell flat on his back into the stream with a tremendous splash that doused both banks.

There, the water was no deeper. But by the time Paul tried to stand, the current had carried him to where the streambed had been floored with stone slabs the size of gravestones. The stones were bright green with weed, and the water was fast but shallow, no deeper than a foot or so.

"Paul, stand up," Val shouted. She'd noticed he was being carried toward the maw of the tunnel. Beyond that was the dark throat of the millrace.

"Paul, stand up!" Elizabeth echoed her mother's cry. "Stand up!"

He tried, but the weed was slipperier than glass. At one point he even sat bolt upright, yet still the force of the current carried him across the slabs.

John watched. A cold dread of the inevitable flooded his stomach.

When Paul tried to roll himself to one side of the stream, the water seemed to bulge upward to push him back to its center.

John raced for the mouth of the tunnel. Rather than compound problems by running into the water himself, he realized the best option lay in reaching down to Paul from the side of the stream, then grabbing him as he passed. The only place he could be sure of reaching him was the very mouth of the tunnel. There, the banks had been enclosed in stone block-work, so at least the sides wouldn't crumble beneath him as he reached out to his son.

John reached the mouth of the millrace. Behind him, both Val and Elizabeth were shouting to Paul to hang onto a branch or simply get to his feet. But the current was swifter here as the banks narrowed, forcing the water to flow faster so it would power the mill.

John leaned over the stream, hearing the echo of water as it vanished under the house. There, in utter darkness, it dashed itself against stone pillars and raced downward under arches to God knows where before surging out the other side. If Paul should be swept under there . . .

"Paul!" he yelled, holding out his hand. "Get my arm!"

Water, accelerated by the narrowing channel, swept Paul faster. Even so, Paul raised an arm, his eyes locked on John's, and John saw an implicit trust there he hadn't seen since his son had been a little boy.

There was no problem in gripping Paul's arm.

The problem was the speed his 160-pound son was traveling. John felt himself spun around, then dragged toward the lip of stone that projected from the edge of the tunnel. The jutting stonework rammed into his chest just below his armpit.

He'd braced himself for a jolt. But he hadn't braced himself against the blast of white-hot agony that raced through his body. He'd never known pain like it. The fist of stone felt as if it had crunched right through his rib cage. Pain radiated outward across his chest and down his arm.

Grunting, he held onto his son's lean forearm. In turn, Paul's fingers closed around John's wrist to grimly hang on. John looked down. With the exception of one arm, the millrace tunnel had swallowed Paul's entire body. Dimly, John was aware of Val running forward to help. But there wasn't enough space on the bank here for her to grip Paul. All she could do was put her arms around John's chest and pull.

He cried out in agony the instant she tugged.

"John? What's wrong?"

"Nothing," he shouted over the water's roar. "Just keep pulling. We need to get him out . . . the force of the water will tear him to pieces under there."

Biting down, he tried to blot out the pain. The pain wouldn't quit. He must have cracked his ribs. It felt like hot iron nails were being hammered into the upper part of his chest. When he tried to tug Paul back, the pain traveled deeper into his arm. He nearly vomited at the intensity of it.

"Keep pulling," he gasped. "Keep pulling."

Then something seemed to reach up from under the house. He felt a tremendous tug on his arm.

When he looked down at the hand that had held his son's wrist, nothing but water lay in its grip now.

Chapter Thirty-four

"Paul's gone."

"What?"

He looked up at Val as the sound of the water drummed in his ear. For a second he didn't even realize he was the one who'd spoken the words. "Paul's gone," he repeated. As John straightened, pain shot through his chest. Breathing in, he winced. A good two or three ribs must have snapped from the force of the blow. But he couldn't let that stop him now.

"We've got to get him out," he said. "There's all kind of debris down there. If it traps him underwater . . ."

Val ran around the house. He followed. Ghost-faced, Elizabeth tried to keep up. It was the dog who reached the other side of the house first. He stood on the banks of the stream and howled a banshee howl.

John and Val reached the outlet together. John stared down, willing his son to reappear, spluttering, sodden, but ready to make a joke of it all.

They waited five seconds, ten seconds. Twenty. Thirty.

Simon Clark

Paul didn't appear.

"Oh, dear God," John breathed. "He's trapped."

"Will Paul be all right, Dad?" Elizabeth's eyes glittered at the outfall of water that emerged in a viscous core as if squeezed from a tube. "I wish I could change places with him. I'm smaller. I'd be all right . . . Dad?"

"Val! Wait here in case he comes through . . . you might have to help him out if he's hurt."

For a moment John considered tearing round to the back of the house, then following his son into the roaring darkness. But God only knows what old timber posts, branches, tangles of barbed wire already lay in the millrace like animal traps. Getting himself trapped wouldn't help Paul one bit. Instead, he ran to the living room, threw himself on his knees, and looked down through the observation glass into the dark pit of the millrace. All he could see were flecks of white foam amongst the swirl and twist of deep shadows. He scrambled across the floor to switch on the millrace lights. A second later he was back at the glass, leaning forward on both hands, staring down into the now-dazzling splash of light that illuminated the observation chamber. He grimaced as the pain from his busted ribs ricocheted through his entire being.

Gritting his teeth, he stared down. This chamber was an access to the millrace in years gone by. But now the glass was well and truly bolted down. Could he break it?

Not a hope in hell. The previous owner had said the toughened glass could bear the weight of elephants. *Damn.* He stared down at flecks of green weed slithering by.

What condition was his son in down there? What if he couldn't keep his head above the surface? What if the water had smashed him against stone columns like a pinball? There must something he could do. . . .

Good God. Just a few feet below him a figure appeared.

A man that had lain dead for years, swathed mum-

340

mylike in green weed, yet still possessing two living eyes that burned up with a terrible fire at him. A hand erupted from the foam. Fingertips slashed at the glass.

Then John knew. "Paul!"

Sheer water pressure must have squeezed his son through the narrower sections of the passage, coating him in waterweed. Now there Paul was: alive—very much alive!—yet trapped in that stone gut. Down there the water must feel cold as ice. The thunder of its passage and that utter gravelike darkness must have disorientated him. But still, he'd looked up and recognized his father.

John saw the mouth open. Paul was shouting, only the glass blocked all sound. In rage John struck the observation window with his fist. His eyes locked onto the terror-filled eyes of his son. For a second Paul struggled against the rush of water, but it was as if dark forces gripped his legs and drew him slowly—as slowly as a funeral pace—from this chamber into the next section of tunnel.

Paul looked up in panic. Water cascaded over his face and those two burning eyes. Constantly, green weed swirled around and over him. Then his waist was drawn into the tunnel, and then his chest vanished. In a gulp his head had gone, too. John saw two hands clutch above the foam, fingers stretching out, as if Paul hoped that even then someone would reach down to pull him to safety.

Then they, too, were gone.

Once more John ran to the front of the house, where Val waited with Elizabeth. The dog had plunged into the stream to stand looking into the outflow.

"He's stuck down there," John shouted.

"John! Where are you going . . . *John*?"

He ran back around the house, then followed the stream up to the lake. At first the torrent had driven Paul to the house, where the tunnel greedily swallowed him. But now the flow of water wasn't powerful enough to force him through the stone bore beneath the house. If he became lodged underwater in the tunnel, then he'd drown before the water pressure drove him through to the other side and freedom.

Gasping for breath, John reached the sluice gate. For weeks now he'd been working axle grease into the rusted cogs and winding shaft, trying to free the locked mechanism without any success. Now he saw that the only way to save his son was to literally flush him through the tunnel and out the other side. Seizing the steel wheel in both hands, he began to turn.

Instantly agony seared his side. His broken ribs must have champed like bloody jaws against one another. Yelling in pain, he heaved at the wheel, straining to turn the thing.

For a moment nothing.

Then, with a scream that echoed his own, the wheel turned. Trying to blot out the pain in his ribs, he forced the wheel around—then around again. Jerkily, the sluice gate began to lift. Water ran faster into the channel. The stream turned black with churned silt. Then, slowly, it began to rise.

Sweating, panting, groaning with a pain that threatened to overwhelm his sanity, he turned the wheel again and again, faster and faster. The ancient mechanism squealed. But it moved. The fucking thing moved!

Howling with a savage exultation, he forced the sluice gate open as far as it would go. Then he turned back to see a tidal wave rush down along the channel. It hit the tunnel mouth with so much force, it sent a splash bursting high enough to wet the bedroom windows. For a second, the waters rose as they hit some blockage beneath the house. Backing up, they spilled over the bank, threatening to form a lake across the lawn.

Then, abruptly, the blockage had gone, allowing water to flow freely into the tunnel.

Shakily now, as if the strength had bled from him, he returned to the outflow on the farside of the house where Val and Elizabeth waited.

Water gushed out with enough force to push the dog back to the bank.

But there was no Paul.

"He can't be far from this end of the tunnel now," John panted. "The water pressure should have pushed him through."

Val bent down to look at the green core of water as it vented from the side of the house. Maybe a good yard thick, it appeared solid enough to slice with a knife.

"I can see him!" she cried. Then she forced her arm into the water. "I can feel his head." She shot John an agonized look. "He's underwater. He won't be able to breathe."

Forcing her arm deeper, she felt for the trapped body.

"He's lodged against something," she shouted. "I'm going to try and turn him."

Then, against the force of the water, she drove her arm deeper, until her shoulder reached the lip of the tunnel. Now water gushed up over her face. She couldn't breathe herself, yet she held herself there, working at her son's shoulder, trying to turn him around inside the narrow passageway.

The sun, like some great watchful eye, glared down. John found himself slipping into a weird detached state of mind. For a moment, it seemed, he left his soaking and battered body to gaze down at three figures standing beside the water that tumbled from beneath a three hundred-year-old house. A black dog shivered on the bank.

This was when life hung in the balance. High in the cemetery a shiver of anticipation ran through long dead bones.

"My God!" Val shouted. *"My God!"*

The sheer emotion in her voice brought him back. He looked into the gel-like water. Spray stung his face. The torrent's roar thundered against his head.

Val shouted in disbelief, "He's moving!"

The outflow stopped just for a second.

Like some echo of birth, Paul's head appeared. His hair was a matted cap; green weed formed a cawl across his face. Water spurted around his shoulders as the pressure built behind him.

The titanic force of the current squeezed him through a narrow aperture inside the tunnel's opening. At last, with a wet sucking sound, he came through, his arms down by his sides; pushed out by the force of water to splash down into the stream.

John, with Val and Elizabeth pulling, too, hoisted Paul up the grass banking to the path.

Then John stood back. Val frantically rubbed Paul's chest and arms, repeating his name over and over. Elizabeth massaged her brother's stomach with both her hands. The dog circled them all, unable to take his eyes off the teenager's face.

Paul's eyes were closed. His face was gray. Very gray.

Chapter Thirty-five

One

Singing. Who can sing in a place like this? A man stood by a water cooler singing to an imaginary audience, his hands held out before him. About fifty years old, with the ringed eyes and overabundant nose of the alcoholic, he sang in a foreign language. He was singing because he was drunk. And he was singing here in the hospital's casualty department because, tired of this world, he'd cut his wrists. Now sutured and bandaged, he waited for a bed in the psychiatric ward.

Only, the staff were too busy. So he stood there. Sang. And held out his bandaged wrists for everyone to see.

John Newton no longer wanted to smack the man in the mouth. But he wished someone would take him away. In whatever language the man sang, he was singing a sad song.

John glanced to his left. Elizabeth sat between him and Val. No one had spoken for a long time. The heat boxed them in. Even though it was close to ten that

Friday evening, it was still light outside. All three were grimy, their hair stiff with sweat and stream water.

Three hours had ticked by since Paul's accident.

They'd taken turns to see Paul. John had wondered if Elizabeth should see her brother. She was only nine years old. But she'd taken the shock better than her parents.

John found himself unable to see Paul as he really was. For some reason he found himself seeing Paul through the filter of a half-remembered sci-fi flick where an android, pummeled by gunfire, spills its gut of wires, tubes, and fistfuls of ribbed hoses through plastic skin. As Paul lay on the ventilator in ICU, John saw wires and tubes snaking from his nose, mouth, arms, and chest, and yet he didn't see his son, but an android with chrome endoskeleton and mock human flesh.

"Paul." Elizabeth had shaken her brother's shoulder. "Paul. We're here. Wake up."

The doctor had fed them strong coffee and explained, "Paul must have been underwater for a long time. We know his heart stopped beating for a while. What we don't know is if he suffered any permanent damage."

"Brain damage?" Val had asked, and the doctor had nodded.

In the lounge area, the man still sang his sad song. The seats were full and the hot air dirty with sweat, dust, and the exhalation of so many people. They'd been waiting hours to have their wounds treated, whether it was a man who'd put a garden fork through his foot or a drunk who'd fallen flat on his face.

John rubbed his forehead. Immediately the movement struck up a whole symphony of pains in his side where he'd cracked his own ribs. Maybe he should get someone to look at them? No. Not yet. He had to be sure Paul was going to be all right first before he could even think about himself.

Yeah. Paul. Why was he letting his attention wander to other people? His son lay with tubes coming out of every hole in his body. John realized his mind still tried hard to evade reality.

The doctor had told it straight. Paul had drowned. Fact. For five or six minutes Paul had been dead. Fact. The paramedics had jolted his heart. It had resumed beating. Nevertheless, Paul's immediate future was uncertain.

Now there were three alternatives.

One. Paul might wake at any moment as fit as any teenager.

Two. Paul might wake with brain damage; this might be slight enough to leave him with slurred speech for a month or two. Or it might be severe enough to put him in a wheelchair forever.

Three. He might not wake up at all.

A nurse took the singing man away. His voice faded down the corridor, until all John could hear were dying echoes. That was the moment when Val took a deep breath. "There's no point in all three of us sitting here," she told John. "You take Elizabeth home. I'll stay here with Paul." She sounded so matter-of-fact.

"I want to make sure that Paul's OK before I go," Elizabeth said in a small voice. "I can't leave him here."

"Don't worry, hon. He'll be all right."

She paused for a moment. "Dad. He saved me, didn't he? If he hadn't got me out of the stream, it would have killed me, wouldn't it?"

Was there any real answer to that one? John hugged his daughter.

It should be me in there instead of him. John half-expected her to say it, but she fell silent. No doubt, however, those very words were going around in her mind.

Perhaps this was where shock would give way to self-recrimination. He winced as the pains speared his side. If only he could have held onto Paul, the boy would be all right now. He'd have climbed out of the stream, grinning and joking about the ducking. Everything would be fine. *But you're weak, John Newton. You*

*could have saved your son. You had a good grip on his wrist.
But you let him go. You're gutless. You never fought to save
him. . . .*

He deliberately hurt himself by taking a deep breath,
the cracked ribs shifting before his expanding lungs.
*That's it, Newton. Try and wash away guilt with pain. But
then, you've never been a fighter, have you?*

Just you wait and see, he told himself. The fight's
only just beginning.

Despite the harrowing evening, he knew the clock
was ticking down the minutes until midnight tomorrow. The letter demanded he hand his daughter over
then to whatever lurked in the cemetery.

No way.

NO WAY!

Two

After leaving the hospital, John drove Elizabeth for a
hamburger. It was close on eleven by now. The place
was crowded with kids in their teens. They were laughing, shouting, having a good time.

But he and Elizabeth sat in silence, as if they'd been
sealed into their own sphere. Outside that, everything
seemed disjointed, people looked like alien life-forms.
John wondered if other people could read the anxiety
on the faces of the little girl and the man who sat pushing French fries into their mouths as if they tasted of
paper. He guessed not. Those young people were so
happy, they'd never notice the melancholy pair in the
corner.

Neither he nor Elizabeth finished the meal. Soon they
were in the car again, heading home. By now night had
fallen properly. The car's lights splashed across the
road. At one point the headlights caught the Necropolis
gates. Headstones were black, soulless eyes staring
down from the hillside. Above them, trees had become
hunched monsters that reflected the car's headlights
with the cold flash of ghost-light.

John drove on. He felt that he had a stone for a heart. It grew even heavier when he pulled into the drive and saw the stream that had taken his son just a few hours ago.

The instant John opened the front door, Sam ran out to the car. When the dog saw Val and Paul weren't there, he returned to the house, his head hanging low.

Mechanically, they got ready for bed. John yielded at last to the pain and swallowed paracetamol. He chased that with a tumbler of whiskey. The painkiller had no effect. He lay there on the bed, gnawed by teeth of sickening pain.

Elizabeth cried for a while in the next room. Then fell silent.

Shadows swarmed across the walls. Once or twice he heard the dog yelp in his sleep.

Long past midnight, he drifted off himself.

He dreamt that a face looked in at him through the window. It was ghost-white with gouged sockets for eyes. A mouth opened that could have been an ax wound. He watched as a pair of eyes oozed out like snake heads through the empty sockets in the skull. They were lined with veins as thick as worms, while the pupils were fierce black points that stood out from the eyes as hard as warts. These were eyes that feasted on the ghosts of children. Hungry eyes that wanted more and more and more.

A voice ran through his head. A nitric voice that sounded burned, whispery, and so low, it vibrated the whiskey glass on the table. *Listen to the sound of the clock, John Newton. It's ticking the minutes away. You know what you must do. Hand over the girl. I want her....*

"No!"

You know what will happen if you don't. You must pay the forfeit.

"I won't!"

What happened to your filthy little son, John Newton? That was a warning. Hand her over....

Beyond the window, the face looked in. The eyes no

longer bulged, but withdrew into the sockets, leaving empty chambers that were as dark as an open grave.

"You're not having her!"

He shouted himself awake. The sun blazed into the room as if a furnace door had opened. Straightaway, he turned to the clock on the bedside table.

Six o'clock.

In just eighteen hours it would be midnight.

Zero Hour.

Chapter Thirty-six

Herbert Kelly had put an ocean between his daughter and Skelbrooke. That had broken the link. Whatever power festered there in the hill couldn't reach them in Canada. Nor, apparently, had it been able to wreak its revenge on Skelbrooke's inhabitants. For seventy years it had retreated back into the cemetery dirt (or wherever it made its home), and it had bided its time before reawakening.

John Newton sat on a garden bench, staring at the Necropolis as it rose above Skelbrooke village, brooding on this and other thoughts. Even though it was not yet nine o'clock in the morning, he'd begun phoning airline offices, trying to get himself and Elizabeth on a flight before tonight. The mobile phone lay on the bench beside him. It was early, the staffs had claimed. There was a glitch with the booking computers. They'd get back to him. So he waited in the shade. The temperature climbed. Soil cracked wide open. Even the branches clicked as bark shriveled in the sun. Already the heat made it difficult to breathe. When he inhaled, his cracked ribs jabbed hard enough to make him wince. Wincing pulled on the cracked bone, hurting like hell. And so the cycle repeated itself.

Elizabeth sat on the grass not far from him. Alongside her lay the dog.

John glanced at his watch. Ten past nine. Why didn't the airlines ring? He needed those tickets now. But what he'd tell Val, he didn't know . . . she was going through a nightmare as it was. How could he just announce he was taking Elizabeth to the other side of the world?

The phone rang. He snatched it from the bench. "Hello?"

He'd expected an airline. Instead, he heard Val's careworn voice. His heart lurched. God knows, he expected the worst.

"John, I'm telephoning to tell you about Paul. He's still unconscious. There's no change."

"Have they been able to give you any more information about his condition?"

"No. They keep stressing it's a case of wait-and-see."

Elizabeth had heard the phone ring. Putting his hand over the mouthpiece, he told her Paul was still asleep, that there was nothing to worry about.

"What was that, Val? Yes, we're both fine. I'll come through in a little while."

"Oh, could you bring me a change of clothes and my toilet bag? They say I can stay here so I can be near Paul."

"Will do."

"Sorry if you can't hear me properly," she said over voices in the background. "It's busy here this morning. Of all things, there's been an outbreak of meningitis in Skelbrooke."

"Christ . . ."

"As if we didn't have enough to worry about. From what I can tell they're trying to identify it. If it's the bacterial C strain of meningitis, then Elizabeth will

352

have to be vaccinated. Apparently there's a couple of children from her school down with it."

"God what a mess." *The cause of the meningitis outbreak? Hell. As if I didn't know. It's you, Baby Bones, isn't it? You came down into the village at night to breathe your poison onto the faces of the children as they slept.*

"John?" Val raised her voice over the voices nearby. "Did you hear what I said?"

"Sorry . . ."

"All hell is breaking loose here—they've just rushed in more cases. I'm sure one of them is Elizabeth's friend, Emma. Damn, this is just what we don't need. John?"

"Yes?"

"Will you keep a close eye on Elizabeth? This epidemic's going through Skelbrooke like wildfire."

"Of course I will."

"The symptoms are headache, nausea, pain in the joints. And if she complains about the light being too bright, get her to the hospital right away. Oh, and there'll be a rash, too."

"Val, don't worry. I know what to look out for."

"I best get off the phone. People are queuing up to use it. Hell, it's like a war zone down here."

"Val, take care of yourself. Look after Paul."

"I will, John. You take care of things at that end. I'll have to go, my money's running out. Love you."

Suddenly, he needed to tell her he was leaving. That it was the only way to take this curse off everyone's backs. "Val. Listen to me. I'm going away with Elizabeth for a couple of weeks. I can't . . ." He stopped, realizing he was talking to the dial tone.

He looked across at Elizabeth, who was dreamily tickling the dog's stomach. She was in a world of her own, praying that Paul would wake from the coma soon.

John slipped the phone into his shirt pocket, then returned to the house to pack.

Simon Clark

Two

By nine-thirty he was on the road to the hospital. Elizabeth sat by his side. The radio played bright pop songs. The guitars jangled his already worn nerves. He glanced at Elizabeth. Stone-faced, she stared forward at the road unspooling before them.

Meanwhile, the car's air-conditioning had already lost the battle against the heat.

His eyes flicked from the road to the mobile phone balanced on the dash, then to the clock. The seconds ticked steadily away toward midnight. Zero hour.

Why wouldn't the airlines ring back? Had the *thing* in the hill the power to reach into the ticketing computers and play merry hell with the programs?

Ring, phone. Ring.

But the phone refused to ring. They arrived at the hospital to find it as Val had described, a war zone. Ambulances arrived, sirens whooping, lights flashing, with more victims of the meningitis outbreak sweeping Skelbrooke.

Avoiding the bustling medics and streams of gurneys, John took Elizabeth to intensive care. He handed Val her bag, kissed her. Then they went to see Paul. He lay inside the spider's web of tubes, wires, cables. Monitors bleeped; screens traced out his vital signs like comet trails racing toward the inevitable.

Paul's breathing, mechanically driven, looked exaggerated. His bare chest rose so high, the skin pulled tight, revealing the bones beneath. There was still grayness about the face. For the first time John noticed bruising around Paul's eyes where he'd been battered against the tunnel walls. There was precious little skin on his elbows too. The millstream stones must have been as abrasive as sandpaper. John felt such a surge of love for his son that it winded him. He had to make everything right for him. If only he'd managed to keep a grip on his wrist . . .

Once more Elizabeth shook her brother's shoulder. "Paul, wake up."

After about an hour or so, John took Elizabeth home. As arranged, Val would stay with her son. When they reached the house they found a dead blackbird outside the front door. The heat had killed it, he figured. But in the underside of his mind he knew that a poison was leaking into the village wholesale.

Events were racing toward their inevitable conclusion. It was nearly midday. Just twelve hours to go until midnight.

Three

When the mobile rang on the bench, he reached out for it so quickly his cracked ribs shrieked in protest. He had to answer through gritted teeth.

At last. An airline. Two seats were available on a flight to Jamaica at three that afternoon. His heart beat faster. He was going to beat old Baby Bones yet. He booked, paying by credit card. The tickets would be waiting at the airport.

He walked back through the searing heat to the house. There were still loose ends to tie. He'd have to leave the dog at the boarding kennels, and though he'd packed for himself and Elizabeth, he'd neglected to hunt out the passports. Forgetting a detail like that would really louse up his plans.

Once more his heart weighed stonelike inside his chest. He'd told Val he'd see her this afternoon. The deception sickened him. What's more, he'd have to telephone her from the airport. What he'd tell her, he didn't know, but he'd think of something.

Just reaching up into the closet where they stored family documents came as a little slice of hell in its own right. The pain in his ribs sickened him. He could hardly breathe. But he gritted his teeth, pulled down the old cookie tin, then riffled through it for the passports.

For one chilling moment he suddenly thought his

had expired. But no. It was good for another six months. And there was his photograph. A younger John Newton, calm blue eyes, wavy hair, and not a care in the world back then.

Sitting on the bed, he spent five minutes checking the credit cards in his wallet, stuffing the passports into his holdall, and generally ensuring he had everything he needed.

"Dad . . . Dad! Come here!"

The urgency in his daughter's voice jerked him to his feet. His ribs jagged so hard that a wave of darkness swamped his mind, sending him thumping down onto his knees.

What's wrong?

It's Baby Bones, all white-faced and wormy-eyed; he's come to claim Elizabeth for himself. . . .

Shaking vertigo out of his head, he blundered out of the bedroom and ran downstairs.

"Quick!" Elizabeth gestured at the back door. "Dad, why are they here?"

"What's here, hon?" Face dripping with sweat, he ran out onto the patio.

Good God.

He stopped and stared. There, covering the back lawn, like a fall of strange fruit, were dozens of black feathery forms.

"Dad, why have they landed here?"

"Don't worry, hon. They're only crows."

"But there's loads of them. Why have they come down onto our lawn? Look! They're all over the roof, too."

In folklore, a flock of crows settling on your home is an omen of death. That an occupant of the house will die soon.

Just for a second his hand closed over the phone in his pocket. He sensed digital radio waves speeding toward the aerial, then coursing through circuitry to trigger the ring tone.

Paul's dead ... the birds are here as messengers of old Master Death himself.

"Can't you scare them away, Dad? I don't like them."

Birds hopped about the grass ... so many black-feathered demons, their coal-bright eyes glaring at the house, their sick yellow beaks opening to fire echoing cries, like the sound of hungry babies wracked by famine. To his eyesight, distorted by heat, and blurred by exhaustion and pain, these night-black crows were holes in the fabric of reality. They revealed dark eternity beyond, where grim-hearted phantoms stalked.

Oh, sweet Jesus ... He felt his mind slipping. The pain unraveled his wits.

He felt Elizabeth's hand slip into his. She said in a low voice, "Something bad's going to happen, isn't it, Dad?"

Four

The time was 12:30. They needed to leave by 1:15. It wasn't a long drive to Leeds airport.

As he laid the cold chicken on the bread, he realized he needed to give Elizabeth some reason why they were leaving. He knew she'd resist. She wouldn't want to leave with Paul lying there in a coma. What could he do? His hands were tied. This was for the best. It had worked for Kelly; it would work for them.

The heat and the pain from his fractured ribs conspired to kick the crap out of him. He found himself constantly breathless now. He tried to avoid taking deep breaths because the pain was so bad. But then he needed to breathe. This was the mother of all no-win situations. He'd already gulped down the usual drug-store painkillers. But he might as well have swallowed sugar lumps for the good they'd done. It felt as if a wolf was chewing on his side.

He labored upstairs to the bedroom. There he found a pack of powerful painkillers that had been prescribed to Val for a tooth abscess. She'd told him with a goofy grin on her face that they were strong enough to anesthetize a hippo. That goofy grin hadn't left her face for hours. They were powerful medicine, all right.

Now he swallowed the big white tablets with the help of a glass of water.

12:45. Half an hour before they left. He carried the holdall downstairs to the car. Elizabeth had finished her sandwich and was washing the plates. She looked flushed. Her eyes had narrowed as if she had the makings of a headache. He tried to recall the symptoms of meningitis.

Meanwhile, the bag had been heavy enough to trigger a whole symphony of jangling agonies in his side. Returning to the house, he sat down to allow the tablets a few minutes to kick in. Once he felt them working their magic, damping down the pain, he'd ask Elizabeth if she felt unwell. Now, those meningitis symptoms? Headache, pain in the joints, a rash . . . Sweet Jesus. He just needed these drugs to kill the pain . . . then he could function again.

Eleven hours to midnight near as damnit. In a little over two hours they'd be airborne. Twenty minutes after that they'd be over the ocean.

"You won't be able to catch us then," he sang under his breath. "You won't be able to catch us, you son of a bitch."

Chapter Thirty-seven

One

John Newton awoke to the sound of the clock chiming seven.

Seven?

He sat up on the sofa. His heart beat hard. Elizabeth sat on the millrace window watching him. He looked at his watch.

The shock was electric.

"It's seven o'clock!" The words tore through his throat in something between a gasp and a yell.

"I know," she said. "You slept all afternoon."

"Elizabeth, why didn't you wake me? We've missed . . ."

"Missed what, Dad?"

He shook his head in disbelief. Jesus Christ, the plane was long, long gone. How could have slept so deeply with all this . . . this shit happening? It must have been a combination of painkillers, exhaustion, and all the crap he'd gone through over the last couple of days. It had knocked him cold.

Hell and goddamn. What now?

He turned on his daughter again. Her eyes were wide. Scared-looking. "Damnit, Lizzie. Why didn't you wake me?"

"I tried . . . you wouldn't wake up. Sometimes you stopped breathing." Her voice grew small. "I thought you'd died."

He paced the floor, shaking his head, clenching his fists, his jaw working but no words coming out. Dear God . . . why was he fighting this alone? Surely someone could help. But down in the village people were milling around like frightened sheep. Yes, they knew what was happening, Goddamnit. But they were too frightened to help in case that great menacing, dark-boned finger of fate pointed at them.

No way was he going to face this alone. He would find help. Or at least punch some slack-fool jaws in the process.

With the blood roaring through his veins, he said to Elizabeth, "Get in the car, we're going down to the village."

"Why?"

"Don't ask, please. There's someone I need to see."

But who?

Who indeed?

Two

He drove as far as Skelbrooke's main street. The road ahead, according to a sign that straddled the white line, was closed.

"Wait here," he told Elizabeth. "I won't be long."

Parking the car at the side of the road, he headed toward the center of the village on foot. It was after seven now; people would be in the pub.

There's only five hours until zero hour, John Newton. Five hours until midnight. The letter demands you leave your

*daughter in the cemetery. What are you going to do, New-
ton? What y' gonna do?*

He walked down the village street. The sun still rode
high in the sky. The place looked deserted. A ghost
town.

Then he saw the cause of the road closure. A truck
stood in the middle of the street. White powder had
spilled from the back of it all across the blacktop, creating an arctic-white scene. A lone workman attempted
to clear the road spill, working away with a long-
handled broom. But he made little headway. In fact, he
seemed to make matters worse.

John walked by the dazzling white blanket of powder.

"I'll be damned," he said to himself, pausing. This
was no accidental road spill. This was deliberate. As he
walked into the road, grains of white crunched like
snow beneath his soles. He reached down, touched the
grains, then licked his finger.

Salt. The frightened people of Skelbrooke were using
the oldest protection against evil in the book. Salt scattered all over the damned place. Salt for the Devil's eye.

The workman wasn't sweeping up. *He was spreading it*.

Ahead, John saw a girl that seemed familiar. Black
hair, dark Latino eyes. The face clicked in his memory.
Miranda Bloom. She was back home? Why? Why, when
her mother had sent her away in a panic after receiving
the letters, had Miranda returned?

Miranda had seen him. Straightaway, she ran across
the salt-covered street.

"Mr. Newton?"

He nodded, and saw that she'd been crying.

"I heard about Paul's accident," she said. "How is
he?"

"It's serious," he said, suspecting he was on the brink
of finding out a truth he was frightened to know. "He's
in a coma. The doctors say the next few hours will be

crucial." He didn't sugarcoat this bitter pill. "They don't know whether he'll live or not."

As if he were carrying some infection, she fell back from him as he passed. Ahead stood the Swan Inn. Not a soul was in sight. But he knew the villagers would be in there. Sheltering together for some imagined protection. Waiting for this particular storm to pass.

Once more he walked across the blanket of salt. The workman watched him. Said nothing. And continued sweeping salt out in a gleaming wash across the blacktop.

He intended walking straight into the bar as he'd done before, then challenging those frightened sheep in human clothing to tell him everything they knew.

John Newton never reached the pub door.

An old man walked out of the building to meet him halfway across the street. They stood in the blazing sun, watching each other for a moment. The old man's white hair shone as bright as the salt beneath his feet.

"John Newton," he said. "You don't know me. I've lived all my life in this village. My name is Joseph Fitzgerald. I'm ninety-two years old."

John tilted his head to one side, his expression grim. He didn't speak, but waited for the old man to say more.

Fitzgerald looked levely at John. "I was a colleague of Mr. Kelly seventy years ago when he received his letter. Now I'm here to tell you your duty."

Three

The two men looked like two gunfighters facing each other along the street of a town from the Old West. The roadway, even if it was salt, not Texas dust, played its part.

Sun reflecting from the white road narrowed the old man's eyes to slits.

"Mr. Newton. There's no easy way. But you must do it."

"Do what?"

Instead of answering, Fitzgerald said, "Seventy years ago, Mr. Kelly at the Water Mill received a series of letters. People down here in the village received similar ones. They asked for trifles—chocolate, beer. Nothing much. Then Mr. Kelly received a demand from—"

"Baby Bones?"

"From something that's had different names down the years. This last letter demanded he leave his daughter in the cemetery on a given night."

"I know," John said levelly. "I've read the copies Kelly made."

"Mr. Kelly fought it. He delayed taking Mary Kelly to the cemetery. He refused to accept responsibility for the consequences. There was an outbreak of influenza in the village. A lot of people died."

"Herbert Kelly was a strong man, Mr. Fitzgerald."

"He was obstinate. Dangerously obstinate."

"Heroic, I'd call him."

"I was a junior member of his teaching staff. I believed he thought highly of me, and people here figured I could persuade him of his responsibilities to his neighbors."

"I hope he ignored you." A dangerous anger was spilling through John now. He knew what was coming.

"He did ignore me. And as I returned home on my motorcycle, I blacked out and the machine ran under a tractor. I paid the price for Mr. Kelly's obstinacy." He raised an arm. The sleeve slipped back to reveal a forearm with no hand, merely a shriveled stump. "Mr. Kelly was an intelligent man. He believed his intelligence would allow him to beat something that had been here five thousand years or more."

"And what is that *something* exactly?"

"No one can say. Any more than you can detail the anatomy of God. But it can make demands of us periodically. And it can punish if we don't comply."

"Well, your filthy little monster isn't going to dictate shit to me!"

363

Simon Clark

"Mr. Newton . . . John. I am sorry. I truly am. But the last letter's come to you. It has demanded your youngest child, hasn't it?"

"You know a lot, don't you?" John clenched his fists in fury.

"Believe me, John. I would willingly take her place. But *IT* demands what it demands. There's no escaping it. You must do what is best for the village. You must—"

"*No.*"

"You don't have the luxury of choice. There has been an outbreak of meningitis in the neighborhood. Ten children are in hospital. Now their lives hang in the balance. They will recover if you meet the demands of the letter. If you don't, the children will die. They will be followed by more. You and your family will not be spared. This has all happened before. You cannot break the cycle."

"Oh, but I can. Do you know something, Mr. Fitzgerald? Stan Price . . . you might have heard of him? Old, senile Stan Price fought hard to get his wits together again, and he came up to see me at the Water Mill. He brought me documents that prove Kelly was fighting the monster . . . *with this.*" John stabbed a finger at his own head. "He fought the monster with his own brain, Mr. Fitzgerald. Now I intend to do the same!"

"No, John. He tried. He tried hard. But in the end he had to admit defeat. He took his daughter to the graveyard at midnight and left her there."

"Wrong again, Mr. Fitzgerald. Kelly took Mary to Canada. He found a way to beat this thing. Now I'm going to do the same."

Burning with rage, John turned away from the old man's pleading eyes. He walked back to the car. He didn't look back.

The time had come. No more prevarication. He'd drive to the airport, then take the first available flight to anywhere that lay over an ocean.

The clock in the Necropolis funeral chapel struck eight. Four hours to midnight.

OK, so he was sitting on a time bomb. Zero hour approached.

But he and Elizabeth wouldn't be here when it did.

Chapter Thirty-nine

One

After the showdown with ninety-two-year-old Joseph Fitzgerald, John returned the car to find Elizabeth standing on the sidewalk watching him.

"Elizabeth? I thought I asked you to stay in the car."

"What did that man want? And why is there sugar all over the street?"

"It was a very old man. I think he's confused. And it isn't sugar, it's salt. Get back in the car, Elizabeth, we're in a hurry."

She did as he asked, perhaps figuring they were on the way to the hospital to see Paul.

John noticed people leaving the pub as he U-turned the car back home. In the rearview, he saw them watching him go. They looked like a bunch of lost spirits.

As he turned onto the main highway, he saw Miranda waiting at the bus stop. She watched him, too. Fear enlarged her eyes into discs that glittered in the sunlight.

"If it gets any hotter," Elizabeth commented hollowly, "we're all going to burn up in smoke."

John swung the car onto the old lane, then powered on up to the Water Mill.

"Wait here," he told Elizabeth. For the first time that day he was clearheaded. He knew what he must do now. He picked up the holdall containing the passports, then, after locking the house, he ushered the dog into the car's backseat. For a second Elizabeth laughed her delight at seeing Sam. Then she frowned.

"Dad. We won't be allowed to take Sam into the hospital, will we?"

"He's not going to the hospital. I'm dropping him off at the boarding kennels."

She was thinking fast. "Where are we going, Dad?"

"Away for a few days."

She spoke in a low voice, but emotion made her tremble. "Don't make me go, Dad. I haven't done anything wrong, have I?"

"No, of course not." John was startled. Had she really thought he was taking her away as punishment? "We'll be gone a few days. Tops."

"I don't want to go. I want to stay here and make sure that Paul's—"

"Elizabeth. I'm sorry. But it's out of my hands. We have to make this trip."

"Are you breaking up with Mum?"

"No, hon."

"This is what happened when Lee's parents divorced."

"There won't be any divorce, hon. Your mother and I love each other. It's just important we go on this trip. I can't explain it yet. Just trust me, sweetheart. OK?"

He leaned across to hug her. She hugged him back. His ribs grated, shooting a pain from one side of his chest to the other, but this time he didn't flinch. He squeezed his daughter tighter, telling her how much he loved her, that everything was going to be all right. "You just see," he told her. "In a few weeks we'll start work on that swimming pool. Then we can have a big opening party with all your friends."

"Can we have a barbecue?"

"Of course. We could even hire a disco."

"And have fireworks."

"Biggest and the best." He smiled.

"And Paul will be home?"

"He will and he'll be back to his old mischievous self." Mentally, he added, *Touch wood*. In the car there was no wood to touch. Was that a bad omen?

It was approaching nine o'clock. Now he was conscious of time racing them toward midnight. Again the image came of the time bomb ticking down to zero hour. A dirty great time bomb that could take out this village. The moment he started the engine the mobile rang. He answered, his heart pounding. It would be about Paul. Bad news . . .

"Good evening. Mr. Newton?"

The voice was as hearty as it was recognizable.

"Mr. Gregory?"

"Yes. Bit of a problem. Sorry to bother you, but Stan's gone walkabout again. As he came up to the Water Mill last time he disappeared, I wondered if he was with you."

"No, he's not, Mr. Gregory. I haven't seen Stan at all this evening."

The annoyingly hearty voice vibrated the mobile in John's hand. "I see. But if he should come up to your house, will you telephone us? Cynthia and I are beside ourselves with worry."

"Of course I will." John didn't feel like explaining that there'd be no one home. All he wanted to do was get out onto the road and drive hell-for-leather to the airport. Barring turning the car over in a ditch, everything should be just fine then. But the monster in the hill did have a long reach. Might it have the power to make a plane fall out of the sky? He closed off the thought, focusing instead on the voice in his ear.

"I'm going out to look for Stan myself now," Gregory

boomed. "But Cynthia will wait by the phone."

"I'll call if I see him," John said. "Good-bye."

Elizabeth made no mention of the call. She stared through the windshield lost in a world of her own. He drove out to rejoin the lane once more. His hand went automatically to the light stalk. A cloud nearer to purple than black had loomed over the horizon to kill the sun, prematurely curtailing the once-bright summer evening. They drove down the lane to be swallowed by shadow.

Two

"Dad, stop!"

Short of running Miranda Bloom down, he had to stop. She'd stood in the road to wave them down.

Now she came up to the driver's door, her dark eyes doom-laden.

"I need to get to the hospital to see Paul," she said quickly. "But the buses don't seem to be running."

"I'm sorry, I'm not going straight to the hospital tonight." A white lie. He wasn't going at all.

"Please. I want to see Paul. I've been going out of my mind with worry ever since I heard."

"Dad, take her," Elizabeth pleaded. "Let her see, Paul."

"All right." He opened the rear door for her, then moved the dog to the far side of the rear seat so she could climb in. "Hang on. We're in a hurry."

He'd only gone about a hundred yards or so when he passed Robert Gregory in the car. Stan Price sat in the passenger seat. Neither noticed John.

That's quick, John told himself. At least that was one less thing for him to worry about. Robert Gregory had found Stan. The old gent couldn't have wandered far after all.

As he drove, he glanced in the rearview mirror. Now that was odd. In fact, it didn't make any sense at all.

Robert Gregory's indicator lights were flashing. But the wrong ones.

Instead of turning left to drive home to Ezy-View in the village, he'd turned right onto a dirt track. And as far as John knew the track led up alongside the cemetery. Nowhere else.

The time approached 9:15. The gloom deepened enough to activate streetlights.

So what on earth was Robert playing at? Why was he driving the old man up to the Necropolis?

John shook his head. Luckily, that was one mystery he didn't have to solve. Hitting the gas, he accelerated away from Skelbrooke and the glowering mound of the Necropolis.

Three

Robert Gregory panted with fear and excitement. No mistakes this time. The dashboard clock read 9:19. As if on cue, dusk drew a veil over the face of the cemetery.

He stopped the car at a gap in the railings. In a separate compartment of his mind he rehearsed the story he would tell the police. At the same time he leaned across the old man to open the passenger door.

Stan's face bled pure bewilderment. Dementia had him in its iron grip again.

"Why are we here?" he muttered. "It's so dark."

"You wanted to see, Harry, Dad." Robert smiled. "He's here."

"Harry?"

"Sure."

"Harry? But I . . ." Confusion quivered in his eyes. "I . . . someone told me Harry had died . . . I remember a funeral."

"Now, Dad. What kind of ridiculous talk is that?"

"But it's been so long since I've seen Harry."

"I know it is. That's why I've brought you here to see him. He's up there on the hill waiting for you." As

Robert helped the old man out of the car, he could see doubt seesawing with hope in his expression. "Harry's come a long way, Dad. You don't want to miss him."

"No, I don't, do I?"

With that little shuffling step of his, Stan Price passed through the gap in the fence into the graveyard.

Robert Gregory waited a few moments. Then he followed.

Four

"Dad, what are you doing?" Elizabeth had to hang on to her seat belt as John U-turned the car with a screech of tires on hot tar. In the back the dog slipped sideward, too, to go sprawling over Miranda's lap.

John's voice was tight. "I need to check on something."

Miranda leaned forward. "Mr. Newton, aren't you going to take me to see, Paul?"

"It won't take a couple of minutes."

This is crazy, he told himself. You need to put as many miles as possible between Elizabeth and Skelbrooke. You're no knight in shining armor. But guilt would gnaw him to the bone because he knew what was going to happen to old Stan Price. It made perfect sense now. Robert Gregory had made that telephone call to John for Cynthia Gregory's benefit, pretending concern that Stan had wandered away from home again. That was all part of the alibi. Robert, no doubt, had already left Stan away from the house in a place where he could easily find him. Then he'd told Cynthia he'd go look for him. Moments later he'd collected Stan. Now he was driving him to the cemetery. And, God knows, the Necropolis is a lethal place after dark.

All the clues were there. Gregory planned Stan's death. The police would hear a verifiable story of an old man lost in his own world of dementia, who would wander away from the house. Only one evening he wandered away to meet with a fatal accident. And, hey presto, Robert not only gets away with murder, he inherits Stan's fortune.

The dash clock pulsed 9:22.

A poet once wrote about "time's maggot on my back." John Newton felt that now. He felt a wormy, itchy presence there. *Less than three hours to midnight.*

Both Elizabeth and Miranda were shooting him anxious looks, as if asking themselves whether he'd gone mad. And when he swung the car right, bouncing it along the dirt track, their expressions of anxiety turned to alarm.

"Don't worry," he told them. "This should only take a minute."

Seconds later, he saw Robert Gregory's car parked just yards from the gap in the cemetery fence.

Stopping, John killed the motor. An unearthly silence stole into the car. This was a lonely place at night. There were no houses nearby. No people. A great hush had settled across the graveyard. Trees stood guard as towering black forms. The sky had darkened, too, the low, oppressive clouds making themselves felt rather than seen.

He wound down the window. Hot night air poured across his face as if to steal the breath from his lungs. Breathing in deeply, he grimaced as pain bit into his ribs.

For a moment he stared through the railings into the cemetery. There was no sign of the two men. Gregory must have taken Stan Price deep inside, well away from prying eyes.

John knew that if he was to save Stan, he had to catch up with Gregory fast. He pulled a penlight from the shelf under the dash.

"Elizabeth. Miranda. I need you to stay here for a few minutes."

"Mr. Newton." Miranda's voice wavered. "What's happening? Where are you going?"

"I'm trying to stop something bad from happening."

He wiped the sweat from his eyes. "Will you wait here with Elizabeth?"

From the gloom in the back of the car, Miranda nodded. Clearly, she wasn't happy with the situation, but she'd stick it out. As John climbed out the car, Sam made as if to follow from the backseat. "No, boy. You stay here—look after everyone."

"Dad?" In the dark, Elizabeth was little more than a ghostly silhouette from which two bright blue eyes regarded him. "Dad, you won't be long, will you?"

The clock read 9:24. "No. I won't be long." He returned to the car for a moment, and she encircled his neck with her arms, hugging him tightly, her cheek smooth against his. "I love you, Dad."

"I love you too, hon." Leaving her at that moment was such a wrench. An aching sense of loss nearly overwhelmed him. "We'll soon be on our way again, hon. Now, lock the doors. I'll see you soon."

She locked the doors from the inside.

As he moved toward the gap in the fence, he glanced back. Her face hung there in the gloom of the car like a white disk. The last thing he wanted to do was leave her. But then he couldn't sit back while the greedy, loathsome Robert Gregory murdered Stan Price.

Feeling as if he was diving into a pool of bubbling sulfur, John gritted his teeth before plunging into the cemetery. He walked quickly, not risking running in here now that the light was all but gone. Grave after grave squatted there in the dark with all the menace of crouching demons. Trees arched over him like monstrous arms thrust upward from out of the earth.

His eyes adjusting to the gloom, he quickened his step. Nevertheless, the grave world he now entered was a disordered mass of shadows, grays, blacks. The days heat had squeezed a bitter smell from the plants that irritated the back of his throat. When he coughed, his ribs burnt with the white fire of agony.

Trying to quell pain by sheer willpower, he threaded his way among dark islands of stinging nettle. As he walked, rotted Christs watched him pass with their dead stone eyes. Grass stalks caught his feet like so many tentacles that had wormed their way from coffins below the sod. Already dark forces, it seemed, were intent on slowing him down.

His imagination, swollen by the pain in his side, and the torrent of events over the last forty-eight hours, supplied leprous images—of tentacle vines, erupting from the ground to entwine around him, snaring his throat, whipping around his arms and legs, before pulling him down into the dirt, where coffins swam through their subterranean world like predatory beasts.

He tripped over an angel that had fallen into long grass. The shock of stumbling to his knees mutated into explosive pain in his ribs. He gagged. Pain became a solid presence that squeezed up through his throat to choke him. For a moment he lay facedown in the grass, struggling to breathe. Every breath plunged him deeper into mindless agony.

It took a full minute to pull his scattered senses together, then rise to his feet.

Time's running out on you, John. Time's running out. Robert's going to crack the old man's skull like an egg, while you crawl about the graveyard like a mewling pup.

Coughing dirt from his mouth, he stumbled to his feet, gagging again on the pain spearing his side.

Gotta move faster, John Newton. Time's maggot is writhing on your back. Midnight's rolling this way like a runaway train. Baby Bones ain't going to be content to stay lonesome forever. Gotta move, John. Gotta move now.

This time he moved at a run toward the heart of the graveyard, which waited like a dark phantom with its arms wide. Waiting for him to enter its lethal embrace.

Five

"Harry, is that you? Come closer, I can't see you in the dark." Stan Price had made it to the top of the Necropolis hill. His legs trembled with the effort. Gloom encircled him, while row upon row of tombstones bore all the noxious presence of decaying teeth. A night bird cried; then again, it might have been the cry of an abandoned baby. After all, the fruit of more than one unwanted pregnancy had been left here before now.

Stan moved on, snapping sticks beneath his feet as if he walked on tiny rib cages.

Snap . . . snap . . . *SNAP!*

Then a thin, hurting cry. Some night predator had found its prey in the dark.

"Harry? Harry?" Stan's voice came as a hoarse whisper. "Harry. Are you there?"

By now Stan had reached the lip of the cliff. Thirty feet beneath him the maze of burial vaults formed a city within the city of the dead. Passageways were canals filled with shadow. A dark shape moved along one of them.

He moved closer to the edge of the cliff so he could look down at that shape swimming through darkness toward the ramp. The sheer drop plunged away just inches from his feet. "Harry. Is that you?"

A rustle came from Stan's right. He turned to see a figure staring at him from the bushes.

Chapter Thirty-nine

John Newton moved into the gulf of shadow that was the Vale of Tears. Adrenaline powered him through the maze of tombs. Door after door flashed by him at enormous speed. Once his hand accidentally brushed a door. The iron chimed with a haunting note, like a gigantic bell touched by a padded hammer.

Through sweat-blurred eyes he glanced at his watch. 9:29. Minutes were racing by. Now he could all but see the hour of midnight hanging over the Necropolis like a vast pair of leathery wings.

But he had a plan. A clear plan. And, good God, it was simplicity itself. He'd catch up with Robert Gregory. Grab the jerk by the scruff of his neck, warn him that if anything happened to the old man, he, John Newton, would see he went to jail for it. Secondly, after leaving Miranda at the hospital gates, he'd race Elizabeth to he airport for the next flight out. If he could put an ocean between Elizabeth and that dark pus-ball of evil inside that hill, then everything would be all right. A billion gallons of salt water would break its hold on the Newton family. Herbert Kelly had beaten the monster. Now so could he.

Sometimes cannoning off the walls like a flesh-bone pinball, he moved deeper into the Vale of Tears. Robert Gregory would take Stan to the high ground, he reasoned. A lethal fall would do the job.

The sound of his own breathing thundered in his ears. He labored to draw enough air into his lungs. But each breath killed him by inches. His cracked ribs shrieked their protest as his lungs pressed against them.

Purple mist bloomed from the tomb walls as his brain struggled to make use of too little oxygen in his blood. That same purple flooded from the iron doors, forming death's-head shapes that ferociously darted forward, their jaws opening wide.

He paused for a second, allowing his oxygen-starved brain time to recover. When his eyes cleared, he saw something that enclosed him in an icy membrane. He stared at it, wondering if his overheated imagination had played yet another trick.

One of the crypt doors yawned wide open. Beyond it, a gulf of darkness, oozing with vile promise. He blinked hard. The image of the door remained. *No, you're not dreaming this. Someone's opened the tomb.*

His eyes raked the stonework above the doorway to find a plaque that named the family interred there: *ELLERBY.*

You will leave her by the sepulchre of Posthumous Ellerby. . . .

That was what the last letter had demanded of him. Now here was the Ellerby tomb. Open wide. Like a hungry mouth demanding food.

No. Not a chance in hell. You're not getting hold of my daughter, Baby Bones. She's staying put. You've bitten off more than you can chew this time. Herbert Kelly beat you. I'm going to beat you, too.

He gazed, hypnotized by the entombed darkness while the silence called his name. Or so it seemed as he stood there, heart pounding, his breath sounding dry as bones.

Moving slowly now, he approached the tomb.

No, don't go inside. Keep moving. Go straight on by. . . .

Darkness called his name: *John . . . John . . . we are waiting. . . .*

He pressed his lips together. Shook his head. Purple growths expanded from the tomb doorway, like drops of blood hitting clear water. His eyes burnt hot as embers in his head, straining to make sense of formless darkness. *Keep walking, John,* he told himself. *Walk by the open doorway; put it behind you. Find the old man. Then drive Elizabeth away from this place.*

But the rasp of his breathing dissolved, then reformed into words in his ears.

No, John. See what's inside. There's something you need to see. Something secret. Something that's been buried here for a long, long time . . .

John moved along the alleyway between the crypts. He intended walking straight on, but another set of feet carried him that night. Before he knew it, he was inside the vault. Beneath him, thick dust. All around him, soft darkness. A darkness that gently burst with those purple blooms. He breathed deeply, trying to squeeze that all-important oxygen into his brain. Momentarily, the pain in his side vanished. He stood there, feeling the stillness of the century-old tomb, and the silence that laid its heavy hand upon the place.

Strangely, he didn't use the penlight. For he sensed he stood on the bridge between ignorance and knowing. And at that moment, standing in darkness in that place of the dead was infinitely preferable to seeing what lay around him. There were more than coffins in the tomb. There was something else, too. A *something* he did not want to see.

He listened to the dark of music of his respiration. A pulse in his brain thudded. He wanted time's maggot to stop right there. But he knew it wouldn't. Midnight rolled with a dreadful inevitability toward him.

Do it, John. It was his own inner voice. Clear. Calm. Insistent. *You've got to see what is in here.* He switched on the penlight.

There, revealed by the splash of yellow light, were the oblong boxes that held the bones and dry skin of the Ellerby men, women, and children. Sprays of funeral flowers, now little more than patterns of dust, tied with black ribbon, still lay on coffin lids.

John played the light into the far corner. He knew that he'd find another occupant of the tomb here. When he saw it lying against a mold-encrusted wall, it no longer came as a surprise. He stepped forward, keeping the halo of light around it, taking in the details—the suit of clothes, the canvas bag used as a pillow, a bottle of blue glass that had once held poison. The white Panama hat beside a fleshless head.

It's been a long time, Mr. Kelly. But we meet at last. The words flowed with toxic menace into his brain. He gazed down at the bones of Herbert Kelly, one-time teacher, one-time resident of the Water Mill, and John knew everything.

Herbert Kelly had lied. He'd deceived everyone. His daughters, his wife, his neighbors, even one John Newton who'd moved into the man's very home seventy years later. Kelly had never gone to Canada. He'd only set clues to make it look as if he'd fled there with his daughter Mary.

The truth was very much darker. Kelly had received that last letter, too. *You will leave little Mary by the sepulchre of Posthumous Ellerby....* And when all his options had expired, he'd met its grim demand. No wonder Kelly had wept against the apple tree in the orchard.

Briefly, John's mind flew back seventy years. He saw with awful clarity the events of that night when Herbert Kelly had crept into his daughter's room, roused her from her bed, whispered that they were going on an adventure, while trying to mask his own sense of dread and horror with a smile. Then, with a suitcase in one hand, holding his daughter's tiny hand in the other, he'd led her to the cemetery. An influenza outbreak was raging in the village. So many lives hung in the balance. Herbert Kelly was the only one who could save them. . . .

And so, talking soothingly to his daughter, he'd walked up the night-darkened lane to the Vale of Tears.

Perhaps a former pupil living in Canada had sent the telegram on his behalf. But what did the details of his deception matter now? Other than he'd thought it important to leave his family and neighbors believing he'd taken his daughter to start a new life in another country. But in reality, he'd taken his daughter to the cemetery, to the appointed place at the appointed time.

What then?

Those events at midnight seventy years ago were entombed in mystery, too. Except that this gentle-hearted schoolteacher had not permitted his daughter to meet the inevitable alone. He'd gone with her, held her hand, comforted her, spoke gently to her as that dreadful time arrived.

What had they seen as midnight struck?

John gazed into those eyeless sockets of Kelly's. They exposed the gravelly remnants of his brain, but of course, the man's memories of that night had vanished with his final breath.

Once it was over, however, Kelly must have drunk the poison, removed his white Panama hat, then lay down here praying death would come quickly, while trying so very hard not to recall what had become of his daughter. Even so, he must have felt his own tears roll down his cheeks in the darkness.

Now, fast forward seven decades.

John Newton stood in the Ellerby tomb. Barely two hours separated him from midnight. Zero hour. *What now, John?* The question ricocheted around the inside of his skull. *What now?*

At that moment he heard a cry. Turning, he stumbled as fast as he could from the tomb.

A terrified voice came from above: "No, I won't go . . . *I won't go!*"

Chapter Forty

One

Robert Gregory gripped the old man's wrist. He pulled him toward the grassy slope that overhung the edge of the cliff in a ragged fringe.

"I won't go." Stan Price's voice echoed from the gravestones. "I won't go!"

Robert Gregory sweated. His father-in-law was a tough old dog. Robert had been starving the man for months. But would he die? Would he hell! Now he fought like a tiger to prevent himself from being hauled over the edge of the cliff. *Damn him.*

"Don't keep Harry waiting," Robert panted. "Come on, Dad. This is the way."

But the deception was over. Stan Price had snapped back into lucidity. His eyes were sharp now as he looked around the darkened cemetery. "No. I know what you're trying to do, Robert . . . let go of me!"

"No frigging way. You're going over the edge." Robert's heart thudded. So close now. Soon all the money would be his. He pulled harder, sliding the old man across the grass. All he needed now was to position him so he was on the lip of the cliff. Then one last shove . . .

In the gloom, Stan's blue eyes locked onto his. Suddenly, he began to speak in a loud, clear voice, "Robert. I know you got the letters. You ignored them. You didn't know what would happen. You've not done what you should."

"Shut up."

"You got the letters, didn't you? They asked for beer and chocolate. You thought it was children playing tricks. . . ."

"Shut up!" Sweating, Robert struggled to pull the old man closer to the dark void above the crypt roofs. *A nice, straight drop. Right down onto hard stone.*

"You should have done what the letters demanded, Robert. You'll suffer for it now."

"Get over here, you old dog. *C'mon!*"

The grass was slippery. If Robert pulled too hard, then his own feet slipped, too. But there it was, just a step away now. *A lovely, long drop that's gonna break every bone in the old dog's body.* He wrestled Stan nearer to the edge. Rivers of sweat poured into Robert's eyes, stinging like crazy, but he'd do it. Come midnight, senile, muddleheaded old Stan Price would be history.

Grunting, he changed his tactics. Now he pulled the man closer to the cliff edge.

Stan Price shouted in a suddenly piercing voice, *"Leave me alone . . . leave me alone!"*

The ferocity in the man's voice was startling enough. But then Robert heard a second voice.

"Hey!"

Startled, Robert glanced back over his shoulder and downward into the maze of tombs. From the center of it a light sprang upward into his face, dazzling him.

With a furious yell, Robert Gregory released his grip on the old man. Now he had every intention of punching Stan unconscious before throwing him over the edge. The hell with subtlety. But he let go so quickly that his balance was lost.

Robert lurched back, putting his foot backward to stop himself falling. But there was no more solid ground. Only the hot night air. He cried out in terror: *"Help me!"* And even caught hold of Stan's outstretched hand to save himself. Only, his own hand was now so slick with perspiration, it was like trying to clutch a hunk of wet soap.

That was the instant when Robert's hand slipped from the hand of the man he'd abused so ruthlessly these last six months. For a second his own panicked eyes met the calm blue eyes that belonged to Stan Price. Then he was tumbling backward into velvet darkness.

The air surged round him, his heart clamored against his ribs. He managed one loud scream before he struck the ground.

That was when the agony began.

Two

John Newton ran from the Ellerby vault to witness the struggle on the cliff. He'd cried out *"Hey!"* and shone the penlight up at the figures. He'd seen Robert Gregory's startled reaction.

A moment later Robert had come tumbling over the cliff like a boulder. The maze of crypts had echoed to the impact. Iron doors had vibrated in a medley of notes, which had sounded like a dozen muffled bells before fading to a metallic hum.

John ran through the maze of alleyways, shining the light in front of him, which ricocheted from walls, doors, and paving slabs like the flash of unearthly eyes.

Then he had found Robert Gregory.

The heavy man lay flat on his back. Blood oozed from his mutilated skull. For five seconds or so he groaned in agony, raising bubbles of spit from his lips. Then the man's whole body jerked as if it had been kicked. After that, he lay still, his eyes wide open.

Whatever dwelt in the hill had just collected another forfeit.

Three

Elizabeth stared out the car window. A girl in a white dress stood watching her from the gap in the cemetery railings.

Elizabeth looked back over her shoulder. The dog was staring at the girl, too. Only his ears had flattened against his head and he'd begun to snarl. When Elizabeth looked back toward the cemetery, she was surprised to see the girl now stood right outside the car looking in.

The girl was about her own age, with fair hair and a pleasant smile.

Sam ran back and forth across the backseat. Miranda cried out as claws dug into her bare legs. It took all her strength to wrestle the dog away from her.

"Sam," Elizabeth said calmly. "Sit down, you're scratching Miranda's legs."

Sam glared at the girl through the window, a snarl rumbling in his throat. The hair on his back had risen into stiff bristles.

"What's got into him?" Miranda said, rubbing the sore scratch on her thigh.

"The girl startled him."

Miranda looked out of the window. "There's a girl? Where?"

Elizabeth looked back out. The fair-haired girl's face nearly touched the glass, her eyes vast and luminous.

Miranda sounded puzzled. "I don't see a girl. Where is she?"

Then the girl spoke softly to Elizabeth. "Your father needs you straightaway."

"I'm not allowed out of the car."

"He's hurt and he needs you, Elizabeth."

With that the fair-haired girl turned and walked away from the car, her long white dress brushing the heads of the wild flowers. Immediately, the dog barked furiously.

Elizabeth unlocked the car door and started to follow. She heard Miranda's startled voice rise above the dog's bark. "Elizabeth? You're not to leave the car. Elizabeth, come back!"

But the stranger said her father was hurt. She didn't want to lose the girl, so she followed the now-white ghost shape that weaved around the gravestones, deeper and deeper into the cemetery.

In the back of the car, Miranda struggled with the dog. He fought to get out of the car as well. Inside the confined space the barks were deafening. At last he slipped from her grasp, and with supple ease slid between the two front seats, then out the front door.

"Elizabeth!" Miranda cried. "Don't go in there!"

But by this time Elizabeth had been swallowed by shadow. Miranda tried to open the car's rear door, only to find child locks held them fast.

Damn. Why on earth has Paul's sister run off like that?

She'd have to go after her. With the rear doors locked, Miranda had to struggle over the back of the driver's seat before climbing out of the car. Precious time had gone. She paused, listening. Nothing but silence now. Even the dog had vanished. Consumed by the gigantic cemetery.

Inexplicably, Miranda felt suddenly cold, as if she was being drawn into some ice tomb underground. She shivered from the roots of her hair downward.

What on earth's happening here? Where's Mr. Newton? Why has Elizabeth suddenly raced off like that? And why has the dog gone crazy?

Oh, Jesus. She didn't like it here alone in the dark. The shadows and the silence crept toward her like the tide of some great nighttime ocean. Trees whispered eerily. Headstones stared at her like so many weird geometric eyes.

Reasoning any illumination was better than none, she reached into the car, hitting the button that activated the hazard lights. The flashing orange bulbs sent a ruddy ghost light into the cemetery to illuminate those monstrous trees that loomed over her, seemingly ready to pounce the moment she stepped inside those railings.

She forced herself toward the entrance to the Necropolis. She had to find Paul's sister. She was responsible for her safety. If anything should . . .

A shape lumbered out of the darkness toward her.

"Miranda? What are you doing out of the car?"

"Mr. Newton?"

Into the field of flashing orange light John Newton appeared. There were two figures, John Newton and an old man she recognized as Stan Price. Both looked exhausted, as if they'd just come down from a mountain.

"Miranda, get back into the car. I need to take Stan Price home."

Miranda was frightened to say the words, but she had no choice. "Mr. Newton. I—I'm sorry, but Elizabeth ran off after some girl. The dog followed her. I don't know why she went or—"

"Elizabeth's gone into the cemetery?" A look of horror transformed his face into a wide-eyed mask.

Miranda nodded. "I'm sorry. I never even saw any girl, but she—"

"Oh, God." His voice dropped to a whisper. "Help Stan into the car. I'll be back as soon as I can."

Then he disappeared into the cemetery, calling Elizabeth's name as he ran, the penlight flashing from headstones, sending shadows racing across the ground.

Four

Where was her father? Had he fallen here in the dark? Was he hurt? But if he was hurt, how could she help him?

The ghostly shape of the girl running along the path ahead of her twisted through the darkness and the headstones with a dreamlike slowness. Elizabeth followed, weaving amongst all those Jesuses and angels whose faces had rotted into ugly, monstrous things that leered as she ran by. Inadvertently, she stepped on a grave. Something clutched at her heel.

Slipping free, she ran deeper and deeper into the cemetery. Trees arched over her, then shadow swallowed her, burying her in darkness.

Seconds later she entered the eerie maze of passageways with iron doors. Behind those, she knew, there were coffins that contained the bones of dead people.

Still following the girl in old-fashioned clothes, she ran along the passageway. As she did so, she happened to glance down and saw that Sam ran beside her, his eyes bright and his ebony body sleek.

Ahead of her, the girl had now stopped outside a tomb.

The door lay open. When she saw Elizabeth, she beckoned her. Then she went into the velvet blackness of the vault.

Why had her father gone in there? Why didn't he wait at the door for her?

Elizabeth decided he must have hurt himself. That was why he hadn't come out to meet her.

With the dog still following faithfully, she went inside.

Five

John moved quickly through the cemetery. The darkness here was all but complete. The penlight cast its meager radiance ahead of him; a little of the light splashed against the tombs.

His cracked ribs chafed against each other as he ran. The pain was immense. That, and the hot airless night, conspired to leave him with a suffocating breathlessness. He strove to take deep breaths, but they only triggered fresh agonies.

He followed the path as it meandered across a landscape scabbed darkly with eighty thousand tombs. Ivy swarmed over them like an infection. Rotting in man-sized cavities beneath the earth, skulls would grimace up at him; eyes that had been devoured by maggots now bulged with mushroom growths; they glared at the soles of his passing feet and gleamed with antici-pation, sensing what was to come.

In a weird, dislocated way his mind slipped free to swoop like some spirit bird down through the brown mist of earth. It glided amongst the burials lying there. He saw it all: *Rotting coffins revealing their occupants that are slowly melting into the soil. And in the casket beneath the humpbacked angel is old Abraham the miller, who'd slipped between his millstones one winter's morning, which ground his skull to splinters. He'd burnt the letters that came to him in the dead of night. Then he'd mixed the ashes with salt and buried them where the gallows once stood at the Skelbrooke crossroads.*

It didn't do any good.

The demands must be met.

John knew that now.

He ran on into the darkening heart of the Necropolis. At every bend in the path, he willed his daughter to be there.

Once more his imagination took him underground, down through the coffins that stretched out for half a mile or more in a single, vast formation. Black lozenge shapes flying through the mists of eternity. His mind's eye flew deeper and deeper into the hill, where some-thing pulsed with a violet light. Something that was old when the pyramids were new. It pulsed, slowly hem-orrhaging its evil out into the dirt, where it spread out-ward, polluting the lives of everyone it touched.

Five thousand years ago it was known by a different name that was now lost to history. A thousand years ago it was Father Bones; five hundred years ago it was Jack O'Bones. Three hundred years ago the name had mutated into Baby Bones. Three hundred years from now it would probably attract a new name. But it would carry on the same age-old business. Slumbering. Waking. Issuing its toxic little demands. Nourishing itself on outbreaks of terror and submission. Then once more slumbering until the next time.

A branch raked John's face like a claw. He shook himself out of the trance. The pain in his chest was worse; his breathing had become so restricted, the oxygen barely reached his brain. Somewhere across the hill, the clock in the cemetery chapel struck twelve.

At last the entrance to the Vale of Tears hung before him, clad in the same darkness that lay between stars. Shining the all too feeble penlight in front of him, he lumbered into the alleyway; ahead of him stretched the crypts with their iron doors.

In one such alley the body of Robert Gregory would lie cooling. John had intended calling the police from his mobile. That, however, was forgotten now.

He must see Elizabeth. He needed it the way he needed breath. It had become a burning demand of his own body.

He moved along between the slumbering tombs, working his way deeper into the maze of passageways that were now held by a dreamlike stillness.

Then he stopped. Ahead stood the tomb of the Ellerby family.

Slowly he approached. Silent, forbidding, secretive, the iron door was now shut. As if someone had closed it to commit a private act.

"Elizabeth?"

He'd intended to shout. But his voice came softly. "Elizabeth?"

He approached the iron door, which was now so firmly sealed against the outside world. He shone the light at it. A few strands of light brown hair that looked a lot like Elizabeth's hung down where the door was closed against the frame.

"Elizabeth." He struck the door with the flat of his hand. The echoes came back at him before slowly dying away.

It might have been a trick of his ear, but as the sound faded, it sounded like the faint bark of a dog receding far underground.

He took a deep breath, then cried out:

"Elizabeth! Where are you?"

This time the stone swallowed his voice; there was no echo. And he knew there never, ever would be a reply.

Epitaph

One Year Later

"Every year thousands of people go missing. Some come back. Some vanish without trace. And you never know—it might even happen to you. . . ."

One

John Newton had one more good-bye to say before he left Skelbrooke forever. With the house behind him, awaiting its new owners, he eased the car onto the old Roman road. If most of the traffic on that two-thousand-year-old highway consisted of ghosts, then his car would be joining them. It would be the last time he would drive on these bone-dry cobblestones.

He passed the spot where he'd found Elizabeth after she'd fallen from her bike all those months ago. Dandelions blazed a bright gold there in the midday sun. He reached the end of the road, then crossed over into the village. There were few people out and about. Not one of those met his eye as he passed by. On the pond in front of the inn, a lone black swan drifted on the water.

For the last year, ever since his daughter had vanished, John had existed in a state of emotional coma. Life went on. But he'd not been connected to it. The umbilical that fastened him to reality had broken the moment he'd seen the door of the tomb closed. That was when he knew that Elizabeth had gone from his life.

First had come the massive publicity of the police search. He and Val had received kind letters from strangers the world over. But they'd been unable to touch him. After three months, the police scaled down their search to a minimalist "leaving the file open." Privately, their expressions told the Newtons that Elizabeth must be dead. Publicly, all they'd state with any certainty was that one Saturday night Elizabeth Anne Newton, aged nine years, had left the family car parked near the Skelbrooke Necropolis. Then, accompanied by the family's dog (also not found), she'd entered the cemetery, never to return.

And so life had gone on. John buttoned up his emotions. He did not cry. His face became a stonelike mask. No one knew that a wound had opened up inside him, a great weeping cut that would not heal.

Of course there was no funeral. No small white coffin. No flowers. In his mind, therefore, he could not lay his daughter to rest.

He finished the book. *Without Trace* made it to the best-seller list. A Golden Dagger award followed, then the television documentary. He deposited royalty checks at the bank, passed the time of the day with the cashier with something on his face that impersonated a smile, but all the time his inner face was turned inward to that vast, weeping wound.

Medical authorities identified the meningitis outbreak as the C strain. Antibiotics stopped the bug dead. There were no fatalities.

Paul made a full recovery. Now he was on vacation with Miranda. They planned to study at university together. This afforded Val some consolation. "It's good to see them so much in love," she'd say after reading one of Paul's cheerful e-mails.

Love hurts. Love tears people apart. . . .

John pulled up in front of the imposing gates of Ezy-View. Straightaway he saw old Stan Price sitting in the shade, still wearing the funny old hat. John climbed out of the car, to be met by Cynthia like a mourner at a funeral, her eyes grave.

"I'm glad you could say good-bye, John," she said, shaking his hand. He noticed that this once-timid mouse of a woman had blossomed since her bullying husband's death. She wore delicately framed glasses, and her hair had been expensively made over; the gray had gone, replaced by a rich chestnut color. For her, life had moved on to a far pleasanter chapter.

She led the way across the lawn to Stan Price. He sat with his hands on his lap, his head slightly down. As John approached, he looked up. No look of recognition lit his eyes this time. Dementia had his mind well and truly nailed now.

"He's like this every day," Cynthia whispered. "He doesn't know anyone. Not even me. Sometimes he'll call me Mother, but it's rare that he speaks at all now."

John crouched down and rested his fingers on the back of a liver-spotted hand. "I'm going now, Stan," he said gently. "I've just dropped in to say good-bye." He gave the hand a squeeze.

"Dad, John Newton's saying good-bye. He's going to live in Los Angeles with his wife. He's working on a movie of one of his books. Hasn't he done well, Dad?"

Yeah, the boy done well.

The open wound inside John Newton bled until it hurt. But his outward expression remained the same.

"Good-bye, Stan. You look after yourself." John stood up.

Cynthia bent down to look in the old man's face.

"Look, he's smiling. I think he recognized you after all."

John wasn't so sure. Not that it mattered. If the old man was in a world of his own now, it was one that made him happy. His face was relaxed, the eyes sleepy. A moment later John returned to the car, leaving Stan Price sitting in the shade on this fine summer's day.

Stan closed his eyes. When he opened them he found himself lost in a dark wood. He was frightened. He'd been lost here for a long time. It was a place engulfed with shadows. Moss-covered trees rose all around him, cutting off his escape, while fungus formed white faces on tree trunks that leered down at him as he passed. He stumbled on beneath the canopy of branches, searching desperately for a way out of that eerie gloom.

As he struggled on through the choking undergrowth, it seemed as if someone far away called his name. He headed toward the source of the voice, knowing it was important he find it.

After a while he pushed his way through a dense curtain of bushes. Sunlight dazzled him as he moved away from the wood to find himself on a riverbank. A suntanned boy turned to look at him. He carried a fishing rod in one hand. A catch net hung from the other.

"What on earth kept you, Stan?"

"Harry?"

"What, me old china?"

"Harry, is it you?"

"Of course it's me, y' daft monkey. Where on earth have you been all this time? No—never mind that now. Come and give us a hand with this net."

Stan looked at the back of his hands. They were healthy boy hands, with dirt under the fingernails, and scrapes and scratches, and all those trophies that go with being ten years old.

"Come on, Stan." Harry grinned broadly. "You don't want to be late meeting the new girl, do you?"

Two

From the village John Newton drove to the cemetery. After parking the car, and taking a bunch of flowers from the trunk, he walked along the overgrown paths to the Vale of Tears. With his heart growing heavier with every step, he found himself approaching the iron door of the Ellerby vault, which was now firmly sealed against the outside world. In their search for Elizabeth the police had opened every vault. There had been no sign of a nine-year-old girl, with the exception of her footprints leading into the tomb. Naturally, there had been some speculation why her footprints had not led back out again. But in the end, no official conclusions were drawn. There were, however, more mysteries for the media to chew over. The body of the retired doctor, Dianne Kelly, had been found in another tomb. While in the back of the Ellerby tomb police had discovered the bones of the long-dead Herbert Kelly. A father, John knew, who had never deserted his daughter.

John stood in the shadowed labyrinth of tombs. He felt as if he was carved from the same dead stone as the angels and the Christs that watched him from the strangling brambles and vines.

For a long time he stared at the implacable iron door.

He'd given what the last letter demanded.

At last he laid the flowers on the ground before the door. Then, leaning forward, until his cheek touched the cold metal, he whispered, "Good night, Elizabeth. Sleep well."

From beyond the door an echo of his voice sighed back.

John Newton drove away. Behind him the great mound of the cemetery hill rose toward the sun. Trees stirred and the whole hillside moved in a series of vast, slow ripples. A haunting procession that continued long after he'd gone and he could see it no more.

He'd driven more than a hundred miles before he stopped at the roadside. Then, at last, he wept into the palms of his hands.

Blood

Crazy Simon
Clark

Saturday is a normal day. People go shopping. To the movies. Everything is just as it should be. But not for long. By Sunday, civilization is in ruins. Adults have become murderously insane. One by one they become infected with a crazed, uncontrollable urge to slaughter the young—even their own children. Especially their own children.

Will this be the way the world ends, in waves of madness and carnage? What will be left of our world as we know it? And who, if anyone, will survive? Terror follows terror in this apocalyptic nightmare vision by one of the most powerful talents in modern horror fiction. Prepare yourself for mankind's final days of fear.

__4825-6 $5.99 US/$6.99 CAN

NAILED BY THE HEART
SIMON CLARK

"One of the year's most gripping horror novels ... Truly terrifying." —*Today* (UK)

The Stainforth family—Chris, Ruth and their young son, David—move into the ancient sea-fort in a nice little coastal town to begin a new life, to start fresh. At the time it seems like the perfect place to do it, so quiet, so secluded. But they have no way of knowing that they've moved into what was once a sacred site of an old religion. And that the old god is not dead—only waiting. Already the god's dark power has begun to spread, changing and polluting all that it touches. A hideous evil pervades the small town. Soon the dead no longer stay dead. When the power awakens the rotting crew of a ship that sank decades earlier, a nightmare of bloodshed and violence begins for the Stainforths, a nightmare that can end only with the ultimate sacrifice—death.

___4713-6 $5.99 US/$6.99 CAN

Dorchester Publishing Co., Inc.
P.O. Box 6640
Wayne, PA 19087-8640

Please add $1.75 for shipping and handling for the first book and $.50 for each book thereafter. NY, NYC, and PA residents, please add appropriate sales tax. No cash, stamps, or C.O.D.s. All orders shipped within 6 weeks via postal service book rate. Canadian orders require $2.00 extra postage and must be paid in U.S. dollars through a U.S. banking facility.

Name_____
Address_____
City_____ State_____ Zip_____
I have enclosed $_____ in payment for the checked book(s).
Payment <u>must</u> accompany all orders. ❑ Please send a free catalog.

PREY

GRAHAM MASTERTON

There's something in the attic of Fortyfoot House. Something that rustles. Something that scampers and scratches. Something with fur. But it isn't a rat. It's something far, far more terrifying than a rat.

Recently divorced, David Williams takes a job restoring Fortyfoot House, a dilapidated nineteenth-century orphanage, hoping to find peace of mind and get to know his young son, Danny. But then he hears the scratching noises in the attic. And he sees long-dead people walking across the lawn.

Does Fortyfoot House exist in today, yesterday, tomorrow—or all three at once? Only one thing is certain—it is a house with a dark, unthinkable secret that threatens to send David's world hurtling into a living nightmare. A nightmare that only David himself can prevent—if he can escape the thing in the attic.

___4633-4 $4.99 US/$5.99 CAN